"FOR THE LOVE OF GOD, GO!"

The ambushers almost on their heels, they all ran flat out for the nearby hill. At the foot of the hill a rock turned beneath Shrewsbury's already weakened foot. He fell heavily. Billi turned and raced back to haul frantically on his arm. An arrow hit her in the forehead and she sat down hard.

I'm killed, she thought. And then: *No, I'm not, or I wouldn't be thinking this. Would I?*

Another arrow moaning past her ear snapped her back from the verge of hysteria. She tore the missile out of her forehead and threw it away.

Shrewsbury was struggling to his feet beside her. He froze at the sight of her blood-washed face. "Billi—?"

She jumped up and grabbed his arm again. "Don't just stand there gaping, you son of a bitch," she shouted, pointing at their fast-approaching attackers. "We've got to *move!*"

RUNESPEAR

**VICTOR
MILÁN
AND
MELINDA
SNODGRASS**

POPULAR LIBRARY

An Imprint of Warner Books, Inc.

A Warner Communications Company

This book is dedicated to Rich Smith, Mike Wellbaum, Bob Prestridge, and Joe Chacon, who went before.

Acknowledgments

A number of people helped us create this book. We'd like to thank them. So, to Professor Jake Spidle, Professor Richard Berthold, Helen Damico, and Professor Fred Ragsdale, Jim Moore, and John Miller thanks for the books, advice, and other less tangible help. For our indefatigable agent Patrick Delahunt special thanks, and greatest thanks of all to Brian Thomsen, our editor, who believed we could do it.

CHAPTER

One

"Crows," Professor Shrewsbury said.

Rafe Springer sipped his coffee and cognac and looked out the steam-misted window. Sure enough, there were two crows hopping around in the snow that covered the median strip, beneath the bare branches of an elm. They were big devils, and seemed as unperturbed by the chill of the late-February afternoon as by the roar and stink of the autos and big white buses rolling along the Kurfürstendamm to either side of them.

"*Nebelkrähen*," he said. "Fog crows. Out of Poland and Russia, they say. Trees down by the Havel are lousy with them all winter long."

A little farther along the block, two SA men, sunken-chested, potbellied, and doleful in their brown leather great-coats and Pullman-porter caps, stood guard over a *Winterhilfe* collection box. Typical Nazi bungling, to stick the winter-relief box in the middle of the street at this time of year. In summer, children would play on the broad, grassy stretches of the median, and old men doze and day-dream on the benches, but in winter people only went to the median in crossing the street or to make snowmen—an activity Rafe didn't notice too much of these days, in this bustling National Socialist age.

On the other hand, maybe the Party bosses wanted to give

the *Sturmabteilung* men something to do and, at the same time, keep them in their place. Rafe noticed the two had covered holsters. If there was anything beneath the flaps, that was a change since the days of the Blood Purge in '34.

"Ugly, great brutes," the Professor observed, and Rafe had to rattle a few loose thoughts back into place before he realized he meant the birds and not the brownshirts. "Why don't they winter down in Spain where it's warm, like sensible creatures?"

Rafe glanced back at the crows. They were just standing there. As he watched, one turned its head and looked at him with glass-bead eyes. He felt an odd tingling at the back of his neck. *Odd how the damned things can almost look intelligent*, he thought.

"They probably couldn't take Madrid," he said quietly, "what with Primo de Rivera's boys tramping through the streets shouting their slogans all the time."

Shrewsbury produced a snort of disdain through his thin patrician's nose. "Scoff if you will, Rafe, my boy. But the Falangists will bring order to Spain. And not a moment too soon, if you ask me."

Rafe smiled. He preferred not to discuss politics, but he was still enjoying this reunion with his old professor of Norse language and history too much not to tweak him a little. So he flicked ashes from the end of his hand-rolled cigarette into the white porcelain ashtray on the polished wood table and changed the subject.

"Odd how the damned things can almost look intelligent." He nodded at the crows. For a moment birds and men regarded one another with deep interest. Then Shrewsbury shifted irritably.

"You're letting your imagination run away with you," he said, and shook his head. "It's that fantastic fiction you're addicted to. That twaddle is rotting your mind."

Rafe had to laugh. "I thought you told me some of your cronies back at Oxford were busy writing some of that 'fantastic fiction.'"

Shrewsbury's dark blue eyes blinked rapidly. "Good heavens, no. Theirs is utterly different. Clive's engaged in crafting a Christian allegory, and Ronald is writing a sort of prose saga based upon several languages he created as a linguistic exercise. It's not the same thing at all. Worlds of difference."

Rafe nodded and let silence settle in. His acquaintance with the professor was of long enough standing that they were comfortable just about anywhere and under most circumstances.

He was an American, but unlike the typical American of European imagining, he was neither rich nor loud. Nor was he especially tall, just a bit above medium height and of compact build. His hair was blond, dried and lightened by the sun, and his face was tan. Despite their lived-in appearance there was something boyish about his features that made him seem younger than he was, an expression of alert curiosity in deep brown eyes that made an odd, but not unpleasing, contrast with his light hair. He was casually dressed, his battered beige trench coat tossed over an arm of the red-and-green-striped armchair, his tie ever so slightly askew, light tan suit coat and slacks neat but not obsessively so. Berlin was still informal enough, and the café's coal-burning stove enthusiastic enough, that he could have dispensed with the jacket. But that would have exposed the intensely illegal Colt Model 1911A1 automatic tucked into a worn leather holster under his right arm, so he preferred to keep it on.

Professor Shrewsbury propped the leather elbow patches of his tweed coat on the table and raised a long finger. "The National Socialists have done a good many splendid things for Germany," he said in his best lecture-hall tone, through the mist rising off his espresso, "but sometimes I believe they take this Party business too far. Take the new director of the University. His appointment was political, pure and simple."

"I thought he was the one who brought you over from England."

"Oh, indeed, indeed. He is greatly encouraging the study of the history and culture of the Germanic peoples, though I think he gives too much credence to the unscientific maunderings of Darré and that ruffian Rosenberg."

"What do you expect? The man's a veterinarian, for God's sake."

Shrewsbury nodded triumphantly. "Exactly. And therein lies the problem. The only areas of the curriculum that really engage his interest are those which pertain to his specialty. The humanities and physical sciences go begging, but the University of Berlin can boast some twenty-eight courses in veterinary medicine!"

Rafe hid a grin behind his coffee cup. "But what of your own dealings with the University?" Shrewsbury asked.

Rafe shrugged. "Haven't added up to anything yet. When I got their telegram in Belgrade, they were hot for me to come and lead an expedition into the Belgian Congo. Now that I'm here, they seem to have cooled down somewhat. They talk a lot about plans and preparations, but not a whole hell of a lot gets done."

"Perhaps they've come to their senses. The idea of grown men chasing through the jungle after some sort of silly dragon the natives claim to have seen..." He shook his head. "Appalling."

"It's not just any dragon; it's Professor Koldewey's Sirrush of the Ishtar Gate. Herr Professor Doktor Edelkranz at the University believes it might be a survivor of some species of dinosaur."

"Balderdash."

"At any rate, it would be a trip to Africa for me—and a healthy fee." He stubbed out his cigarette. "Maybe I could make an appointment with the *Rektor* in person. Bringing back a new species of animal would open up whole new vistas of veterinary science...."

A gust of cold air swept through the café as an old man in a lamb's-wool hat, floor-length coat, and extravagant Ludendorff whiskers—whiter than the sooty snow outside and waxed into minarets flanking his nose—pushed through the glass and polished-brass door. The other oldsters paused, then set aside their newspapers and coffee cups as the old man hung up his coat and hat and made a circuit of the room, gravely shaking hands with his contemporaries. Ignoring Rafe and the professor, who were obvious foreigners and therefore not worthy of notice, he finally lit by the espresso machine, an immense gleaming contraption of mirror-bright aluminum, brass, and white enamel, which looked as if all it needed were big wheels and a wagon-tongue to be driven off to fight fires. He ordered a stout pastry from the spotless chrome and glass counter, selected the day's *Börser Zeitung* from the rack, and settled down to the grim business of stuffing his face with *Kirschtorte* and grumbling over the news. Rafe watched in fascination as the oldster, after each bite, wiped whipped cream from his mustache and carefully licked his gnarled finger.

Shrewsbury set his cup down as the other old men went back to their papers. "Seriously, Rafe, my boy, when are you going to settle down?"

"I don't anticipate doing so," Rafe said. He frowned. The room was redolent with the cloying scent of pastries and the awful stuff Germans smoked in their pipes. The smells were beginning to get to him. He pulled a little pigskin bag from the inside pocket of his jacket, produced a packet of papers, and commenced rolling a cigarette.

The professor shook his head, his lips pressed into an exasperated curve. "You could be anything you want, boy." Rafe was actually thirty-six, well past boyhood, but that was the way Professor Shrewsbury had always addressed him, and, no doubt, always would. "You're a trained engineer. Your family owns land off in the far reaches of your Wild West. When you read under me, you displayed a fine, keen mind, if one sometimes lackadaisically applied. You've a touch for languages. You could be anything you want to. Yet you wander aimlessly about the world." His long, slender hand made a disgusted circle in the air between them. "Always haring off after mythical beasts in Africa or fossils in Manchukuo."

Rafe winced and spilled a few shreds of tobacco in his lap. "I only wanted to build a dam," he said defensively. In a checkered career his recent venture in that part of the world, from which he'd been returning to the West when the University of Berlin's telegram caught up with him, had definitely been among the black squares.

"Is it that you're trying to find yourself, boy?" Shrewsbury had had a Welsh grandmother, and sometimes when

what he was saying caught him up, his voice acquired a
Celtic lilt.

Rafe shook his head firmly. "I know what I am." He
licked the paper and rolled it into a neat cylinder with his left
hand, an action at which he'd been adept since the age of
seven. "I'm a professional student, if you like. I've just chosen the world for a classroom."

"You've too much romance in your soul," the professor
said. He sighed rather theatrically. "I suppose it's too late for
you to mend your filibustering ways—"

"Rafe? Rafe Springer! Is that *you*?" Both men turned their
heads at the sound of a feminine voice coming from the
direction of the door on a blast of icy air. Shrewsbury didn't
miss the way Rafe's left hand rose toward his right armpit,
then transmuted the motion into an absent brushing of his
lapel.

A petite young woman stood on the step down to the
street with the door held open and the wind flapping the tail
of her long coat about her ankles. Her cheeks were pink
from the brisk air, and a small toque perched rakishly amid a
riot of red curls, its long feather brushing her shoulder.

The old *Junkers* were beginning to glare past their *Vol-
kische Beobachters*. The proprietor chugged out from behind
the pastry counter, ready to remonstrate with this unruly
young woman for spoiling the blast-furnace atmosphere of
his establishment. She let the door swing to behind her, and
he found himself helping her off with her coat instead.

Rafe was on his feet as she walked over to the table.
"Billi," he said, grinning broadly. "You haven't changed a
bit."

Removal of the bulky coat revealed a brown velvet suit
with a knee-length skirt and a short jacket over a fawn
blouse that sported a jabot pinned at the throat with an antique filigreed gold pin. The outfit showed her trim figure to
good advantage and indicated both taste and wealth on the
part of the wearer.

"You haven't either, Rafe," she said, coming forward to
take both his hands in hers and kiss him on the cheek. "You
seem to be ageless, like the Alps or the Eiffel Tower. I

should be jealous." She threw back her head and grinned, accentuating the foxlike quality of her triangular face.

"He's simply cultivated the art of protracted adolescence, my dear," remarked the professor, who had unfolded himself from his overly deep armchair by now. "I don't believe I've had the pleasure of meeting your charming friend, Rafael."

Rafe laughed. "Billi, allow me to present Professor Melbourne Shrewsbury. He taught me Old Norse when I was at Oxford and made a valiant, if wasted, attempt to teach me chess as well. Professor, meet Wilhelmina Forsyth, formerly of Boston. She's a reporter for UPI and an old friend."

Billi extended a gloved hand. Shrewsbury took it and raised it to his lips. Billi's eyes widened at the Continental courtesy, so out of character for the tweedy English don she seemed to be presented with. They were large eyes, very green.

"Delighted, Miss Forsyth."

"The pleasure's mine, Professor, and my friends call me Billi. No one calls me Wilhelmina after the first try."

"The Professor hasn't called me Rafael in twelve years," Rafe said. "Sit down and have something to take the edge off the cold."

"Thanks." She allowed Shrewsbury to hold a chair for her and sat down facing the misted window. "What're you gentlemen drinking?"

"Coffee, my dear," the professor said, resuming his seat to Billi's right. "Rafe sees fit to spoil his with brandy, but I'm content with cream."

She arched a brow. "Coffee? Not tea?"

"Can't stand the stuff."

The proprietor had arrived at the table now. "I'm with you, Professor. I don't believe in diluting what I drink. *Kognak, bitte.*" She stumbled slightly over the German. The proprietor bobbed his balding head and went away.

"How did you happen to meet our Mr. Springer, Miss—er, Billi?"

"I was doing a piece for *National Geographic* in Southern France. I ran into him in Nice where he was up to some sort of shady dealings." She shot Rafe a teasing glance. "Scott Hudson, my photographer, knew Rafe from some caper in

North Africa." She shrugged and stripped off her gloves. "We've been bumping into each other off and on ever since."

Reaching into her purse, she produced a cigarette case of yellowed ivory and took out a cigarette. Rafe gave her a light from a badly dented lighter. As she puffed the cigarette to life she studied the professor out of the corner of her eye.

He was a tall man, inches taller than Rafe. He had gray-blond hair and dark blue eyes and a schoolboy's complexion, and she noted with approval that as far as his somewhat baggy garments revealed, he had a slender, fit figure, with no scholarly sag about the middle. There was decidedly something intriguing about the Professor, she concluded. For one thing he didn't dress as carelessly as she would have expected. He had the obligatory don's clothing: loose trousers, tan sweater-vest figured with brown rectangles, brown tie, tweed coat. But they were new, not threadbare and patched, and looked as though they may have cost a bit. She saw a flicker of disapproval pass over his face as she puffed her cigarette alight, but it was gone at once.

The old men glared briefly as Billi drew in smoke and let it out. Then, as one, they turned their heads back to their papers and pastries. This was Berlin, after all, and the woman was obviously foreign, besides.

Rafe coughed. "Still smoking those Gauloises, eh?"

"Picked up the taste for them in Paris. Once you're hooked on them, nothing else will do." The waiter arrived with her cognac and refills for the two men. "But don't allow me to interrupt what you gentlemen were talking about."

"We were discussing Rafe's rather checkered career."

Billi laughed through a blue cloud of smoke. "Watch yourself, Professor. Dear Rafe's quite the raconteur. If you listen long enough, he'll have you believing he's the long-lost cousin of Manfred von Richtofen . . . the Red Baron."

"Indeed." The professor gave Rafe a sidelong look. Rafe shrugged.

Billi settled back in her armchair, holding the brandy snifter under her nose in both hands. She glanced moodily around the stuffy café and at the traffic outside, churning the snow into slush. Following her gaze, Rafe noted two crows —the same ones?—still standing outside on the median of the Kurfürstendamm.

"Ah, Berlin." Billi sighed. "It used to be so wonderful here, so lively. All the shop windows filled with bright colors and the latest fashions from Paris, and all the cafés filled with handsome young people talking art and revolution. Now that's gone. Outside everything is bustle, bustle, bustle; the young intellectuals are all off building the new Reich or rotting in some squalid jail, and the cafés are left to the old men." She shook her head. "The heart's gone out of the city. The Nazis have brought terrible changes, and I'm afraid the worst is yet to come."

Shrewsbury stiffened. Rafe sucked on his cheeks and studied the light-glints skittering across the surface of his coffee. The warm seductive aroma of cognac caressed his palate as he waited for the explosion.

"I cannot agree with you there, I'm afraid, young lady," Shrewsbury said, leaning forward with his patches planted firmly on the table. "I should have to say that the National Socialists have brought a new spirit to Germany. A spirit rising like a fresh, clean wind from the ashes of defeat and the anarchy of the Weimar days."

Billi stared at him as if about to arch her back and spit. "But they're murderers and thugs!"

"Certainly they have their ruffianly elements, and I, for one, cannot understand their silly obsession with the Jews. But they are revolutionaries, mark my words; revolutionaries in the best sense of the word. They've wrought much-needed change, though often in an imperfect, even crude, manner. Their vision of the future is rough, I grant you. But it works."

"But how can you call them revolutionaries?" Billi sputtered. "They've gone to the greatest lengths to destroy any vestige of real revolution. The concentration camps are filled with Social Democrats, to say nothing of the Communists and trade-unionists. The working man has no rights, the public is crushed under ever-heavier taxes to support all this illegal rearmament and a social-welfare program in which the bureaucrats eat up a full quarter of the funds meant for the needy. Artisans and tradesmen are caught in a tangle of regulation designed to benefit the industrialists and big capitalists who gave so heavily to the Nazi Party before it seized power." She gave her head a passionate toss. "Germany's far worse even than Italy!"

Shrewsbury pursed his lips. "The Duce has done a great deal for that unfortunate nation, my dear. His reindustrialization program is working wonders, so much so that the Americans are copying it as part of Mr. Roosevelt's New Deal. He's made the trains run on time, as they say."

Billi turned to Rafe in exasperated disbelief. "Rafe, you tell him. You've been around; you know how things really are. *Tell him.*"

"Well," Rafe said mildly, "for one thing, Mussolini hasn't made the trains run on time. They're always late—just like the German ones."

She glared at him. "Rafael Springer, how can you be so prosaic? I'm talking about brutality and violence and repression, and you're prattling on about *trains*. If you could just see . . ."

She let her words trail away because Rafe was no longer listening. Instead he was looking fixedly past the flying buttress her pheasant feather made from her hat to her left shoulder.

An extremely tall and extremely blond young man stood behind Billi's garishly upholstered chair. Another one had materialized behind Shrewsbury. A third stood by the door, and Rafe sensed another hovering behind his own armchair. He'd never known they'd entered; they must have slipped in through the back, bringing with them a chill that had little to do with the temperature outside.

They were dressed oddly alike, these tall, fair young men. They all wore ankle-length greatcoats of gleaming brown leather and jaunty little green fedoras. The ensemble wasn't a uniform, exactly, but its meaning was all too clear to any German or knowledgeable visitor.

It meant Gestapo.

CHAPTER

TWO

"Good afternoon, gentlemen, Fräulein," said the smiling youth, who stood behind Billi in accented but clear English.

Billi looked around and did a take at the young giant looming over her. "What's the meaning of this?" the professor demanded, starting from his chair.

A tingling seeped through Rafe's body. The chunk of iron under his right arm seemed to have grown white-hot. If the *Geheime Staatspolizei* were of a mind to, they could make his life very ugly for possession of the weapon, the fact that he held a passport issued by a friendly power notwithstanding. But then again, if the Gestapo wanted the three of them, it would take them, and neither the professor's British passport nor Rafe's and Billi's American ones would be of the slightest help.

"A regrettable incident," the Nazi explanation would read. "Three foreign nationals, detained on suspicion of illegal activities, met with an unfortunate accident while in the custody of the State." Foreign Minister Ribbentrop would issue condolences to the families and countries of the unfortunates, along with assurances that such a thing would never happen again. But it had before, and would again.

Is it going to happen now? Rafe wondered. For just the finest sliver of a moment he thought about going for his pistol. He could use the Colt like an extension of his arm;

the debonair thug behind Shrewsbury and the one back of Billi's chair would never know what hit them. The others ... but no. He doubted the four in the café were all the Gestapo had on the scene. Even if he managed to shoot a way clear, the only border the three of them had a prayer of making was the one with Poland. And the Polish government had been making recent loud noises about its eternal solidarity with the German Reich in the face of the awful Bolshevist menace. They'd doubtless hand the fugitives right back.

As if to confirm his decision not to act, he saw the coffin snout of a huge Daimler pulling up into the slush by the curb outside, black as the devil's waistcoat and gleaming in what dull light filtered through the clouds. The nearer of the crows met Rafe's gaze with a black, sardonic eye, and both the birds took wing.

"I beg your pardon for this intrusion," the young Gestapo man said amiably, "but I must ask that you accompany me."

Shrewsbury stood with his back to the window, legs well spread and braced, and Rafe recalled that he'd done some boxing in his youth. "For God's sake, man, leave the girl. She's got no part in this business, whatever it is." He seemed to have forsaken his role as the Lincoln Steffens of the Third Reich and appeared ready to fight to keep Billi out of the clutches of the Secret State Police. Presumably they were one of the "ruffianly elements" he'd referred to. Rafe got slowly to his feet, hoping to Christ and the Virgin of Guadalupe that the professor realized all three of them were already in the Gestapo's clutches and that resistance at this point would only make things worse.

Billi was on her feet now, too, fixing the spokesman with a haughty green gaze. "I presume," she said frostily, "that you gentlemen have come to conduct me to the interview with the Führer, which I have been requesting for so long."

"Alas, no, Fräulein," the agent said after only an instant's hesitation. "And now I must suggest that we proceed. We have no wish to disturb the other patrons, have we?"

The old men at the other tables had laid down their papers and pastries and were glaring with hostile boars' eyes at the

foreigners who had caused this disturbance. The Gestapo
man by the front door had moved up near Shrewsbury, and
the one who had stood behind the professor had shifted to
place himself between Billi and the Englishman. Billi looked
at Rafe and held out her arm.

"Shall we?"

"Nice day for a ride," Rafe said, and took her arm.

The two were ushered into the black Daimler Rafe had
seen drawing up outside. Shrewsbury was steered to a second vehicle behind the Daimler, this one an equally gigantic
and equally black Mercedes. *The Nazis might not have much
taste*, Rafe reflected, *but they sure know how to make an
impression*. He and Billi climbed into the back while the
polite spokesman slid into the passenger seat in front. The
door slammed shut, and the car glided out into the traffic
flow, the Mercedes following closely. On the sidewalk pass-
ersby glanced at the two big cars, then turned frozen faces
to the front and marched on about their business.

Inside, the car smelled of leather, stale smoke, and soap,
the latter of which seemed to beat in waves from the fresh-
faced youth behind the wheel. The Daimler moved northeast
along the Ku'damm toward the Zoo. Rafe watched the windows of boutiques and cafés slide by outside.

Along the elegant Kurfürstendamm you didn't see the
queues of people lined up for a dole of whatever commodity
was hit by a spot shortage that week. Here along the city's
most fashionable thoroughfare the effects of the new guns-
before-butter Germany were to be seen mostly in the window displays that didn't change as often as they used to, and
in the dust that gathered on last fall's latest and the smiling
mannequin who modeled it. In the cafés it was as Billi said:
the old had supplanted the young.

Rafe eased back against the leather of the seat, forcing
himself to relax. *They haven't even frisked me,* he thought.
Are they being cagey—or just careless? He shrugged and
reached for his pouch and papers.

Settling her coat about her shoulders, Billi opened her
purse, took out a Gaulois, and lit it herself. The driver,
whose hair was shaven to a whitish plush and whose hat was

buttressed by two outstanding ears, gazed at her with surprise in the rear-view mirror.

"But, Fräulein," he said in broadly accented German, "how can you do that to yourself? Don't you know that tobacco ruins the constitution? Think what it might do to the sons you will bear."

Billi had recovered enough of her composure that her grasp on common sense was beginning to slip. She leaned forward and directed a thin stream of smoke into the driver's left ear. To his alarm Rafe realized that Billi understood German far better than she spoke it.

"Do your people hand out nice bronze medals to bunnies," she asked sweetly, "the way you do to women who produce huge litters?" The young man coughed. Rafe winced.

"Don't mind him, Fräulein Forsyth," said the Gestapo spokesman, smiling icily. His coat was finely tailored, not off the rack like the driver's, and he gave off a delicately expensive aroma of some French body wash. "He came into the Gestapo from the SS."

He spoke in English, with a significant look at the youthful driver. "And with you it was the other way around?" Rafe asked in the same language, presuming it to be unknown to the prudish driver and grateful for an excuse to sidetrack Billi.

Approaching the big intersection at the corner of the Tiergarten, where the Kaiser-Wilhelm Memorial Church stood like a pseudo-Gothic island in the midst of the traffic streams, the driver was beginning to weave a bit, what with trying to watch the faces of his superior and Rafe, ogle Billi, and drive all at the same time. The Gestapo man nodded.

"What on earth are you talking about?" Billi demanded.

They were in the Budapesterstrasse now, the trees and pavilions of the Zoo sliding by on their left, nebulous through breath-fogged windows. "Himmler likes to recruit strapping blond boys of peasant stock for the *Schutzstaffel*," Rafe explained. "He's very big on peasants. So a lot of his SS men are country boys like the Thuringian hillbilly who's driving. Whereas many of the Gestapo are men he inherited from Göring, who only joined the SS after Himmler took over the Secret State Police. They're from Berlin, mostly, and far more sophisticated." The man in the passenger seat said nothing, but showed Billi a smug smile.

Eight Prinz Albrechtstrasse was a sprawling eighteenth-century palace built in the restrained Dutch manner, light gray granite with slate roofing. This part of the Mitte, the government and bureaucratic district at the center of the vast expanse of Berlin, teemed with palaces from the 1700s. Hitler's Reichskanzlei occupied one. Though of no particular architectural interest, 8 Prinz Albrechtstrasse nevertheless exerted a peculiar fascination. Here were located the headquarters of the dreaded Gestapo.

The Daimler drove between ramrod-erect sentries in damp SS black, through wrought-iron gates, and into the cobbled forecourt. The driver brought the vast machine to a halt in front of an arched doorway. He climbed out and opened Billi's door. She smiled suggestively at him and laughed when he blushed to the tips of his ears.

The Mercedes drew up behind the Daimler as a light, powdery snow began to drift down from the grayness overhead. Rafe took Billi's arm and firmly steered her to meet the professor as he emerged from the second car, lest she torment the youthful Gestapo man any further. Country boy or not, he was still a member of the all-powerful secret police.

The urbane Berliner in the tailored coat led the three of them up the steps, past two SS men in helmets with the lightning-flash shield of their order painted on the sides; looming silent statues in their black greatcoats, with Bergmann machine pistols slung around their pillarlike necks. Billi halted in front of them, dragging on Rafe's arm like a refractory foal.

"You know what these two remind me of, Professor?" she asked Shrewsbury. "The poem 'Ozymandias,' by Shelley."

"Jesus," Rafe muttered.

The smile on the thin lips of the English-speaking Gestapo man stretched until it wasn't exactly a smile anymore. "*Bitte?*" His friendly air had changed to feral alertness.

"The young lady is, ah, comparing your men to a certain glorious monument of antiquity," Shrewsbury said. Without waiting for the secret policeman's reply, he took hold of Billi's other elbow and, with Rafe, hustled her into the dark hallway of the Gestapo headquarters.

His smile back in place and only a degree or two chillier than before, the elegant officer led them along a corridor smelling of varnish and disinfectant. To all appearances it was just like any other office building in Germany: rows of doors with frosted glass windows flanking an inadequately lit hallway, some open to reveal agonizingly neat young women clattering industriously at Olympia typewriters the size of washing machines. Billi frowned at the sheer innocuousness of it all.

"Where are the torture chambers?" she asked Rafe, sotto voce.

"In the basement. If you try hard enough, you might get to see them."

She cast him a challenging look, but something in his face made her swallow whatever rejoinder she'd been about to make. They were led up two flights of stairs to the gabled third floor, the three agents who had accompanied the officer into the *Konditorei* following unobtrusively. At the end of the corridor they came to an oak-paneled antechamber. A strapping young adjutant in a black uniform leapt to attention behind his desk and snapped off a Party salute.

The officer sketched a reply. "*Heil Hitler.* Kindly inform the Reichsführer that the foreigners he wished to see are here."

The young man's collar badge identified him as a captain. He licked invisibly thin lips. "But, Standartenführer, there were to be only two—"

"Tell him." He didn't raise his voice. Simply cracked it like a whip.

The captain gulped and disappeared through a huge oaken door carved in oak-leaf designs. Shrewsbury's face was pale and tight. Billi was looking around with her usual pugnacity. The fact that she had yet to so much as see a rubber hose, much less be beaten with one, seemed to have convinced her she was indestructible.

The Berlin-bred officer—Colonel, the adjutant had called

him—switched on his smile. "Please feel free to remove your wraps and hats. Dürer—"

One of his silent companions stepped forward to help Billi out of her coat. With an angry heave of her shoulders she twisted away and removed the garment herself. Shrewsbury uttered a dry cough.

They had no sooner hung up their outer garments on the wooden coat-tree than the ornate door opened. "Standartenführer Klein, the Reichsführer wishes a moment with you alone."

The colonel arched a slender eyebrow. "If you will excuse me?" He disappeared in turn behind the door, while the white-blond Hauptsturmführer resumed his place behind the desk in the Spartan antechamber's sole chair and resumed writing.

Rafe's mouth was dry, and he itched for a cigarette, but he knew better than to roll one. He noticed Billi fishing in her handbag, caught her eye, gave his head a peremptory shake. A brief frown furrowed her brow, but she removed her hand.

Presently the door opened and the Standartenführer emerged, his poise chipped a bit at the edges and his smile out of place. Rafe saw beads of perspiration up near the roots of his tousled blond hair. "In," he said curtly, then in German to his subordinates, "No. You three wait out here."

Billi and the professor looked at Rafe. He shrugged and started forward. The dapper Standartenführer stepped in front of him. Rafe froze.

"*Moment, bitte,*" the officer said. He reached inside Rafe's open jacket and deftly removed the .45 from its holster. "Don't worry," he said sardonically. "I'll keep it safe." He stood aside, and Rafe went through the door.

The room beyond was spacious and would have been well lit by the two tall windows had the sun been giving a better account of itself. What milky light did straggle in was given a boost by unfinished light-oak paneling that covered the walls to a height somewhat above Rafe's head and by a shaded lamp that burned atop an immense desk of burnished oak. The occupant of the room sat behind the desk, his hands folded neatly on the blotter before him, his mouth set in a curious V-shaped smile.

"*Grüsse*," said Heinrich Himmler, Reichsführer SS, in the fashion of his native Bavaria. "I'm so very grateful that the three of you could come to see me. Please, please be seated."

With his heart beating double-time somewhere in the vicinity of his epiglottis, Rafe waited for Billi to observe out loud that they'd had little enough choice in coming to see him. But she kept silent and allowed Professor Shrewsbury to help her into one of the three leather-covered armchairs that had been placed facing the Cyclopean desk.

"Forgive me for not shaking hands with you," Himmler said in his soft South German accent. "There's a dreadful epidemic of flu going around, and I fear I am most susceptible."

"Quite all right," said Shrewsbury, his politeness reflex taking control. Billi shot him a poisonous look. Himmler beamed at him.

A staccato rap came at the door. "*Ja*?" Himmler said. The adjutant entered and crossed to the desk, boots rustling on the woven coconut-fiber mats that lined the floor, and placed a folder on the desk before his chief, alongside two already resting there. He left.

"Excuse me," Himmler said, and opened the new folder. A gray-pink tongue-tip protruded between his lips below his almost invisibly small Hitler mustache as he began to read. Watery gray-blue eyes flicked rapidly from left to right, magnified by the round wire-rimmed spectacles perched on his thin nose. His three involuntary guests exchanged nervous glances but said nothing.

Not one German in four knew who he was. He wasn't even the official head of the *Geheime Staatspolizei*; that honor remained with fat Hermann Göring, who had founded the Gestapo and from whom Himmler had assumed actual control in early 1934. When the Nazis seized power in 1933, he had not even been offered a cabinet post, though his rivals Göring and Goebbels and lesser lights had. But this colorless little schoolmaster of a man was the head of the black army of the SS, mailed fist of the Nazi Party, and its hated and feared tributaries, the Gestapo and the little-known but elite *Sicherheitsdienst*. He was conceivably the most powerful man in the Reich, after Hitler himself.

Confirmed academic that he was, Professor Shrewsbury still knew enough of German politics to be aware of Himmler's existence, and of his importance. As a member of the foreign press, Billi also knew of him, for the Reichs-führer was a favorite bête noire of the correspondents. But only Rafe, who had ties to Germany both above- and under-ground, really grasped the scope of Himmler's power.

On this gray day the Reichsführer wore a field-gray dress uniform with the distinctive silver oak-leaf badges of his rank on either stooped shoulder. On the wall behind him, flanking him as he read, were a bronze bust of the Führer and a Hummel figure of a pink-cheeked drummer boy—a curious Victorian-housewife touch. A hothouse orchid, mauve with a yellow throat, drooped in one window. The room did not look like the office of a man who could at a word make anyone disappear into the concentration camps. No more than Himmler looked like a man who could do such things.

At last he finished, looked up with those Mongol eyes, and favored his guests with that isosceles smile. "Forgive my rudeness. I confess I was surprised at being honored with the presence of Fräulein Forsyth—or should I better say Frau Paillou?" Billi sat up stiffly in her chair. Shrewsbury gave her a puzzled frown.

"I found it necessary to acquaint myself with your dossier, Fräulein. I had already perused those of Captain Springer and Herr Professor Doktor Shrewsbury before you arrived. Marvelous things, dossiers, absolutely marvelous. Indispensable tools for a well-ordered mind."

He readjusted his pince-nez and looked down at the open folder. "'Forsyth, Wilhelmina Helena. Born 9 February 1905 in Boston, Massachusetts, U.S.A.'" He smirked at Billi. "Do forgive me for being so ungallant as to reveal your age. 'Graduated with a bachelor of arts degree'—cur-ious, your educational terms—'from Vassar in 1926. Moved to Paris the same year and married Alain Paillou, a notorious French anarchist. Divorced in early 1927, after six months of marriage.'" He shook his head and clucked reprovingly. "Divorce is always a regrettable business, but in your case one can well sympathize. Doubtless the scoundrel concealed his hateful and disgusting tendencies before you married him, and that caused your estrangement."

"Not at all," Billi said testily. "He wasn't disgusting enough to hold my interest."

Himmler blinked, then went on as if she hadn't spoken. "'Held various jobs since; now employed by the Berlin bureau of the United Press.'"

He closed the folder. "A splendid job Gruppenführer Heydrich's young Captain Schellenburg has done, don't you agree?" He smiled obliviously into the full blaze of Billi's glare and turned to the professor, opening the gray-green cover of a second dossier.

"'Professor Melbourne Shrewsbury. Born in Gloucestershire, England, in 1885, on the estate of his father, Sir Reginald Shrewsbury. Educated at Oxford, stayed on as a lecturer after graduation. Married a Miss Anne Durham of Kent in 1908. Served in British Military Intelligence during the war, subsequently returned to Oxford. Widowed in 1921, natural causes. Currently lecturing at the University of Berlin as part of its expanded curriculum in Nordic history and culture.' Accurate, Professor?"

"It touches the high points, as the Americans would say."

"And speaking of Americans—" he opened the third folder—"you, Herr Hauptmann, have a most remarkable history—almost as remarkable as your genealogy. As I understand it, your grandfather, Doktor Ingenieur Hellmuth Springer, Professor of Engineering at the University of Leipzig, emigrated to North America in the early 1880s to participate in a cattle-raising scheme promoted by his cousin, Walter, Freiherr von Richtofen. That's a noble name in German history, a noble name indeed." Billi looked to the professor, who raised an eyebrow and shrugged. Himmler leaned forward sympathetically and in a confidential tone said, "I'm sure it was a source of sore distress to you and your family when your cousin Frieda married that degenerate Jew scribbler, D. H. Lawrence."

Professor Shrewsbury snorted. Billi scowled. "We were able to contain our indignation," Rafe said dryly.

"You may certainly take pride in the deeds of your other cousin, Wolfram, the current Freiherr." Solicitude dripped from the Reichsführer's words. "He has experienced quite a meteoric rise in the Luftwaffe."

He turned his myopic gaze back to the dossier and primly cleared his throat. " 'When the catastrophic blizzard of 1888 wiped out his and many others' cattle, Dr. Springer moved to the then Territory of New Mexico where he had other relatives. His son, Richard, likewise became an engineer and a professor at your Vocational University, now known as Uplands.' "

"That's *Highlands*."

Himmler blinked rapidly in concentration and licked his lips. "I'm terribly sorry, truly I am. It's a mistranslation . . . someone shall pay for this." He scowled, as though resolving to keep a problem student after class. Then, brightening, he continued, " 'In 1897, Richard Springer married one Juana Consuelo deBaca Ramírez, daughter of a prominent local family.' " He tipped up his spectacles to look at Rafe. "I understand the deBaca family is a highly distinguished bloodline, for the Spanish."

"We like to think so."

"Of course, there is nothing inherently wrong with Spanish blood. It can be very virtuous when it has been kept clear of the Moorish taint. Indeed, my very good friend, General Yagüe . . . but I digress. You were born Rafael Domingo Santiago Springer y deBaca, to quote what I'm told is the full form of your name, in Las Vegas, New Mexico Territory, in 1899."

Billi's eyelids were showing a tendency to droop, but Himmler plowed heedlessly on under a full head of pedantic steam. "In 1914, you entered Princeton University to study engineering like your forebears. In the summer of 1917, you enlisted in the artillery and were sent to officers' school. You served with distinction in combat—the true test of a man— and were wounded in July of 1918 during Feldmarschall Ludendorff's Marne offensive, receiving the Silver Star for your gallantry. Recovering sufficiently by September to vol-

unteer for active duty, you were sent with the British General
Sir Edmund Ironside to serve as artillery officer for the
American 339th Infantry Regiment, then fighting the Bolsheviks with the British and French before Archangel. You
were again wounded, during the withdrawal from Nijni Gora
in January 1919. Let me congratulate you, sir; it is a great
honor to meet a man who has shed blood defending civilization from the Red hordes. I myself had a hand in no few
brawls with the Bolshevist rabble, back in the Weimar days,
and hope that I may yet see more."

This was clearly a lie—whatever else Heinrich Himmler
was or had been, a brawler he was not—but Rafe didn't
really hear him. His attention had turned inward, and he
heard the keening of the Arctic wind, and rising above it the
harsh voices screaming, "*Uhra! Uhra!*" like the hammering
of surf on rocks; saw the lines of bearded men rising from
the snow in the meager light of dawn, smelled burning cor-
dite, felt and saw and heard the world explode in one white
flashing-searing-shattering roar, and knew blackness and
stillness and the cold, the cold, the burning, biting, mind-
killing cold. . . .

"After release from hospital, you returned to university,
graduating with honors in 1921. You spent two years at Oxford and then drifted away from the academic life, true to
your restless nature as a man of action. Since then I understand you have been a bit of everything: prospector, journalist, expedition guide." His lips angled into a man-to-man
smile. "Not always on what one might call the proper side of
the law, I understand."

Rafe sat back in his chair. "Depends on your definition."

"Oh, indeed. I agree absolutely," replied Himmler, who
clearly had no idea what he meant.

"Herr Reichsführer," Professor Shrewsbury said with a
touch of exasperation, "not that I fail to be impressed with
the research your investigators have done into all our back-
grounds, but do you think you might possibly give us some
clue as to why you've, ah, *invited* us here?"

"Oh. Of course, of course." He steepled pudgy fingers
before his face. "You, Professor, and you, Hauptmann
Springer, are uniquely suited to participate in an expedition

we are very shortly about to undertake. And, as I think about it, you also, Miss Forsyth." Billi raised her brows at him. "I confess I was rather nonplussed when my fine young boys brought you along with your male companions. But now I see in it the workings of that Providence that cares especially for Germany and her Führer. I begin to see the part that you will play in this grand undertaking."

"And just what undertaking might that be?" Billi asked sardonically.

Himmler leaned forward, and his drab eyes glittered in the lamplight. "To recover the spear of Odin, father of the gods," he whispered.

CHAPTER

Three

For a moment Rafe wrestled with the compulsion to laugh out loud. They had been detained by the Gestapo, hauled off to the most feared address in all Berlin, and ushered into the awful, if not exactly prepossessing, presence of the Reich's chief secret policeman, just so they could be asked to go chasing off after some mythical toy?

"Preposterous!" Professor Shrewsbury blurted. "The spear of Odin is a legend, nothing more. How can one 're-cover' something that does not exist?"

Himmler leaned forward, his round suet-pudding of a face bland as always, but his eyelids flickering furiously, as though his eyes were dim gray-blue signal lanterns.

"Professor," Billi said, leaning back in her chair and ostentatiously crossing her slim silk-stockinged legs, "I came here in a Daimler, and I don't particularly want to leave in an unmarked van. Before you give us all a lecture, shouldn't we hear what the man has to say?"

"Good idea," Rafe murmured.

Shrewsbury looked from Rafe to Billi as though they were students who had just contradicted him. Then he realized what he'd said and whom he'd said it to. The healthy pink of his cheeks faded to the color of Berlin sidewalk.

Himmler beamed at Billi. "My dear, the reaction of your British friend was perfectly natural for one of a cautious, academic frame of mind. And well might one dismiss this matter as 'preposterous'—unless one were aware of the startling evidence my Gruppenführer Darré's researchers have unearthed."

He reached down and opened a drawer of the massive desk. Shrewsbury caught Rafe's glance and rolled his eyes. Rafe gave him back a taut nod. Argentina-born Walter Darré was one of the prime Nazi racial theorists. He had written a book called *The Peasantry as the Life Source of the Nordic Race*, which had impressed Hitler so much he had made Darré Minister of Food and Agriculture for the Reich in 1933. The book happened to corroborate exactly Himmler's passion for the Aryan peasant and his natural mode of life. Moreover, Darré was obsessed with the mythology of blood and soil, having written a book on that subject too. He introduced the good Bavarian Catholic Himmler to the "blood religion" of the German people, the worship of the old Teutonic deities. In reward Himmler had given him high rank in the SS, which he held concurrently with his cabinet post.

From the drawer Himmler withdrew a folder and laid it on the desk. Rafe's eyes widened, and Billi craned her neck with open interest; none of the three had ever seen a dossier anywhere near as grand as this. No common manila-hemp or rough card-stock folder for *this* dossier. It was bound in gleaming black leather, embossed at the top in gold with the Nazi eagle clutching the *Hakenkreuz* in its claws at one corner and the lightning-bolt twin *S*'s of Himmler's Order at the other. Across the front of the folder were bold gold-inlaid characters:

$$\text{ᚠᚢᚾᚠᛏᛁᚱ}$$

"Gungnir," Shrewsbury read aloud, frowning a little at the effort of deciphering the curious symbols upside down.

Billi looked blank. "It's written in the later, pointed runes," he added, as if that explained everything.

"Gungnir was Odin's spear," said Rafe, coming to her rescue. "The runes are an old Norse alphabet."

Himmler nodded approvingly at him. "As you are all no doubt aware," he said, folding his hands on top of the gleaming dossier, "General Darré is head of the *Rasse und Seidlungshauptamt*, the Race and Settlement Office, though that office is of course subsidiary to the *Sicherheitsdienst*." His listeners' eyes began to glaze. Not even Rafe could follow the complexities of the Party's secret-service *apparat*.

"The foremost task of the RuSHA is to screen the genetic background of the prospective brides of SS men. We take great care with the pedigrees of our young supermen; it wouldn't do to have, ah, mongrels jumping the wall as it were, heh heh." He gave a dry titter. Then, seeing his humorous sally bounce off the three foreigners, he blinked rapidly, removed his glasses, and spent a moment polishing them on his violet-scented handkerchief.

"However," he continued, replacing the pince-nez on the narrow bridge of his nose, "the Race and Settlement Office is also charged with researching the past of the Aryan race; more specifically, its Nordic branch. The sacred mysteries of Blood and Soil.

"Recently Darré's men came across an ancient Norse prose manuscript, authored in the thirteenth century by a Norwegian named Bjørn Eyjolfson. It told how Eyjolfson and a bold party of adventurers followed legends, whose origins were even then lost in antiquity, to Greenland, in pursuit of a fabulous treasure." He whipped the dossier open in a dramatic gesture. A sheaf of vellum pages promptly fell into his lap. "Oh, stuff," he said pettishly, and, gathering the pages back up, replaced them in their resplendent folder.

"Ahem. Bjørn and his daring companions faced many trials as they crossed the ice to a range of smoking mountains. They arrived at last in a secluded valley, in which they found a trove that exceeded their wildest dreams: the Gold of the Gods."

"How curious," Shrewsbury said quellingly.

"More glorious than all the gold and jewels shone Gungnir, the Runespear, weapon of Odin, whom we Germans worship as Wotan." The Reichsführer blinked moistly, shaking his head as if caught up in a transport of emotion. "Such was the treasure that lay within their grasp. Yet before they could claim it, they were beset by hordes of otherworldly creatures. Only a handful escaped; by the time he reached the coast and the waiting ships, Bjørn Eyjolfson was the sole survivor of the band that had ventured inland."

"'Otherworldly creatures'?" Billi repeated, arching a skeptical eyebrow.

"Fearful, is it not?" Himmler shuddered. "Trolls, beyond question. They must have stolen the spear at some time in the distant past, when the gods of the Aryan race still walked the earth."

Shrewsbury looked pained. "Don't you find that interpretation rather farfetched, Herr Reichsführer?" he asked in a languid drawl. "The word Eyjolfson used, no doubt, was *skraelinga*, meaning 'screamers.' While it was applied to what you termed otherworldly beings, it was also commonly used to refer to the Eskimos and the Cape Dorset people." His smile held more than a trace of donnish condescension. "Now, don't you think the passages describe indigenous savages rather than . . . *trolls*?" He got the last word past his tongue with obvious reluctance, as if afraid it would taste bad.

Himmler's thin lips had disappeared altogether into a stubborn line. "The reference very clearly refers to their dark and awful countenances. My researchers translated the word as 'trolls,' Professor. They would not commit such an error." *They would not* dare, he didn't say. But it came across all the same.

"But the Eskimos, being darker-skinned than the Norsemen, might have appeared—"

"Undoubtedly the chronicler was describing trolls," Rafe said loudly. "*Isn't that so*, Professor?" He stabbed Shrewsbury with a baleful look as he spoke. The professor stuck out his underlip like a rebellious child and opened his mouth.

"Where do we fit in, Herr Reichsführer?" Billi asked quickly.

"Professor Shrewsbury is an internationally recognized authority on Norse culture—the history, traditions, languages, and religion of our noble pagan forebears. Am I correct, Professor?"

"Oh, well, I—" Shrewsbury blushed modestly and dropped his eyes. "Why, actually, yes."

"And you, Herr Springer"—a pudgy finger swung to bear

on Rafe—"you enjoy a considerable reputation as a guide and arranger of expeditions. In the summer of 1934, I believe, you led a Royal Dutch Shell exploration team into the interior of Greenland in search of oil deposits."

"Which they never found. But, yes, you're right."

"*Natürlich*. You know the land, the people—you're even conversant with their barbaric tongue, I understand."

"I have a smattering of the local Eskimo dialect, yes."

"And you are also not unversed in Norse culture, having been a student of the esteemed Herr Professor. So: who better to lead an expedition into Greenland's icy heart to recover this holiest of relics?" Himmler clasped his hands and gazed devoutly at the baroque ceiling. Not for nothing did Hitler call him "my Loyola."

Billi was frowning. She started to say something, but just then the look of near ecstasy on Himmler's face was displaced by a ripple of pain. "Oh," he said. "Oh, my." He picked up the handset of the white-enamel and gilt telephone on his desk and spoke a few words into it. He had barely replaced the receiver when the door opened and in came the adjutant, bearing a silver tray, teapot, and four cups.

"I'm afraid excitement disagrees with me," Himmler said with a sickly smile as the adjutant set the service on the desk before his master and poured a steaming cup of brownish liquid. "Though my diet is most carefully regulated—I stringently avoid meat and all artificial products—I am tormented with the most horrid stomach pains. The cares of my office." His thin shoulders rose and fell in a sigh. "Would you care for some of this herb tea? It's a special blend I invented myself. Settles the stomach splendidly." He lifted the cup, little finger fastidiously extended, and sipped.

The adjutant proffered the tray to Billi. "Fräulein?" She shied away like a horse from a snake.

"No thank you," Shrewsbury said with a wave of his hand and a barely perceptible pinching of his nostrils. "Can't abide tea of any sort. Sorry."

Rafe could have used some refreshment; at that moment he'd have done almost anything for a smoke and a shot of whiskey. That wasn't the sort of thing you said to Reichsführer Himmler, however, for any number of reasons. All the same, he turned down the potation too. It smelled exactly like wet cut grass that's begun to rot, sweetly putrid.

The young captain left. Before the door closed, Rafe caught a glimpse of several men waiting in the antechamber.

"What part do I play in this grand scheme, Herr Reichsführer?" Billi demanded. "I've never laid eyes on Greenland or an Eskimo, and I wouldn't know a Norse god from a haberdasher."

"Yes," Himmler said, removing his glasses and wiping them. The steam off his cup had fogged them over. "But you are a correspondent for a respected foreign news service. Because of the envy of our foreign enemies and the Jew-inspired calumnies they've heaped upon us, our own domestic news services are—how shall I say?—no longer taken with the utmost seriousness by readers outside of Germany. Not that I lay any blame for this lamentable state of affairs at the feet of my distinguished colleague Herr Goebbels, of course. Not at all. At any rate, who better to tell the world the epic tale of this expedition than someone who by no stretch of the imagination could be considered a mere mouthpiece for the Party?" He smiled. "You see, now, why I discern the clear workings of Providence in what seemed the error of my men in bringing you here with your companions."

"All well and good," Billi said, "but what's in it for us?"

Himmler looked pained. "My dear girl, I believe you are in some danger of allowing your mercantile background to overpower your fine Ayran genes. I warn you: That way lies the path of becoming a mere tool of the Jews."

She tipped her head back so as to look down her nose at him. "You, for example," he said, "would have exclusive access to the story of a grand adventure, and at its end a scientific discovery of the utmost importance. This is the story of the century I'm offering you, Fräulein."

"Bigger than Lindbergh's landing in Paris?" she asked sarcastically.

Himmler nodded enthusiastically. "Indeed, indeed. And the professor would have the honor of being the first to examine the find—the first modern scholar to hold in his hands the true and indisputable relic of the gods. And, of course, such a trove must contain myriad other items of the greatest scientific and historical interest."

Shrewsbury had been looking progressively more bored throughout the presentation, but now he managed to summon up a smile of polite interest.

"And you, Captain Springer. What better way to assert your preeminence as a practical explorer than by leading this vitally important expedition to its successful conclusion?"

Rafe didn't trust himself to answer that one. Himmler squared the thick ivory pages of the dossier. "And, finally, for each of you, the sum of ten thousand English pounds, in gold—unless Herr Springer would prefer to accept payment in another currency, since his country's laws forbid him to possess gold?"

"I'm sure I'll find something to do with the gold," Rafe assured him.

"Does that mean you accept?" Himmler leaned forward eagerly, like a chipmunk begging for food.

Rafe looked at his companions. Shrewsbury was staring up at a corner of the ceiling. Billi met Rafe's eye and shrugged.

"Well—" Rafe began.

"Excellent!" Himmler exclaimed. He snatched up the telephone with such enthusiasm that he knocked over a gilt-framed photograph of his wife, a stout women with rather a more successful mustache than his. "Ask the Gruppenführer if he could step into my office now," he said into the mouthpiece. He smiled around at his guests and fidgeted in his black leather-upholstered chair like a small boy who has to go to the bathroom.

The door opened with no preliminary knock. A man walked in with quick swinging strides. Billi gasped. Rafe almost did, too—for a totally different reason.

Billi saw a man so tall that his field-gray cap brushed the top of the door frame as he entered. His head was narrow, with a high prow of a forehead and aquiline features as pale and perfect as anything carved in marble by Michelangelo. His eyes were the blue of a winter sky, narrow, and, like those of his chief, slightly slanted. Himmler's eyes sometimes gave him the appearance of being somewhat retarded; not this man's. His were the eyes of a wolf on the prowl.

He took off his fawn-colored greatcoat and the high cap with the death's-head in front and handed them to the adjutant, who came fawning in at the heels of his mirror-polished jackboots. Like Himmler he wore a field-gray dress uniform. The hair combed immaculately back along the long skull was blond, the shoulders broad, his carriage haughty and erect. Altogether he looked as if he might have stepped out of an SS recruiting poster; he was everything most of the Nazi leaders, Hitler and Himmler and Goebbels, were not: a beautiful man with a greyhound's physique. The only dissonant touch was his hips, which were as broad as his ribcage.

He raised a hand in the sketchiest of Party salutes. The fingers were slender and unusually long. *"Heil Hitler,"* he said to Himmler. He looked around at the strangers with a smile that widened perceptibly when his eyes fell on Billi. "Good afternoon." His voice was oddly high, coming from such a big man, the words clipped and sharp.

Billi gazed at him raptly. She obviously thought him the most magnificent man in Germany.

For Rafe's money he was the most deadly.

"Captain Springer, Professor Shrewsbury, Fräulein Forsyth—allow me to present my honored and invaluable assistant, Gruppenführer Reinhard Heydrich."

The tall man took Rafe's hand. "An honor to meet such a distinguished warrior," he said in German. His grip was strong, and cold as the crystals of ice that had begun to form on the windows as the temperature dropped outside.

"A pleasure to meet you, sir," he said in crisp British-accented English as he shook Shrewsbury's hand. Then he caught up Billi's hand in his and bent low to kiss it. *"Enchanté, mademoiselle."* His fingers lingered on hers. Billi blushed and looked as if she would melt and run down through the cracks in the floor. Rafe caught the flash of irritation that passed over Shrewsbury's face.

Reverently Himmler closed the black-bound dossier. "Gruppenführer Heydrich will explain the details of your commission to you. A very good day to you all. It was a pleasure to meet you. A very great pleasure," he concluded hurriedly.

He sat there hugging the Gungnir file to his chest like a hymnal, smiling sweetly. Rafe saw sparkles of sweat near the lines of his thin, dark hair. Apparently the Reichsführer grew uncomfortable if he spent too much time in the presence of other human beings.

Having been abruptly dismissed, the three rose and made for the door. Heydrich himself opened it for them—or rather, for Billi—with a quick half bow and a resounding click of his polished heels, all the while mocking himself with a sardonic smile.

"Herr Springer." Himmler's high-pitched voice halted Rafe in the doorway. "Your people are landowners, are they not? I understand you grew up on a farm."

"A ranch," Rafe corrected. "We raised horses and cattle."

Himmler's face fell. "Well, perhaps we can have a discussion over tea someday, as one yeoman husbandman to another. But your dossier *said* you grew up on a farm, and I was so looking forward to talking with you about the organic method of gardening." He looked down at the offending dossier, eyes blinking as if to beat back tears of disappointment.

"Perhaps after the expedition's return, Reichsführer," Heydrich said. "You and he can . . . They'll be very busy until they depart."

"Oh, very well."

The looming Gruppenführer winked at Rafe as the American went by. Rafe nodded. It was a strange experience to feel a flash of gratitude to one of the few men in the world he feared without reservation.

"Reinhard, dear fellow, I must talk to you a moment," Rafe heard Himmler say. The ornate door shut.

The Standartenführer was sitting on the young adjutant's desk, ignoring that worthy's glances of petulant hatred. He was discussing the bicycle races with a middle-aged man shaped like a beer barrel, dressed in standard Gestapo mufti. By the wall stood a young man in Wehrmacht uniform, rather painfully trying not to look ill at ease at being in the stronghold of the Armed Forces' despised rivals.

When the door closed, Klein pushed himself off the desk. "This way, Fräulein, gentlemen." He nodded to the man he'd been talking to and led them down the hallway, past a woman with wild hair the color of old piano keys and dressed in severe black and white, who was scrubbing the hardwood floor on her hands and knees.

He stopped at a door. Like all the doors on this floor, it was carved and stained dark. He held it open. "Go right in. The boss will be with you in a minute."

They entered a room dominated by a long oaken table, which was surrounded by high-backed chairs. The walls were dark-paneled, giving the room a gloomy, portentous aspect that wasn't relieved by either the two windows that gave off on the forecourt or the not particularly inspired portrait of Henry the Fowler in its silver frame at one end of the room.

As soon as the door closed on the three of them, Shrewsbury snorted. "I will agree the man's degenerate, but to call D. H. Lawrence a Jew is a positive outrage!"

After a mistrustful look at the Nazi eagle crowning its back, Billi swung a chair out from the table and sat. She shot Shrewsbury a fierce look. "Lawrence was a fine writer. Only a . . . a reactionary could call him degenerate! And why is it so offensive to call him a Jew? Professor, you almost make me think you're no better than that horrid little man in—"

Standing at the window with his back to the two combatants, Rafe loudly cleared his throat. "I suppose you both realize this room is no doubt wired like a studio at Broadcast House?" Silence fell with an almost audible thud. Hands in his pockets, whistling a jazz tune to himself, Rafe watched the breeze send spindrifts of dry, new-fallen snow around the boots of the guards at the gate.

The door opened. "Sorry," Heydrich said in his perfect public-school English. He held up the massive black folder. "The Reichsführer wanted to be certain I had all the pertinent information at my disposal." Rafe thought he detected an edge of irony in the words.

Heydrich strode quickly to the head of the table, gave Henry the Fowler a skeptical glance, hooked one heel around the leg of a chair, pulled it out, and propped his boot on it. "Feel free to smoke. You, too, Miss Forsyth. I lack my superior's scruples as to diet and health. He fears for me constantly."

He threw the dossier down on the table, took a rolled map from under his arm, and whipped it open on the scarred oak. "Our Bjørn Eyjolfson gave a good account of his journey. Solid. Our researchers were able to pinpoint the landing place of the expedition. Here." A long finger stabbed the map of Greenland, just past half of the way up the eastern coast of the island. "Near the mouth of the Waltershausen Glacier. In what's now Andréesland. They proceeded northwest"—the finger moved—"traveled twenty days. To *here*."

Rafe whistled. "That's a hundred and sixty kilometers—a hundred miles—into the sort of territory where they used to put pictures of monsters on the old maps." He had wandered from the window to bend over the table.

"Impressive," Heydrich agreed. "The Vikings were hard men. Especially since they had to fight savages every step of the way."

"The natives don't generally range that far from the coast," Rafe remarked. "And they aren't particularly savage."

Billi had risen from her chair and now stood next to Heydrich, looking tiny beside him. "What did they find, Herr Gruppenführer?" she asked.

"You must call me Reinhard. All of you." A camera-shutter smile, then back to the map. "They found a range of mountains. Apparently volcanic."

Rafe snorted. "That's not far from the path of the Koch expedition of 1913. They didn't report any mountains."

Heydrich's icy eyes met his. "It's my understanding that strange things happen to vision in the Arctic ice fields, Captain Springer."

"True enough. But it's still hard to believe. The inland ice cap is ten thousand feet thick in places, Grup—er, Reinhard. Over three kilometers of cone would have to build up to so much as show its tip."

Heydrich's eyes bored into him like icicles. "Are you

saying it's impossible, Rafe?" Professor Shrewsbury asked. He had gotten up to stand very near, on Billi's left.

"No." Rafe shook his head. "Hell, I can't say for sure *what's* there. He's right; vision's tricky out there, over any kind of distance at all. And until there's some kind of comprehensive survey of the interior, there could be entire lost civilizations out there for all anybody knows, like something out of Burroughs."

"So what if there are mountains there or not?" Billi demanded. "I can't see tramping across a hundred miles of glacier after fairy gold."

Heydrich laughed, an abrupt sound, like rapping knuckles. "I appreciate your concern, Miss Forsyth." He took his foot off the chair, swung it around, and sat. "However, the Eyjolfson account has a good deal of the ring of truth in it. You're familiar, perhaps, with the narratives of Marco Polo? Embellished. But containing no little truth."

Shrewsbury cocked an eyebrow. "You're saying you believe in this Gold of the Gods rubbish?"

"I believe in gold, Professor. As to gods"—a whippet shrug—"what I say is that a number of Norse chieftains accumulated substantial treasures over the years. One of their favorite ways of amassing wealth was to prey on each other. Perhaps one took extreme measures to safeguard—" His words snapped sharply off. It was a speech pattern Rafe was already getting used to, that of a man too impatient to finish a sentence once its import was obvious.

He rubbed his chin. "I don't believe the Reichsführer intends us to go to Greenland just to bring back treasure," he said.

"He does rather seem to have his heart set on possessing Gungnir," Shrewsbury agreed.

Heydrich sat back, crossing one long leg over the other. He tapped a forefinger in slow cadence on the table. "The Reichsführer is a passionate believer in the dark and ancient mysteries of the Aryan race, as I believe you're all aware. A great man. Who's done as much as any but the Führer himself to bring Germany to her present greatness." He shrugged. "His fierce love of our race, the unimaginable burdens of his office—who might not be susceptible to a bit of wishful thinking, eh?"

He folded his hands on his knees and looked from one of them to the other, positively caressing Billi with his eyes. An uncomfortable blush rose in her cheeks. "For all his talents as an administrator and policeman of a troubled land, there is one thing Reichsführer SS Himmler is not: an archaeologist." Heydrich smiled. "I seriously doubt he would be able to tell any sufficiently large and gaudy spear of Norse origin from the mythological Gungnir."

"What about Darré and his researchers?" Billi asked.

The smile widened to incorporate Heydrich's eyeteeth. "His researchers are SD, which means they belong to me. Though perhaps the esteemed Gruppenführer Darré entertains different ideas. As I said, it seems certain that what Bjørn Eyjolfson actually discovered was the trove of a Viking chieftain. One he didn't have the chance to despoil." The fine head nodded. "I think I can guarantee you'd have no trouble getting the spear authenticated by the RuSHA."

Billi moved away from him and sat down. "Aren't you getting ahead of yourself, Herr Heydrich?"

"Reinhard," he reminded her softly.

"Er, Reinhard," she amended quickly, and fished nervously in her purse for her cigarette case. "We haven't agreed to go yet."

Heydrich laughed and held out an arm to light her cigarette from an elegant silver lighter embossed with the death's-head on one side and the letters *SD* in diamonds on the other. "The Reichsführer offered you a substantial sum of money."

Billi puffed the cigarette alight. "Money doesn't matter that much to me," she said through the pungent, bluish smoke.

Heydrich shrugged. "A pity you don't wish to be part of this undertaking. I can imagine little that would please the Führer more than granting an exclusive interview with a young woman, foreign at that, who had been so intrepid as to go along on such an important and arduous expedition."

The draught of smoke seemed to catch in her throat. She patted her breastbone and coughed. "I suppose there's no harm in considering the matter," she said, trying to sound nonchalant.

"Your speculations do change the complexion of the matter, certainly," said Shrewsbury, bent over to study the map intently. "To find an authentic Viking chieftain's trove, unspoiled over the centuries . . ."

"The chance of a lifetime," Heydrich said. "For a serious scholar such as yourself." He turned to Rafe. "Your move, Captain *Springer*."

Rafe laughed shortly. His name meant, among other things, a knight in the game of chess. "I don't play, Gruppenführer."

"I should say not," Shrewsbury murmured without looking up.

Rafe stuck his hands in his pockets. "I'm game," he said. "I'd like to see your chimerical mountain range in the middle of the Kong Frederik Land ice sheet. And I can't complain about the pay Herr Himmler offered."

Regretfully Shrewsbury shook his head. "I fear I must decline the invitation, Herr Gruppenführer," he said with real effort. "I am obligated to remain at the University of Berlin until my leave runs out."

Heydrich studied manicured nails. "Perhaps the *Rektor* would see reason if I were to speak with him. Don't you think?" He looked at Rafe. "You needn't make the objection you've in mind. Consider the inexplicable cooling of interest on the University's part in the Congo expedition they had planned—"

"What about my wire service?" Billi asked.

Heydrich shrugged. "Not German. You'll have to deal with them yourself."

He skimmed the map toward himself with his fingertips and rerolled it quickly. "Time you met two of the men who'll accompany you."

No sooner had he spoken than the door opened and the smiling Gestapo colonel escorted in the two men Rafe had seen in the antechamber of Himmler's office. He noticed that Heydrich could not forgo a look of triumph; Rafe was duly impressed by the arrogance and power it took for Heydrich to say the things he had about his superior in a room he

knew full well was wired. Of course, the men operating the
recorder at the other end of those wires were Heydrich's
creatures. But in the shadowy world of the Party secret police, even that was no guarantee of Heydrich's safety.

Heydrich waited until Standartenführer Klein had ab-
sented himself and shut the door before introducing the new-
comers. "May I present my colleague, Oberführer Ernst
Waldmann? And Leutnant Joseph Kampfer, of the Eleventh
Gebirgsjäger-Regiment." He had reverted to German. "Gentlemen, Fräulein Forsyth, Hauptmann Springer, Herr Professor Doktor Shrewsbury."

The two men nodded; they had obviously been briefed in
advance. They were as disparate as it was possible for two
men to be. Leutnant—the rank was equivalent to second
lieutenant—Kampfer was a beautiful youth, though beautiful in a different way than Heydrich. His was not the type
the Nazis put on posters. He was not tall, no taller than
Rafe, though he carried himself with athletic grace and wore
the gray-green Wehrmacht uniform quite well. He was of the
dark Teutonic type, scarcely less typically German than the
stereotypical blond. His skin was olive, his face finely
sculpted, the eyes hazel, the neatly parted hair jet black. His
shoulder tabs were the light green of the mountain troops,
and Rafe was intrigued to see on his sleeve a cloth patch
sporting crossed skis intertwined with oak leaves: the cov-
eted *Ski-Jäger* badge. He clearly belonged to the elite, even
among the elite mountain troops.

He gave Heydrich a snappy military salute—not the *Heil*
and Party straight-arm. Theoretically, the Wehrmacht was
beyond the reach of the Party and its secret police forces, the
SD and Gestapo; its members were subject only to military
law. But both of the secret agencies were under Heydrich's
control, and in this building, as in his own headquarters
around the corner on the Wilhelmstrasse, Reinhard Heydrich
was the whole of the law. The boy had nerve, Rafe thought
as Kampfer firmly clasped his hand. But not much sense,
perhaps.

Waldmann, who nearly broke his arm giving the stiff
Party salute, was no less beautiful in his own way. He was
short and fat and bullnecked, with a perfectly round face,

Hitler mustache, and thinning gray hair combed straight back over his cannonball head. He wore an ill-fitting brown suit and shook hands curtly all around, withdrawing his hand smartly, as if fearing contamination from these foreigners. He was everybody's conception of a Nazi thug. Beautiful.

"General Beck, the Chief of the General Staff, has been kind enough to consent to lend me the lieutenant and five of his men to provide military escort for this expedition," Heydrich explained when everyone had seated themselves around the long table.

Shrewsbury's eyebrows rose. "Military escort?"

"I thought the Eskimos were peaceful," protested Billi.

Heydrich merely cocked an eyebrow at Rafe. "Most of them are," Rafe said, "but it isn't wise to generalize. Some of the Greenland tribes are pretty harsh. And the Danish colonial authority hasn't always done the best job of public relations."

"I see," the professor said.

"So you're ready to consent to shooting our way into the interior?" Billi flared.

"By all means, if the savages attempt to bar our way," the professor said severely.

"I'm not eager to try to force my way through anybody's territory," Rafe said. "But the interior's sparsely settled, if at all. I doubt we'll have much opportunity to trespass."

Throughout the exchange he watched the two Germans who were to accompany them from the corner of his eye. Young Kampfer, ramrod-erect in his chair, looked uncomfortable and unhappy, but it did not seem to be in reaction to the conversation; something else was eating him. Waldmann looked on with beefy disdain.

Looking amused, Heydrich said, "Oberführer Waldmann will be in charge of the expedition."

It took the bombshell a moment to detonate. Rafe and the professor sat still for a moment, Rafe frozen in the act of rolling a cigarette, Shrewsbury gazing at Billi in an unfocused way. Then both their heads snapped toward the SD chief. "What?" Rafe said, while the professor harrumphed, "Out of the question."

"If you could state your objections one at a time—" Heydrich said with heavy irony.

Rafe and Shrewsbury both began talking at once, shut up, and looked at each other. Rafe nodded. "I had assumed that my academic credentials would entitle me to lead this expedition," Shrewsbury said.

Instead of answering, Heydrich swiveled his aristocratic head to stare questioningly at Rafe. "What's your background, Oberführer?" Rafe asked, turning to look at the fat man.

"I was an inspector in the Bavarian State Police for a number of years," Waldmann said in stiff German. "I joined the *Geheime Staatspolizei* in 1934, when Reichsführer SS Himmler took over from Herr Göring." He spoke the latter name with apparent distaste.

"A flatfoot," Rafe said in English. "What kind of experience is that for a man who's going to lead a hazardous expedition into the heart of terra incognita?"

"Oberführer Waldmann is an old comrade of the Reischführer himself," Heydrich said in the most arid of tones. "He enjoys the Reichsführer's utmost confidence."

"In other words," Billi said brightly, "we're stuck with him."

Heydrich smiled. "Admirably put, Miss Forsyth. Besides, Professor, what manner of organizational and administrative expertise have *you*, really? That's as vital a qualification as either field experience or scholarship, I daresay. As for field experience, that's what you're being paid to provide, Captain Springer."

"I vill run a taut ship," Waldmann enunciated painfully, in ghastly music-hall Hun English.

Billi blew a smoke ring. "Great."

Waldmann glared at her. Heydrich cleared his throat softly. Waldmann pulled his head down into his shirt collar like a turtle withdrawing into its shell.

"Another thing to consider, Professor: You're not German. Nor are you, Captain Springer, though you are *Volkdeutsch*. This is a German expedition, to recover a German national relic. We could hardly put an outlander in charge. Could we?"

Shrewsbury stared at the tabletop. "No. No, I suppose not."

"Splendid." Heydrich bounded to his feet like a great hound. "I shall issue orders at once to set the final preparations in train. Standartenführer Klein will see that you are driven to your new accommodations—"

"*New* accommodations?" Billi looked up in surprise.

"Of course. This project enjoys the highest priority. As such, it's bound to attract a certain amount of invidious attention from those who mean ill to our Reich— or our Reichsführer." He scooped up the dossier and snapped it shut. "We've made arrangements to house you in adjoining rooms in a hotel so that we may better protect you."

"House arrest, huh?" Billi blew smoke at Waldmann. "You're housing us at the Aldon, of course."

Heydrich grinned at her. The Aldon was Berlin's premier hotel. It was also Berlin's most expensive. As Billi well knew, since the hotel bar was a favorite watering hole for the foreign press corps. "Of course," Heydrich said.

Waldmann's head retreated deeper into its shell. Rafe halfway expected it to disappear altogether, the broad lapels of the jacket closing over the opening like a plastron. He could guess the source of the Gestapo man's discomfiture. Heydrich had lied through his perfect teeth about arrangements being made at the Aldon. But now they were, thanks to the Gruppenführer's casual affirmation of Billi's cheeky suggestion. And it would be Oberführer Ernst Waldmann, as case officer for the expedition, who would have to answer to the SS comptrollers for the added expense.

Rafe grinned and settled back in his chair. It promised to be an interesting journey.

CHAPTER

Four

"In those clothes, Rafe, my boy," Professor Shrewsbury remarked as the two stood in the crowded lobby of the Hotel Adlon, "you contrive to look almost respectable."

Rafe grinned boyishly. "Thanks." He had on a gleaming black tailcoat, white shirt, and white tie. A lofty silk hat sat tipped at a jaunty angle on his head, and his hands were in the pockets of his trousers. "Heydrich had them sent around. His spies were able to ferret out my measurements, it would appear."

Shrewsbury nodded. "They seem very efficient."

A party of reporters in trench coats and battered fedoras pushed their way out of the bar and walked through the lobby, conversing in loud, abrupt English. They attracted no more attention than did the quieter pair in evening dress in this most cosmopolitan of Europe's grand hotels. Rafe shrugged. "Will Rogers remarked it was a good thing the American taxpayer didn't get all the government he paid for. Germany gives you a good feel for how right he was."

"Now, now, you mustn't be so cynical—but here's our lovely Miss Forsyth."

Lovely was scarcely an adequate description for the vision that glided down the stairs and across the plush red carpet toward them, with two trench coats lumbering dutifully along behind. One of the watchdogs was uncomfortably juggling a black mink stole and a small black silk purse. Billi Forsyth wore a floor-length black silk dress that fit her like skin. Tiny rhinestone straps supported the confection.

She stopped before the two men and pirouetted, flashing a tantalizing glimpse of thigh through the flaring slit in the gown. The plunging back presented an expanse of creamy skin dusted lightly with golden freckles, and shoulder blades etched like wings beneath firm muscles. She held out a gloved hand, a delicate diamond bracelet glittering against black. Matching diamonds swung from her earlobes, and a single marquise-cut stone nestled in the hollow at the base of her throat.

The professor deftly caught the proffered hand. "Your beauty is so incomparable," he murmured, bending low to kiss her hand, "that words cannot capture it."

"Flattery." She smiled. "But I think I'd like to hear you make the attempt sometime." She sent a sideways glance up at him from beneath her lashes, a look that was both maddeningly innocent and breathtakingly sultry. "You're not exactly an eyesore yourself, Professor."

He harrumphed in an unsuccessful attempt at modesty. "Thank you." The fact was, he looked splendid and knew it. The tight cut of his tailcoat and trousers showed what trim shape he really was in, and he wore evening dress with marked panache.

Rafe Springer managed to look comfortable in his formal attire, totally composed and at ease. Professor Shrewsbury, on the other hand, managed something Rafe could admittedly never quite achieve: he was truly elegant. The way Billi's eyes caught his and lingered as he released her hand showed how well aware she was of the fact.

Somewhat hurriedly she turned to Rafe. "Rafael Springer, you're enjoying all this." She swept an arm out to encompass the lobby, Berlin, perhaps all of Germany itself. "Aren't you? And don't try to deny it, standing there grinning as if your teacher had just stuck her hand into a drawer where you'd hidden a frog."

He laughed. "I won't deny it. I wouldn't miss this for the world."

The professor pursed his lips reprovingly. "Come now, Rafe, be serious. This is no pleasure outing."

"It's not?" He cocked a skeptical eyebrow at the professor.

"Why, of course not. My interest in this . . . this fantastic business is purely scholarly. If it weren't for the glimmering of hope that up there in Greenland might await a find of truly significant historical value, I'd throw over this whole charade in an instant."

"He has a point, Rafe," Billi said. "This isn't a game, you know."

"Really." He shook his head. "You two disappoint me. We're standing in the lobby of one of the great hotels of Europe, in the capital of a strange and fearsome empire, a city that lies at the center of a network of intrigue that stretches clear around the world—a web, if you'll permit me the cliché, in which we find ourselves caught at the moment. We are on the verge of embarking on a voyage into the unknown, in search of a fabled treasure, in the face of supposedly supernatural resistance. We're wearing borrowed finery and waiting on the pleasure of one of the deadliest men alive.

"Whatever happens, whether this is a quest in search of fairy gold, whether or not any of us survives—whatever, we're experiencing something the like of which few people could even dream. We are *living* a storybook adventure. And I know both of you altogether too well for there to be any point in pretending *you* aren't enjoying this every bit as much as I am."

Billi laughed. Shrewsbury sniffed. "Storybook adventure, indeed. You've been reading too much of that Burroughs stuff. It's made you almost as mad as Herr Himmler."

Instantly Rafe's cheerful manner dropped away. "In one way you're right," he said in a terse, narrow voice neither of them had heard him use before. "We're in a game, but the stakes we're playing for are very real. And if we let it get out of hand, it can turn ugly quicker than either of you can imagine."

"Whatever do you mean?" Shrewsbury asked, dumbfounded.

"I mean, you'd better be awfully careful who hears your reflections on the sanity of certain prominent citizens of the Reich."

"Don't be ridiculous, boy! No one can hear us. There must be a hundred people in this lobby—"

"And how many of them are plants?" Rafe rapped. The professor hemmed and hawed a moment, and dropped his eyes. "We're not just tourists anymore. We've gotten ourselves *involved,* and if we get into deep water, we can't exactly expect the British or American embassies to be able to fish us out. So tell me, Professor—who among the hundred people in this lobby is here for the express purpose of watching us?"

"Now, Rafe, how can you expect me—"

"I *know* what you did during the Great War, Professor," Rafe said quietly. "Put your Intelligence training to work, and never mind the gentlemanly disclaimers."

Shrewsbury colored. Then he looked around, his light blue eyes coming suddenly to life, flickering around the room while he continued to hold his head as if he were listening attentively to his younger companions, taking in the Persian rugs and potted plants, the sky-blue busboys bustling back and forth, the business barons and celebrities and relict nobles.

"A man over by the wall in that leather armchair," he said shortly, his voice pitched low, "pretending to read the *Deutsche Allgemeine Zeitung.* Over your left shoulder, Miss Forsyth—that's a good girl, no, don't turn and stare at him." She arrested the motion midway and turned back, flushing angrily. "He can cover the entire lobby and the entrance to the lounge."

He grinned sheepishly. "Thanks for giving me the nudge, Rafe. I'd quite forgotten myself." His cheeks had taken on a pink glow, like those of a man riding to the hounds through the chill of an early autumn morning.

"Very good," Rafe said, grinning at the visible change in the professor's demeanor. "Who else?"

"The desk clerk," Billi said, almost spitting out the

words. "He's a poisonous little creature, and he keeps giving us the fish-eye. Not that he's here *expressly* to watch us. But I'll bet he's been told to keep tabs on us too." She turned to Shrewsbury. "And I'm not a *girl,* Dr. Shrewsbury."

Shrewsbury blinked, taken aback by her vehemence. Rafe nodded. He had thrust his hands into his trouser pockets. "There's at least one more," he said. A smile tugged at the corners of his mouth, but his manner was stone serious.

Billi and the professor exchanged looks. "How do you know that?" Billi demanded.

"Call it a sixth sense."

The woman looked skeptical. Still grinning, Rafe pulled a bag of tobacco and a packet of French-made papers from an inner pocket of his Gestapo-supplied tailcoat and began to roll a cigarette. Billi's eyes opened wide. She looked at the professor. Knowing Rafe better than she, he merely shrugged. Rafe was simply unaware of the incongruity of a man in full evening dress rolling himself a Bull Durham smoke in the lobby of the Hotel Adlon. One-handed, no less.

"The man standing there, beyond the counter," he said. "Small, trim, monocled, wearing a Russian greatcoat with mink collar. Acting as if he's got nothing better to do than watch those out-of-work Russian noblemen over by the double doors lambast the bolsheviks in courtly French."

Shrewsbury studied the man a moment, then frowned down his nose at Rafe. "Really, he's obviously a gentleman. You'd not expect him to bustle here and there like a common tradesman."

"Common tradesman?" Billi echoed sweetly. "Do journalists fall into that category, Professor?"

The professor's face flushed. "Perhaps not," Rafe said, a trifle louder than necessary. He wasn't sure why he was bailing Shrewsbury out; if they were all going on an expedition together, the Englishman was going to have to learn to cope with Billi Forsyth's mercurial ways, cloistered don or not. Besides, Rafe knew perfectly well that Melbourne Shrewsbury wasn't all that cloistered.

Nor was he precisely sure what made him finger the

well-dressed, late-thirtyish man in the fur-trimmed coat and Astrakhan as another agent. Just that "sixth sense," and a certain familiarity with the way Reinhard Heydrich picked his *corps d' élite*.

A sudden impish urge made him lift his head and stare directly at the man. Blue eyes, bright in an ascetic's face, met his, held them. The man in the Russian coat smiled and pushed off from the wall, walking directly toward them.

"Are you quite sure that was wise, my boy?" Shrewsbury murmured from the corner of his mouth.

"No."

The small man stopped before them. "Joachim Heinz, Graf Kinski, at your service." He clicked his heels, offset it with a self-deprecating nod. "A pleasure to meet you, Captain Springer," he said, offering a hand as impeccably manicured as his English.

Rafe took it. "I'm not a captain any longer," he said, "but beyond that, the pleasure's mine, Count. I presume you know Miss Forsyth and the professor as well?"

"Only through the medium of their dossiers. Quite dry, by the way. One cannot receive a rounded picture of an individual of any merit from the reports of an army of shabby transom-peepers compiled in a manila folder, in spite of what certain influential parties may believe. If you will permit me?" He held out a silver lighter, flicked a flame alive, held it up to Rafe's hand-rolled cigarette. The blue eyes danced. Rafe bowed his head to accept the light, wondering if the others had caught the implications of the count's studied insolence. His implied contempt for the dossier-loving Reichsführer confirmed Rafe's guess as to which service he belonged to. "For example, no verbal description could do justice to your beauty, Miss Forsyth."

"So I'm told," Billi said, extending her hand for him to kiss. His grin was quick and boyish.

"And you, Professor—a pleasure to meet so distinguished a man of letters."

"It's always gratifying to meet a man of your obvious breeding and discernment, Count," Shrewsbury said warmly, accepting a pale hand worked with a tracery of fine blue veins.

"You're really not very subtle for a Gestapo man," Billi said.

Shrewsbury choked. "Forgive my companion's indiscretion, Count. She's young—and a woman—and, ah, American."

"You do me less than justice, Fräulein," the count said with a smile. "I have the honor of serving my Reich and my Führer as an officer of the *Sicherheitsdienst*."

Shrewsbury frowned and moistened his lips with a pink tongue tip. "Really?" he said, taken aback. "I had rather thought SD operatives were more . . . surreptitious."

Kinski laughed. "You were about to say 'ruffianly,' were you not? My friends, we leave that to our esteemed colleagues of the Prussian State Police—or whatever it is they're calling themselves these days."

"Best not speak too loud, Count," Rafe said, willing enough to play straight man to this charming little aristocrat for the time. "You might offend your two colleagues."

A slim eyebrow arched microscopically. "Indeed—just so," Kinski said after a moment's hesitation. "That's why I made no attempt at secrecy. I knew Captain—that is, Herr Springer's keen eyes would pick me out at once. Besides, I am to be your SD case officer. To play games of hide-and-go-seek would be foolish, is it not so?"

"That seldom seems to slow you Germans down," Billi said at her most poisonously sweet. "Are we to have representatives of every bureaucratic fiefdom in the Reich stumbling into us and introducing themselves as our guardians for the next few days?"

It was Rafe's turn to wince. If Billi insisted on playing her impudent little games with Heydrich, they might soon learn just how much stock the elegant Gruppenführer put in his master's Greenland scheme. But not even Billi Forsyth's candy-coated venom could wither the count's cheerfulness.

"Indeed not, Miss Forsyth. That's one of the reasons I have been assigned to you. To help insure that you are not subject to such . . . intrusions." His eyes darted sideways, and Rafe had the distinct impression they had subjected the thick back of the neck of the man in the armchair perusing his *DAZ* to a quick but penetrating scrutiny.

"Will you be accompanying us tonight?" Rafe asked.

Kinski shook his head. "I regret not. I find Wagner rather heavy going. The light touch, the classical touch: this is what I favor—but here's the Gruppenführer now."

The doors swung open to admit a gust of cold, wet air and the chief of the SD. Heydrich strode in with his quick light-stepped march, resplendent in a dress uniform of gleaming black, a black greatcoat flapping like a cape from his shoulders. The locust buzz of conversation that filled the lobby died abruptly as he entered. As he passed people whispered behind their hands.

He made straight for Billi, catching her right hand up in both of his and bending low to press it to his lips. "Miss Forsyth, you are a vision. Indescribable."

Billi blushed, an act Rafe hadn't known she was capable of. "She knows," he murmured half intentionally, as much to forestall a witticism on her part as for any other reason. Heydrich flashed a quicksilver grin.

"Indeed she must. And you—quite the gallant, Herr Springer. And you, Professor. What a brave company we shall make."

He turned to Kinski as if noticing him for the first time. "I see you've made the acquaintance of our charming count. Good evening, Joachim."

Kinski clicked his heels again—not quite as sardonically as before. "Gruppenführer."

"My car awaits your pleasure, my lady . . . gentlemen." He helped her on with her wrap, then turned and crooked an arm. Billi's teeth brushed her upper lip, a sketch of hesitation. Then she linked her arm through his and smiled boldly up at him.

I don't know whether she's being brave or not, Rafe thought. Even without the immense mana his quiet but near absolute power gave him, Heydrich was quite the type to turn ladies' heads, and did; they turned under feathered hats and faces fair and otherwise showed jealousy through black net veils. Male heads turned to look at Billi, too, some of her fellow journalists with interest, but the Germans maintained an almost Buddha-like inscrutability. One did not display envy or any other encroaching emotion toward

Gruppenführer Heydrich—though, Rafe reflected, he'd probably revel in it if they did.

But if one was Melbourne Shrewsbury, Rafe noticed, one didn't entirely manage to hide a look of irritation as Heydrich strode back along the somewhat mud-tracked maroon carpet with Billi gliding along on his arm.

Repressing an imbecilic urge to break into a soft shoe, or perhaps waggle his eyebrows, twirl his cigarette as if it were a cigar, and duck-walk after them in approved Groucho Marx style, Rafe nodded a good evening to the urbane Count Kinski and followed. He could feel the professor seething behind him. He empathized with the older man but felt little concern. Shrewsbury was not the sort to risk his life indulging in jealous petulance.

A couple of strapping SD men had come in behind Heydrich and stood flanking the door. This pair lacked Joachim, Count Kinski's polish; more obvious gunsels Rafe had seldom seen. He ignored them as studiously as did the lobby loiterers and pushed through the door.

Outside, a thin snow had begun to sprinkle down, dusting the cobbled courtyard like white powdered sugar on a pastry. The doormen cracked to attention as Heydrich swept by with Billi on his arm and bowed her into the backseat of a Mercedes landau. She scooted across; he folded himself in beside her. A black-clad driver shut the door and scuttled around to clamber into the driver's seat.

CHAPTER

Five

"Gentlemen?" Rafe turned at the insinuating voice. A slight man in a black death's-head cap hovered nearby. His gloved hand gestured to a second Mercedes. "If you please. I'm your driver."

He skittered back to hold the rear door open. Rafe got in and slid across the leather seat. Professor Shrewsbury got in after him, looking unhappy.

The door slammed. "Of all the nerve," Shrewsbury sputtered. "Absconding with Miss Forsyth and leaving us to ride behind like footmen."

Rafe shrugged, drew on his cigarette. The driver slid in behind the wheel. "I'm Walter," he explained, racing the engine and letting in the clutch. The car bucked and lurched forward as Heydrich's landau purred onto Unter den Linden. "I'm SD, too, assigned by *him* to be your driver. He doesn't trust you with that Gestapo trash."

Rafe's cheek twitched as the driver, head turned over leather-clad shoulder to address his passengers, steered the big car straight for a granite gatepost. "My good man—" Shrewsbury said in alarm, pointing at the approaching wall.

"No sweat," Walter said blithely, deigning to turn his head in time to veer right, swinging out through the wrought-iron gates and directly in the path of a Mercedes lorry, which fishtailed on the slick street with a scream of

brakes. He turned right, away from the looming Branden-
berg Gate, and shot down Unter den Linden toward the immense square of the Forum Fredericianum, surrounded by
the looming monoliths of the University, the opera house,
and several baroque palaces. Despite shortages and inclement weather, the business-and-bureaucracy district of the
Mitte teemed with vehicles at this hour of the evening.
Walter lunged the massive car in and out of the traffic flow
with the aplomb of a drunken gondolier.

He turned back again as they passed through the shine of
a snow-haloed streetlight, briefly illuminating a sharp face
with black eyes and a prominent, sensitive-looking nose.
"That's quite a piece the Gruppenführer had on his arm, eh?"
His upper lip twitched into a wet leer. "The Crown Prince—
that's what we call him in the Service—he's got a reputation
as quite a swordsman, and not just like at Heidelberg, either."

Shrewsbury's eyebrows crawled up his high forehead like
outraged blond caterpillars. "My *good* man!" he repeated,
voice rising as sharply as his brows.

Rafe had sunk back into the protection of his voluminous
camel-hair overcoat. "Steady, there," he told Walter. "That's
his sister."

Walter blinked, then snapped his head forward again just
in time to keep from piling into the rear of a Citroën.
Shrewsbury stared at Rafe, his look of indignation shifting
outlines into one of puzzlement. Rafe ignored him, peering
out the window at the gray buildings sliding past outside, the
multichambered granite heart of the Reich rendered ghostly
by gusting snow, and listening to the hiss of tires on slush.
After a moment Shrewsbury sat back, but he didn't relax.
Rafe could feel him wound as tight as the guy wires of a
suspension bridge.

He had more important things to consider than his old
professor's putatively wounded feelings. For example, for
what was ostensibly a Gestapo-run operation, the SD was
certainly thick on the ground. Rafe didn't entirely understand the labyrinthine workings of the German intelligence
and security services—but then neither did any other man
living, probably including Hitler's Loyola and his demon

acolyte. Rafe gathered it was the Führer's intention to keep his watchdogs too busy watching one another to have the leisure to plot against their master. In any event, there was pronounced rivalry between SD and *Geheime Staatspolizei*, in spite of the fact that they shared a leader. What part that rivalry might play in this expedition Rafe couldn't guess. But it did little to reassure him.

And who was the extra man in the leather coat? Kinski was good, but so was Rafe Springer, and the count had been startled to learn he had spotted two tails. Who could horn in on a Sicherheitsdienst operation—as Kinski had indicated the surveillance at the Adlon to be—with such apparent impunity? The Gestapo? The minions of Heydrich's mentor turned mortal enemy, Admiral Canaris? Agents of some clandestine Nazi organization not even Rafe had heard of? Even foreign intelligence wasn't out of the question.

Heydrich's car drew up before the Staatsoper and halted. The State Opera House was another late-baroque relic, a great granite mound with soot-streaked muses slouching forlornly along the roofline, gazing in dismay at the glittering ranks of the National Socialist elite debouching from their motorcars below. Heydrich had Billi up the steps and through the portico before Walter skidded the second Mercedes to a halt. Rafe felt Shrewsbury's temperature rise a few more degrees.

Heydrich was waiting for them inside the buttery-warm embrace of the theater lobby. Billi stood at his side, her hand on his arm, a flush to her cheeks that may not have been caused by the cold. Heydrich nodded. "Gentlemen. Forgive me. I could not very well keep the lovely Miss Forsyth outside. . . ." His words trailed off, as they tended to do. He smiled engagingly.

"I quite understand," the professor said, charmed in spite of his irritation.

A couple of acres of white marble lobby glittered under the light of five massive chandeliers. Along the ceiling's edge plump, naked cupids gamboled among gilded plaster garlands and bunches of fruit. No less resplendent than the setting were its occupants. Clinging floor-length dresses with swooping bodices were the order of the day for the women, whether or not their figures merited such close attention, and unless a lot more glints were from rhinestones than Rafe suspected, some elements of the Reich's population were less struck by economic hard times than others.

Rafe and the professor stood out; uniforms were as prevalent for men as off-the-shoulder dresses for the women.

"In the new order uniformity shall be the rule—everyone and his dog shall have a uniform," Rafe said sidelong to Shrewsbury.

"Now, now, Rafael. Your cynicism is showing."

"Think so?" He nodded to a portly old party with monocle and billed cap and a hawser-thick gold braid strung across his portmanteau. "Then tell me that's not a more elaborate version of the outfit the garbage collectors wear."

Shrewsbury peered hard at the man. "Well, I can see— that is—well, yes, I do believe you're right."

Several Party functionaries, Golden Pheasants in full plumage, were exchanging insincerities with Heydrich. Billi drifted over to Rafe and the professor. Shrewsbury took her hands in his. "Are you all right, my child?"

Instead of flaring back at him, as Rafe expected, Billi caught her underlip briefly in her teeth and nodded. "The Gruppen—Reinhard is a very, ah, *emphatic* man."

Before Shrewsbury could strain his imagination over that one, Rafe gave them a quick rundown of what he'd seen. "But that's absurd, Rafe," Shrewsbury protested. "Who might be spying upon Herr Heydrich's men?"

"Any number of people. Who could get away with it is the question that worries me."

Shrewsbury shook his head. "The Gruppenführer mounts a thoroughly professional operation, one must give him that. I—"

Billi started as Heydrich caught her by the arm and twirled her like a waltz partner. "I've been inattentive. Forgive me. Those tedious Party drones..." He looked over thickly massed caps. "But here: Our companions..."

Stumping his way through the gorgeous crowd like a walrus through a pack of gaudy seals was Oberführer Ernst Waldmann. Like Rafe and the professor, he sported tailcoat and white tie, which he wore with the panache of a disgruntled sausage maker. At his side walked young Kampfer in *feldgrau* uniform with his cap tipped to a defiant angle. Obviously under orders to stay close to the stumpy Gestapo man and obviously unhappy about it, he kept as much distance between them as possible, producing an effect like two desperately incompatible circus animals, a polar bear and a tiger perhaps, harnessed together by an invisible cord and trying their best to escape one another.

Waldmann cracked his heels together with a sound like a Parabellum shot. Heads snapped around all over the lobby, and Rafe saw fear standing naked on several faces: *My God, have they started executing people in the lobby of the State Theater* ?

"*Heil Hitler!*" Waldmann bellowed, shooting his arm out from the shoulder.

The look on Heydrich's patrician face suggested the presence of spoiled meat. "Please, Oberführer. We take your loyalty to the Führer as given. Leutnant."

A curt nod to Kampfer, who clicked his heels and bowed. The young officer didn't salute. Rafe knew what he was thinking—black dress uniform or not, fancy title notwithstanding, Reinhard Heydrich was not a member of the German Armed Forces and hadn't been since Grand Admiral Raeder cashiered him from the Navy in 1931. Like every member of the SS, which included the SD and most of the present Gestapo, he belonged to an armed auxiliary of the National Socialist Party, not the Wehrmacht, a distinction the Armed Forces were at pains to maintain.

Though Heydrich's face showed no response to this studied impertinence, Rafe once again wondered as to young Kampfer's judgment. He hoped he would show better sense on the ice.

Then Kampfer kissed Billi's hand. "A pleasure to see you again, Fräulein." Heydrich's wide lips compressed briefly. Take it easy, boy, Rafe wanted to tell the youth.

"This crush becomes irritating. Shall we go?" Heydrich's arm snapped out, indicating the wide staircase leading to the upper lobby and the first level of box seats.

Without waiting for assent, he tucked Billi's arm beneath

his and strode up the steps, masses of humanity parting for
him like water around a particularly large boulder. The small
snack bar on the second floor was doing a brisk business
selling *Saltzbrod* sandwiches and champagne by the glass.
The overheated air was redolent with Speck, the cloyingly
sweet perfume favored by most German women, and the
ill-disguised scent of infrequently washed bodies.

Heydrich led them through the crowds of working jaws to
a small red velvet door. Waldmann leapt forward, held it
open, then frowned in irritation when Rafe and Shrewsbury
entered before him.

The box was arranged with three rows of chairs. Heydrich, Billi, and Shrewsbury arranged themselves in the
front three, Rafe and Kampfer took the two directly behind,
and Waldmann found himself shunted to the backmost chair.
No admirer of opera, Rafe would just as gladly have traded
places with the portly Gestapo man, but he decided that he
would spare Kampfer any further contact with the man. Besides, this chair let him keep an eye on his more erratic
companions.

Heydrich's blond head was bent solicitously over Billi's
red one. His lips were moving, but Rafe couldn't catch the
words. Billi was making a great show of studying her program, but the heightened color in her cheeks indicated she
was not as oblivious to the Grupperführer's words as she
would have liked him to think. Shrewsbury's aristocratic
nostrils were pinched like those of an angry Arabian horse.
Rafe was relieved when his old professor turned his attention
to the great maroon velvet curtain and the crowds milling in
the orchestra below.

With that punctuality the Germans always managed when
it didn't matter, the lights went down precisely at eight fifteen, and the overture to *Tristan und Isolde* engorged the
hall. Behind him Rafe heard the rhythmic creaking of the
chair as Waldmann kept time with energetic bobs of his
spherical head. Kampfer had slumped down until only the
base of his neck and his tailbone were touching the seat.
Like most professional soldiers, he seemed prepared to grab

sleep where he could find it. *Not a music lover,* Rafe thought. *Or maybe he can't take Wagner, either.*

Wedged between Reinhard and Shrewsbury, Billi had the growing sense that the opera house was becoming a good deal warmer, and all the air retreating to the gilded vault of the ceiling. She was no blushing miss, she had had her share of men; she could not mistake the sexual energy flowing off these two.

She slid eyes toward Heydrich. He was looking at her full face. It was like a physical impact. He smiled that devil's smile. Her gaze darted away. Shrewsbury next. His feel was steady, comforting yet somehow exciting. She lifted her program from her lap and began to fan herself. Shrewsbury quickly plucked it from between her fingers and took over. It was a courtly, old-fashioned gesture, and in a perverse way it pleased her.

Intermission at last, and Billi bolted for the lobby. Shrewsbury followed, looking concerned. "Billi, are you feeling quite the thing?"

She gave a tight, brittle little laugh. "Yes. It's just so stuffy in there. Could I have something cold to drink?" He bowed and went, and Billi had time to consider Heydrich. She was both relieved and piqued that he had not followed her from the box, and wondered where he'd got to. *Probably off setting up another plump doe for the kill,* she thought, *and do I care?* She wasn't sure.

The Gruppenführer had in fact followed, at a more leisurely pace than customary, relishing what he considered the foregone conquest of the redheaded little American. He found Rafe standing with his back to a pilaster, restoring his fluid balance with champagne on the SD's tab. "Herr Springer."

Rafe nodded. His eyes were hooded.

"You fear me." It was a flat statement. "That reassures me. Prudent. But you have no awe of me."

He slapped the American on the shoulder. "You have no idea how refreshing that is."

* * *

A chime signaled the beginning of the second act. Billi
and Shrewsbury returned to the box to find the rest already
there. Empty through the first act, the Imperial box was now
the center of frenzied activity. A crowd of twittering women
were gathered about the box, and Billi recognized the portly
form of Hermann Göring bending eagerly, if not easily, forward over the rail to sign the programs they were fluttering
at him. His wife, former actress Emmy Sonnemann, sat at
his left with a somewhat fixed smile on her wide, soft face.

How does she stand it? Billi wondered. *I'd kill something
if my husband looked at another woman—hell, women—the
way that fat pig is.* The lights dimmed. Cheeks flushed,
blowing kisses after the disappointed ladies who had failed
to secure his autograph, the Marschall, in his resplendent
sky-blue glad rags, promised to remain available during the
next break.

Billi slid another glance to Heydrich and found that he,
too, had been observing the goings-on in the Imperial box.
His narrow lips had thinned almost to invisibility. His nostrils pinched fastidiously as he watched the Luftwaffe chief
busily nuzzling Emmy's suety neck.

Heydrich had seemed somewhat bored by the opera's first
act, but with the opening strains of the *Liebesnacht* he turned
his full attention to the stage. The lush, almost unbearably
erotic music of the love duet washed across the hall, and
Billi again divided her attention between the don and the
Gruppenführer.

This time Heydrich did not return her scrutiny. His lips
were compressed, one long, white hand fingering out the
first violin part. Billi remembered that in addition to being a
first-ranked fencer, Heydrich had a reputation as a fine vio-
linist. But she found something almost repellent about those
long, white fingers walking across the red velvet covering
on the balustrade. They kept reminding her of albino
spiders. The image forcibly brought to mind Rafe's trope of
their being trapped in a web. Imperceptibly she drew closer
to Shrewsbury, drinking in the fresh, almost baby scent of
the man and contrasting it with the bittersweet after-shave

affected by the Nazi officer. For some reason the contrast of odors brought to mind innocence versus power.

Maybe I like innocence better. She gave Shrewsbury's arm a quick squeeze. He shot her a surprised glance, then settled back with a certain smugness on his face.

But still, Heydrich's such a handsome devil. Damn him.

"Well, that was unrelievedly depressing," Billi announced as they shuffled toward the door. She clung to Shrewsbury's left arm like a burr. Waldmann glared and muttered under his breath. Billi gave him her poisoned-sweet smile in return.

"I take it you are not fond of tragedy, Miss Forsyth." Heydrich's pale eyes flicked like a whip over the crowd, searching for a quick exit. "Waldmann," he finally snapped in German. "Clear our way."

The Gestapo man bulldozed into the crowd, ruthlessly opening a path to the door. Fine feathered dignitaries voiced discreet resentment. Complaint quickly faded as Heydrich rushed down the cleared lane.

The two Mercedes were still parked out front. Heydrich bowed to Billi and indicated the front car. Her face crumpled momentarily, and her grip tightened on Shrewsbury. But the tremor of intent passed quickly, and with jaunty grin set firmly back in place, she climbed into Heydrich's car.

"Poor child," grumbled Shrewsbury as he followed Rafe to the other Mercedes. "It was quite clear she wanted to stay with me."

"Fortunately she had the good sense to acquiesce to the Gruppenführer's invitation."

"I should have been more forceful. Let him know that we do not approve of this sort of emotional intimidation."

"You really think playing tug-of-war with Reinhard Heydrich would be the way to accomplish that?"

Walter slid in next to Rafe. His ears were bright pink with cold. "By the way, Captain," he said, "there's a little something you left behind."

"What's that?"

For reply Walter tossed something with a heavy thump on the leather between them. Rafe stared at it as if it were a dead animal. It was his big Colt pistol in its scuffed shoulder holster.

CHAPTER
Six

"You are interested in aviation, Fräulein Forsyth?" Heydrich asked over salad. "Excellent. You must come flying. I've a new aeroplane, the latest from the Bavarian Aircraft Works. Typhoon, they call it. Willi Messerschmidt design. Smashing."

Around them, forks rang discreetly on fine china like so many wind chimes, and waiters moved like breezes among ferns and diners dressed to the nines, endlessly reiterated in the mirrors covering the walls. Restaurant Horcher, in Lutherstrasse near the Zoo, was the undisputed place to go for a fine dinner after the theater, or at any other time. Herr Horcher himself had met them at the door, and Heydrich had stood there smiling like a wolf as the proprietor had hustled them in ahead of some wealthy burgher and his hefty Frau.

Rafe repressed a smile as Billi glanced first to him and then to the professor. Billi had never hidden the fact that she found him attractive, yet one way or another they had never found their way to bed. Now her attention was wavering between Shrewsbury and the predatory Gruppenführer. Never one to let himself be drawn into rivalry, Rafe was mostly amused. He did hope Billi was worldly enough to know just what she'd be letting herself in for if she gave in to Heydrich's charms, however.

The glass armor of her poise snapped into place. She

reached out and moved the elaborate floral centerpiece out of the center of the table, placed it near her right elbow. She gave Heydrich a sparkling smile.

"This thing is so irritating. I can't see my other handsome male companions. And, yes, I'd be delighted to fly with you, Reinhard." Shrewsbury stared glumly at his plate. "Perhaps on our return . . ." She let the words trail away as if in unconscious parody of Heydrich. The don glanced up again, suddenly hopeful, and Rafe found himself wishing Billi would stop playing with his old teacher.

Glass in hand, Heydrich turned to Shrewsbury, on his right, with some question Rafe couldn't catch. He guessed it had to do with the professor's work, because Shrewsbury brightened visibly, sitting up a little straighter and answering, with animation, to Heydrich's nods of apparently avid interest. Like a Renaissance prince, Heydrich prided himself on mastery of arts and sciences, conversation not least among them.

Seated on the other side of Shrewsbury from the SD chief, trying to maintain that mellow, alcoholic glow without getting too drunk to safely carry the weapon Walter had inexplicably—and unquestionably on Heydrich's orders—returned to him, Rafe felt a flare of insight as to what Heydrich was about. If he won the British don's friendship, it would make it that much more poignant when he had his way with the woman Shrewsbury was so blatantly smitten with.

A waiter materialized at Billi's elbow to replenish the wine in her glass. Rafe was startled by the way its level kept dropping. She'd never been a very hard-drinking type.

"Herr Springer."

Rafe glanced at Kampfer, seated to his right, studiously ignoring Waldmann, who was stacked on the other side of the young officer like a dour herring barrel. If he noticed the unnatural hump beneath the right arm of Rafe's dinner jacket, he wasn't giving anything away. Probably he'd burned his eyes too raw on Billi to see.

"Leutnant."

"I understand you were raised on a ranch out, ah, out West."

"Word gets around. It's true, I was."

"And did you know cowboys?" His eyes shone.

Rafe nodded, laughed. Another good German youth raised on Karl May Westerns and therefore filled to the brim with images of white-hatted heroes and noble Indians. It would have soothed old Rousseau's breast.

Rafe might have told Kampfer that where he came from, cowboys were basic manual laborers, enjoying about the same status in society as stevedores, but he didn't have the heart. Instead he said, "I was one myself," and that was true too. For all their aristocratic background, both his parents believed in offspring making themselves useful.

So now, of course, nothing would do but to regale Kampfer with stories of life out West. Heydrich and Shrewsbury broke off to listen, and even Waldmann showed signs of interest.

Entrées arrived while he was on the subject of one of his mother's uncles. "He had a thirty-two caliber rifle sawed off at stock and barrel, with a little stud soldered onto the side of the receiver that fit into a hole in a plate in his belt and acted as a swivel," he was saying. He was a little surprised at himself; this wasn't a story he generally trotted out in company. Maybe he was hitting the wine a little hard. "He used to ride out with the thing hidden under his *sarape*. When he caught Indians crossing his land, he'd reach inside, swivel the piece up, and shoot them down where they stood. Needless to say, that caused a certain amount of talk, but no one ever did anything about it."

"Barbaric," Heydrich said, smiling, shaking his head with admiration. "Your West breeds men, Rafe Springer."

Billi was settled back with a tight little half smile, figuring he was spinning out yarns for the benefit of these cowboy-mad Europeans and maybe a bit miffed at no longer being the center of attention. "Your veal, mademoiselle," the waiter said. She glanced up as he leaned forward to place her plate before her.

As he moved away, Rafe's eye caught a furtive flash of motion, and one of the flowers in the centerpiece quivered. *That's where she's putting all that wine,* he realized. *The proverbial potted-plant trick!*

"*Fräulein*," Waldmann said, "you've spilled your wine."

Billi froze with the glass poised beside the table's white-linen lip. "The waiter." Waldmann stared at her like a toad gauging the range to a fly. "He bumped my arm," she amplified breathlessly, sensing that the Gestapo man did not believe her.

"What's this?" Heydrich asked, his fine brow lowering.

"You!" Waldmann barked at the waiter, who plainly didn't understand English and was still passing out plates in blithe ignorance. "What's your name?"

"Why, Kranz, sir."

"First name."

"Johann, sir." A catenary of sweat drops decked his retreated hairline. He had no idea what was going on, but he knew Gestapo when he saw them.

"Perhaps," Heydrich said, his normally shrill voice pitched down to a buzz as ominous as a wasp on a warm summer day, "you should apologize to the young lady for your clumsiness in jostling her arm."

"But I—" He bit the sentence in half. Contradicting the Gruppenführer was no way to stay healthy.

He turned to Billi. "Forgive me, Fräulein, I swear it was unintentional. I only hope that you can forgive me, I . . ."

All the color in Billi's cheeks had drained away to somewhere within her tight black bodice. "Of course," she said, almost choking. "It was only an accident, not your fault at all."

Anxiety and guilt hadn't helped Billi's faltering German; perhaps the man didn't even understand her. "Really, *es war nichts*—oh, damn this language!" She grabbed his hand with both of hers, squeezed tightly.

He piped down, looking at her with the eyes of a frightened horse. "Leave us," Heydrich rapped. Relieved, the man practically stumbled to the kitchen.

Around them the cricket chorus of silver on china commenced again. "Really, I should think Herr Horcher would hire more competent help," Heydrich sniffed as Billi studied her hands. Her fingers were so tightly laced that the blood showed like lavender crescents beneath the nails.

Beside her Waldmann gave Rafe a look as hard and flat as armor plate. He knew what she'd done, knew Rafe had seen it too. The gray eyes shifted a few seconds of arc right, toward Heydrich, and Rafe sensed Waldmann's contemptuous amusement that the vaunted Gruppenführer had not noticed the trick. Whatever else he was, Heydrich was an amateur at police work. Whatever else *he* was, Waldmann was a pro.

They started in on the main course, Billi with little appetite. Heydrich resumed his conversation with Shrewsbury as if nothing had happened. Presently Waldmann excused himself, made his way to the front of the crystal chamber.

"He'd better not come on too strong to Herr Horcher," Kampfer said from the corner of his mouth. "*Der grosse Hermann* will have words with him." Rafe grinned at the kid's use of the Berliner's punning nickname for Göring— classically it referred to the ancient leader Arminius, who beat the Roman Legion at the Teutoburger Wald, but it also meant Fat Hermann. Horcher's was the Marschall's favorite eatery.

Presently Waldmann came lumbering back to resume his place. "Are you feeling unwell, Herr Waldmann? Perhaps you ought to go home," Billi suggested, all solicitousness.

He touched his throat with a thick forefinger. "Only a bit of fish bone."

"Pity you didn't choke on it," muttered Billi in English, and in an undertone that unfortunately fell in one of those inexplicable conversational lulls that can blanket a room and so carried easily to every member of the party.

"Miss Forsyth!" Shrewsbury exclaimed. His English comprehension unequal to Billi's aside, Waldmann just frowned. Rafe felt a headache coming on.

Dessert arrived, baked Alaska of inordinate size, served by Herr Horcher himself with obvious pride. Appetite revived, Billi was just attacking it when a scream rang out, audible even from the kitchen: "Dear God, don't! *Let me go!*"

Rafe was on his feet with his .45 in his hand. Diners dove under tables as he raced for the kitchen. Shouldering past a waiter turned to stone in the swinging doorway with a laden tray upraised above his head, he caught a glimpse of Billi eeling out of Professor Shrewsbury's frantic grasp to follow.

The kitchen was hot and humid and full of faces the color of boiled linen. The advent of a wild-eyed American waving a gigantic gun didn't even faze the cooks and busboys standing around. "What happened here?" Rafe demanded.

A chef's hat nodded at the back door, desultory snow-flakes filtering in through its yawn. "Kranz, the waiter. The Gestapo just came in and grabbed him. Just like that."

"An outrage!" somebody said. "When the revolution comes—"

"Shut up," the chef said.

"But this is Berlin!"

"It's also *das dritte Reich*. You'll live longer if you keep that in mind."

Rafe turned back to find Kampfer and Billi jammed into the doorway, the professor bouncing from foot to foot behind. Viciously Rafe thrust the pistol back into its holster and stared at Billi very hard.

Her face crumpled. She lowered her chin to her throat and squeezed her eyes so tightly shut her cheek muscles quivered. Rafe pushed past and walked back to the table, hands in the pockets of his jacket.

Heydrich was waiting with a big cigar and a bigger grin. "You're quick with that thing, friend Rafe. Are you good with it?"

Rafe shrugged.

Heydrich nodded. "I was right. As always. I feel much safer with you at my back."

Billi returned, supported by the professor and Kampfer, shooting barbed glances at each other over the top of her head. "Well, my friends," Heydrich said, running the tips of his fingers rapidly once over his open palm, "are we ready for further diversion? I know a little club—quite the place. The entertainment—most cosmopolitan." He leered at Billi quite openly.

She held her head well up to the full extent of her neck,

shook it in short arcs. "Not tonight, Reinhard. I find the evening's events have quite fatigued me."

Heydrich's face pinched momentarily. The venison Rafe had eaten began an uneasy polka with the lingonberry sauce and Bordeaux down there in his stomach. He would not have picked Heydrich as a man to take well to refusal. In his line of work he wouldn't have had much practice at it.

Heydrich's brow smoothed and he turned away. "Very well," he said, speaking as if Billi had just been transformed into a chair. "My driver will return you—Gentlemen? Are you with me? This cabaret—you've not seen anything like it."

Rafe, who'd been in Havana, doubted that. He shook his head. "Miss Forsyth's right. It's been a pretty eventful day. Guess I'll turn in too."

"My thoughts precisely, Rafe," Shrewsbury said. "Truly, Gruppenführer Heydrich, you've been a most gracious host."

Heydrich snapped his head up and down. He jerked his head at Waldmann and Kampfer like the lord of the manor summoning his grooms and strode out of the restaurant, barely pausing to allow Herr Horcher to help him on with his greatcoat. Waldmann gave the foreigners a last, bleak look, then vanished into a swirl of snow.

"Well." Breath gusted out of Billi in a sigh. "It's been quite the . . . educational evening." Her eyes met Rafe's for a brief instant, then dropped.

"Indeed," said the professor.

Jaunty grin back in place, Billi looked from one to the other, crooked both elbows outward at her sides. "Gentlemen—shall we?"

Since Heydrich had been in his Medici mood when he ordered housing arrangements, each had a room to him or herself on the third floor. Rafe and the professor were next to each other, Billi several doors down. Rafe suspected the setup was deliberate, to cut Billi out from her male companions. He kept the opinion to himself, bade his friends good night under the watchful eye of a pair of Gestapo heavies holding down the carpet in the corridor, and went to bed.

In her room Billi quickly stripped down to garter belt and hose. Backless or not, the evening gown had begun to feel just a bit clammy, and the ever-solicitous Adlon staff had cranked the radiator all the way up, so that the air was like hot, wet felt.

She went into the bathroom—the Adlon was a very posh hotel indeed, and a very modern one, so her room in fact came equipped with a private lavatory, complete with commode, bidet, and an enormous bathtub with eagle's feet clutching gilded globes. She brushed her teeth and thought about Reinhard Heydrich.

Should I have gone on with him? Part of her regretted that she hadn't, though she was under no illusions as to just what sort of entertainment the Gruppenführer had in mind to cap the evening, either at his cabaret or afterward. She was no innocent little girl, no matter what Professor Melbourne Shrewsbury liked to think.

Heydrich gave her a delicious feeling. She couldn't deny it; she liked the aura of danger that pulsed around him like heat from that confounded radiator singing to itself in the other room, the air of almost conscious evil he affected.

For all that she viewed the world as a place where fat capitalists spent much of their time conspiring to oppress the workers, just about all the people she'd ever encountered in person spent *their* time trying to do what they thought right, the best they could.

Heydrich was the only man she'd ever seen anywhere but on a movie screen who wore villainy like a cloak. The Gestapo in their leather coats and jaunty little fedoras, the Party bureaucrats the Berliners called Golden Pheasants, their tunics crusted with medals and stretched to sausage tautness over bulging paunches, even that drab, oddly pathetic little man in his office at 8 Prinz Albrechstrasse, who could snuff a thousand lives as easily as a candle flame—they all thought what they did was right, just and natural. Sometimes it required mental gymnastics, or selective blindness, but they were all, like Brutus, honorable men—so Billi realized when she was being honest with herself, as she was tonight.

But not Heydrich. He made no excuses. Her scruples notwithstanding, Billi found such forthrightness damned attractive.

The good are such bores.

Yes. In the end she would have gone with him. But the incident with the waiter had been like cold water thrown in her face. Hard to admire evil when it came crashing into the real world from the abstract plane, right before your eyes. Reality was tough on romance.

Enough of Reinhard. Her refusal had irked him, and he had dismissed her; the hell with him. She spat into the sink, rinsed her mouth, and felt refreshed and relieved. In truth, she might have had a narrow escape.

She opened a jar of cold cream, began to remove her makeup. *The Professor's wrong,* she told herself. *You are definitely not a girl.* She was thirty-two; the skin of her face was a bit drier, fine lines just visible around mouth and eyes.

"And what have you done with those years, Wilhelmina?" She could hear her mother ask the question. Not what her family had intended for her, that was certain: early marriage to some well-scrubbed Harvard boy, discreet children, the clubby life. Would that have been better than what she had? Sometimes she had to ask the question too.

Well. Maybe this wild-goose chase to Greenland would somehow prove worthwhile. Give back some sort of definition to her life. Resting her hands on the edge of the basin, she leaned in close and studied her image in the mirror. In her mind's eye it was a shattered cubist picture that stared back. Maybe it would be more than she could take; maybe the uneasy consensus that she felt was herself would come apart in endless Arctic twilight, beneath the weight of a challenge she couldn't escape.

Isn't that how you've lived your life? Running from one crisis to the next, skipping from one experience to the next like stones across a stream, never getting your feet wet? Never really living. But what will you do when the next step's a hundred miles of ice?

She ripped tissues from a box and scoured cream from her face, shaking the thought away. For some reason she thought of Rafe Springer, and the flick of irritation his image summoned perversely made her feel better, as it often did.

The hell with you, Rafe. When Professor Shrewsbury treated her like a child, that was one thing. When Rafe did it, it had another meaning—that she could do better, could do without her glass-brittle games. She felt his unspoken faith in her basic capability as an affront: how could he think better of her than she did herself?

She changed to a flannel nightgown, turned down the hateful radiator, and went to bed. She shut the bedside light like a door on the mock-baroque elegance of the room and pulled the covers to her chin. The comforter promptly slid off onto the floor.

She sighed. The comforter was an inevitable article of German bedclothing, a vast buff-colored feather-inflated blimp universally excoriated by foreigners. She bent out of bed, grabbed a handful of seam, dragged the thing on top of her.

She lay on her back until she could make out the elaborations of molding at the fringes of the ceiling. Restless, she rolled onto her side.

The comforter slithered onto the floor.

She retrieved it. It was like manhandling the carcass of a horse, desiccated to near weightlessness and somehow pliable, but all but unmanageable. She pulled the sheet to her ears and drew her knees almost to her breasts.

Berlin night overwhelmed drawn curtains with its relentless glow. The radiator pinged random notes like a man playing a modern composition with a collection of partly-filled water glasses and a mallet. When it began to feel as if each beat of her heart was driving the ball of her hip into her like a tent peg, she straightened her legs—and was not quite quick enough on the grab to prevent the comforter's making good its escape.

"Damn," she said.

The light let all the baroque back into the room. She rose, went to the bathroom, where she stripped out of her bulky gown and reapplied her makeup, misted Shalimar onto breast, thighs, and backs of knees. Back in the bedroom, she withdrew a frothy sea-green confection from her bag, slipped it over her head. Lace peignoir, her key in her-pocket. She patted her hip, a self-reassuring little gesture, stepped into the hall.

Down at the end of the corridor a middle-aged man with thinning hair and jug-handle ears sat reading a newspaper and ignoring attempts at conversation by a strapping youth whose blond hair was shaved to firebreaks above his ears, who stood over him endangering the glass flower of a light fixture with his head.

At the sound of Billi's door shutting, the blond boy jerked his head around and cracked the back of it smartly against the curving brass stem of the wall lamp. He caught her just as she reached the professor's door. "Fräulein! You're not supposed to be out at this hour of the night."

She gave him a look.

"Wait!" He tried to interpose himself between her and the door as she raised her hand to knock. He reached for her, and his hand jittered in air like a bird facing an uncertain landing. She was a guest of the Reichsführer and a woman, besides; actually *touching* her could have the direst consequences.

Still waving his hand as if to distract her attention from the forbidden door, he pointed off down the hall with the other. "Dere," he said in clubfooted English. "Your toor. Down dzat way. T'at where you belong, *ja.*"

She pulled her shoulder blades together and pinned him with her eyes. "For God's sake, don't you have the decency to let me seduce a man in peace?" she asked in imperious if scrambled German.

His face exploded in pink. He shrank from her like ice cream from a hot poker. Down at the end of the hall his companion uttered a single *Nebelkrähe* caw of laughter and went back to his paper.

The door gave way before Billi's knuckles. "What in God's name is this confounded racket—oh. I do beg your pardon, Miss Forsyth."

"I was just requesting that this ragamuffin permit me to seduce you in peace, Professor."

"Well, I should certainly say that you're quite within your —I *beg* your pardon?"

She smiled sweetly.

"I, ah, I'm afraid I fail to understand."

The Hitler Youth poster boy had mustered his courage. "It's forbidden for you to leave your rooms at night," he announced, feeling once more secure in the embrace of Orders.

"The ways of the heart will not be denied," Billi said in German. She committed an outlandish wink. Shrewsbury raised an eyebrow. "I cannot sleep for thinking of this man."

"I do beg your pardon?" the professor said again.

Billi's left eyelid worked like a signal lamp. He stood there enriching her comprehension of the word *dumbstruck*. "I ant-way to alk-tay," she said, "and is-thay erk-jay ouldn't-way et-lay e-may."

Shrewsbury frowned at her. She considered kicking him in the shin, but then he blinked and said, "Ah! I begin to see."

The kid was trying to work his way between them again. "For Christ's sake, come away and let them fornicate in peace," his partner called down the hall. "You'll rouse the whole floor."

"But we're Gestapo!"

"*I'm* Gestapo, you little prick. You're a country lout with the pig shit still between your toes—and between your ears, by the way you act."

Seemingly on the verge of tears, the boy lurched back from the door. Billi squirted inside and slammed the door behind her. "I was beginning to wonder if maybe you weren't half bright, Professor."

"Well, you have to admit you chose rather a shocking subterfuge." His cheeks were the same color the juvenile secret policeman's had been. "Might I offer you something to drink?"

"Whiskey would do nicely. Or don't you drink that, either?"

"Don't I? Oh. I see. You're referring to this afternoon, when I mentioned I don't care for tea, and—"

"Professor."

"Yes, Miss Forsyth?"

"You're running on. And call me Billi."

"Yes, I suppose I was—Billi. But you must admit you gave me rather a surprise."

He pottered down the brief hallway into the room, went to his suitcase, drew out a bottle of Irish. "Fortunate that I prevailed on Rafe to teach me your pig Latin when he read under me at Oxford. Interested in languages, don't you know."

There were glasses on the bureau. "I've no mixer."

"I'll take it straight."

Shrewsbury looked doubtful. "You really are a most unorthodox young woman," he said, pouring two fingers. "I must say, that was quite a cunning ruse you concocted. But risky of your reputation, don't you think?"

Billi looked at him. He had on white pajamas with pale blue pinstripes, a blue dressing gown over them. His temples were dabbed with gray. He was really quite striking.

She propped an elbow against the wall and shot her hip. Her eyes were very large.

"And what," she purred, "makes you think it was a ruse, Professor?"

CHAPTER
Seven

"God, this exploration business is exciting," Billi drawled. She was dressed in slacks and a café-au-lait silk blouse, perched on the narrow sill of a window in Rafe's room, staring out at the denatured morning sunlight.

Rafe, the professor, and Leutnant Kampfer were clustered around a table covered in maps and notebooks, hammering at logistics. For some reason, expedition head Waldmann had not been invited to this morning-after planning session. "Now, Billi," Shrewsbury said solicitously, glancing up from where he stood next to the young lieutenant, "this needn't be of any concern to you. Why don't you just run along?"

"Because I'm part of this team, dammit!" she snapped. Shrewsbury recoiled.

"Little testy this morning, aren't we?" Rafe remarked, blowing at the black coffee he'd just poured himself from the huge flowered porcelain pot that room service had sent up. There was some new tension between Billi and the professor. He didn't welcome the development.

Shrewsbury stood watching the edge of the table with apparent interest. "Fräulein," Kampfer said, all solicitude, "perhaps you should reconsider. This journey will be full of very great hardships. More than a woman should be asked to endure."

She stubbed her cigarette viciously in an ashtray on the

sill beside her. "Great. Another overgrown Boy Scout. I know what I'm getting into, Lieutenant. I'm not the helpless hothouse flower everyone seems to think I am." She cast a fierce look at the radiator hissing beneath the other window. "Including the staff of this damned hotel."

Kampfer looked wounded, confused. "But, Fräulein, the physical rigors will be extreme."

"When I was growing up, I spent my summers on a farm in Vermont. I am not a Dresden doll, Lieutenant, no matter how much certain parties wish to make me into one." She shot a smoldering glance at Shrewsbury.

"Billi." It was Rafe, speaking quietly from the depths of his chair. "If all goes well—which it won't—the trip overland to these magic mountains and back needn't take more than a few weeks. But they'll be the most grueling weeks you've ever spent. That I promise you."

He flicked his eyes to Kampfer. "With all due respect, Lieutenant, I wonder if *you* realize just what you're letting yourself into. What kind of experience do you and your people have?"

Kampfer drew himself erect. "My men and I have just completed a winter-warfare training course in—ah, *under* the most exacting conditions. I was allowed to pick the six best men from my platoon for this detached service, and we have also a winter-warfare instructor, a Finn, who will accompany the expedition. Like myself, all possess the *Ski-Jäger* badge."

"Which they don't hand out in boxes of Cracker Jack. I know. But ski training isn't the whole story. Have you done glacier work?"

A rocker-arm nod. "On the Great Aletsch Glacier, Herr Springer."

"No work with dogsleds? I thought not. Well, the ice work helps—but crossing the Greenland cap compares to that the way swimming the Channel compares to doing laps in some *Sportpalast.*

"This is not an ideal time for our little jaunt. We are going to have the tail end of the winter storms rolling over us. Our eyebrows will crust over with ice, and the snow is going to blow constantly into our faces like a desert sandstorm. Exert yourself, sweat a little, and you cook inside your parka. Since the sun came up at that latitude two or three weeks ago, when the storms let up we'll have some hours of daylight each day, which means the danger of snowblindness. The warming means the ice is going to be active, crevasses opening up right beneath our feet."

Kampfer couldn't keep his lip from curling. "We are perfectly inured to such conditions, Herr Hauptmann."

"Yeah. But not for a month at a time. And manhandling the sleds—it's really too bad Dante didn't know about them, because running the dogs is a special kind of hell. The sleds are heavy when they're loaded with supplies. We'll be using European-made ones left over from one of that crackpot Wegener's expeditions—steel runners so we won't have to waste time polishing the native ones, which are made of bone. They can break your foot if you aren't wary. You have to help push the things up hills and dig in your heels to brake going down; unless you've actually done it, it's hard to imagine just how unwieldy they are.

"On the flat there's an exhausting rhythm to be maintained. First you run behind the sled, then trot along with it at about three miles an hour to warm up. Then you do a quick sprint, running in front of the dogs to encourage them, being careful not to let your lungs freeze in the icy air. Another minute behind the sled, holding on to the *napariaq*, and you run forward and jump onto the sled from the side. But you'd better make sure you don't miss it. Happened once to a friend of mine. As he sat in the snow he watched his sled vanish into the night. The dogs are kept hungry, so they'll race on in hope of a camp or prey—and race on they do, whether you're along for the ride or not."

He sat on the table edge. "Ah, yes, the dogs. They're savage bastards. The Eskimos generally treat them with a brutality that is going to turn your stomach, and as I said, they starve the beasts. Not uncommonly they eke out their diet with one another; if you're not alert, they won't hesitate to supplement their diet with you.

"Finally there are the Eskimos themselves. We'll be hiring guides and dog handlers with teams. They have a lot of admirable qualities, but some of their practices you are not

—any of you—going to find much more congenial than their notion of humane treatment of animals."

Professor Shrewsbury let go a long, unsteady breath.

"Oh, gosh, oh, gee, Mr. Springer," Billi cooed. "This sounds *sooo* scary. Maybe I'd better pack up and run right back to Boston where I'll be safe."

She blew smoke through her nostrils and pinned Rafe with a glance. He made a sour mouth. "Just one little question. Which one of you heroes is going to volunteer to tell Himmler I'm not going on this little pleasure cruise? He seemed quite set on the notion."

There was a moment of uncomfortable silence, then Kampfer, ignoring Billi's spiteful interruption, said, "Fair enough, Herr Springer. But what of you three? What experience have you, to qualify you for such an ordeal?" His olive cheeks still showed two spots of color.

"I've been to the interior," Rafe reminded him.

"Don't forget I'm an intrepid girl journalist," Billi said. "I've done my share of skiing, downhill and cross-country. I've competed in the Langlauf a couple of times. *And* I've some acquaintance with mountaineering, Lieutenant."

Kampfer nodded. "And yourself, Herr Professor?"

"Well, ah, I'm an active hiker. I've always been most concerned to keep myself fit. Keep the wind and legs from going, don't you know?"

"In other words," Rafe said, rolling a smoke, "he doesn't ski."

"We're going to have to carry you on our backs, Professor?" Billi asked.

Shrewsbury tossed her a hurt look. "The professor does appear in excellent shape for one of his advanced age," said Kampfer, attempting to come to the aid of a fellow male embattled. Shrewsbury gave him a look too. Rafe tried not to grin too overtly.

"My team does include one of the foremost ski instructors on the Continent," Kampfer went on. "A few days with Uurtamo will see you running on skis as if you were born on them."

"Cross-country techniques aren't hard to pick up," Rafe said to the professor, who was looking distinctly dubious.

"And we're going to be at least a week outfitting—if we can do it that quickly, which seems unlikely."

Kampfer tapped the lists they'd spent the morning poring over with his fingertips. "Aside from the sleds, which the University has in storage, there's nothing here private outfitters don't have on hand right here in Berlin." One thing Heydrich had made clear at the initial meeting the day before was that their equipage would be purchased from civilian dealers with SS funds, instead of being SS- or military-issue. "This project is dear to the Reichsführer's heart. Things will be expedited."

Shrewsbury nodded knowingly. "The legendary German efficiency."

"Which largely belongs to the realm of legend," Rafe said from his armchair. Kampfer looked hurt. Despite the earlier flare he'd directed at Rafe when he felt the competence of himself and his men was being questioned, he generally acted quite in awe of the older man. To his active Bavarian imagination Rafe Springer was a figure out of romance: war hero, adventurer, and most exalted of all, cowboy. Actually, in weaker moments, Rafe felt pretty much the same way about himself, but that was one of very few self-truths he would have died before admitting.

On the other hand, their supply requirements were pretty straightforward: winter clothing, medical stores, preserved food. Rafe was a follower of Arctic explorer Vilhjalmur Santesson (himself a former cowboy), but Santesson's "friendly Arctic" of plentiful food supplies was coastal. The inland ice was a desert far more devoid of life than Death Valley. Still, with the exception of the special sleds, which the University fortuitously had to hand, all they needed should be easy to come by.

"You're the experienced hand, Rafe," Shrewsbury said, "but I believe we've covered everything in terms of what we'll require." Kampfer nodded agreement.

Rafe sighed, slugged the rest of his coffee, stood. "Now comes the fun part. We get to take our wish list to our fearless leader, the Oberführer."

Billi pushed off the sill and hit the floor with a sharp little tick. "This is where I get off. Have fun with Herr Kugel-kopf."

Kampfer laughed. "Where are you headed?" Rafe asked guardedly.

A flip of the head set her short-cropped curls to bouncing. "Out."

"The watchdogs are going to want more of an answer than that."

Her eyes flashed at him, but she said, "All right. I want to get in touch with my bureau. I have responsibilities."

"But Billi," the professor said, "the Oberführer expressly forbade you to communicate with your news agency."

"Watch me." She grinned, came up to him, stretched on tiptoe, kissed him on the lips, and patted his cheek. Then she went out, heels tapping like a hot drum solo.

Melbourne Shrewsbury shook his head like a bull beset by *picadors*. "For the life of me, I cannot make that child out."

Rafe patted him on the shoulder. "Don't brood about it, Professor. Neither can she."

There were four leather trench coats holding down various patches of carpet in the hall when Billi emerged from her own room with her coat over her shoulder. She was amazed at the amount of energy that was being devoted to this ludicrous scheme. *Shouldn't the police have better things to do in a police state?*

She smiled sweetly at them as she passed. They nodded back politely. Two matter-of-factly joined her in the elevator. She ignored them.

In the lobby she paused, scanning the room, trying to ascertain whatever ineffable something it was that enabled Rafe Springer to finger undercover cops. Unfortunately it took her very little time to realize that with the tubes of her imagination well warmed, *everybody* was an obvious spy. The two businessmen with thick necks emerging from the entrance to the cellar bar; the painfully thin woman in feathers and fringe a decade out of date, the kohl around her eyes augmented by sleepless bags; the tall, dark, slender man in Savile Row suit and blue turban (what made them think they could fool her with such a disguise?). The powder-blue busboys, clearly all in the pay of the Master Spider, Himmler.

She started for the door. As she reached it another Gestapo agent arose from behind an elephant ear to one side and intercepted her.

"*Guten Morgen, Fräulein.* Where might you be going?"

"Shopping."

"Do you require anything?" one of the tailing watchdogs asked. "We would be more than happy to provide it for you."

"It would save you having to face the inclement weather."

Billi crooked a finger at them. They leaned in. "Sanitary napkins," she whispered.

The two blushed to the tips of their prominent ears. The bifurcated nature of the Gestapo to the rescue again: these were more of the Reichsheini's rural boys, whose training had been geared to make them merciless but never prepared them to be rude to beautiful foreigners of unmistakably Aryan extraction; who had an Old Testament horror of Unspeakable Female Matters.

No doubt the Adlon didn't omit to have such items available for its clientele, but this pair didn't know that. She just blew past them like a gust of the chill air filtering around the brass-and-glass revolving door.

Outside was not so forbidding as advertised. The sky was milky-bright, and the wind pushed cold hands up under her coat in an unwelcome familiar way, but today had the feel of early spring, to yesterday's late winter; the gauzy sunlight was enough to skim the top off the snow, fill the gutters with sooty freshets and the streets with slush. She wished she had exchanged shoes for boots; her pants cuffs were going to be soaked by the time she reached her office. She went out the big wrought-iron gate onto Unter den Linden, turned toward the fountains of the Pariser Platz, gaily playing on, with the Brandenburger Tor topped by the Quadriga driver in a cloak of grimy snow. Almost at once she took a right around the flank of the Adlon's granite sprawl, down Wilhelmstrasse with the British embassy on her right.

She was aware that the Gestapo who'd accosted her in the

lobby were following a bit breathlessly. She breathed deep
and fought the urge to break into a run. Deep down inside a
voice was telling her that playing tag with the *Geheime
Staatspolizei* wasn't the most prudent thing to do, no matter
what her status. But it wasn't just the cold buffeting of the
breeze that brought the flush to her cheeks. She was *enjoying* this, and damn Rafe Springer anyway.

Her mind was freewheeling, trying to spin out some cred-
ible plan of action. The lion-topped gateposts to the Presi-
dential Residence were across the street, the Ministry of
Justice bulking ominous on her left. She sensed the Gestapo
men behind her, pacing her. Sooner or later they would fall
into step, she knew, inquire again where she was going.
Then, ever so politely and circumspectly, they would shep-
herd her back to the hotel.

A bus groaned by, a two-decker, white and blocky with
paint chipped here and there to show gray metal, like a bathtub in a cheap hotel. *Here we go*, she thought, making herself walk deliberately as it wheezed and creaked to a stop
thirty meters ahead.

The bus disgorged a flock of briefcases and dark hom-
burgs. Billi leaned into a sudden sprint. The doors were just
shutting when she popped inside. The conductor, a pinch-
faced woman with a Party eagle in her lapel, came forward
to take her ticket as the vehicle pulled away from the curb,
leaving the Gestapo shadows standing on the curb while a
passing lorry soaked their shins.

There was the usual tiresome wrangle because she had
not first purchased a ticket at a kiosk. Billi was too exhila-
rated by her escape to be impudent, and her readiness to pay
at least convinced the woman she wasn't intending to ride
free. It was still a breach of regulations, but Billi was an
obvious foreigner—and the conductor a *Berlinerin,* albeit
Party.

It was late morning and not crowded. Billi got a seat by
herself and sat looking unseeingly out a window smeared
with oily residue. *You were certainly hard on the professor
this morning, girl,* she thought.

She knew why: that maddening head-patting paternal solicitude of his. He'd abandoned it readily enough the pre-

vious last night, but she couldn't let him think she was his property now. He looked like a man who favored commitment. Terrifying thought, that. Something to be avoided as carefully as her Gestapo shadows.

A couple of quick switches, accomplished with much head-turning surveillance in case her bird dogs had managed to get to a car in time to pursue the bus, brought her to the Kurfürstendamm. The cafés were swarming already, and out among the bare trees of the median clumped a whole gang of fog crows, looking like nothing so much as a bunch of brownshirts looking for a Jew to jump.

The Berlin UPI office was a few blocks down from the Potsdamerplatz, only a block or so from the *Konditorei* where she'd run into Rafe and the professor, which fact was to blame for her embroilment in this bizarre affair. She pushed through the door, stood for a moment smelling the paper dust and cigar smoke and listening to the chatter of teletype machines in the back.

Ulrich, the front-desk man, emerged blinking pinkly beneath his eyeshade. "Fräulein Forsyth," he said. "And how are you this typical Berlin morning?"

"Well enough. Yourself?"

He sighed. It was the question he always waited for. "Not well, Fräulein. I have conjunctivitis today, as you can plainly see, and I have to tell you, it's giving me fits—"

He raised his soft face toward the door and forgot to finish the sentence. Cold air eddied around Billi as she spun.

A pair of men stood there, one in a leather jacket and worker's cap, the other in gabardine trench coat and tan fedora. They smiled. "Miss Forsyth," the one in the trench coat said in English.

"I don't believe I've had the honor."

"The honor's entirely ours. This is Richard; you can call me Julius. You've led us a merry chase, Miss Forsyth."

She raised a hand to her throat. "You're Gestapo?"

Leather-jacket's pointy face wrinkled. "Please."

"We're colleagues of Count Kinski. He sends his regards."

She glanced back. Ulrich was dry-washing his pudgy

white hands and looking less healthy than usual. Nothing like a visit from the SD to give a real edge to hypochondria.

"I'm afraid you've been naughty," Julius went on. "Didn't Oberführer Waldmann direct you to stay in your hotel except on official business?"

"This is official business—for me. And Waldmann doesn't run my life."

The SD pair had a good chuckle. "Very well, Miss Forsyth. Would you mind telling us what manner of business you had in mind to transact here?"

She looked from one to the other. Their apparent friendliness seemed somewhat more genuine than the Gestapo brand, but she didn't doubt they were perfectly capable of picking her up and carrying her bodily to the big car double-parked in front of the office. "I wanted to send a message to my head office. Explaining that I . . . I was going out of the country for a while . . . following a lead of my own." She hated herself for the hesitation.

Julius had a face a bit like Walter Gropius, squarish and sober with piercing gray eyes and graying brown hair that rather looked like the top of a tent peg that had curled down at the edges from being pounded on. It rumpled thoughtfully. "Telephone?" he asked Ulrich in sharp German.

Swallowing, Ulrich nodded him to a set on a desk at the back of the room, beneath an aerial photograph of the city. He dialed quickly and spoke likewise, shading his mouth with his hand.

"How did you find me?" Billi asked the driver, Richard.

"Followed you, Fräulein."

"But that's impossible! I was on buses the whole day after I ditched the Gestapo—" She sharply shut her mouth, wet her lips.

"But, Fräulein Forsyth, you did not ditch *us*. We were parked down Unter den Linden from the Adlon and followed you every meter of the way—at a discreet distance, of course."

Billi looked down at the black-shot water pooling on lino-leum around her feet, felt the clammy cling of wet material about her ankles. She'd been so eagle-eyed on the lookout for the two Gestapo men that she never noticed someone else

following her. Feeling sick, she realized she had no clue
how to pick possible tails out of the welter of Berlin midday
traffic; it was like trying to pick out one particular swallow
from the masses due to return to the Tiergarten woods in a
few weeks.

Julius hung up the receiver with a precise click. "It's arranged, Miss Forsyth. You may send your telegram—but
only if you omit all details of just what the story is you're
pursuing."

Her reflex was to arch her back and spit, but somehow
she lacked the stomach for it. She didn't like this game anymore. Meekly she stepped forward to the desk, drew a pad
of telegram forms to her, sketched a brief message under
Julius's Weimeraner eyes.

He peeled the sheet from the pad, handed it to Ulrich,
who was blinking more rapidly than pinkeye alone could
account for. "Send it."

He turned to Billi, offered his arm. "Shall we go?"

She turned to the door, lips compressed. The door jumped
open and in tumbled the two Gestapo tails, one missing his
fedora. They stared at the SD men with slack expressions.

"We were just leaving," Richard said, elbowing past.
Firmly holding Billi's upper arm, Julius steered her in his
wake, pausing at the door to tip his hat to the rival secret
cops.

"My regards to Oberführer Waldmann. Tell him not to
overwork himself, won't you?" And they were gone, leaving
the Gestapo men looking very hard at Ulrich.

CHAPTER

Eight

Waldmann had a fit.

Billi had scarcely closed her door on her SD escorts and stripped out of her mud-splashed slacks when a ham-fisted hammering endangered lock and hinges. She slithered quickly into a skirt, holding it closed at the waistband, and peered into the hall. There stood Waldmann himself, large and stumpy as life, his round face a curious mottled purple, like a plum past its prime. "Fräulein Forsyth," he said with a stiff correctness that crossed his lips and tongue like a razor blade.

"Why, Herr Oberführer, whatever do I owe the honor of this unexpected visit to?"

He made a sound that seemed to come out from behind his ears and started to bull into the room. She put out her arms to block the way and gave him her very sweetest smile, the one that made her look like a precocious ten-year-old child. "Do it," she said, "and I'll cry rape so loud they'll hear it in the Palatinate." The unzipped skirt started to settle, and she shot one hip to hold it precariously in place.

He started to bulldoze ahead, then braked. Billi's convictions aside, he was not a stupid man. Accusations such as what she threatened would usually be of small concern to a man of his standing. But she was under the Reichsführer's protection. And that devil Heydrich—*he'd* make it an Imperial case, he would, with the sharp-toothed zeal of a ferret arresting a fox for stealing chickens.

He scraped together his composure. "I must talk with you, Fräulein. At once."

"Oh, very well." She sighed, the rasp of the zipper edging the boredom that laced the words. "But I insist that the Herr Professor and Captain Springer be present."

It was more impertinence than he'd been served in the whole two years since he came to Berlin, but he had no choice but to follow her down the hall to Rafe's room. A glance to the watchdog goons as she waltzed past, and Billi began to sing: "Happy cows, as you browse."

It was one of the more insipid lines from one of the more cloying ballads from *The White Horse Inn*, Hitler's favorite operetta. Waldmann stiffened, and Billi threw him a limpid glance.

Rafe answered immediately and blinked as if to clear his eyes at the sight of Waldmann looming over a still-humming Billi like a thunderhead. He and the professor, rising from a chair behind him, had just returned from an instructive half hour at the former arts-and-crafts school at 8 Prinz Albrechtstrasse. A meeting at which Waldmann had bitterly complained that the first planning session had been held without him—the expedition chief's—being invited or even informed. He'd griped even louder about the projected costs of supplies, though Rafe pointed out that given the modest scope (if not aim) of the expedition, they were getting off quite cheaply.

So they all sat around Rafe's room while the Oberführer, controlling his vehemence by courting apoplexy, declared that Billi's jaunt had been an *intolerable* breach of security, which threatened the integrity of the *entire expedition*, news of which had to be prevented *at all costs* from reaching *unfriendly ears*. Finally, worst and foremost, Billi had displayed *an inexcusable lack of discipline* for a prospective member of a German expedition.

Through the whole tirade Billi just sat there with silk-stocking legs crossed and a cigarette smoking languidly in a back-tipped hand, just like Marlene Dietrich in *The Blue Angel*, while the professor stood behind her and now and then gave her shoulder a reassuring squeeze. At last Wald-mann wound down, declared that none of the foreigners *under any circumstances* were to leave the hotel except on official expedition business and with an official escort— dark hints of the catacombs beneath Gestapo HQ—and stumped out.

Rafe had sat through the entire performance, rolling and smoking cigarettes. "Billi," he said, stubbing the last as the slam of the door was still reverberating off the windowpane, "what in God's name made you do that?"

"I had to send a telegram to the head office of my wire service."

"You could have done that at the front desk, for God's sake."

She shook her hair. "I didn't want these ridiculous people thinking they could push me around."

"Hijo de la chingada."

"Now, Rafe, you've no call to be so hard on the girl. I think what she did was jolly good. It showed fine spirit."

Rafe's eyelids descended heavily, like cement doors. "You people go away," he said at length. "It's just occurred to me that I have to get drunk."

He was not as good as his word. An hour later, when Count Kinski knocked at his door, he was cold sober.

Shortly the other two were gathered yet again in Rafe's room. Billi sat in a chair near the window with Shrewsbury perched protectively nearby on the corner of a dresser. Rafe lay on his back on the bed with his feet on the floor, staring at the ceiling.

"Miss Forsyth," Kinski said without preamble, "you've been indiscreet. And you've upset Oberführer Waldmann terribly, into the bargain."

She sat and watched him, half lidded. He was more her type than the barrel-shaped Bavarian flatfoot; there were class affinities between them. She would at least listen to him.

"You may also," he went on, drawing smoke through a long ebony holder, "have exposed yourself to immediate physical danger."

"What? From Waldmann's thugs?"

"Our associates in the Gestapa"—he used the official acronym rather than the colloquial *Gestapo*—"are charged, as I am, with assuring the secrecy and success of this expedition. They would not harm you. But there are others who might. Particularly if word of this expedition were broadcast."

"But why?" Shrewsbury asked. "What could be more innocuous than an expedition to recover Viking relics in Greenland?"

Kinski trailed smoke through nostrils like tiny china cups. "Our National Socialist revolution is not without enemies. You'd be surprised at the lengths to which . . . certain parties . . . might go to head off anything that might gain it prestige."

Billi frowned off toward the window, uncomfortable at the reminder that she was involved in a scheme that could indeed bring credit to the Reich. "Surely not to the extent of doing us harm," burst out the professor.

Kinski looked at him. His pale, narrow eyes were set at a slant in his skull, lending his face an exotic, vulpine look. "You might be surprised, Professor—though it's my job to insure that you're not surprised, shall we say, too drastically."

He took a sip from the whiskey Shrewsbury had poured for him—a refreshment, oddly, not offered the expedition's nominal leader on his earlier visit. "Ah. Excellent stuff, this. Understand, Professor, Miss Forsyth, Berlin is the focus of secret operations by at least a dozen foreign powers, most of them none too friendly, some of them decidedly less than scrupulous in their methods."

"The Red menace," Billi said, languidly sarcastic.

"Our colleagues to the east are active in such matters. They're jealous of revolutionary rivals—and it wasn't for nothing that the Social Democrat Brüning once termed us 'Brown Bolsheviks.' But there's no need to look so far to the east. Our neighbors the Poles have an expansionist's eye and have launched several irruptions against the European peace since the debacle at Versailles—against the Soviets no less than ourselves. And the gentleness of their methods may be judged by the ceaseless streams of Jews pouring into the

Reich from Poland to escape maltreatment, though we scarcely receive them with open arms.

"Then there are our old friends, the French. And the Bulgarians, and the Italians—the list is lengthy. Even your countrymen, Professor, might decide it worth their while to interfere, if they caught wind of the project."

"But England's not hostile to Germany. And the notion that Englishmen might actually injure us—preposterous."

"Those engaged in clandestine activities are frequently impatient with the restrictions imposed by the government they nominally serve. Nor are they always overly stable, emotionally. Some may indeed choose to take matters into their own hands."

He held up two fingers. "But I don't mean to indict your countrymen, Professor. I have the greatest admiration for the English. There are elements native to German soil who might interfere actively in this project."

Billi produced her patented Daring Lady Brahmin snort. "I know how little you've got in the way of any kind of resistance."

Kinski smiled, nodded. "I accept that as a compliment, Miss Forsyth. It's my job to keep such resistance to a minimum."

She drove her cigarette out in a cut-glass ashtray. "Damn you, anyway, Count. You're so beautifully spoken, it's all too easy to forget what you are. A secret police thug."

For a moment the Count sat looking at her, fingering his chiseled chin and looking pained. "Miss Forsyth, you're a woman of strong political convictions, are you not?"

"I believe in social justice."

"Very well. You acknowledge that certain elements in your—in American—society oppose your program of reform? Of course, I know you do. Indulge me for a moment: stipulate that you or those who feel as you do accede to power in your excellent country. Since, therefore, the whole of your society does not embrace your just and necessary reforms, what then do you do to those who do not cooperate?"

"Why, legislate. Enact laws to bring about reform—in an

orderly manner, without armies of roughnecks battling in the streets."

"Ah. I perceive you refer to the excesses of the *Sturmabteilungen* in the early days of our movement. They are a shame we must bear, just as you Americans bear the onus of slavery. Curious, was it not, that when our government finally acted to bring those universally despised ruffians to heel, it reaped its bitterest international censure to date?

"But to return to my disquisition—and pray forgive its length—what will you do to those who do not obey your just new laws? Who pay their workers less than they should or compete too vigorously in the marketplace?"

"Throw them into jail," she said firmly.

He nodded to steepled fingers. "Precisely, Miss Forsyth. And quite rightly. And just as you must rely on the coercive power of the state to promote and protect your reform, so likewise do we of the Third Reich." A small sound like a strangled kitten erupted from Billi. "My employment as a secret policeman is part and parcel of that process."

"This is a fascinating debate, Count," said Rafe, climbing to his feet from the bed and going to gaze out the window with his hands in his back pockets. "But somehow I don't think it's what brought you here."

Kinski laughed. "Perceptive as always, friend Rafe. But I find your conversation so stimulating that it's all too easy to put off the unpleasant part of my task."

Six eyes were suddenly watching him very closely. "It is with great regret that I tell you it has now become necessary to insist that you never leave the premises of the hotel except under immediate supervision. If our agents find it necessary physically to constrain you to prevent a repetition of this morning's performance—laudable as it may have been in spirit—they now have orders to do so."

Visibly Billi gathered herself to explode. "However, there is no intention to immure you here—except on the part of the unfortunate Oberführer, who in his choler proposed rather stringent measures indeed. In addition, therefore, to what transportation may be required by preparation for your departure it pleases me to place at your disposal a car and

driver to convey you on whatever personal or recreational
excursions you like, compliments of the *Sicherheitsdienst*."

He tossed off the rest of his whiskey—a respectable dollop for a man his size—and stood. "Well, then. The mun-
dane details are out of the way, and good riddance. May I
beg the honor of your company at dinner tonight? Horcher's
isn't the only splendid restaurant Berlin has to offer."

Next day, the first plenary meeting of the expedition took
place in a lecture hall of the University. Billi wore a sharp
little black dress with short jacket and veiled hat that made
her look like a naughty widow, but she had her pencil and
pad ready to record details for posterity. Shrewsbury looked
like a sedate greyhound in his tweeds. Rafe, in tan, loose,
and venerable trousers and jacket that looked like something
he might have worn surveying, trailed smoke from his cigarette. It hung at just above head level in air thick with resid-
ual aromas of sweat and varnish.

Leutnant Kampfer was there, his squad with him: five
Germans with ski-bum tans in sharp contrast to the usual
Berlin-winter pallor, and an almost offensive emanation of
boisterous health. They seemed to range in age from late
teens to perhaps thirty. They sat in the front row of studiedly
uncomfortable wooden chairs in their uniforms of *feldgrau*,
—field-gray, that amorphous gray-blue-green color that de-
fined the German army—fidgeting and talking behind hands
like fraternity boys, practically glowing with repressed ebul-
lience that seemed to spring from something beyond excitement at the upcoming mission.

To one side, quietly chain-smoking, sat a diminutive
blond man with slanted sea-green-eyes. He had on a Wehrmacht uniform with warrant officer's insignia and an enam-
eled pin on his tunic's lapel, a blue cross on a white field.
This was Unteroffizier Uurtamo, the ski instructor on loan
from the Finnish army.

Waldmann mounted the stage, fat and immaculate as a
pork cutlet in a butcher's glass display. In the wake of whatever transports of diplomacy the dapper Count Kinski had
performed the day before, he seemed to feel he had gained a
signal victory over the fractious *ausländer* and had met them

that morning with his earlier anger replaced by heavy avun-
cularity. Now he wedged himself behind the lectern and
beamed around at the assemblage with the bonhomie of a
slightly suspect scoutmaster.

"My friends, I am certain that like myself you are buoyed
with excitement at the coming adventure we are to share,"
he said, glancing now and again surreptitiously over the
bulge of his cheeks at the notes he'd laboriously prepared the
night before. "Destiny shines before us like a beacon. The
time approaches for us to reach out and grasp it with both
hands."

Billi emitted a hiss like a deflating bike tire and subsided
farther in her seat, glaring furiously at Rafe when he nudged
her in the ribs. Fortunately the Oberführer didn't notice.

"I am honored beyond words that our Führer and Reichsführer SS Himmler have seen fit to entrust me with command. I trust that you all shall obey orders fully and
promptly and that success shall crown our efforts. Thank
you."

Sweating as if he'd just scaled the *Zugspitze*, he retreated
hurriedly from the podium. Billi blinked in surprise, then
leaned forward, enthusiastically clapping her black-gloved
hands. "Bravo! Bravo! Splendid speech!" Waldmann halted,
then, beaming, bowed at her. Over the tipped top of her
pillbox hat Shrewsbury cast Rafe a look. Rafe shrugged and
sent up more smoke.

Next Kampfer got up and said a few words, even more
tongue-tied than Waldmann. Then Rafe, quite pulled together, got a hickory pointer and made appropriate fencer's
arabesques at a huge map of Greenland pinned over a parti-
colored map of Europe rolled down behind the lectern, describing the point at which they'd make landfall and their
projected route to Eyjolfson's alleged "smoking mountains."
He reiterated the warnings he'd earlier given his friends and
Kampfer about the rigors they faced. The Germans sat with
politely skeptical expressions on their bronzed faces. *Well,
let them learn the hard way,* he thought. Uurtamo, at any
event, was listening.

"This all sounds to me," Rafe said, summing up, "as
implausible as the floating continents of the later Herr We-

gener. Who, by the way, is by way of being our host; he was quite an enthusiast for Greenland and died on his last expedition to the island in 1930 or '31, where even now his body lies entombed in a glacier."

He stood for a moment, meditatively tapped the pointer against the blank whiteness where their destination supposedly lay. "Still, there's no telling. Continents may drift after all, and in the immensity of the Greenland ice sheet, vast areas of which no man has seen, we might just find a smoking mountain and a Viking treasure trove."

He stepped down to polite applause. "Your turn," he said to Billi, jerking his head at the dais. She blinked in surprise, then bounced up.

"You've all been making much of what no *man* has seen," she said. "Let me remind you no woman has seen it either. Or maybe she has, and the males, in their arrogance and ignorance, just ignored her. A threat you gentlemen should take seriously, I might add—since it's this woman who's going to be chronicling your masculine derring-do for a putatively breathless world. And her feminine derring-do as well."

The soldiers cheered and stamped uproariously as she returned to her seat. She took it very coolly, realizing she was being applauded for the fine lathing of her figure more than what she'd said, that she could have recited "Mary Had a Little Lamb" in pig Latin and evoked the same response. But as she resumed her seat Rafe caught her eye and gave her thumbs-up, and the professor murmured, "Well said" in her ear, and she flushed happily behind her veil.

Last of all it was the turn of Professor Melbourne Shrewsbury to give them all some background on the object of their quest. "As you all no doubt know," he began with practiced professorial ease, "certain of Reichsführer Himmler's researchers have unearthed a document that purports to be the account of a Norwegian expedition in the early eleventh century deep into the Greenland interior."

Sitting up front with his men, young Kampfer was fidgeting ever so slightly in his chair, as if he needed to relieve himself. Shrewsbury propped an arm on its leather elbow patch on the podium and said, "Yes, Lieutenant? You have a question?"

"Begging the Herr Professor's pardon—"

"Go ahead, lad. No need to be shy."

"Herr Springer emphasized the hardships we'd encounter in traveling to our objective. Why should the Vikings have gone to the trouble of such an arduous journey?"

"Few hardships slowed the Vikings down if there was the prospect of loot at the end of them, as I'm sure everyone here knows. Eyjolfson and his companions seem to have had information that a fabulous—perhaps literally—treasure trove awaited anyone bold enough or hardy enough to reach it.

"You may well ask what made them believe it. The eleventh century was a turbulent time—its latter years saw the end of the Viking movement as we know it. Bjørn Eyjolfson and his companions were in the main refugees from Olaf Tyrggvason's heavy-handed Christianization of Norway. Now, even at the best of times, Vikings, especially returning empty-handed from the south, were none too scrupulous about preying on their brethren who had enjoyed better hunting. It did not, therefore, strain Eyjolfson's credibility that a raider chieftain, an exile himself perhaps, might have chosen to cache the bulk of his wealth in a location as inaccessible as our objective and then been prevented by some cause—death being the customary one—from returning to claim it."

Waldmann's brow had begun to beetle, his eyes to gimlet; his arms were folded across his chest. Shrewsbury cleared his throat. "I might refer here to Reichsführer Himmler's interesting theory, which indeed gibes with the narrative itself, that the Eyjolfson party were bound in search of nothing less than the treasure of the gods of Asgard, stolen perhaps by trolls. The outstanding artifact of this supposed hoard is nothing less than Gungnir, the spear of Odin, Wotan in Old German, chiefest of the Norse gods."

Billi's hand shot up. "Just what's the story behind this Gungnir, Doctor? Asking in my capacity as expedition reporter, of course." She poised with knees crossed and pencil and notebook pertly ready.

Ever so slightly the professor frowned. She had neatly whipsawed him. She was tweaking him by making him expand on Himmler's Gungnir theory, which he regarded as so preposterous it was embarrassing to talk about. On the other hand, she was encouraging him to expound on his very favorite subject in the world: Norse mythology. It was consummate Billi, as Shrewsbury was beginning to realize. That's why he frowned.

"The goddess Sif," he said, "had long, golden hair of which she was quite proud. One day, for reasons that need not concern us, Loki cut it off—that's the sort of chap he was, Mischief Maker they called him; and why the Aesir tolerated him is far from clear. Unfortunately for him, Sif's husband, the war god Thor, got wind of it. Now Thor was a robust sort of fellow, none too bright, whose sense of humor ran to jokes about bodily functions and cracking skulls—"

"Must have been a German," said Billi, sotto voce.

"—but he didn't see the humor in this at all. He caught Loki and offered to crack *his* skull unless he set matters right. So Loki nipped round to the Dark Elves—or Dwarves, the legends are none too clear which, or indeed whether there's any real difference—and got them to whip up a new head of hair for Sif made of real gold. In the process he inveigled them into creating a plethora of wondrous items, including a golden boar, the ring Draupnir, Thor's hammer Mjöllnir, and Gungnir. Gungnir is the spear with which Odin started the first war in the world and will fight the last battle at Ragnarök, and which has the useful property of never missing its mark, of never ceasing its thrust without striking home. I trust that answers your question, Miss Forsyth."

She finished her note with a flourish. "Quite well, Professor, thanks. And now, what about these trolls that drove Eyjolfson and his companions away from the treasure? Just what are they?"

This time he scowled. "I am quite sure the references in the manuscript, which I have myself now examined, pertain to hostile natives. The same word—"

"Ah, but Reichsführer Himmler's quite keen on their

being trolls, not Eskimos. Surely you can tell us something about them."

"Oh, very well. The first beings to appear in the Norse cosmos were the giants. Though the Aesir, the gods, sprang from them (with some help from the cow Audhumla), the giants and gods are perpetual enemies. Now, the giants were known by a variety of names, including *jotunn, ettins, thursar,* and trolls. Whether these names refer to specific kinds of giants or the breed as a whole is none too clear. In any event, giants came in all descriptions, from Loki, whom legend tells us 'was fair to look upon,' to shape-changers and monsters. Not all of them were even gigantic. It does seem clear that there were certain distinct varieties of giant, such as stone-giants, frost-giants, and fire-giants, who are in essence elementals."

He shifted his weight from one foot to the other. Clearly —to Rafe, at least—he longed to point out that the reason for the discrepancies of nomenclature was that they were dealing with the local superstitions of a far-flung culture, each little pocket of which had its own beliefs. That this wasn't history, after all, but mythology.

On the other hand, there was the question of what tolerances might be being approached behind the ponderous placidity of Waldmann's face. Cop of the hard-boiled school as he so obviously was, it was hard to estimate how much of Himmler's loony cosmology he actually believed. His belief in the Reichsführer's *authority,* on the other hand, was unquestioned and unquestioning. So it would not be prudent to poke at Himmler's hypotheses too vigorously.

"Additionally there are various other supernatural creatures hostile to gods and men, such as the dwarves and *svartalfr,* Dark Elves. Then there are *jutuls* and goblins, who are types of trolls, which is to say giants. On the whole, it seems convenient to speak of malignant supernatural beings of colossal size, such as Ymir and Utgardaloki and Surt, as giants, and those of lesser stature as trolls. And above all, not to worry overmuch, since they belong, after all, solely to the world of mythology."

"Thank God for that. I'm having enough trouble with

some of the *people* on this expedition," Billi said, snapping shut her notepad.

As if that were the gavel to adjourn, the little audience began to stir and stretch.

"Oh, not you, Professor," added Billi in an undertone as she stared up at him shifting uncomfortably from foot to foot on the stage.

"You comfort me. I had begun to think otherwise."

"Hasn't Rafe warned you not to pay attention to anything I say?"

"Er, no."

"Well, he really should have."

"My dear chi . . . lady," he amended as her eyes sent a warning. "I should have thought such a remark would offend—"

"It depends. I'm very erratic . . . where my emotions are concerned."

"Billi—"

"Later." She blew him a kiss and moved off, the net of her veil fluttering.

"This Gungnir sounds like a fine weapon, Herr Springer," said Bauer, the big Bavarian sergeant with the single black eyebrow. He stretched like a bear after a good hibernation. "Almost as useful as a Maxim gun, eh?"

"If the spear's there as advertised," Rafe said, likewise stretching, "that means its supernatural guardians are too. So it might be even more useful than a machine gun, Sergeant."

Kampfer clapped him on the shoulder. "Ah, Rafe. Always the comedian."

Chewing on the inside of his underlip, Rafe looked at him. "What makes you think I'm joking?"

CHAPTER

Nine

Rain had returned to Berlin. It raised silver-gray halos on the humped backs of the cars and lorries goosing each other along wet brick streets and made a constant white-noise patter on the roof of the Mercedes in which the inevitable Walter was lurching and jouncing Billi on a shopping expedition.

Billi had had a trying few days. On the heels of news of the February 26 uprising in Japan, she'd received a telegram from the UPI head office tartly informing her that substantial, if as yet unknown, developments were afoot in Germany, and that she was to stay put and wait for whatever story was in the offing to break.

Infuriated, she had whistled up Walter, their SD chauffeur, and set off like a duchess in high dudgeon for the UPI offices on the Ku'damm, as if she could better give her employers a piece of her mind over their own wire. She found a strangely subdued Ulrich, who barely grunted a greeting, much less launched into his usual torrent of infirmities. He kept his face averted.

In no mood for mysteries, she'd grabbed him by the chin and turned his face toward her. It was a mistake. One whole side of it was a black-and-purple mess, the eye puffed virtually shut, the lid split and crudely sewn together.

"My God," she'd gasped. "Who on Earth did this to

you?" He hadn't answered. On the ride home Walter had refrained from his standard magpie gabbling, shamefaced. And Rafe and the professor had tactfully refrained from putting words to the obvious, that the Gestapo had vented their irritation at Billi's giving them the slip on the nearest target at hand.

Chastened though Billi may have been by the misfortune her impulsive behavior had brought first on the Horcher's waiter and then on Ulrich, it didn't prevent her firing back a telegram to her employers telling them precisely what they could do with their wire service. Consequently she was, as they say, between jobs at the moment. She claimed not to care, but her temper wasn't sweetened by unemployment.

So: shopping. It wasn't as if she *wanted* to go. In point of fact, she despised herself for descending to such stereotypically feminine behavior to pare away some of the time weighing down on all their backs. But what had to be done to prepare for the expedition had been done, and now they had to wait for the last of the gear to be made ready.

Shrewsbury had retreated into the photostats the RuSHA had made of Eyjolfson's manuscript, Rafe into a thick stack of fantastic-fiction pulp magazines with titles like *Weird Tales* and *Amazing* that he'd conned somebody at the American embassy into smuggling in for him in a diplomatic pouch. Given his proclivity for dressing and acting like a rumrunner, it was hard sometimes to remember he was an Ivy Leaguer who'd made some remarkable contacts during his Princeton days.

They'd all begun to snarl at each other like big cats in a too small cage. Billi had to get out, and every time she'd tried to do something of substance, she'd gotten somebody beaten to jelly by the *Geheime Staatspolizei*. So she went shopping.

In the Adlon lobby she had overheard a couple of women with American society accents discussing the *most marvy* little antique store down in Potsdam, so that's where she was bound. Not that she had any fondness for antiques. Her mother had a great house full of the things, all named after one or another imbecile Bourbon king or fat English queen, rooms full of chairs under no circumstances to be sat in, bureaus not to be leaned on, tables most especially not to set things on. It had been like growing up in a museum for Billi and her sisters and her idiot older brother, Gill, whose great pecuniary success (buying up breweries during the depths of Prohibition and the early Depression years in partnership with Joe Kennedy) had done more than anything to solidify her conviction that mental and moral debility were positive assets in capitalist pursuits.

But in her extremity of boredom and propinquity she was fleeing to the southwestern suburb of Potsdam. It was as much to get out of Berlin's massy Mitte, dour gray by day, crystal-neon at night, and the breezy, unlikely mix of Paris cosmopolitanism and high-starch *Gemütlichkeit* of the Kurfürstendamm.

I sure picked the day for it, she thought. They were almost to their destination, passing through the forests of the Wannsee district, rounding the tip of the lake itself, which hung like an appendix off the Havel River. Rain pitted the uneasy surface of the water while the wind whipped it up in unlikely ridges and rills of beaten lead. Despite the wretched weather, the white isosceles of a sail pitched to and fro in the middle of the lake, intermittently obscured by a gouache of rain. Some people were determined to have fun if it killed them.

It was getting on toward noon. Perhaps she'd detour briefly for luncheon in some café in the movie colony that had sprung up around the UFA studios in Neubabelsberg. Perhaps she'd get to see Emil Jannings throw one of his fabled temper tantrums.

Growing bored for the hundredth time with the view of the back of Walter's close-cropped head—at least the back and sides were, though he wore it longer on top, in a rakish Luftwaffe/Student Prince cut that went queerly with his prominent ears and bad teeth—Billi let her attention drift around and out the back window of the Mercedes. *Odd,* she thought. *Haven't I seen that car before?* It hung forty or fifty yards behind them, a great gleaming black Porsche. Immediately she shook her head, deriding herself; Berlin was nothing if not full of great black automobiles, and all of them were gleaming in the rain.

But no, it was familiar. For some reason it had caught her attention as they turned right onto Leipzigerstrasse in front of Wertheim's department store, and again when they angled southwestward past the old ladies hunched beneath umbrellas among hothouse flowers and moss-filled baskets, and the rusty smoke streaked barrels filled with glowing coals and roasting chestnuts in the Potsdamer Platz. Downtown the traffic was thicker, and the car was quickly lost in it, as though obscured by a quick rain squall. But here it was again, following at a leisurely, but very measured, distance.

She leaned forward, tapped Walter's shoulder with a gloved hand. He turned back, smiling and veering, showing teeth packed with gray-brown matter at the interstices. "Walter," she said in halting German, "do you believe it's possible that car is following us?"

The corners of his grin tipped to reassuring-deprecating angles. Instantly she felt a fool: *This is ridiculous, I should have kept my mouth shut.* But she was still smarting at being shown up by the SD in the UPI office and still very alive to the possibilities of being shadowed.

Still grinning his now-now-little-girl grin, Walter glanced up into his mirror. The expression sheared away. He stiffened his arms and slammed down the accelerator. The back of his leather driving jacket kissed the darker leather of his seat with a slick smacking sound, and Billi went flying all over the back as the Mercedes took off like a rocket from a field in Reinickendorf.

Tires sang on wet asphaltum. The car rocked from side to side on its suspension as Walter cranked it in and out of the sparse Leipzigerstrasse traffic. Seasick, Billi got hold of the strap and pulled herself upright.

She looked out the back. The Porsche was loping along behind, effortlessly keeping its interval like a sleek black panther chasing a water buffalo. Walter was fumbling inside his jacket, bringing out a chunky Mauser pistol and looking in the rearview with herbivore eyes.

The big car shot into Potsdam as if breaking a membrane between centuries. A military lorry emerging from a tree-crowded lane slammed to a halt like a conger eel half out of its lair in a reef, conscripts with white heads and wide eyes tumbling out from under their coal-scoop helmets in the open back. The Mercedes cleared its blunt snout by inches, fishtailing and wailing, then streaked into the center of town, scattering pedestrians from the broad square for the safety of the domed town palace and the elaborate Havel-side colonnades.

Walter dived down a lane that was scarcely more than an alley. An old man baled off his push-bike with a wail. Billi screamed and covered her eyes. The bike beat on the under-carriage like futile metal fists as the Mercedes ran it down. Fearful, Billi looked back to see the old man picking himself out of a puddle—and diving back in as the Porsche howled down on him, avid with pursuit.

The car clattered over cobblestones as if caught in a hail-storm. *Am I having an adventure?* Billi wondered. She couldn't figure out for the life of her why she'd ever wanted to have one. At the moment it seemed that nothing could be worse.

"He finally lost them," she said, snapping a cigarette in half and spilling tobacco in little dry clumps and disks on the zeppelin on Professor Shrewsbury's bed. "But not until after that lunatic Walter had gone screaming through the grounds of San Souci Palace. I think we shook them when we bounced off the side of that windmill, but I'm not sure."

She threw the broken cigarette aside, got out together, only bending this one slightly in the middle. Rafe hastened to light it for her with a match flicked alight by his thumbnail.

"Thank God you weren't hurt," the professor said.

She nodded jerkily, flooding herself with smoke. "I thought I was being silly, just a bad case of the jits. But Walter took one look at that car and came utterly to pieces. I daren't imagine why." She shook her head. "You know, this may seem strange, but I actually think Walter drove *better* when he was scared green."

Shrewsbury petted her shoulder and made basso cooing noises, like an immense pigeon. She shrugged him off like a fly from a horse's flank. He pulled his hand back slowly, looking at it and her as if she'd burned it.

A pink nodule pushed out between Rafe's lips. Billi and Shrewsbury suddenly fixed their eyes to him, canaries with a cobra. The pink bud grew, expanding in a rough sphere, growing milky and then translucent, then, the size of a baby's head, popping to hang in pink rags from his lips. Unperturbed, he poked the rubbery wreckage back in his mouth.

Shrewsbury released the breath he'd been holding. "Just what in the name of God was that?"

"Bubble gum," Rafe said. "Bazooka. You know, Joe Palooka." He held up a little rectangle of wax paper, crimped from quarter-folding, printed with a little smeary four-panel cartoon that wound up with a big man in yellow boxing trunks punching somebody in the jaw.

"Are you mad, man?" Shrewsbury demanded.

"It's taken you this long to ask that question?" Billi wanted to know, starting to get her composure back. "What in the hell are you doing with that junk, Rafe?"

"Got it in the same package as the science-fiction magazines," he said, chewing. He waved the cartoon. "Insurance."

Out of their friendship for him, Billi and Shrewsbury were about to ask just what he was talking about before calling in the authorities to remove him to an asylum. A knock on the door stopped them. Shrewsbury answered it. Kinski stood there, an umbrella tucked under the arm of his greatcoat, rouge-spots of color burning high up his cheekbones.

He clicked his heels, bowed. "May I come in?" Correct as always, his tone didn't encourage refusal.

"Why, of course. Come in, come in."

"Fräulein. Herr Springer." He smiled concisely at Rafe, who was just tucking his .45 back inside his jacket. "A prudent precaution."

Shrewsbury smiled an unusually uneven smile. "He's not the only one to take precautions," he said, producing an ancient broom-handled Mauser as long as his forearm that he'd been holding down beside his leg, out of sight of the door.

Billi craned. "Where'd that come from, Prof?"

"He had it under his pillow," Rafe said as the count entered and availed himself of an offered armchair. Somewhat self-consciously Shrewsbury set the Mauser down on a dresser and perched himself beside it.

"War memento, don't you know," he said, half abashed.

"I understand you had an unnerving experience this afternoon, Miss Forsyth," Kinski said. "I've spoken to your driver already. Now I'd like you to tell me everything you can about the incident, if you will be so kind."

For once in no mood to talk back to the voice of authority, Billi gave him the story. She sounded very calm and collected, recounting the alarming events as if they'd happened to someone else.

"You have a very precise eye, Fräulein," Kinski said when she finished.

"I am a reporter, after all."

He nodded vaguely, rubbed at his eyes with thumb and forefinger, and Rafe saw he had bags beneath them. *"Das Haus gegenüber,"* he murmured.

The House Opposite. "What's that, Count?" Shrewsbury asked, a trifle more sharply than he intended. Mentally Rafe saw a quick picture of the count's face when he'd pointed out the extra watcher to him in the Adlon lobby.

A wave of irritation, seemingly at himself, rippled across Kinski's face. "Nothing, nothing." He stood, scooping umbrella and Astrakhan off the round table beside him. "I perceive I don't need to tell you that what happened this afternoon was most serious. It's possible your life was in danger, Miss Forsyth."

He gave that a few beats to seep in. "I understand that you are to depart Berlin in two days. Until that time I fear I must ask that you not leave the premises except under the most pressing expedition business, and then only under guard. A very good afternoon to you all." And, not omitting to bow briefly over Billi's hand to kiss it, he went out.

As the door closed, Rafe said, "Well, I know what I have to do now. I was afraid I would, all along."

They looked a question at him. He blew another bubble.

CHAPTER

Ten

Lorenz Adlon had torn down a palace to build his hotel.

The general consensus of Berliners held that they had lost an architectural treasure but gained physical proof of Berlin's stature as a world city. Or perhaps, Rafe mused, as he left his room the next morning, a pair of Gestapo guards falling silently into step behind him, they merely liked the display of personal aggression that had built the world-famous hotel.

The original Schinkel house had been part of the entailed estate of the aristocratic Redern family, protected by law from transference of ownership. But the holder of the title in 1870 was a reckless gambler who had lost his entire fortune in one week to the King of England. He was desperate to sell his palace, and Adlon was eager to buy. It had taken the intervention of the Kaiser to demolish the building, but it had been accomplished, and now the Adlon stood in splendid, sprawling opulence.

Esthetic considerations notwithstanding, at the moment the granite warren of the hotel suited Rafe just fine. Its maze of halls wasn't enough in which to lose your better class of official shadows but sufficed to separate the men from the boys, so to speak.

The original pair was still behind him, though farther back and breathing heavily, when he stepped out into Wilhelmstrasse from a side exit. He sauntered south, hands in his pockets, inevitable precautionary umbrella tucked under his arm, hat pulled down to a casually rakish sweep across his eyes. On Behrenstrasse he took a left, heading downtown.

The sun shone fitfully. The clouds looked like thin batter stirred across a pale blue sheet. Off to the west the looming stacks of the Klingenberg drooled a gray scum of smoke into the sky. The Gestapo hounds had calmed down, seeing he wasn't making any further moves to escape, and strolled along behind, almost casually, but parting desultory ranks of Berliners like a battle cruiser nonetheless.

Rafe's constitutional was clearly on the black, *streng verboten,* but these were no hicks from the Mecklenburg sticks. This was the first team, real cops who'd been with *Gestapa* since Göring invented it, and plainclothes dicks were of the Prussian State Police before that. They were men of the world, willing since the Reichsführer smiled on this man to smile along and let him have his head. It was a lovely day when it wasn't raining, and Berliners themselves, the flatfeet happily joined the multitudes enjoying the Berliners' pastime of walking the city's streets, taking advantage of every errant sunbeam.

Berlin, Vienna, Prague: in every Eastern European metropolis it was the same. Walk through a deserted, rainswept park. Let the clouds part, however momentarily, and instantly the benches filled with old people nodding over their canes, mothers with prams, young lovers lying in the grass. Start the rain again, pause to adjust your hat against the moisture, turn back and they would all be gone, spirited away like phantoms in a sorcerer's dream.

At the Deutsche Bank Rafe cruised south again, ambling nowhere in evident particular, pausing to peruse ties in a portable kiosk out in front of a men's shirt shop, hawked by a round-faced youthful street vendor of the sort the Nazis were always trying to put out of business. Rafe made a leisurely feint toward Gendarmenmarkt, just to make life difficult for what he took to be the *Sicherheitsdienst* shadows in their sporty beetle-green Merc, trying to pace him unobtrusively while buses and taxis piled up honking on their rear

bumper. Then he drifted south and west again as if blown by
gusts carrying bracing slaps of rain, past the furniture stores
and all-weather Italian-ice sellers and signs plugging Patzen-
hofer Beer, Berlin's Own Brew.

Eventually his steps carried him, as if of their own voli-
tion, to the mullioned *massif* of the Wertheim department
store, as the noonday crowds began to spill out into another
sun shower. And inside, between ladies' notions and radios
ranked in silent rows like hunchbacked dwarves with curious
faces of flat cloth and wood, his escorts lost sight of him for
good.

There was a whole squad of Gestapo and no one knew
how many of their silent SD partners shuffling frantically
through the bargain-hunting crush twenty minutes later,
when a panel truck rolled unremarked out of a loading bay
and turned north, headed back for its warehouse in Pankow,
its box empty but for Rafael Springer deBaca, smoking a
cigarette and reading *Weird Tales*, his pockets heavy with
Bazooka Bubble Gum.

"So, Rafi," Rudi said. "So it's been a while. So what can
I do for you?"

He yawned, stretched slightly, scratched himself under
his right armpit. Rafe sighed. All along he'd known it would
come to this, and now it had: a consultation with his horrible
pimp cousin.

"I need some information, Rudi."

Clipped between index and third finger, Rudi's cigarette
described a smoke arabesque in the gloom of the little café
on the Friedrichstrasse north of the Weidendammer Bridge.
"If it's happening in Berlin, I know it. My girls hear everything. And if they hear it, I hear it." He produced a wet leer,
somehow suggestive of leather strops and straight razors.

He was a small man, lithe, round-faced, and pointy-
nosed, who looked like a shaven-cheeked and brilliantined
weasel in his dinner jacket with gray wear spots at the
elbows, his stained highboy collar, his striped pants, and his
spats—or maybe *The New Yorker*'s masthead man at the
wrong end of a two-week binge. He had obviously just

crawled out of bed when Rafe knocked at the door of his third-floor flat in the theater district, just shy of one o'clock.

A neurasthenic waitress affecting *démodé* Paris chic— black stockings that emphasized the thickness of her legs and kohl beneath her eyes—brought Rafe his brandy and set down a *pouisse café* in front of Rudi. Seven layers of sweet liqueurs lay in rainbow bands in the tall glass, and Rafe's stomach did a slow acrobatic roll as his cousin took a slurping sip of the multicolored decoction.

"Anything for my long-lost cousin from America," Rudi said grandly. "Gossip, girls—whatever."

He leaned forward, produced a wink with an eye startlingly black in a face whose complexion suggested it might dissolve to dust at contact with sunlight. "You saw those girls, in those photos on the walls of my flat? You can have your pick of them. Any of them. All of them. Just say the word, dear boy."

Rafe had seen the girls. A score of them, some so beautiful that they made his breath rasp his palate like sandpaper, all of them naked but for little fetishist grace notes, from your standard Blue Angel garter belts and stockings to corsets and dog whips to the redoubtably popular Indian Princess number, a dark-haired, slightly plump young woman decked out in a tomahawk, a beadwork apron of sorts, and a feather duster on her head, that always caused Rafe to scrunch his lips against his teeth to keep from cracking up. Some of them might actually even work for Cousin Rudi.

"Not today, Rudi. Just information."

Rudi's fingers circled in front of his lapel. "Whatever. If you change your mind—really you should, my boy—just say the word. And price? Did you mention price?" Rafe hadn't. "It's free. Of course. You're family, Rafe. From *America.*"

Rafe sighed. It wasn't that he couldn't be tempted by some of the women stuck to Rudi's walls (which in between the cheap frames peeled as though suffering an exotic tropical skin disease). He just didn't like making himself beholden to his cousin.

"Speaking of coming from America." He dug in a pocket of his coat, rapped his closed hand down on the table before him. Rudi's button eyes widened slightly. "I brought you something." With a conjurer's flourish he took his hand away.

Rudi's eyes widened some more. "Joe Palooka," he breathed, all reverence. The first name came out *Tscho*. His hand shot out like a mongoose, captured the dozen little colorful slabs and crammed them into a pocket, then fished one out again. Carefully he unwrapped it, popped the pink-dusty tablet into his mouth, then held the comic sheet from inside the wrapper two inches from the moist-looking tip of his nose—trust Rudi to be too vain to wear glasses—and read it with the utmost earnestness while his jaw worked and his lips moved. Rafe was fairly sure he couldn't read the rudimentary English; he wouldn't bet anything past 1923 marks he could read German.

At last Rudi folded the comic fastidiously and stuck it in a pocket. "Ah, Rafi." He pronounced the name *Roffy*. He slapped his cousin on the biceps. Rafe resisted the urge to check for spots. "Thanks, huh?"

Well, he'd known the gum would come in handy. As a rule, Rudi insisted on payment in advance for services rendered. Rafe respected that as he did nothing else about his cousin; in his experience, people who refused outright payment still expected a return, which, since never made explicit, tended to be disproportionate in the end. Endlessly reiterating that family rode for free, Rudi would be offended if Rafe offered to pay for information; he clung to the point of honor as only a man who suspects he has little can. The bubble-gum lagniappe kept accounts squared.

"So," said Rudi, leaning forward and breathing a fruity miasma of stale smoke and food and alcohol and Joe Palooka into Rafe's face, "what is it you want to know?"

"Is anything causing an unusual stir at the high levels of the Party?"

Rudi tapped the side of his long nose with his finger, which made him look cross-eyed rather than wise. "You came to the right place, baby." It was true enough. Whether or not the highest ranks of Party and military could actually be numbered among his clientele, he was firmly plugged into the pillowcase-gossip switchboard.

"Something's shaking. Big military move coming. Going to rip a page out of that damned Versailles rag, maybe." Like most Germans and John Maynard Keynes, Rudi hated the Versailles Treaty. He tried to blow a bubble, succeeded only in popping the gum half out of his mouth.

"The Prussians are like brass monkeys about what is actually in the offing, mind. But they can't help tittering about the black eye they're going to give the English and the French—those who aren't too windy to make it past half mast, if you catch my meaning, at the thought that things might get out of hand. Why, old von Seeckt, the Chief of Staff, was with one of my girls just a few days ago, dressed as a French maid he was, and—"

Rafe was shaking his head. "That's not it. What about the SS? Or do your contacts reach that far."

Tut-tutting. Rudi shook his head. "Rafe, Rafe, you wound me. Really. I have contacts everywhere. Those SS supermen are human too—and some of them a lot less than super in some departments, let me tell you." He rubbed his cheek. "Well, the Reichsheini does have some new bee under his bonnet, and a little bird tells me it's crazy even for him."

Rafe leaned forward. "Don't tell me Himmler's one of your clients?"

"No, no. Not that one. It's said he's queer, and I don't deal in that sort of meat. Some say . . . but some lie. Surely with all those pink-cheeked farm boys he brings in he'd never have to pay, don't you know." He stubbed his cigarette in an ashtray caked with something Rafe couldn't identify. "I don't think he does it at all, myself."

"About his new notion . . ." Rafe said with a touch of desperation.

A shrug. "Something the longhairs came up with. A document of some kind. I don't have the details on that, either, it pains me to say. But it's got the cloak-and-dagger types thoroughly riled, let me tell you."

"Why? If it's such a crazy idea, that is."

"That's just the way the game is played, Rafi. If Heinrich wants something, a lot of people think it worth their while to take it away from him. Of course, it takes very big boys to play that game, very big. Or ones with rich uncles—in London or Paris, say. Or . . . points east."

His accent was rising through the social strata as he warmed to his subject. Rafe considered for a moment. "Two of my friends and I were the guests of Gruppenführer Heydrich at the opera last week." Rudi's mouth made a soundless *O*. "As we were going to dinner our SD driver passed me my pistol, which I'd left in my hotel room. Struck me as pretty damned peculiar at the time. Do you think it had anything to do with these game-players of yours?"

To his astonishment Rudi laughed. "No, no. You know the unpleasantness of a couple of years ago, when the *Sturmabteilungen* fell off their perch?" Rafe nodded. "Well, Heydrich was in that, he was in it to the eyebrows. Some of their dear departed leader's bun boys who somehow escaped the ax have sworn vengeance on him. The Avengers of Röhm, they call themselves. Dearest Reinhard hates having bodyguards trailing along behind him—gives people the idea he can't take care of himself. So he likes to have more discreet gunslingers in his party. It gives him kind of a thrill, if you ask me."

He shook his head. "Ah, that Heydrich! Such a devil. The things I could tell you! Even if it was all political, when he was thrown out of the Navy—all that rubbish about an industrialist's daughter, pah! Who's ever heard the girl's name? Who's seen the transcript of the court of honor that gave him the heave-ho? No one."

He swilled vigorously at his *pouisse café*. "Now, there's a man for you, Heydrich. The Blond Devil, they call him, and they're not half right, are they? I remember one party I helped cater—that tableau he designed himself, with the twin Parisiennes and the defanged cobra—masterful!

"There's an idea we've kicked back and forth between us once or twice—Heydrich and myself, that is," Rudi went on, leaning forward conspiratorially. "He knows what ideal sources of intelligence whores are. So he says to me, 'Rudi, what if I should open a brothel of my own and generously invite, say, the foreign corps to patronize it at a discount rate? And those stiff-necked Prussian generals who think they're so superior to us Party trash. We might learn a thing or two, eh?' and I said, 'Reinhard, old cock, that's brilliant. Let me tell you one thing about those *Junkers,* once the top tunic-button of their uniform's unfastened . . .'"

He noticed Rafe sinking into his coat like a snowman melting in the sun. "Forgive me. I'm talking shop again. Must be frightfully boring."

"Not at all," Rafe said without conviction. Under other circumstances he would have been interested, though he was pretty sure his cousin was pulling the long bow about his own role. He had a perversely vulgar fascination for the peccadilloes of the powerful. But he had too much on his mind this afternoon.

He swirled the lees of his brandy, drained them. "Who does the SD call the House Opposite?"

Rudi turned half profile to his cousin and one-eyed him. "You've had run-ins with that lot, then?"

"It's a possibility."

Rudi pursed his mouth. "Very dangerous. That's the Abwehr, don't you know. Military intelligence. Bitter rivals of the Reichsheini's side. And their chief, Kapitän Canaris, harmless-looking little chap with apple cheeks, cares fuck-all for anyone but his damned dachshunds—he's dangerous as a snake. They say he escaped from an Italian prison during the Great War by pretending to take an interest in converting to Catholicism. When the prison chaplain came to wrest his soul from Luther, he strangled him and made off in his cassock. Navy boy, of course. Old crony of Heydrich's."

"Friend of his?"

"He'd squash Heydrich like a bug if he could. Reinhard would return the favor gladly." He flicked a gilded lighter, lit another cigarette. "They say Abwehr and Gestapo agents in foreign countries aren't above turning each other over to the local secret police. And there have been bodies found in the back alleys of Berlin itself—

"A word to the wise, Rafe. Stay clear of Canaris's boys."

"I'll do that," Rafe said, rising.

Rudi came up halfway with him. "It's been a pleasure, Rafi. And if you change your mind about the girls"—he gave Rafe's coat sleeve an admonitory triple tug—"just say the word, huh?"

CHAPTER
Eleven

Mock Oriental carpeted floor lurched beneath Billi's feet as if somebody were banging it with a hammer as she made her way back along the car, toward the uniformed men clustered in the doorway of Rafe's first-class sleeping compartment. They were laughing and calling encouragements into the cabin in soft South German accents. As she approached, one of them brandished a bottle of cognac held by the throat. "Drink, Fräulein?"

"Passauer, you pig"—a basso grumble emerged from inside the compartment—"she's a lady. She doesn't drink from the mouths of bottles." It was "Brummbär" Bauer, showing off the growl that helped win him his name.

Of course, she couldn't resist. She grabbed the bottle from Passauer's square hand, put the mouth unwiped to hers, and took a healthy swig. "Thanks," she said with half a voice, "that hit the spot." She was trying to keep her eyeballs from rolling up in her head like a frog swallowing a cicada, and the track seemed to have developed some roller-coaster whorls, but it was worth it. The corridor echoed to appreciative laughter, Unterfeldwebel Bauer's booming out louder than anybody. The sergeant was a man who appreciated jokes, even on himself.

The four soldiers gave way to let Billi up to the door. This was no Train de Luxe, on this night run to Bremerhaven, but it didn't do too badly. The compartment was all hand-rubbed mahogany and silver fittings, very nice. Bauer's bearish bulk was perched on a stool, up against the curved door that concealed the washbasin. Next to him was Maurice Chatenois, who fortunately was on the skinny side. Across from them Rafe and Leutnant Kampfer sat on a muted green settee with cards in their hands.

The lieutenant tried to bounce to his feet, blushing to the opened throat of his tunic, clearly embarrassed at having been caught in such unmilitary state by the Fräulein. The two across from him tried to follow his lead, with the result that all three got jammed in half erect.

"Here, here, sit down," Billi said, patting the air. Her stomach was calming down, but her throat still felt seared. "We're all friends here."

Sheepishly Kampfer subsided back onto the leather bench. The other two followed his lead. Rafe sat there steadying the table with his hand.

"Mind if I watch?" Billi asked.

"We'd be honored, Fräulein," said Chatenois. He was a trim, self-possessed young man with a shock of straw-colored hair. An Alsatian whose family had declined to be awarded to France after the Great War as part of her reward for being rescued by the British and Americans, he had a nobleman's manner—except when Billi had initially greeted him in French, a language he refused to speak or acknowledge understanding. His squad mates called him "the Freiherr," though he was no better born than the rest of them.

Billi declined his offer of a seat and stood braced in the doorway as play resumed. She could only hold her tongue for a few moments before she burst out, "Hearts?" in disbelief. *"Hearts?"*

"Na ja, Fräulein," Bauer said, beaming. "It's a wonderful game." Though he was a sergeant and he was nicknamed Grizzly Bear and though he did in fact resemble nothing so much as a black bear that had shaved its face and donned a stolen uniform in hopes of slipping unnoticed out of some zoo, he was a predominantly gentle, soft-spoken man whom Billi liked immensely on short acquaintance.

"I'd think a real Western he-man like you would play poker or nothing," she shot at Rafe.

"But I *like* Hearts."

"Better that than bridge, young lady." She turned to find Shrewsbury standing behind her with his head all but lost in a haze of smoke from a veteran brier pipe. "He's worse at bridge than even chess."

"You're a bridge player, Professor?" Billi said coolly, surprised into asking.

He nodded. "Yourself?"

"I'm an addict."

Relations between the two had been strained for the last day or so. At the last moment before boarding the train for the overnight trip to the North Sea port from which they'd take ship for Greenland, Billi had dug in her heels and refused to budge until the waiter she'd gotten arrested at Horcher's was released. Waldmann spoke firmly to her, but neither his heavy-footed attempts to reason with her, his double entendre threats delivered from behind a fat smile, nor his red-faced bellowing had budged her. After he stomped off, trailing a cloud of threats, Shrewsbury had reproached her as if she were an unruly child. She tore strips off him.

Late that night Joachim Count Kinski turned up, all urbane, and after hearing Billi out offered to see to the unfortunate man's immediate release. Billi, with matching urbanity, had thanked him but was leaving nothing to chance. Her distrust of the Nazis was not lulled by even the count's charming manners, and she insisted on personally seeing the waiter back on the job before she graciously consented to depart on the evening train, having delayed the expedition twenty-four hours.

Needless to say, Melbourne Shrewsbury had spent the previous night alone and all the time since the blowup ensconced in Billi's icebox. But instead of mooning around or whining for forgiveness, he'd been very calm and matter-of-fact to her, and that impressed her despite herself. Also, he looked so damned distinguished in that sweater.

Billi kibitzed for a while. The game was actually Black Lady, in which the queen of spades was as great a liability as the whole suit of hearts, and in which each player got to pass three cards off on his neighbor. Chatenois played volubly but with more flair than strategy. Kampfer was quiet, and Billi got the not unpleasurable sensation that her nearness was cramping his style, restraining the exuberance he might display if no lady were present. His fidgety decorousness did slip to the extent of an anguished squawk when he discovered on the next hand that his loyal sergeant had slipped him the Black Bitch.

All the while Billi was acutely aware of Shrewsbury's nearness, the rather strong pipe tobacco mingling not unpleasantly with the fresh verbena scent he always wore. For his part, the professor was resolved not to think about her at all; he was a mature man, after all, and no point in losing his head over a mere slip of a girl. And there was Anne's memory. . . .

He was able to divert himself by marveling yet again at the casual intimacy of officer and men displayed by Kampfer and the troopers. For a British officer of even the most progressive views to be found at cards with enlisted men—*particularly* his own—was simply unheard of. Though his military intelligence days were two decades behind him, he stayed au courant enough with German military affairs to know it couldn't be passed off as an anomaly arising from the squad's elite status.

Adolf Hitler's political opponents traditionally jeered at him for having held the rank of corporal in the War to End All Wars. Though his admiration for the Führer was a long way from unqualified (what he said when Billi got his back up with her fuzzy leftist sentiments notwithstanding), he thought such aspersions folly. Alone among world leaders, the German dictator had experienced war as a private soldier—not even a noncom; Hitler's rank of *Gefreiter* was equivalent to the British lance corporal and the American private first class. Though even his squad mates considered him a daft old man (he was twenty-eight when the war ended), Hitler had earned the Iron Cross First and Second Class—and those weren't exactly handed out as prizes on Guy Fawkes Day.

Among the many crabbed convictions Hitler had carried

out of the Great War with him was a hatred of the *Junkers*, the aristocratic Prussian officer caste, as savage as any Georg Grosz caricature. He was determined that in *his* army the class system would be abolished. He had, in fact, performed a major revolution in narrowing the gap between officer and ranks in the German army until it was least of any army in the world, including the American. An officer's authority was still virtually absolute, but he was to exercise it as paterfamilias, not from a lofty perch of privilege. What in another military organization would have been considered unforgivable fraternization was an officer's duty in the Wehrmacht. The easy, obvious bonds of affection among Kampfer and his men only strengthened Shrewsbury's conviction that German arms were stronger for Hitler's reform.

Bauer took the hand, leaving Kampfer and Chatenois tied for last. The other soldiers drifted off to find their own amusements. Quicksilver, Billi slid away from the professor and made her way to the dining car, early for their reservation. Presently Rafe, who'd taken the game, arrived with Shrewsbury and Kampfer, just in time. Not because of the reservation—there was hardly anyone in the car—but because here came Waldmann, puffing and Walrus-and-Carpenter jovial in an ill-fitting suit, to join them.

Dinner was excellent. Billi picked at hers. Waldmann produced a sheaf of snapshots of his family, a beer-keg Frau and no fewer than six daughters, blonde hair knotted in excruciatingly tight pigtails and all lined up in perfect size place. Billi found the hearty intimacy ghastly, and was appalled when Rafe leafed through the pictures with apparent interest, making amiable noises.

"How can he *do* that?" she inquired behind her hand of the professor, who somehow had wound up seated to her right. "If I thought for a moment Rafe was capable of insincerity, I wouldn't be half so shocked."

"Well, that's Rafe all over," Shrewsbury remarked loftily. "He is half Spanish, after all."

The comment infuriated her so much she couldn't even dream up a comeback. She spent the meal's remainder in basaltic silence and refused dessert to retire to her sleeping compartment, pleading exhaustion. The rushing-water sound of the train flowed over her, bore her down into sleep.

Hours later she awakened to find her head whirling like a carousel and herself being dragged down the passageway by strong, unfamiliar arms.

Fully dressed, Melbourne Shrewsbury lay on his back on the bed which the conductor had made of his settee while he dined. It seemed to him he was too old a dog to be kept awake by something like this. How long had it been since he was accustomed to anything but sleeping alone? Yet here he was, still wakeful with a young man's discomfort.

The train jounced him with repeated impacts along a line from shoulder blades to tailbone. The tempo was too brisk to lull him. Besides, in a matter of a few hours they would be at Bremerhaven, poised on the brink of departure. Shrewsbury had never been one to rest before a journey; anticipation always stirred him up. And, of course, there was Billi—or, rather, there was *not* Billi. . . .

He sat up, flipped on the reading lamp in its silver sconce above the bed. There was a table at the foot of the bed, the drawn curtains of the window rippling soft as summer wheat above. He stoked up his faithful old brier and began in an abstracted way to sort through the mail one of Count Kinski's men had brought from his flat as they were debarking. It was all the usual rubbish—appeals from charity, missives from former students beseeching letters of recommendation or introduction, one from his solicitor in London which doubtless concerned the never-ending fuss his wretched sisters were putting up over their father's estate, which bid fair to continue well into the 1950s. Greenland insolation would more than make up for the discomforts of Greenland ice, he reflected, and started to toss the sheaf of mail aside.

Belatedly the Oxford postmark registered on his brain. He rooted back through the envelopes, drew out one addressed in the familiar small, almost childlike, handwriting of his fellow Inkling and enthusiast of Northern tongues, Ronald Tolkien.

> *Dear Mel,*
> *I am sorry for the long delay, but the holidays*
> *were excruciating (every one of the family laid*
> *low by influenza), and we are just finally back to*
> *normal. One bit of brightness to light this dull*
> *winter day.*
> *I don't know if you remember Susan Dagnall,*
> *she's a former graduate who's been working for*
> *the publishing house of Allen & Unwin, but she*
> *cast an eye over* The Hobbit, *and has encouraged*
> *me to finish the story and offer it for publication*
> *at her house. Too early to predict yet, I've only*
> *just picked up before the death of Smaug, but one*
> *can hope.*

Shrewsbury was pleased for his friend; he thought the
piece charming but a bit naïve. He was also put out, ever so
slightly. He had penned some epic verses on his own, but no
one in publishing had shown the least interest in *them*.

> *Edith sends her love, and like many of us, is*
> *uneasy by events over there, so do be careful.*
> *One War is enough for any man, but I fear it shall*
> *come to that. I'm glad I have Edith, my*
> *companion in shipwreck. You should perhaps*
> *consider remarrying. It does the heart good to*
> *have a safe haven. . . .*

Shrewsbury found he couldn't concentrate. Billi's face,
with its downturned eyes and that secret smile that had become so familiar in so short a time, insisted on poking into
his consciousness.

Slowly he folded the letter, slipped it back in the enve-
lope. He could imagine Ronald's comments on his liaison
with the pert American. Tolkien was adamant in his belief
that this was a fallen world, and that what he termed the
dislocation of the sex instinct was one of the chief symptoms
of the Fall. He would, perhaps, view the affair as a betrayal.

And that uncomfortable thought brought Shrewsbury

round to Anne. He always thought of her, almost by reflex, when the American girl entered his mind. He had no idea why. They were unlike as could be. Anne had been tall, deliberate, with an austere beauty—a trifle horse-faced, in truth, but that lent her character—hazel eyes, hair the color of the splendid wood that paneled the compartment. A woman who looked well in tweed, who presented the grave mien appropriate to a don's wife and aged, it seemed, by infinitesimal degrees—until the cancer began to have its way with her, of course. In the public duties of a faculty wife she was so reserved that many privately thought her more dignified than her husband, who wasn't always capable of hiding the secret boyish enthusiasm for his work and life that always bubbled inside him.

That was public Anne. In private she was dry wit, slow laughter, a wild nocturnal abandon that had shocked him at first, if only briefly. She was a very physical woman, who loved hiking and riding and tennis, whose firm but gentle nagging had led the normally indolent professor to keep himself fit, which he still did, by way of honoring her memory—one of many ways. She shared his curiosity and his love of learning, though Greek and Latin classics held more appeal to her than Norse eddas and sagas. She was an accomplished mathematician who had given up what despite her family's opposition promised to be a brilliant career in that field to be with him, and sometimes still he chided himself for permitting that—but no, that was absurd. She had known that her place was by his side, and though she continued to work on her own, she never tried to publish her results.

He loved her. That was, finally, all he could think to say about it. He loved her, and her death had been an amputation. And this was how he honored her memory: with a caustic chit of an American girl who smoked cigarettes and talked like a sailor (he had never spent much time with sailors).

For a time he flogged himself with Anne's memory, while the train ratcheted west across the Lüneberger Heath. Tiring at last of that, he climbed back into bed and opened a copy

of Spengler's *Decline of the West. That* seldom failed to put
him to sleep, but tonight his eyes stubbornly stayed open.
The bottle of Irish stashed away in his bag began to call to
him. He resisted; there had been a time, when Anne was
fading and after, when he'd only been able to sleep curled up
in a bottle. He'd grown unkempt, his hair long and his
clothes odoriferous, his sense of himself gaseous and vague.
He was still unsure how he'd found within himself a stanchion of solidity to seize and hang on to and draw himself
together again. He still drank on occasion but only lightly;
he dreaded any surrender or loss of self-control, even to help
relax himself into badly needed sleep.

Voices filtered in from the corridor. Something in their
tone drew his concentration like a compass needle. He lowered his spectacles, staring at the door as if to force his
vision through the solid wooden door.

A muffled impact, a grunted curse. Sounds of scuffle,
and a female voice raised in outraged protest. *Billi!* he knew
in sudden panic.

He leapt up, banged his knee on the table. Cursing, he
steadied himself with one hand, rooted in his Gladstone
while the train's motion jounced the top half up and down on
the other like alligator jaws. In his mind he flagellated himself—he should have known there'd be trouble, they'd had
ample warning . . . his fingers closed around the smooth
round wooden butt of his Mauser. He snatched out the unwieldy pistol, chambered a round, and flung himself at the
door.

Lunging into the corridor, he ran smack into a stranger,
bulky in a camel-hair greatcoat. "Do forgive me, frightfully
sorry," he murmured, at once feeling an utter fool. He raised
a placatory left hand, hoping fervently the man wouldn't see
the pistol. It could cause no end of uproar.

The stranger grunted and brought up his own right hand.
It was black-gloved. Faint yellow shine from the overheads
skittered along the blued barrel of the pistol it held.

In frantic reflex, Shrewsbury hacked downward with his
left hand. He felt the impact of radius bone against his
palm's edge, and the gun went off.

* * *

Once she realized what was happening to her, Billi's response was immediate: she drove an elbow behind her with all her wiry strength.

It hit something yielding. The man holding her doubled over with a satisfactory grunt, and the grip on her arms relaxed. Instantly she started to shimmy free, but another hand clamped on her biceps like the steel claw of one of Rossum's Universal Robots.

She twisted. Two heads loomed over her, faces backlit and shadowy-obscure. "Let me go, you son of a bitch!" she screamed.

A hand clamped over her mouth. Naturally she bit it. Its owner snatched it away, grunting, "Damn."

The other man—younger, she sensed—who had possession of her arm raised his free hand as if to strike her. His partner fended him off. She went limp—she hadn't battled Paris riot cops back-to-back with her worthless ex-husband André for nothing. That almost got her free again, but the younger man stooped and got her under the armpits in an almost-nelson and began to drag her backward down the corridor with her bare heels trailing ridiculously along the carpet.

Tonight she was dressed for sleeping, not effect, but her ancient faded pink flannel nightgown was hiked all the way up around trim, muscular thighs. The older man bent past her to pull the gown primly down again, and she caught a brief impression of a thick, florid face that clashed terribly with brick-colored hair.

The door to the next car banged open behind her, and cool air ran down the back of her neck and up her bare legs like a million refrigerated spiders, and she was in the covered accordion passage between cars with the coupling banging underneath like a metal giant that wanted in, and Rafe popped out into the hallway in his pajama bottoms, and it suddenly occurred to her that the captor she'd bitten had cursed in English, and the door closed.

CHAPTER

Twelve

Rafe felt just exactly like Captain Spaulding, the African Explorer: *when I was in Africa I shot an elephant in my pajamas. How he got in my pajamas, I'll never know.* Tension made him giddy.

The *wagon-lit* door slammed shut just this side of Billi's toes. Through the glass he saw the far door open into the dining car beyond. Whether Billi's captors—he'd counted two, hoped he hadn't missed any—had seen him, he couldn't say. As soon as they'd cleared the covered passage between the cars he raced after them.

He was in the bucking, noisy passage when he heard the distinct hammerfall rap of a shot behind him. He glanced back. At the far end of the sleeping car Professor Shrewsbury was wrestling with a big man in a greatcoat. Rafe looked right. Billi's captors had her halfway through the dining car, already set up for breakfast with gleaming tablecloths and crystal water pitchers. Friendship struggled with chivalry.

The door opened behind Shrewsbury and his antagonist, and Leutnant Kampfer appeared from the second-class car next in line. With reinforcements on hand, chivalry won. Rafe pushed on into the dining car. As he did, he heard another shot, but by then it was too late to change his mind.

* * *

The sound of the gunshot exploded the rhythmic train-noise from Shrewsbury's ears, leaving ringing residue. The flash was dazzling. After what seemed a distinct interval he felt a sharp impact on the instep of his left foot, which instantly went numb.

He glanced down. The knee of his trousers was smoldering, and the stink of burning wool clogged his nostrils. *I'm shot,* he thought, and his knees went pliable beneath him as he tried to bring the Mauser to bear.

His assailant raised his pistol. The door opened behind him. The man spun and fired. Young Kampfer cried out and sagged out of the passageway, face ashen, a dark brown stain filtering into his tunic like ink into a blotter.

The strength came back to Shrewsbury's legs as the assassin fled the car. He hurled himself in pursuit. Fumbling, he got the gangway door slid open as his quarry slammed through into the second-class sleeper. He caught that door before it shut and found himself with a clear shot at the broad back from less than an arm's length.

Instead of shooting, he launched himself in a classic rugby tackle. The two of them went down into a swearing, squirming tangle. Shrewsbury hacked at the man's gun hand with the butt of his Mauser. The rounded end of the broom-handle grip caught him where his thumb bone met the rest of his hand, and he dropped his weapon.

Shrewsbury smiled in triumph. The old dog had a few bites in him yet. He started to raise himself up.

The other man threw himself sideways, carrying the professor with him as if he were weightless. Shrewsbury's elbow cracked the wall, his own fingers turned to jelly, the Mauser skittered away across the flower-printed carpet like a frightened animal. The man in the camel-hair coat rammed his fist into the pit of Shrewsbury's belly, knocking the breath from him with such force his eyes almost popped from their sockets.

His assailant got to his feet, dragging the professor upright with a hand wrapped in the front of his cardigan. The professor fought to pry some air into his lungs. His opponent didn't look much younger than he, but was larger.

Very much so. A huge, balding brute with a long lip and an often-broken nose.

The big man twisted the latch on the door to the outside, slid it open. Icy air hit Shrewsbury like a blast from a fire hose, and the night rushed by with a voiceless howl. *My God, he means to throw me off,* Shrewsbury realized. Breath or no breath, he grabbed for the thick throat. His opponent pulled his head back. Shrewsbury tangled long fingers in the collar of the man's coat and clung for all he was worth.

"Hold it!" Rafe shouted in German, bringing the .45 up before him in a two-hand grip.

"Bastard!" shouted the younger man. He let go Billi's arm, stepped to the side between two tables crusted in silver and crystal, raised his arm, and fired without pausing.

Glass exploded from the window in the door sliding shut behind Rafe. He squeezed the trigger. The big Colt rode up in that heavy ocean-wave way as the slide slammed back and forward again.

The bullet hit the would-be kidnapper like a mule kick in the sternum. He went back, seeming to fold in the center of his chest, arms whipping around before him, slack-jointed, extended like a diver preparing for the plunge. His pistol wheeled away, smashed through glasses like a bowling ball, shattered a pitcher. Water cascaded, a torrent carrying glittering sharp floes of glass.

The man fell back over the table behind him, half turning. Fingers clutched red-spattered linen, and he subsided, drawing cloth and silverware and dishes clattering around him like the last trick of an incompetent magician. Billi screamed once, struggled, then went deadly still as her captor's arm tightened across her throat.

Rafe pivoted as the big pistol fell off from the recoil. The front-sight blade seemed to come to rest against a ruddy cheek, right of center in a broad, battered face that looked as if it customarily rode in easygoing lines. There was nothing easygoing there now in the pale gray eyes; the wide, hard-set mouth, lipless with tension; the high wide forehead lumped over almost invisible brows, sweat beads strung catenary along a line of thinning pink-red hair. His far cheek and much of his chin were obscured behind disarrayed sprays of Billi's hair. The muzzle of a Spanish automatic jutted out at Rafe from beneath Billi's right armpit.

"Let her go and you get to walk out of here," Rafe said. "No questions." The sights rode up and down to the tempo of the track. Rafe felt for the timing.

Billi seemed to have shrunk, the points of her shoulders drawn in toward her breastbone. She stared fixedly at the gap between tables where her younger assailant had fallen. Her face was white as a mime's.

"I think not," her captor said. "I hold all the cards, don't you know. Drop the gun."

The car jounced, the .45 rose. Rafe fired.

"Sod you," gritted the man in the greatcoat. Shrewsbury was hanging from his neck like the Ancient Mariner's albatross; if he was going off the train, he was by God not going alone.

The bulky man caught hold of the door frame with a stubby hand and drove the other fist in under Shrewsbury's short ribs. Shrewsbury's eyes bugged, and he bit his tongue; he felt as if he'd swallowed a broken magnum bottle. But he hung on.

Another punch pistoned into the professor's belly. His vision faded, came back unfocused. He was holding his body cramped, half from pain, half from design, to keep his attacker from getting good shots at him. *Perhaps I'm too old for this, after all*. The joints of his fingers seemed to be dissolving like cheap glue in the rain.

He heard the passageway door slide open. His attacker took a step back, turning to face it. Shrewsbury cramped forward around the dull fire in his belly and collapsed in the blast of air from outside as Leutnant Kampfer, the right side of his tunic soaked with blood, stepped into the car and shot the man through his camel-hair coat with a Luger.

The man grunted and took a backward step as the copper-jacketed bullet went through him. Kampfer slumped, seemingly held up by the sliding door, hair falling sweat-lank in his face. He fired again and again. The big man dropped to his knees with a thump and a groan. Kampfer shot once more, and the man fell onto his face.

"Great God, man," Shrewsbury forced out, "did you have to keep shooting him?"

Kampfer nodded. A strange green light burned in his olive eyes. "*Ja*. For Brummbär."

At his nod Shrewsbury turned his head to look down the corridor. Not five feet from his attacker lay the burly Bavarian sergeant, sightless eyes staring at the silent second-class doors, and the back of his head smashed in.

Rafe turned the pistol over in his hand. ASTRA UNCETA Y CIA S. A. GUERNICA-SPAIN was stamped into the dark blued receiver. "No clues here as to where our friends came from. These things are floating all over the known world."

Sitting in the dining car as the train hurled past the cows and empty hayricks of North Germany outside, and a couple of ashen-faced stewards worked to repair the damage the brief battle had done before the breakfast rush, Kampfer nodded. All three of the intruders had been carrying Spanish pistols, wearing clothing off some bourgeois rack in Berlin, and carrying no papers. The few passengers who would admit to having exchanged words with them said they spoke German with an unidentifiable accent, which Rafe could personally confirm. They could have come from anywhere.

The surviving soldiers were all gathered in the car, drinking coffee and being very quiet. Brummbär Bauer had been popular. But he'd been in the wrong place at the wrong time; too bad. Rafe drank deeply of his own black coffee and wished it were stronger. It might wash some of the taste from his mouth.

"Well, I suppose that fat slob Waldmann will wring the truth out of the one the lieutenant shot before he gives up the ghost," grumbled Dietrich, the Schwabian miner with the movie-star looks and the dense wrestler's body. The others called him Black Peter, for his dense black eyebrows and his beard, which could never be reduced past blue stubble by any means known. "That Gestapo lot could make a bronze statue of Bismarck confess. Swine."

He made as if to spit. Kampfer stopped him with a raised

eyebrow. The sergeant was being missed already. Maintaining the hairline balance between *esprit* and discipline had been his task.

Chatenois pushed himself up, took two steps down the car and two steps back. Normally languid, he tended to get very wound up when nervous. "I hope Fräulein Forsyth is all right."

His comrades looked at him, except for Uurtamo, off chain-smoking in his own world. They lacked heart for the banter such solicitude for a member of the opposite sex— especially from the Freiherr—would normally evoke.

"She's taking this quite well," Kampfer said. "I'm more concerned for the professor."

Rafe nodded. Billi had taken everything quite well indeed. In fact, when he went to help her up off the floor, he was the one who was trembling. She was very calm, almost too calm.

"I'm fine, just fine," she said, before he could ask the obvious question. She scraped a damp forelock off her face. "What's the matter with you?"

He sat down. His legs felt very weak. "I'm sorry."

"For what? You saved me."

"I shouldn't have shot. Might have hit you. Too . . . too much of a risk."

She frowned down at the torn shoulder of her nightgown and hitched it higher. "Nonsense," she said, and tried to make a joke of it. "I know you too well, Rafe. You never miss."

"Everybody misses. It's too damn easy."

And then the door to the first-class car banged open and in came Waldmann in his nightshirt with the soldiers behind him, and that was when Billi threw up.

Things got very confused for a while. Rafe sat there with his .45 in hand, feeling shocky, and the chaos just sort of ebbed around him as the conductor went banging on doors looking for a doctor and somebody draped a coat around Billi's shoulders and Waldmann stomped around doing police things. He'd killed men before. It wasn't his favorite thing to do. Worse was the chance he'd taken with Billi's life—the bullet had combed her hair, and what if he'd misjudged the train's rhythm, or it happened to hit a rough spot in the track in the wrong slice of a second? He'd let the stories and strange happenings get to him, had reacted to a threat without sufficient thought.

. . . Or had he? Somebody was playing a high-stakes game here, high enough that Feldwebel Bauer had been sapped simply for stepping out of his room to check on his men at the wrong instant. Anybody willing to play by such rules, be they Abwehr or OGPU, was not going to be too scrupulous about the health of Wilhelmina Forsyth if they got her off the train. Maybe he'd done the right thing, after all. The thought failed to bring much comfort.

Chancing to overhear that both Kampfer and the professor had been wounded brought him out of it. *I'm not doing too good a job playing the hero, am I?* he thought. *Moping around while my friends are hurt.* Tough to live up to Sapper and John Buchan, let alone Robert E. Howard.

The conductor's best efforts had flushed out a dentist, who wasn't a lot of help and kept asking Shrewsbury to open his mouth. He covered well, claiming he wanted to see if the professor was spitting up blood, which fortunately he was not. Kampfer sat to one side of the professor's compartment smoking a cigarette, shirtless, the right side of his rib cage wrapped in bandages. Neither his gunshot wound nor Shrewsbury's was serious; one nine-millimeter *largo* slug had cracked one of the young officer's ribs and glanced off; another had laid open Shrewsbury's right instep to the bone and split his shoe. Luckily the dentist had been equal to dressing them.

What worried Rafe was the beating Shrewsbury had taken. "Professor," he remarked, "you look like you've just been drug through a knothole backward, as the cowhands used to say."

"Thanks awfully, old man," said the professor ironically. He *did* look like he'd been drug through a knothole backward. His hair stuck out in tufts, his complexion was reminiscent of various types of French cheese Englishmen won't eat, and his eyes looked as if they were being carried in sooty slings. "That Southwestern American idiom of yours is really quite colorful. I must devote some study to it some-day. Confound it, man, get your hands away from my mouth! I'm not a pit pony being let for sale."

"But, Herr Professor Doktor, I have found a problem."

Rafe's heart sank. "Well?" the professor demanded. "Out with it, then."

"Plaque."

At that moment Billi came charging in, a risqué, disar-rayed Clara Barton in a torn nightgown, still reeking of the chloroform with which her would-be kidnappers had tried to keep her under, and waving a .25 Beretta. The dentist squeaked and started to dive under the settee. Rafe caught a handful of suit coat and hauled him back. Every-one stared nervously at the weapon as it executed arcs in the air.

"Why, Billi," the professor said, "whatever are you bran-dishing that for?"

Billi flushed. "I have been drugged, dragged, hit, shot at..." She paused, searching for more indignities, and, finding none, concluded, "And I'm by God not going to let it happen again."

Shrewsbury stepped to her side, gently relieved her of the pistol. Rafe stiffened for an explosion. To his surprise it didn't come.

Billi pulled her gaze from Shrewsbury's battered face and chivvied them all out, the dentist still adjuring the professor to floss regularly and avoid sweets. Rafe thought he heard her sob as the door swung closed, and shut it with a gentle-man's firmness.

It wasn't a sob. It was an hysterical giggle, half swal-lowed. "You look like a little boy jumped by the school bully on the playground," she told the professor.

The simile tweaked his professorial dignity, but on the other hand, being called boyish stroked his vanity, so he just blinked at her like a bewildered owlet.

She threw herself at him with such force he recoiled, grabbing him and cradling his head against her breast. "Oh, Melbourne, what did they *do* to you?" Then she did sob.

* * *

The train stopped in some North German tank town to take on a real live physician and a troop of Gestapo heavies. Despite the conductor's howls of protest, the bodies were left on board; no one and nothing was getting off the train before Bremerhaven. Waldmann was determined to keep the lid on.

The doctor had to play Oedipus to Billi's Sphinx, convincing her he knew his trade, before she'd let him at Shrewsbury. He wasn't able to amplify much on his predecessor's diagnosis: the gunshot was superficial, not dangerous unless infected, and the professor wasn't showing any signs of internal injury from his beating. Yet. Likewise the doctor had confirmed that Kampfer's injury was more painful than serious.

Now an hour had passed, and Rafe and the soldiers were killing time in the dining car, waiting for word on the interrogation of the single captive, whom the doctor had brought around enough for some kind of communication. Rafe had firmly refused Waldmann's invitation to participate. He was distinctly of two minds about this. He didn't approve of torture and was under no illusion as to how gently Waldmann would press his questions—hell, no cop in the enlightened modern world of 1936 would hesitate to beat answers out of somebody in a case like this, much less the Gestapo.

On the other hand, the man and his friends had kidnapped Billi, taken a potshot at Rafe, and murdered Unterfeldwebel Bauer, and the prisoner himself had tried to kill the professor and Kampfer. In a lot of ways Rafe was not going to mourn if they pulled off his goddam arms and legs in order to get answers. Still, he felt this squeamishness. Overall he preferred not to know what was going on. It was cowardice, he supposed.

He was prodding these thoughts around in his brain when one of their little friends in the fedoras and trench coats came into the dining car and jerked a summons with his head. Everybody got to his feet.

"Just you two," the Gestapo said to Rafe and Kampfer. He turned and went out.

Kampfer's neck burned. Rafe slapped him on the shoulder. "Tactful sonofabitch, isn't he?" The lieutenant turned him a hot-eyed look, then grinned.

They followed the secret cop back to Professor Shrewsbury's compartment. Waldmann and the doctor were there already. "We got the truth out of him," the Oberführer said with heavy satisfaction.

Billi was sitting on the bed next to Shrewsbury with her legs drawn up, ignoring the professor's discomfiture and Waldmann's scandalized expression alike. Now she looked at the Gestapo officer as if he were a poisonous serpent. "We did not need to employ coercive means," the doctor said quickly. He was sweating profusely for such a dry-looking little man. "The . . . the subject was delirious. He responded quite readily to our questions, as long as he was lucid."

He took off his glasses, scoured them with his tie. "I was unable to save his life, unfortunately."

Billi squeezed her eyes briefly shut. "Okay, then what didn't you torture out of him?"

Waldmann's brow lowered. He looked hard at her, then at the professor, then at Rafe and back to Billi, as if he knew that each of them was personally responsible for leaving a tack on the Führer's chair. *"Engländer,"* he said shortly. "They were Englishmen."

Shrewsbury stood up, brushed past Rafe and Kampfer, and limped out of the cabin. Billi started to follow, only to be stopped by Rafe.

"No, I can handle this better."

Her expression disputed that, but all she said, in tones of loathing, was, "Boy talk," and flounced back to the bed.

Rafe caught up with the professor in second class. "I know what you're feeling."

Shrewsbury looked at him, his face desolate in the yellow glow of overheads. "They were my countrymen, Rafael. I helped kill them."

"They weren't backward about trying to kill *you*, Professor. Nor me, for that matter. Nor abducting an American national or murdering a citizen of a country with which England doesn't happen to be at war. Don't eat yourself alive, Professor."

Shrewsbury removed his glasses from his shirt pocket, put them on, then, with almost the same motion swept them off again. "There's more to it than that," he said, gesturing with the folded spectacles. "They were almost certainly in Intelligence—Foreign Office, Military, it really doesn't matter. They were acting as representatives of the Crown. Am I a traitor, Rafe?"

"No."

Shrewsbury shook his head, pinched the bridge of his nose, and shut his eyes. Rafe saw tears among the lashes. "You know what my cousin told me," he said. "Our expedition's attracting a lot of attention. I think these boys got wind of it and decided to look into it, and wound up going off half cocked. You've been in the field yourself, Professor. They made a right royal balls-up of this thing. Doesn't that bear all the earmarks of some overgrown schoolboy deciding to play the hero on his own?"

Shrewsbury sighed. "You've a point, Rafe." He sounded at least half convinced.

"So I don't think you bear any moral stigma for this—an Englishman has the right to defend himself, after all. And given the many illegalities our friends perpetrated on this little outing, I can't imagine you're going to face any legal ramifications from this on the home front. Though—" Rafe clamped his mouth shut just in time. He had just been about to say too much.

Rafe had not just been blowing smoke; he would have been surprised had His Majesty's government known anything about what these three of its servants had been up to in the wee hours of this March morning. But the deceased might have had comrades, other grown boys playing cloak-and-dagger games, who knew of their self-appointed mission and might conceivably try to avenge them.

The prospect didn't trouble Rafe particularly. He'd had representatives of his own government—some of whom could have given Oberführer Waldmann a lesson or two—after him during the recent unpleasantness of Prohibition, when he'd been putting his convictions into practice by providing people with the option of deciding for themselves whether or not to drink. During his recent misadventure in China he'd been dodging gunslingers from the Comintern, the Kuomintang, the Japanese, and, as a matter of fact, the Abwehr. He knew his way around.

The professor was a more settled type. Law-abiding. No point giving him something extraneous to brood about; this Greenland jaunt looked as if it was going to be unnerving enough as it was.

"Though what, Rafe?"

He gripped his old friend firmly on the arm. "Nothing," he said, and led him back to Billi's waiting arms.

Coldhearted light of North German dawn dribbled in through the curtains as Waldmann perused the telegram he'd just composed for dispatch to 8 Prinz Albrechtstrasse. He did it with satisfaction. "These damned foreigners have had things their own way for too long," he told himself aloud. "Now we shall see about reining them in. Yes, indeed we shall."

Worst—the most undisciplined—was that confounded American woman. Like a spoiled child, she had refused to accept the reasonable strictures he'd laid down as expedition head. And her games had come to this: the mission compromised, the German peace shattered, good German blood spilled.

Wilhelmina Forsyth, late of Boston, would never have to look Frau Bauer in the eyes and tell her that her three children were fatherless because she'd decided to flout authority by playing fast and loose with security. A vein at the side of Waldmann's forehead twitched like a windup soldier at the thought. His face was flushed, and he felt an anger even the blood of three foreign criminals could not quench.

Very well; let the object lesson be directed at Miss Forsyth. He smoothed an imaginary wrinkle from the pale blue form and read again the message directing that the wretched waiter from Horcher's, whom she'd staged her little pet to get released, be rearrested and shot as an enemy of the State, photos to be forwarded to Bermerhaven by air. It was irregular procedure even for the Gestapo—even in the wake of the massacre called the Night of the Long Knives, which broke the *Sturmabteilung*—but Waldmann had been given absolute discretion in this affair by Reichsführer SS Himmler himself.

With a puff like a locomotive brake bleeding steam, he rose to seek out the conductor.

CHAPTER

Thirteen

"There she goes again," Rafe said, peering out the grimy window.

Billi checked her wristwatch. "Got it. Care to make a wager, gentlemen? The last three times in a row, she's been back on the pavement in fifteen minutes to the second. Can she do it again?" she added in that breathless tone that radio sports commentators affected when a batter was coming up three-for-three.

Shrewsbury frowned up from his book. He was ensconced in a mammoth wingback chair whose arms were covered with discreet, though grimy, lace doilies. Its upholstery was a floral print fit to water the eyes. The springs were shot, which meant that both the professor's knees and his nose occupied approximately the same altitude.

"Really, Billi," he sniffed, "this is hardly a fit subject for a lady to concern herself with."

Billi laughed, came away from the window through which she and Rafe had been watching the streetwalker conduct her business across the little street in the waterfront district adjoining Bremerhaven's Old Harbor to massage Shrewsbury's shoulders from behind. She had to reach around beneath the wings and prop her chin on the back to do it: a startling effect, *Sartor Resartus* starring Salome.

"Don't fret yourself, Mel. I'm hardly fit to be called a lady."

He snorted, refused to look at her. She laughed with musical malice. "You're so cute when you pinch those aristrocratic nostrils like that. Here, what're you reading?" She leaned in over his shoulder, hands sliding down the prickly wool of his sweater.

"Gibbon, if you must know."

She nodded sagely. "Ah, yes, wherein Roman emperors are always being debauched, and *zikk*!"—she drew a forefinger across her throat—"that's the end of them. I have fond schoolgirl memories of Gibbon . . . no wonder you're such a bluenose today, dear, reading that."

Shrewsbury harrumphed. Billi laughed again and kneaded his shoulders harder. His forehead scrunched down deeper and deeper into a frown as he fought to keep from responding to the animal pleasure of it, until his face seemed in danger of cracking and flaking off like cheap plaster from the stress.

At last the professor's resolve crumbled, and he lifted his head to give Billi an exasperated smile. She kissed him on the forehead and sashayed back to the window, glowing with slight triumph.

Rafe stood with his foot on the windowsill, smoking and ignoring their byplay. This was their second day spent languishing in the little *pensione* the SD kept as a safe house in Bremerhaven. He was at least as bored as the others, but bore up better.

"How's she doing?" Billi asked.

He pulled out his pocketwatch. "Seven minutes."

She turned and sat on the sill. "The least they could've done was put us up in a decent hotel, instead of across the street from some cathouse."

"Count Kinski thinks we're best off somewhere out of the public eye. For what it's worth, I agree."

"I do, too, I guess. I don't want to attract any more attention of the sort we've been getting. I've had enough excitement to last me a lifetime."

She sighed smoke through her nose. "At least this sort of thing's easier to take from the Count than from that creepy

Waldmann." She shook her head. "On the other hand, in a way Waldmann unsettles me less. He's more the way a Nazi *ought* to be."

"Maybe you need practice separating the man from what he believes."

"Can you really do that, Rafe? And should you?"

It was his turn to shake his head. "I don't really know." Then he showed her half a grin: "I give you the benefit of the doubt, though, so I might as well keep doing the same for Kinski."

As Billi's eyebrows crept up toward the top of her head, the professor rose and sauntered over. "Very well, you've got me curious. Will the confounded woman be punctual again?"

With a poisonous look at Rafe, Billi glanced out the window again. "Why do I get the impression," she asked, "that everywhere you two go, the same two crows always turn up?"

"Whatever do you mean?" Shrewsbury frowned at the two big black birds standing on the stoop of the dowdy brick building across the street.

"Weren't you two crow watching when I ran into you back on the Ku'damm?" Billi asked.

"Why, yes, but surely you don't believe this is the same pair?"

"There's something familiar about those beady-eyed stares."

"All crows have beady-eyed stares, my dear," Shrewsbury scoffed. "I wonder what they're about down there."

"Maybe they're timing our friend the businesswoman too."

"I wonder," Rafe said thoughtfully, "if they're really crows."

"What? You think maybe they're bluebirds in blackface?" Billi said.

"No. I wonder if maybe they're ravens instead."

"What's the difference? A crow's a crow."

"No, my dear, crows and ravens belong to entirely different species of the genus *Corvus*," the professor said in his best lecture-hall tone.

"Why is it that you always call me 'my dear' when you're patronizing me, Melbourne?" Billi asked sweetly.

"At least we now know what the momentous political event brewing in Germany was," Rafe said, rather louder than the drably but serviceably furnished confines of the sitting room required.

Ponderous might also have been an appropriate label for the furnishings, as if the proprietor, fearing that her predominantly sailor clientele would take it into their minds to brawl, had chosen furniture that was immovable or, failing that, indestructible—or, finally, cheap. There were tables as heavy as a German breakfast, sausage-fat chairs, an imposing cabinet radio off in one corner, its polished wood, gleaming brass dials, and honeycomb speaker making it look like some kind of exotic organ. The chair Shrewsbury had vacated was backlit by a tall pole lamp with a white-enameled standard and a fringed and overly large shade that irresistibly reminded one of a too thin, too old hootchie-koochie dancer.

Billi sighed, turned away from the window, and thrust her hands deep in the pockets of her tan slacks. "Yeah. And why I'm out of a job." She was still put out over the abrupt parting of her way from the wire service's.

The morning they'd arrived in Bremerhaven, yesterday, had been March 6—the day Hitler marched the Wehrmacht into the Rhineland, in contravention of the Treaty of Versailles. The country was on alert in case the Allies decided to take active exception to the move; only military traffic was moving on the rail lines and in and out of the harbors. Even the luxury liners plying in and out of the transatlantic Columbus quay a quarter of a mile from the boardinghouse were frozen.

Until travel restrictions were lifted, the great Greenland Gungnir Expedition was stuck in Bremerhaven. Not because they couldn't have swung the clearance—if the dark lord of the SS and Gestapo said they could go, they could go—but because any vessel warping out of harbor under these circumstances that wasn't the brand-new *Scharnhorst* or her sister ship, the *Gneisnenau,* was going to be a trifle conspicuous. So the travelers got to cool their heels.

Billi checked her watch again. Their conversation had finally worn through and dumped them on a slab of silence like cold cement. A few minutes limped by, and then somebody knocked at the door. Suddenly Rafe wondered if he should have left his pistol in his room, and Billi leapt to her purse and started fumbling around for her .25.

"Who is it?" Shrewsbury called.

"Kinski." The door opened to admit the little count, dapper as always. "I bring fortunate news."

The three stood. "Our breath is bated, Count," Billi said.

"I've always found that expression most peculiar, Fräulein Forsyth," Kinski said with a slight frown on his fox's face, which almost instantly smoothed into a smile. "But you'll be pleased to know that we'll have this spot of bother over with almost before you know it. Travel restrictions are being lifted tomorrow; you sail at ten."

Rafe applauded; the professor nodded judiciously. "If you weren't a Nazi," Billi said, "I'd hug you."

"Billi," Shrewsbury said reprovingly. Kinski sadly shook his head.

"I regret that you feel that way, Miss Forsyth." He stepped forward. "Were you looking at something out that window?"

"We've been timing—" Billi began.

"Ah, we've just been having the most stimulating debate about the identity of those birds across the way," Shrewsbury overrode her. "Whether they're crows or ravens, don't you know."

Kinski raised a brow at him, then leaned forward to peer out with the air of someone humoring a respected associate who has suddenly begun showing signs of incipient madness. "We had great flocks of both types of birds on my family's estate in Silesia," he said, "but I never could tell one from another."

Abruptly the birds unfurled their wings and took off up the street, voicing cries like ripping muslin. Kinski brightened. "Ah. There you have it."

"Have what?" Billi asked.

"Your mystery solved. They were ravens, no doubt about it."

"I thought you couldn't tell them apart," Billi said suspiciously.

"Oh, I can't, not by looking at them. But you heard them. Crows caw. Ravens have a harsh call like—well, like that."

"You learn something new every day," Billi said. The door before which the birds had been standing opened, and out walked the prostitute. Behind her emerged a man in the uniform of the German merchant marine, taking advantage of a day's unexpected liberty and buttoning his fly.

"Fifteen minutes," Billi announced, "on the dot. What did I tell you, Rafe? And you say there's no German efficiency."

At her footstep he failed to turn, sitting as he was in the great, garish chair with an open bottle of brandy between his knees, rocking it all but imperceptibly so that the liquor shed auburn highlights in the light of a single exiguous lamp with a fake Persian shade. "Having trouble sleeping, are you?"

Rafe Springer lifted his head without looking back. "I'm not the only one, unless someone's somnambulating. Have a seat. Have a drink." He gestured expansively with the bottle.

"I'll take you up on the first offer." She came and sat on an ottoman near him. She wasn't playing Salome tonight; heavy robe over a pink flannel nightgown, no frills, no peekaboo. "I think you could use some company besides that bottle."

He held it up, regarded it in the light, such as it was. "You're right." He capped the bottle and set it on the table by his elbow.

"So what gives? I can hardly believe you're nervy about the prospect of our little pleasure cruise."

"I always have trouble sleeping the night before a trip."

"Nonsense."

Shrug.

She sat and looked at him. For some reason her eyes seemed unusually large in the wan lamplight. "Evasion isn't like you, Rafe Springer," she said finally.

"A prisoner of my self-image, am I? All right, you win. I'm feeling second thoughts."

"You? The intrepid adventurer? The rumrunner, the steely-eyed gunslinger, the builder of dams in the middle of Chinese nowhere, knows what it means to have second thoughts?"

"I should hire you as my publicity agent. And you of all people should know I'm anything but steely-eyed." He looked down at the knees of his trousers. "I see I'm not going to get off the hook by wriggling. Billi, we have our differences of opinion—"

"Tell me about it. Benefit of the doubt, indeed."

He held up a warding hand and a brief laugh. "I should have known you'd remember that. But what I mean to say is, I don't care for our employers any better than you do."

"What do you mean?"

"Our paymaster, Himmler. The whole Party structure of which he's a central pillar. They are not nice people, Billi. They're not villains in the sense you perceive them, conscienceless bullies and thugs—at least, not the ones who count. Hitler, Himmler, Goebbels, even Göring, though he's been pretty much a buffoon since he got shot in the ass in Munich in twenty-three. They're men with a vision of a better world—"

"How can you say that!"

"It's true. They're believers in a greater good. And they don't care how many people they have to kill to serve their holy vision." He raised a hand to his eyes, massaged temples with thumb and forefinger. "It's always been that way, Billi. It sounds outrageous, but it's true: great evil, really major atrocity, springs from the purest of motives. Look at Torquemada, the Inquisition—the whole bloody history of religious savagery. Real, bone-deep, committed idealism leaves no room for compassion. Burns it from the soul with a white-hot heat."

"Very poetic," Billi said, crossing her legs primly, and cramming her arms into the sleeves of her robe as if chilled by his premise.

"I'm drunk. Indulge me." He waved a hand. "The National Socialist German Workers' Party has done terrible things. I have a feeling that before they're done, they'll get up to something a thousand times worse—you can smell it on them, the odor of sanctity, the lust to force morality by setting the torch to unbelievers if need be. Sooner or later they'll quit sniffing around the Jews like a snarling dog, and then—" He made a cleaving motion with his hand.

"And not just the Jews. I don't think the Nazis can catch Comrade Stalin, whom all the intellectuals back home love so loudly, when it comes to murdering millions. But I have a horrible feeling they'll give him a run for his money."

Billi shivered. "But what is this all about? Really?"

"We're working for them. I mean, even though this whole Gungnir tale's one of Himmler's more fevered fantasies, I'm sure he can find some way to parlay whatever results the expedition brings back into a propaganda coup. The more so if we follow Gruppenführer Heydrich's thoughtful suggestion about handing Himmler a regular Norse spear as a stand-in for the real thing."

"So what, Rafe? It's probably better if we *do* present Heini with a counterfeit Gungnir. Imagine what the press is going to say when he comes out with what he says is the one and original Spear of Odin. He'll be the laughingstock of the entire world." She set her jaw thoughtfully. "Of course, we might wind up looking mighty silly, too, but we can always try to disassociate ourselves from whatever Himmler claims."

"It still gripes me to be helping him in any way."

"Well, for God's sake, Rafe, what the hell were we going to say, anyway, after he dragged us into his lair? 'Well, gosh, gee, sorry, Mr. Himmler, best of luck finding your spear'? Principle's a fine thing, but are you going to throw your life away to keep from going on a scavenger hunt for some fairy-tale toy?"

Slowly a smile chipped away at the grim set of Rafe's mouth. "You know, you have a point."

"Of course I do. Besides, the only upshot of this little publicity stunt—aside from making Herr Himmler look ridiculous—is going to be to stir up bad blood between him and Goebbels. The little clubfoot is going to see this as an attempt to score points off his own propaganda boys."

Rafe eyed her through the gloom. Her aggressive disregard for common sense made it all too easy to forget just how sharp she was. Maybe Billi was starting to grow up.

"So quit moping around. No one's asking you to help beat up Jewish shopkeepers. Our taking part in this escapade is not going to increase the power of the Nazi Party, or anyone's misery. At least, nobody who hasn't asked for it—I don't see you losing much sleep over shooting somebody who shot at you first."

"Not much. But some."

"Well, I think better of you for it. But maybe this damned country has brutalized me, at that. What happened on the train was horrible—I'll carry it with me to the end of my days—but I just can't find it in me to feel too sorry for those men, after what they did to poor Brummbär. Even if they were English."

She shook her head. "So much for my enlightened liberal convictions."

She rose to stand beside him, very close. He looked up, speculation in his eyes. She brushed back a wisp of disorderly straw-colored hair from his forehead. "You're an attractive man, Rafe Springer. I suppose you know that. No, don't go tense on me—I'm not going to give you a chance to stand on your gallantry and carry on about how you'd Never Do That to your dear friend and mentor Melbourne..."

"Just as well."

"... but I feel I owe you some kind of explanation. Or rather, I don't; I'm not some loose artifact you happened across, that you're entitled to because you saw it first—and I *know* you don't feel that way, don't interrupt when I'm being rhetorical or I'll punch you in the snoot—but I'll give you an explanation, anyway, because we've been friends for years."

"Whew. My breath, as someone said earlier, is bated—and come to think of it, that phrase has always made me queasy too."

She laughed. "There you are, Rafe. There's your problem." He cocked an eyebrow at her. "You're too damned analytical. Always looking past things—be they political beliefs or the meanings of words. You're too damned much a realist.

"It feels strange to say that. If I've ever known anyone who fit the role of knight-errant, it's you. But somehow you don't really believe in all those old, comfortable romantic myths. Melbourne does." She laid fingertips lightly on his shoulder. "And that's what I see in him. He's handsome and thoughtful and kind, and I do enjoy listening to him, much as I love to tease him. But I think that's what attracts me to him . . . that he sees windmills as giants."

Rafe laughed softly. "That doesn't cast me in a very flattering light—Sancho Panza doing Don Quixote's tilting for him, knowing full well he's going to bust his lance against a wall and get swept from the saddle by a vane, and there aren't any damned giants, anyway."

"But it does—cast you in a flattering light, I mean. That's your kind of nobility, Rafe. But I'm more . . . comfortable with Mel's kind."

They sat for a moment in a more relaxed kind of silence than they'd known that afternoon. "Don't sell the professor too short. He has a way of getting to the truth in spite of himself." She looked at him quickly, her eyes keen and strange. He gripped her forearm. "And don't sell yourself too short, either; don't be afraid of what he'll see if his eyes clear."

He let go her arm and stood. "Well. We'd better get to our rooms before Herr Waldmann comes down and lectures us about outraging German respectability." He strolled off toward the door.

"Rafe." He looked back. "Thanks. I don't really believe you, but thanks."

"I'm the one who should thank you."

She held up the bottle. He shook his head. "You keep it. Or leave it for the maid." And he tipped her a one-fingered salute off his left eyebrow and was gone.

CHAPTER

Fourteen

"Nietzsche's the most poorly understood philosopher in the world," Rafe said to Joachim Heinz, Graf Kinski, who sat in the front seat of the big brown Mercedes. "It's as much you Germans' fault as that of your English-speaking former enemies."

Sitting on the leather-covered rear seat, Professor Shrewsbury sniffed. "An immoralist."

"He's the Nazis' patron saint, Rafe," said Billi, as seriously as she could, sandwiched between the professor and Rafe with her skirt hiked up over her knees. "He thought up the whole notion of the *Kulturkampf* that was behind the Great War."

"Oh, no, he didn't. He spent most of his time ridiculing German *Kultur*. 'Wherever Germany extends her sway, she ruins culture,' is one of the kinder things he had to say on the subject."

"He was a warmonger," Billi persisted. "Didn't he say the best thing about peace was that it should be short?"

"Sure he did. He suffered from the same sort of affliction as Dr. Johnson and our own domestic Mr. Mencken: he loved sound and fury in expressing himself and tended to forget people weren't necessarily going to look past the surface to get at what he really meant. His martial-sounding rhetoric referred to the battle for mastery over oneself. He

145

was pretty much a pacifist, especially after he served as a medical orderly in the Franco-Prussian War and got a good look at what war did to people. And he had a vigorous distrust of the all-powerful State."

"That's not what the Nazis say," Billi said, winded, but still game.

"No, it's not." He lifted an eyebrow at Count Kinski. "And the worst disservice the National Socialist intellectuals do Nietzsche is to associate him with anti-Semitism. He hated anti-Semitism—his hatred for it was literally insane, in fact; the last letter he wrote during his breakdown concludes, 'I am just having all anti-Semites shot.'"

"We base our scholarship on the valuable work done by Nietzsche's sister—"

"—who falsified his work, perverted his actual writings, and cobbled together new ones to suit her own fancies."

Kinski gestured easily. "It may be as you say. Nonetheless . . . in the modern world the needs of the State are paramount; must be, to preserve order and keep bestial human nature in check. Thus, when it serves the State to tailor reality to its needs—isn't that really for the greater good?"

Rafe was visibly gathering steam for his reply, but Shrewsbury broke in: "Really, isn't it too splendid a day to be going on like this?"

Rafe grinned and let out a long exhalation. "You're no doubt right, Professor. It is a marvelous day."

Actually it was a day piled high with clouds, though the sun was momentarily bright. But they were on their way at last, off to meet the German contingent at the Danish freighter chartered to take them to Greenland and, they hoped, a modest outdoor adventure.

Even Billi lacked the spirit to prolong what promised to be a good argument. She gazed left and right as the SD driver wound the car through the narrow streets. Bremerhaven was the port proper of the *Hansastadt* of Bremen, having sprung up in 1827 when the increasing draught of cargo ships made it difficult for them to venture farther up the Weser River to the old seaport. It was a pleasant enough town, neat brick and frame buildings—but, on the other hand, this was the waterfront and consequently on the mean side, dingy and huddled close about itself.

"I wonder what was eating old Waldmann this morning," she remarked. "He was going around looking as if his pet rat just died."

Shrewsbury sighed audibly at her gaucherie, but Kinski produced a restrained laugh. "He takes his work too seriously. We of the *Sicherheitsdienst* cultivate a cavalier's heart: always laughing."

The Danish freighter *Holger Danske* was moored at a wharf a fair distance from the ritzy Columbus docks in more than physical terms. The loading area was a cobbled clearing between looming broken-windowed warehouses. It and the ship, an old swaybacked six-hundred-tonner with red and white stripes in peeling paint around her single stack in honor of her native country, showed no signs of life; the last cargo had already been swayed aboard.

Kinski had the driver, a big thick party with a rumpled face, pull up near the foot of the ramp that ran down the rusty hull. The travelers emerged, eyeing the ship with a marked lack of enthusiasm. Billi squinted carefully at the mooring lines dogged about huge cleats sunken in the cement top of the stone seawall.

"What do you see, Billi?" Shrewsbury asked.

"I'm looking for rats."

"Going aboard?"

"Coming ashore."

From beneath the front seat Count Kinski produced with a flourish a bouquet of roses, long-stemmed and white as the clouds stacked above the Frisian Islands out beyond the mouth of the bay. "A token of my esteem for you, delightful lady. Despite our differences of opinion."

Billi moistened her lips. She knew what white roses signified: the pure love of the medieval troubador and the knight-errant of romance. She blinked rapidly several times. "Count, I—"

Low and black, two big cars roared onto the dock behind them from between two warehouses. One broke left, the other right, and they came to a halt with a squeal of tires on gravel. A man in a leather coat stepped out of the one on the right.

"The House Opposite sends its regards," he said. With a gloved hand he pulled back the bolt on the submachine gun he held and fired a burst at the SD car.

The driver was reaching inside his jacket when the slugs caught him. He grunted, fell back against the car, slid with agonizing deliberation to the cobblestones.

The cars disgorged a half dozen armed men as Rafe dragged Billi down behind their vehicle. Shrewsbury ducked beside them, fumbling inside his tweed jacket. Kinski fired two shots from his blunt Mauser 7.65-millimeter and joined them.

Billi fought to her knees, ruining her stockings. "Let go of me, dammit. We have to get up the ramp."

Rafe locked a hand on her wrist. She spat like a bobcat, tried to pull free. Another burst cracked over their heads with a sound like ripping canvas and raked the gangplank. Billi went flat on her stomach again.

"I hate you, Rafe Springer. You're always right." She began digging frantically through her purse for the Beretta.

Bullets were slamming into the big car like the hammers of bodywork elves, but the Abwehr attackers hadn't pulled far enough forward to flank them. Rafe heard at least two machine pistols blazing away out there; probably they hadn't felt much need for subtlety.

He duck-walked to the rear of the vehicle, .45 in hand. The man in the coat was still standing right next to the low-slung Daimler touring car, methodically pumping bullets over the SD car's hood from a stubby Schmeisser with a perforated barrel and a side-hung magazine, trusting to superior firepower to keep the quarry's heads down.

He'd misjudged. Left-handed Rafe Springer was in perfect position to poke his Colt out and fire past the steeply angled boot of the car without exposing much of himself. He shot twice.

The man in the leather coat rocked back on his heels, took two steps back, sat down hard. He laid the machine pistol on the cobblestones beside him with great care, felt carefully at his chest, and fell over.

With a sound like an infuriated kitten Billi upended her purse, dumping wallet, pillbox, cigarette case, lighter, compact, five tubes of lipstick, a shower of ticket stubs, and a bottle of nail polish onto the cobblestones. The shiny little automatic bounced twice on the hard stones and went off.

Rafe winced as the round poked a hole through his hat brim, barely missing the back of his head. "Jesus *Christ*, I'm one of the good guys, remember?"

"I'm sorry!" she screamed, retrieving the pistol.

"Don't *ever* leave a round chambered when you carry the goddam thing in your—"

From the Porsche to the left came the wasp-vicious snarl of a broom-handled Mauser Model 1932 on full auto. Rafe ducked back in a spray of rock chips.

Shrewsbury had finally battled his own unwieldy Mauser out of the shoulder holster Kinski had insisted he wear even to the dock and was crunched down behind the hood just in front of the passenger door. Unfortunately his weapon was a souvenir of the Great War and lacked selective fire. Kinski crouched at his side, keeping the engine between him and the third machine pistol that had begun yammering for their blood. His roses were scattered about his feet.

Billi, on her knees between the professor and Rafe, lifted her head to peer through the window of the car's rear door. A submachine gun responded instantly. She ducked down in a spray of shattered glass.

"Billi!" the professor gasped, reaching for her. "Are you hurt?"

She batted his hand away, brushed glittering glass snow from her shoulders and hair, screamed, "Shit!" and popped up to empty her Beretta across the backseat so rapidly it sounded like a machine pistol itself.

There was silence as she ducked down again. "Did I get the bastards?" she asked breathlessly.

Rafe was flat on his belly, peering past the rear tire. "You missed," he said, "but you shocked them into putting their heads down." He blasted a shot to discourage an Abwehr boy from lunging out from behind the Daimler to recover the dead man's Schmeisser.

Another shuddering burst of automatic fire blew out the

rest of the SD car's remaining glass. "For the moment, anyway," Rafe added.

The fight had settled into stalemate. The attackers had numbers and firepower, but they were all huddled under the cover of their two vehicles, clearly unwilling to do anything too heroic.

"This can't last," the count said. "When their confidence comes back, they—"

Two men broke from behind the car on the right, racing for a pile of crates stacked against the weathered flank of a warehouse from which they'd be able to enfilade the four. As they broke, the two machine pistols blazed furiously away, and another hardy soul made a dive from the rear bumper, recovered the fallen weapon, and opened up from behind his comrade's body.

Kinski came up onto one knee, holding the Mauser with both hands, the pink tip of his tongue peeking from between thin lips, firing with deliberation at the running pair. One went down rolling, cursing, and clutching his shoulder. The other reached the crates, then reeled back and fell to the cobblestones.

A tall, skinny man stood up behind the open driver's door of the Daimler with a Bergmann machine pistol at his shoulder. The weapon chattered. A nine-millimeter bullet caught Kinski in the left shoulder, spun his slight body around to receive the full force of a burst that sent him sprawling among the fallen roses.

Professor Shrewsbury rose to one knee and shot the submachine gunner through the right eye. He dropped in a heap like a string-snipped marionette. "I got him," he said wonderingly. "I—"

Billi grabbed him by the left sleeve and hauled him down just as a fusillade ripped into the hood. Bullets cracked where the professor's head and chest had been a second before. "That's one you owe me, Prof," she said, then wriggled back like a serpent woman at a county fair to try to help the injured count.

"How many of the blighters are there?" Shrewsbury asked, breathing heavily.

"I count at least six."

"Seems we're in a bit of a tight spot. Well, Rafael, I must say it's been jolly good—"

The sky burst open above their heads.

Shrewsbury dropped flat, cut off in the midst of his over-the-top-and-to-eternity speech, as a thunderbolt smashed the Daimler and drove it down on its springs like a giant hand. Glass exploded in jeweled clouds to either side.

Silence fell like a guillotine blade. It was instantly shattered by another end-of-the-world roar. The Schmeisser gunner went rolling out from behind the body of his fellow, the weapon flying from his own hand in turn. The car shuddered to repeated impacts. A man popped up from behind it, racing for the shelter of the warehouse. Puffs of dust and chipped stone seemed to pace him, five meters to his left, and then the spurts caught up with him. He screamed, stumbled, went flying, coming apart like a rag doll in midair.

The second car fired up its engines and screamed backward out of the loading area with Abwehr men trying to scramble into it like the Keystone Kops in reverse motion. From overhead the startled foreigners heard the hard slams of military rifles. The Porsche squealed around in a creditable bootlegger turn that crumpled its boot against a brick building corner, shot away down the narrow street. Thunder cracked again, spraying it with pink-white brick dust, and then it was gone, leaving two more bodies lying still behind it.

Slowly, scarcely able to breathe, the two men stood. As one, they looked up at the rail.

Lieutenant Kampfer stood right above them, cheeks flushed like a schoolboy's, cradling a long, skinny machine gun with a fat flash suppressor and flamboyantly flared buttstock in his arms. Several of his squaddies stood with him, lowering their Mauser rifles with expressions of satisfaction.

Resting his weapon on deck on its extended bipod, Kampfer led his men down the gangplank. The Daimler slumped on flattened tires, its cab cavernously devoid of glass, one headlight gone, the other tipped askew, steam filtering out around the fringes of a hood sprung by the machine gun's onslaught.

Billi was sitting on her knees in a scatter of fallen petals like giant snowflakes, Kinski's head in her lap, crying bitterly. The count's coat lay open. The front of his once white shirt was a scarlet morass.

Pink lung-blood frothed at the edges of aristocratic nostrils. "I—am glad—to see you unharmed—Fräulein. And you, Professor . . . Captain Springer."

Rafe knelt beside him, methodically unwrapping pink slabs of bubble gum, pressing colorful wrappers over the springs of blood bubbling in the count's chest. "Don't talk."

"Rafe, what in God's name are you doing?" the professor demanded, dumbstruck. He moved to interfere. Black Peter Dietrich caught his arm with a hand like a drill press.

"No. He's doing the right thing. Sucking-chest wound."

Kinski raised his hand and looked at Rafe with eyes as pale blue as his native Silesian skies. "It's too late, don't you know," he said clearly. "But thank you—" Abruptly he squeezed his eyes shut, lowered his head to Billi's thigh.

His own eyes filled with tears, Rafe fumbled a bubble-gum packet, tore the wrapper in pieces, and threw it down. "Damn. Just damn."

The count's breath began to come in short chops, and his slight frame shuddered. Billi picked up a single intact flower, laid it on his chest, gently folded his hands across it.

He clutched the stem, ignoring the thorn that pierced his flesh. "One white rose—" He gasped, and died.

The freighter's horn hooted three times. White-faced sailors had come thumping down the gangplank and were hurriedly casting off the mooring lines. Freiherr Chatenois's face appeared at the rail.

"Captain says he's sailing now. Come aboard this moment or stay behind."

Moving with exaggerated care, Billi eased herself out from under the lifeless count. The hand that had placed the rose was covered with blood, and she wiped it on her skirt. She noticed the plaid was already splashed with blood and uttered a single low moan. Kampfer and Shrewsbury helped her to her feet. The horn shrilled again. They left the dead where they had fallen and hurried up the ramp.

CHAPTER

Fifteen

Still unsteady with reaction, Rafe, Billi, and the professor made their way onto the bridge fifteen minutes later as *Holger Danske* shouldered through the crowded harbor. It was cool and dark. Waldmann stood to one side with a radiotelephone in hand, bellowing at the harbormaster, who apparently had had the temerity to ask why the freighter was departing ahead of schedule.

Captain Poulsen was a tall, heavyset man with tightly curled black hair and beard liberally streaked with gray. He stood tipped slightly forward as if leaning into a wind, peering over the shoulder of a young towheaded helmsman with sleepy, slightly protuberant blue eyes. He turned to greet them.

"Good morning," he said in gruff, densely accented English. "I understand you have a bit of *halloj*—you say 'excitement,' yes?"

"Excitement, yes," said Billi bleakly. She had changed into her Merry Widow outfit, only this time she had added black-figured stockings, and the "merry" seemed to be missing. Her cheeks were still flushed, her eyes unnaturally bright. "I understand you were planning to drive off and leave us standing."

"I'm sure we're all quite pleased to make your acquaintance, Captain," Shrewsbury said firmly. "Please excuse Miss Forsyth. She's had rather a frightful morning."

Poulsen produced an ursine shrug. "She's right. I did not sign contract to have my ship in fighting. But, since you here, welcome aboard."

Waldmann threw down the handset, grumbled "*Arschloch*" beneath his breath.

"Who won?" Billi asked sweetly, as if there were any doubt.

Ignoring her, Waldmann planted himself in front of Poulsen. "As soon as possible, give me an officer to interpret and have your men report to me for questioning. I must be sure all of them are fully reliable."

A light seemed to glimmer back in those deliberate eyes. "I vouch for them."

Waldmann waved a dismissive hand. "This attack proves matters are more serious than I imagined. I must insist on interrogating your men."

Poulsen turned back to gaze placidly out the port. "This is a Danish vessel, *tysklander,*" he said in German considerably more fluent than his English. "If you try to impose on my crew, I'll have you thrown over the rail."

Waldmann's whole head turned the color of a boiled beet. He turned to the hatch. "Kampfer!" he bellowed out over the deck. "Come up here at once."

The lieutenant exchanged glances with Chatenois and Passauer and came ambling up the ladder while Waldmann got purpler and purpler. "He looks like he's headed for apoplexy," Billi said in an optimistic stage whisper.

Kampfer sauntered onto the bridge. "What is it, Herr Expedition Head?"

Waldmann pointed to Poulsen, sitting on his stool puffing a meerschaum. "Arrest that man. He threatened me!"

Kampfer looked at Poulsen, shrugged. "I can't."

"What are you talking about?" Waldmann almost screeched.

"This is a Danish vessel. And I'm no policeman."

"Arrest him at once. That's a direct order."

"I can't accept it."

Waldmann looked as if he were about to pop like an

overfilled balloon. "What? I'm your superior. Orders are orders!"

Kampfer snapped to attention. "Begging your pardon, sir, but you are not my superior, sir. I am a member of the Armed Forces, sir, not one of your Gestapo scum. I am attached to an expedition under your command, sir, and bound by my oath as an officer to obey all lawful commands. Ordering me to arrest Captain Poulsen is not a lawful command, sir."

Waldmann's hands bunched into fists like small hams. "When we get back, I'll—"

"You'll what, sir? Wehrmacht members are outside Gestapo jurisdiction, sir."

Raging, Waldmann stamped past him and bounced down the ladder like a leaden ball. Poulsen looked at Kampfer and chewed his pipe stem.

"Bravely said, son. But I wonder if you haven't overplayed your hand."

Kampfer grinned, shrugged, to show how little it mattered to him.

"You a drinking man?" Poulsen asked. "I've a bottle of aquavit in my stateroom that I think's gotten old enough. When I get the *Holger* into a clear channel I'll be putting it to the test. You're welcome to join me, if you will—and your friends."

Rafe tramped down the ladder with Kampfer at his side. "Just what the hell was that you saved our bacon with? Not that I'm complaining, of course."

White teeth gleamed in the tanned olive face. "MG34. The very latest model light machine gun, just accepted into service. We'll be subjecting it to cold-weather field testing in Greenland."

"Not on the Eskimos, I trust?" Kampfer laughed. "How much does that thing weigh, anyway?"

"Twelve kilos."

"Well, if you want to lug twenty-six pounds of machine gun plus God knows how much ammo all over the ice pack, it's all one to me. It's not *my* expedition."

Kampfer looked wounded. "You disapprove?"

"Let's just say I wouldn't do it."

They stepped out on the deck. Rafe walked to the rail and craned back. He could just make out considerable activity on the dock they'd vacated.

"Who on earth were those men, Rafe?" Shrewsbury asked, joining him. His voice was less than steady, and his cheeks had lost most of what color the Berlin winter had left them.

"Remember what my beloved cousin Rudi told me, about the killing rivalry between Heydrich's SD and Canaris's House Opposite? Bodies in the alleys of Berlin."

He tipped his head toward the distant dock. "Now they're turning up on the Bremerhaven waterfront. I wonder what the local constabulary is going to make of all the stiffs and ruined cars? Whatever the *Geheime Staatspolizei* tells them to, no doubt."

He sighed. "First the British, then the Abwehr. I'm glad we're finally out of reach—it'd be like waiting for a three-legged man to drop the final shoe, waiting for the Russians to make *their* play at us."

Kampfer laughed and clapped him on the shoulder. "From here on in, it's all *Strudel mit Schlag,* my friend."

Rafe faced him with a sunken-eyed look that made the boy recoil. "It's nothing of the sort, Lieutenant. If you show the same overconfidence on the ice that you showed in that showdown with Waldmann, you're a dead man, no matter what kind of merit badges you have sewn on your blouse."

He turned and walked off to his cabin, leaving the young officer blinking at his back.

Clad in undershirt, shorts, garters, socks, and gleaming shoes, Waldmann sat on his bunk, laboriously turning the crank of a hand-wound phonograph. The day was still cool, but down here, not far from the boilers, in the cabin assigned to Waldmann from among the dozen or so passenger compartments rather optimistically nestled here and there throughout the vessel, it was airless and hot.

Waldmann did not need any help feeling hot under the collar. The insufferable impudence of the Danish captain, and that confounded Wehrmacht pup's insubordination, were only the latest of the aggravations he'd faced this day. The least, in fact.

Even today's attack didn't enjoy pride of place among his woes. Thank God they were in the charge of that fop Kinski, he thought, and sweated with even more enthusiasm at the thought that it might have come while *he* was responsible.

The crumpled telegram was still weighing down the pocket of his suit coat, hung on a peg against the bulkhead: the terse reply to his message ordering the rearrest and execution of that damned Horcher's waiter. It canceled his order, advised him to leave off seeking scapegoats for his own incompetence, and made it clear that a second slipup would cost him dearly.

It was signed, Gruppenführer Reinhard Heydrich.

Heydrich! That bastard Saxon upstart. Waldmann reached into the suitcase lying open on the bunk beside him, took out the cardboard jacket of a phonograph record, reverently pulled out the disk, put it on the turntable. His hands shook when he lifted the arm; he pulled them back, wiped them on his hairy thighs. Forcibly reminded that he wasn't dressed, he grumbled, rose, and carefully rewiped his hands on the baggy seat of his shorts. It wouldn't do to scratch the record, but it would be just his luck.

What could the Reichsführer be thinking? He had placed him—him—in personal charge of this expedition. Waldmann was Himmler's comrade-in-arms from the high old days of the *Lauterbacher Freikorps*, when they sent the terrorists of the Münchener "Red Army" packing. He had been at his right hand when Himmler was first Acting Police President for Munich and then Political Police Commander for all Bavaria. When Himmler made his move to Berlin and *Gestapa* in 1934, Waldmann was his strong shield arm, helping ward off SA attacks and Göring's intrigues, while bringing much-needed police professionalism to the largely ineffective *Geheime Staatspolizei* fat Hermann had invented.

Of course, even then that weasel Heydrich was on the scene, insinuating himself. What was Heydrich? A glossy rogue with the morals of a goat, who had been cashiered from the Navy for bad behavior. A former crony of that swine Canaris's, whose Military Intelligence plotted constantly to replace the Party apparatus in Hitler's favor. Who was to say the bad blood between them was really real?

It would not surprise Waldmann in the least if Heydrich had in some obscure way been behind the attack at the wharf. Had the assassins even been Abwehr? If they had, of course, Canaris would smilingly disclaim responsibility, produce irrefutable evidence that the dead men had never been connected with 72-76 Tirpitz-Ufer. Which would, of course, prove nothing.

One thing was certain: Heydrich was gunning for him. For all the Blond Devil's nominal suzerainty over *Gestapa,* the *Sicherheitsdienst* was his personal fiefdom. In the Gestapo he was an outsider. Heydrich was always conniving means of increasing SD's influence at the expense of the Secret State Police.

From the pit of his capacious belly a sick feeling spread like spilled ink soaking into a blotter: Heydrich never intended this expedition to succeed. He had played upon the Reichsführer's . . . well, obsessions . . . gotten him to conceive the idea of this ludicrous jaunt to the ends of the earth, and then saddled *Gestapa* with responsibility for making it succeed. Much as Waldmann admired his old comrade and current chief, he did not for one moment believe the Spear of Odin was to be found in Greenland, or anywhere else outside the pages of Norse mythology.

They were intended to come back empty-handed, that was suddenly clear—leaving Ernst Waldmann to explain matters to an *exceedingly* disappointed Reichsführer.

The sick feeling erupted in a gargantuan belch that set his belly to quivering and left a foul, bitter taste on the back of his tongue.

He fumbled in the suitcase, brought out a portrait of Frau Waldmann and their assorted daughters in a gilt frame, set it up on the little nightstand next to the bunk. Then he lifted the stylus again and poised it above the silently spinning disk.

A thought hit him like a blow from behind: Heydrich's telegram would not have been sent without the Reichsführer's personal approval. Not even the crown prince was so bold as to try to take such a step behind Himmler's back; where the Greenland expedition was concerned, no artifice of Heydrich's, cunning as he was, would suffice to prevent Himmler's reading any message long before its recipient did. Not for nothing was Himmler the Master Spider.

Which meant . . . he could not bear to face what that meant.

He dropped the tonearm. It bounced once with a squawk, and then he sat staring blindly at the paint flaking off the bulkhead while Wagner's "Siegfried's Rhine Journey" washed over him like a warm sea.

Sea travel is intrinsically pretty boring, and *Holger Danske* was no luxury liner, with offensively tanned and eager activities directors always chivvying one to the shuffleboard courts and paying too much attention to the more moneyed dowagers. Kampfer turned out to be a juvenile chess whiz, so the professor was lost in a protracted tournament with the officer. There was only so much time Rafe could pass playing cards and shooting the bull with the other soldiers, listening to Chatenois's bantering wit or the bordello braggadocio of Passauer and Kurt Hoff, or Black Peter Dietrich, dour and voluble by turns—and to Rafe's surprise a committed Communist, who seemed to see no contradiction in serving the Third Reich in the Wehrmacht. Whenever he tried to broach the subject, the soldiers passed one of those aggravating German *Besserwisserei* smirks among themselves, that said they knew something Rafe didn't know, and refused to say more.

He spent some time trying to get better acquainted with Uurtamo, the ski-warfare instructor, but the Finn's reserve was so great even Rafe could make only glacial progress toward drawing him out. It drove Rafe nuts; he didn't know much about Finland or the Finns, and he was morally convinced Uurtamo had some fascinating stories to tell, of his people and himself. But the instructor just sat on his bunk, staring at vistas only he could see and smoking.

That pretty much left getting drunk with Captain Poulsen, listening to Jäger Eblinger, a nice man but boring, enthuse about his stamp collection in his Harz Mountain accent;

moping with Waldmann in his Wagner-drenched cabin; or fighting with Billi, who was peeved because the professor wasn't paying enough attention to her. And pacing the decks staring out to sea.

The third day out, he left the Hearts game down in the soldiers' cabin sometime after seven bells of the first watch for a turn around the deck, to clear his head of schnapps and stale smoke. The weather was moderate for a nighttime North Sea at this time of year, which is to say there was a brisk chop, and cold rain randomly lashed the decks from ragged-edged clouds that skidded across the gibbous moon like broom-mounted witches.

It suited his mood. He was feeling trepidations again. Premonitions, perhaps — that the worst still lay before them, that some menace waited in Greenland over and above the dangers of the inland ice. He'd mentioned the feelings to Shrewsbury, locked in chess, who'd dismissed them as superstitious relics of his childhood in the legend-haunted Sangre de Cristo mountains and castled kingside.

Rafe smiled thinly, took a drag on the cigarette he sheltered in his cupped palm. *He's probably right.* He walked aft, past a cargo crane, an unearthly tower of shadows and moonlight glints, watching the fitful sea.

The back of his head exploded in a shower of blue-white sparks.

Without knowing how he got there, he was on his knees with the deck hard, cold, and wet beneath. His head and stomach whirled in contrarotation. His eyes refused to focus. *I've been sapped from behind,* he realized muzzily. The thought was like a small lead figure lying in a vast bed of gauze. *What a Saturday-afternoon serial thing to happen.*

Hands caught him under the armpits, lifted him up. Nausea swamped his belly, enervating him, robbing him of power over his limbs. He made a feeble move for the pistol inside his coat, but his hands were already the stiff, cold members of a drowned man.

Grunting, the unseen assailant heaved him up, propped him on the rail. He gazed down with dispassionate interest at the waves, which seemed to leap at him like a pack of feral dogs. *He's throwing me overboard. That's not very nice.*

He heard an exclamation, and then he was falling—back onto the deck. He rolled over with his shoulder against a stanchion. *I'm delirious*, he thought.

Because he imagined he saw an enormously broad man in the striped jersey of a common seaman hoist a grown man over his head as if he weighed no more than a child, while the man squirmed and lashed out ineffectually with a spring-loaded cosh. The giant held him there a moment, then leisurely tossed him over the rail. A falling scream, rounded with a splash.

Rafe rolled, tried to stand. His head rang like a forge. From the corner of his eye he caught a glimpse of his benefactor standing over him—not a giant, he saw, no taller perhaps than he, but with the disproportionate breadth of shoulder and chest of a weight lifter or stevedore. In the darkness he absorbed an impression of a silver-shot black beard and an eyepatch. The turmoil in his stomach bubbled over, and he vomited.

When he could open his eyes again his benefactor was gone. Unsteadily he got to his feet. His legs were India rubber. He stank. His stomach still felt like a trying morning after, and so did his head. *I dreamed the whole thing,* he told himself. He knew how perverse the effects of a blow on the head could be. He must have stumbled, struck his head on something, hallucinated the whole attack and surreal rescue—

His eye lit on a gleam. Lying against a stanchion was an eight-inch blackjack, its wet black leather glistening like steel in the moonlight. Whistling tunelessly, he scooped it up, stuck it in the pocket of his jacket. *No one is going to believe me, anyway,* he thought, *so I won't even trouble them with this little tale. I slipped and banged my head on a hatch coaming, that's it.* Besides, he'd always wanted to use the word *coaming* in a sentence; it had such a lovely sound.

On uncertain legs he went off to find the ship's doctor.

"Today, Billi, you are going to receive a shooting lesson," Rafe said, squiring her aft to the taffrail after breakfast the next morning. An interested group of onlookers trailed along, offering helpful comments.

"Why? I know how to shoot pretty well already."

"I'm going to teach you to use a weapon that's liable to be a bit more useful in a pinch than that ridiculous BB gun you've been carting around in your purse. And may I remind you again, just in case you missed it in all the excitement in Bremerhaven, don't *ever* carry a pistol in your purse with a round chambered."

She eyed him with suspicion. "Why do I have the feeling this has to do with that goose egg you're sporting on the back of your pumpkin head?"

He swallowed his fried eggs and cold salmon a second time. "It has—why, it has everything to do with my little, ah, mishap. It reminded me that we're headed into a situation filled with unknown dangers, and we need to be more alert than ever."

"What does your falling on your silly conk have to do with me learning to shoot?" she demanded.

"He's addled his wits, my dear," observed the professor, walking a few paces behind with his hands in his pockets. "He's raving."

She rounded on him. "Why are you tagging along, anyway? Aren't there pawns to queen and rooks to rook this fine morning?"

"Friend Rafe confided to me what he intends to do this morning; I wouldn't miss it for the world. Besides—" he nodded over his right shoulder—"my esteemed opponent is also planning to spectate."

"Great. Do I at least get a cut of the concessions?"

It was an achingly clear day, and the sea was mild. Rafe carried several empty institutional-size food cans he'd cadged from the cook under his arms. He set them down on deck next to the taffrail, put out a hand to steady himself against a brief surge of dizziness, and pulled a Colt .45 automatic from the pocket of his coat.

"And now," he said, handing the angular black weapon to Billi, "you're going to learn to shoot a real pistol. Fortunately, I carry a spare—it's not modified to left-hand use; consider it a gift."

Frowning, Billi weighed the three pounds of cold iron in her hand. "Do I shoot this thing or throw it at the bad guys?"

"Best throw it at them, Fräulein," the Freiherr said from behind them.

Rafe heard a familiar raging-boar bellow and glanced forward to see Poulsen walking toward them, puffing his pipe like a circus bear, with Waldmann trotting after him like an obese terrier. "The wireless message this morning confirms my suspicions, Captain," the Gestapo man was saying. "The missing seaman's real name is Radnov. He's a known Bolshevik agent! What do you say to that, *Herr Kapitän*?"

A shrug. "I say he was not much of a seaman. He won't be missed."

"'Was'?" Waldmann pounced. "Aha! So you know something—" Poulsen frowned down at him as if he'd just found him stuck to his shoe, subconsciously tapped the binoculars slung about his neck. "I know there aren't many places to hide on a ship this size. Not when the searchers know where to look. He got drunk and went over the side."

Rafe swallowed.

"You say he signed on in Bremerhaven. How do you justify hiring such a man?"

"He had his union card," Poulsen said placidly. "I do not inquire too closely into the antecedents of my hands. Otherwise I should find myself sailing this ship by myself."

He strolled past the lifeboat hanging in davits and nodded to the assemblage. "So, Frøken Forsyth, you actually intend to try to fire this young cannon unaided?"

"I suppose you telegraphed Walter Winchell so he can keep Mr. and Mrs. North and South America and all the ships at sea abreast of things too?" She held the pistol up, still lying on her palm like a dead thing. "I still want to know what's wrong with my Beretta."

"It's insufficient to drop anything bigger than a ship's rat, and not one of those if he's determined. You hit a man with one of these—" Rafe jutted his chin at the .45. "—he's likely to want to leave you alone thereafter."

"It's awfully big." She fit her hand around the grip.

"Use both hands. Like so." He folded the fingers of her left hand over the right, tucked her thumb down out of the way of the slide. She frowned momentarily, then pushed out her underlip and nodded.

"You know, I kind of like it," she said, raising it. Gently Rafe pushed the muzzle so it no longer pointed at the tip of his nose.

"She's actually going to shoot it," a soldier said.

"Better lash yourself to the railing, Fräulein Forsyth," Kampfer offered helpfully. "You'll save yourself a nasty fall when that goes off."

"Really, Rafe, whatever are you thinking of?" Shrewsbury said. "Billi can never hope to control such an enormous pistol. It's too much for most men; she'll never hit anything with it, and be lucky if she doesn't hurt herself into the bargain." He held out his hand in unspoken command. Billi nailed him with a glare and continued to inspect the pistol.

"I don't know how that myth got started. The .45 doesn't have that bad a recoil. It's just a big, slow push. Billi can handle it; she's a sturdy young woman."

"I think I resent that," Billi said. Experimentally she tried to work the slide. It refused to budge. She bit her lip, grabbed it from the top, tried again. It slid out a fraction of an inch, then snapped back. "Damn!" she yelped as it pinched the web of her thumb.

The spectators guffawed. "Here, Fräulein," Kampfer said, stepping forward with his hand held out, "before you hurt yourself, give it over."

She gave him the same hot-eyed look she'd bestowed on the professor and jacked the slide with a quick, determined motion. "There!" she said, throwing back curls the slight breeze kept tossing in her face. She straightened her arms before her. "Throw a target overboard, Rafe."

Rafe grinned and pitched a can into the sea. Billi braced against the ship's deliberate roll, raised the gun. "There, Lieutenant Kampfer, get ready to catch her—" the professor began.

Billi fired.

Bobbing on the propellor swirl a few yards aft of *Holger Danske*'s blunt stern, the tin leapt straight into the air. There was much silence.

The pistol had ridden up clear over her head. "I see what you mean, Rafe. The recoil's not bad, but I can't hold the thing down."

"Nobody can. Just keep a firm grip on it." This time he threw the second can high into the air over the rail.

Shrewsbury was shaking his head. "Beginner's luck. Anyone can—"

Bang. She took the second can on the down slide of its arc, and it jerked and fluttered from the large hole blown through the tin. Billi brought the pistol down and blew a thin wisp of smoke from the barrel. "Damn. I *like* this."

Rafe nodded. "Just as I thought. You're a natural—even though you've done some target shooting before."

The mob of onlookers was beginning to break up into groups looking everywhere but at Billi, who stood there triumphant, upholding her pistol like a modernized Valkyrie. "All right, bring on the trolls," she shouted. "I'm ready for 'em! Calamity Jane's got nothing on me."

Shrewsbury's mouth wrinkled. "Well, Rafe, you've proved your point, but you may live to regret what you've released upon the world."

Rafe grinned. "But she's right. Calamity Jane had nothing on her. As a matter of fact, she looked like nothing so much as Gertrude Stein in a cowboy suit—"

A cry in Danish brought heads around. A seaman stood pointing dead astern. The travelers could just pick out a pair of black dots hanging against the felt-board blue of the sky.

"What is it, Captain?" Shrewsbury asked sidelong.

Poulsen raised his glasses. "Crows."

Holding the pistol with the barrel tipped up, Billi sidled over. "Why are the sailors so worked up?"

"They're a superstitious lot," the captain said dismissively.

"Isn't it unusual to find crows so far from land?" Billi asked.

"They're probably bound for Ireland."

"We've passed north of Ireland," Shrewsbury observed.

Poulsen shrugged. "Birds got lost too." He turned away.

"Your glasses, Captain," Rafe said. "Might I borrow them?"

Poulsen handed them over. Rafe brought them to his eyes, dialed the birds into focus. "Ravens," he said softly, as if unaware he spoke.

"What's this?" Billi demanded. "In Bremerhaven you couldn't tell ravens from crows across the street. Now you can identify them from a quarter-mile off. Did you get a quick correspondence course from the Audubon Society?"

Smiling, he shook his head, handed the glasses back to their owner. "Let's just say I know these are ravens."

Before she could say anything he picked up another can and hurled it over the rail. "Here. Try for three out of three."

Far astern, the black birds drifted.

CHAPTER

Sixteen

"It's too early in the year," Captain Poulsen grumbled with a dragon puff of condensation, "and too close to the permanent ice."

The *thrum* of the *Holger Danske*'s big diesels came up around them, muffled and ominous in the frigid fog that wrapped her like a moist gray blanket. Shrewsbury stared in fascination as the vessel's prow nosed into the dark streaks of water like jigsaw cuts between the irregular ice floes, driving them apart. For the last hour they had been bashing their way into Fosters Bugt by main force. At times Poulsen would back off and send the ship charging at the ice barrier, the bow climbing onto the ice like an aging elephant seal, running with water. The air would fill with a nails-on-blackboard squeaking, rasping noise as ice and metal contended, then with a crack the floe would collapse, and they would advance another few yards.

Now Poulsen had come down to the foredeck for a closer look at the mist-shrouded surface of the fjord. Leaning on the railing with one foot propped on the lower bar, Rafe gazed thoughtfully off into the mist. Shrewsbury stood to one side, looking like the Michelin tire man in his bulky parka. The captain made do with the fur-lined collar of his greatcoat pulled up and his beaked cap pulled low, puffing his meerschaum as if trusting the smoke to insulate his face from the wind's bite.

Shrewsbury stared in fascination as an ice floe appeared out of the mist, starkly white against black water. It bumped the bow like an affectionate whale calf, sending a shudder up through their boot soles, scraped its way aft.

"My word," he said, turning pale beneath the flush the cold wind had laid across his finely chiseled features. "Are you sure it's quite safe, banging the ice about like that?"

The captain took the pipe stem from his mouth. "No. If we strike a large growler, we'll go straight to the bottom."

Rafe grinned. "Don't worry, Professor. It'll be quick. A man doesn't last more than half a minute in these waters before hypothermia gets him."

"Really, Rafe, sometimes your humor is too morbid for good taste."

Fosters Bugt bent inland between the southern flank of Hudson Land and several big, bleak islands to the tiny village of Narwhal where Waltershausen Glestcher met the sea. It was unusual for the channel to be passable this early in the year—or at all; frequently the bight lay inside the year-round ice. Only two days ago *Holger Danske* had received confirmation by wireless from Lindhof, the Danish government man in Narwhal, that the channel was navigable, if risky. A bit of luck; Waldmann was visibly relieved when he learned they would not have to make landfall at Mesters Vig on Scoresby Land a hundred miles south, or even in the formidably named Kangertittivaq a hundred miles south of that. Not only were they close to their destination, but Rafe got the distinct feeling this journey was not taking place with the entirely informed consent of the Danish government.

Billi walked up, hugging her parka around her with mittened hands. The sharp wind had chapped her cheeks until they were the same shade of pink as the cunning little ski parka she'd wanted to bring along, until Rafe pointed out that temperatures on the ice got down awfully low and she'd freeze stiff as a board if she insisted. Tendrils of windblown red hair mingled with the long white fur that lined the hood of the bulky outfit, which she claimed made her look like the Abominable Snowman. Rafe wondered with amusement

what the locals—both Eskimo and European—would make
of her.

"Are we in sight of land yet?" she demanded. "I'm dying
to see a real igloo."

As if on command, the fog parted before them to reveal a
rocky, dirty beach like an unkempt hem to the bleak and
pitiless land beyond. To one side a mass of ice crawled down
to the black water like a vast dirty-white worm.

"Walterhausen glacier," Rafe said. "Falls in the crack
somewhere between Kong Frederik VIII Land and Kong
Christian X Land. That's our route into the interior."

"'Kong'?" Billi asked with upraised eyebrow. "They
raise large apes hereabouts?"

"It means 'king,' Billi," Shrewsbury said in his usual tone
of exasperation.

"I can't see either king wanting the place. Where are the
damned igloos?"

Poulsen unslung his glasses and handed them over to her.
"See for yourself."

Eagerly she peered through them. At once she let out a
squawk of outrage. Gently Rafe relieved her of the binoculars and looked for himself.

Twenty or so low structures of stone and black peat
squatted like unsightly mushrooms at the base of a high em-
bankment, kayaks resting on frames out front. Blossoming
among them like flowers from a dung heap were a pair of
brightly painted red-and-yellow European-style frame
houses with steeply pitched roofs. To one side sprawled a
large stone building that no doubt comprised both trading
post and government office, an impression strengthened by a
Danish flag snapping briskly on a tall metal pole at one end.
Even at a mile's distance he could see the shore was littered
with rags, broken crates, bones, and old pots.

"Where are the *igloos*?" Billi repeated plaintively.

"Those *are* igloos," Rafe said. "Those lumpy things."

His companions gave him blank looks. "You're thinking
of the *illuliaq*, the temporary snow house. Those are usually
used only on long hunting expeditions. The Greenland Eskimos use peat houses for permanent dwellings: igloos."

"And another long-cherished illusion bites the dust,"

grumbled Billi, waving away Rafe's offer to return the glasses.

"Dingy sort of place," sniffed the professor.

"Not much up here to instill a sense of *joie de vivre,*" Rafe agreed. "But never fear: you'll like it less up close."

"What on earth are we doing here?" Billi wailed, crestfallen at her betrayal by igloos. "There's nothing here but miles of nothing."

"Not so, not so," brayed Waldmann from behind with that hearty good humor that Billi found so appalling. "Gungnir's here."

Pointedly Poulsen turned and walked back toward his bridge. "Or at any rate, that crank Himmler thinks it is," Billi fired back.

The Gestapo man's face darkened within the circle of his hood. She gave him her shoulder. The dreary little settlement, so utterly overshadowed by the glacier and the continent-sized dome of ice rising inexorably behind, brought starkly home just how far from civilization she was. Since "civilization" in its broadest sense included the effective sway of the Gestapo, she no longer saw any reason even to be polite to the Gestapo man.

Waldmann scowled at each foreigner in turn, as if to make sure each knew he or she was *on his list,* stumped aft to pester Kampfer and his Jägers, down in the hold checking over crates of provisions and arms.

"Billi," began Shrewsbury.

"Melbourne, please don't lecture me. We're not in Berlin now, and the sooner that creep realizes it, the better. And if he doesn't, I'll push him down a crevasse."

She started to flounce off. Rafe blocked her path. "That's not funny, Billi. The ice is two miles thick; Greenland's heart is cold and deep and unforgiving. Out there we're on the same side—all of us."

"Ooooh, my Mel will protect me. He's my hero." She clasped the professor's arm in both hands and gazed up into his face with an expression of imbecilic adoration. Shrewsbury harrumphed and looked away, his cheeks tinged carmine by embarrassment and cold.

"What if he's out of reach when a crevasse opens up

beneath your feet? What if the only man near enough to help is Oberführer Waldmann? If you keep riding him—"

The clatter of the anchor chain running out effectively silenced him. As *Holger Danske* lost way a launch left a dilapidated jetty built of imported lumber and came putting across water which was more open here inshore. As it came alongside, a Danish sailor threw a line to the boat while another dropped a rope ladder over the side. Rafe stared at the two with the same half-abashed scrutiny with which he'd regarded all the crew members since that eerie night on the afterdeck. It was a waste of time; nobody aboard resembled the one-eyed man he'd seen in his hallucination. A bearded man swarmed monkey-agile up the ladder, exchanged bantering Danish greetings with the crewmen, headed off toward the bridge to talk to Poulsen while other sailors stripped tarpaulins off the hatch covers, preparatory to transferring the first boatload of provisions.

Once more Rafe scanned the faces of the seamen . . . just in case.

"You there, get away," Leutnant Kampfer bellowed at the dozen Eskimo children who stood staring in moon-faced awe at the pile of provisions growing on the rocky beach. "Get out of here. *'Raus!*"

They stared at him with eyes like obsidian disks. A little girl, after much deliberation, stuck her thumb in her mouth. Shaking his head, Kampfer turned away. "Subhumans," he muttered.

Billi flared like a safety match. "Lieutenant! How can you talk that way? They're people, just the same as you or me."

The lieutenant's handsome young face clenched. "Not like *me*, Fräulein," he said, and stalked away with stones scrunching under his boot heels, to perch watchfully next to the stores, waiting for the launch to put in with another load.

"Really, I expected better from him," Billi said, shaking her head. "I expect that kind of—of filthy nonsense from Waldmann."

"Can't really blame young Kampfer," commented Shrewsbury, having a go at lighting his pipe against a razor-edged breeze. "They are the most dreadful thieves, these Eskimos."

"Personal experience, Professor?" Rafe said.

Shrewsbury flushed and looked a bit belligerent. "All the authoritative books on the subject agree on that point. I may not have your firsthand knowledge, Rafe, but I do read."

Rafe nodded. "And do you have any idea *why* they steal, Professor?"

"The morality of savages is hardly my concern."

Billi made a noise at the base of her throat and turned her back on the professor. "The Eskimo steals because by his standards the white man is fantastically rich. He sees him lightly throw away items that seem rare and wonderful to the Eskimo, and he assumes this disregard applies to all items. Don't take my word for it, Professor; you'll find much the same explanation in *People of the Twilight*, by Diamond Jenness.

"Only, don't be too quick to rely on anthropological texts as the last word. The people who write them tend to forget their informants are intelligent people—frequently with a pretty lively sense of humor."

"You mean they lie to anthropologists?" asked Billi.

"To nosy, supercilious, and frequently just plain rude outsiders who casually ask the most intimate questions? Now, why would they do a thing like that?"

"That's my house over there." An arm the size of a beech tree swept out as though to brush back the already gathering twilight from one of the colorful Danish-style houses. "As far as local sights go, it's about the sightliest, though there are those who hold out for Lindhof's place."

Axel Geisler had piloted the motor launch and now was acting as their guide. He was a man of medium height and maximum breadth, whose dense, curly hair was black liberally mixed with gray and whose skin had the consistency of dried leather from too many years in the Arctic cold. His eyes were dark blue and turned down at the outside corners. He spoke a rough-and-ready German that went with his manner.

"Have you been up here long?" inquired the professor.

"Twenty years. Lived with the natives for most of them,

then decided I was too old for trapping and set up here. I run the trading post, Lindhof the government office. He's involved in the post, too, but prefers to say he isn't. Thinks it looks better if his superiors think he's only ministering to the Eskimos' miserable needs." His laugh was like his voice, booming as though to compete with the ceaseless wind.

"Your wife lives up here too?" asked Billi. She had noticed a gold band on one finger.

"Where the hell else would she live?" Another snorting bellow of laughter. "Oh, you think I'm married to a white woman. No, no, dear lady. No self-respecting white woman'd live up here. In fact, I haven't seen a white woman since I was in Godthab four years ago." He leered. Billi grimaced and shied away. "No, I got my old woman couple of years ago. Does well for me too. 'Specially now that I've taught her to bathe."

Billi arched an eyebrow. She clearly didn't think much of the quality of his tutelage in that department, since the reek of dried sweat, fish, and stale tobacco was rolling off Geisler in waves like fog off the glacier. But his boisterous, earthy manner still had her too off-balance for her usual snottiness.

"Podluq! Hey, Podluq!" Axel bellowed, walking up to his house. A small, plump young woman of twenty or so stepped onto the stoop. She was pretty in a lantern-jawed, rounded, exotic way, with large, liquid brown eyes and hair that almost rivaled Billi's in its copper fire. Billi blinked, pushed back her hood.

Podluq stared at the American's white skin and green eyes, then touched a hand to her own hair, pointed to Billi's, and gave a crow of delighted laughter. Billi gasped; Podluq's teeth were stumps.

"What happened to her teeth?" she demanded.

"Wore 'em down chewing skin for boots and clothes. They're all like that, child. Podluq's better than most because living with me, she doesn't have to chew so much."

"Well, I should hope not!"

By now the entire village was in an uproar. Dogs howled and were kicked into silence by their masters, who emerged from the peat igloos to peer at the strangers from a cautious distance. Eskimo voices babbled excitingly in their strange language, at once liquid and guttural, like the sound of a stream running over stones.

Christian Lindhof stood waiting at the door of the stone structure. He was an enormously tall and lanky man with a surprisingly small, prim mouth tucked beneath a prow of nose, eyes the color of standing water, limp dark blond hair grayed to the shade of old straw. He had an aggressive overhanging jut of brow that fit poorly with his demeanor, and a complexion that managed to remain sallow despite the climate.

"Welcome to Greenland," he said in English. He sounded hesitant, perhaps because he lacked familiarity with the language. Rafe suspected that the arrival of a troop of German soldiers on Danish soil might have had something to do with it. He wondered just how this little visit had been arranged. It didn't seem tactful to ask.

He invited them into his administrative office, a largish stone room occupied by a square iron stove, a desk, and a few military-looking metal chairs. *Trust bureaucrats to send metal chairs to the Arctic,* Rafe thought.

He introduced himself, Billi, and the professor. "Herr Waldmann and the others are busy erecting their tents and seeing to their supplies," he explained in answer to Lindhof's unspoken question. "They'll be along presently."

"Oh, they can sleep in the trading post. You three may have my house—there are, ah, two rooms," he said, looking pointedly first at Billi, then at her two male companions. "I shall stay with Geisler and his wife."

"By no means," announced Geisler, who clearly understood enough English to follow the conversation. "They shall stay with me, and you may sleep in your own imported feather bed. And the *tysklanders* can sleep here, as you say —little for them to steal."

Geisler went off to see the troopers settled in. Lindhof pulled a large pot of coffee off the stove, filled four mugs. After a heartbeat's hesitation he added a dollop of brandy to each, passed them out, and settled with a sigh into his chair. His manner was sharp contrast to the robust Geisler's.

"I can't tell you the difficulties I encountered trying to engage native help for you. I'm correct in my understanding

that you are—for what reasons I'm sure I can't imagine—
heading inland to the northwest?"

Over the steaming rim of his mug Rafe batted a look from
the professor to Billi. "That's correct, Herre Lindhof,"
Shrewsbury said.

"What's the problem?" Billi asked. "I suppose the area's
taboo or something."

Lindhof shook his head as if his hair were wet. "But, yes.
that is the very problem. In fact, they refused to consider
undertaking the trip until last night. I'm sure they held one
of their heathen rituals to come to the decision."

The incongruous brows pinched together. "I'm sure the
trade goods offered for their services helped change their
minds. These folk are far more ready to accept our material-
istic Western values than the truth of the Scriptures, I fear."

"You're a missionary, Mr. Lindhof?" Billi asked, cocking
her head. He nodded. She donned an expression like a mongoose presented with an especially fat, old, and sluggish
cobra.

Rafe rolled his eyes heavenward. Agnostic himself, he
didn't talk to the Virgin of Guadalupe too often, but with
Billi about to start preaching dialectic materialism to some
devout Lutheran who was not only their native liaison but
sole representative of their host government into the bargain,
it seemed a good time for it.

The great debate was forestalled by a peremptory knock
that rattled the door on its hinges. "Could that be the ham
first of Gestapo Waldmann I hear?" Billi wondered.

It was. Clearly afraid of what the *Ausländer* would get up
to without him, he had bustled over straightaway when
Geisler turned up with the invitation. Kampfer stood behind
him with the hood of his snow-white parka down.

Lindhof invited them in, and introductions were completed. "I was just telling your associates of the difficulties I
encountered securing native guides—" the official began in
German.

"They want more money," Waldmann cut him off flatly.
He may have had a head shaped like a cannonball, but he
was nobody's fool.

Lindhof blinked moistly. "Why, yes. Precisely. It seems the area into which you're headed is taboo, and—"

"Superstitious savages," Kampfer said, elevating his fine, straight nose. Billi glowered.

"Or greedy," Waldmann said. "Do they think to make fools of us?"

"Please, please, gentlemen. I have arranged for six local Eskimos to serve as guides and dogsled drivers. I had to offer them a good deal of money, which you are, of course, free to repudiate. But I warn you, for less they probably won't go."

Waldmann started to blow.

"Do you know how to handle a dogsled?" Rafe asked. "If we don't have natives to drive for us, we may as well pile back on the *Holger Danske* and head back to Germany. What do you say? I'd just as soon spend the night on the ship, myself. It's warmer."

"And *you* can explain to Reichsführer Himmler about why we didn't bring him back his spear, " Billi added cheerfully.

A line of sweat droplets had appeared here and there around the edges of Waldmann's face, though the stove was not exactly overpowering. "This quest is too important to turn back now. We will meet their price," he forced himself to say, as if the difference were going to come out of his pay—and it might be, Rafe reflected.

"May I ask what precisely is your object in this expedition?" said Lindhof, folding his hands on the desk.

Waldmann bristled. "That is none of your—"

"Archaeological research," Shrewsbury interjected smoothly. "My speciality is Norse language and culture. We are searching for Viking relics."

Lindhof pursed his lips. "Need I remind you that any artifacts you may discover are the property of the Danish crown—to be held in trust for the natives of this land, of course." His eyes glittered.

"Of course," Waldmann said with heavy irony. "We shall be more than happy to provide the Danish government with a full account of our discoveries."

"Well. Honesty compels me to admit, gentlemen—

frøken—that I fear you've come on a fool's errand. Still, I suppose it is just barely possible that some early Viking chieftain might have established some type of cache . . . "

After the cumshaw silence had gone on long enough, Billi shifted in her chair. "So when do we meet the guides?"

"Why, now, I should imagine."

Outside, drawn either by telepathy or more likely by Geisler, six men squatted in a circle sharing a pipe carved of bone. A man rose as they emerged, inclined his head to Lindhof. To the foreigners' surprise he was a tall man, almost as tall as Shrewsbury. He had great doorknobs for cheekbones and a broad, flat nose and skin that seemed to have been shrunk to fit them. His eyes were flattened triangles. He had wisps of mustache at either end of his broad, firm mouth, and a shock of long hair, jet-black despite the fact he was clearly in his fifties, whipped across his face in the wind. He had the dignified bearing of a man who knows where the center of the world lies.

"This is Number One," Lindhof said.

"Number One?" repeated Billi.

"His Eskimo name is very long and difficult to pronounce. Since it translates to Number One—he was his parents' firstborn—that's what we call him as well. It's also very apt. He is the headman of this village."

"And he's willing to come with us?" asked Shrewsbury.

"Yes," replied the Eskimo. "It time to drive out evil to the north. Nerrivik tell me this."

Shrewsbury started. "You speak English?"

Number One nodded. "English father teach me."

"A Jesuit who lived here for a time," said Lindhof with evident distaste. "Unfortunately English is all he taught him —or fortunately, perhaps. Number One is also the shaman for the village. Apparently he's been communing with Nerrivik, goddess of the waters. They do cling to their beliefs."

Billi noticed that the headman's left hand was tightly bandaged. "What happened to him?" she asked, journalistic instinct winning out over courtesy.

"He was mauled by a bear," Lindhof explained. "Two weeks ago. He shot it, but only wounded the creature. It attacked him, knocked his rifle from his hands. He killed it with his hunting knife, but not before it bit off his thumb."

"You poor man," Billi exclaimed. "You lost your thumb?"

To her surprise his face split into a grin, showing teeth twisted from a life spent chewing *muktuk*, the tough skin of whales harpooned from kayaks or washed ashore. "No, no lose." He held up a small sealskin bag on a thong around his neck. "Keep it right here." She turned an interesting shade of chartreuse.

In Greenland Eskimo, Rafe said, "May we not know the names of our other companions?" Or tried to; it was a tongue seldom mastered by foreigners. The other five, stocky men more typically Eskimo in appearance than Number One, the broadness of their faces accentuated by the hoods of their *kapataks*, exchanged laughing comments until their leader quelled them with a look.

The headman turned back to regard Rafe with interest. "They say you speak our tongue like an imbecile child," he said in his own language, speaking slowly and clearly. "This is true, but they are fools for not realizing how you display your superiority to other whitemen, who have no knowledge at all of human speech."

He raised his good hand, indicating each of the others in turn as he named them off: "Iggianguaq. Pualuna. Olipaluk. Mitsoq. Qavianguaq."

"I think we'd better come up with a few more nicknames," Billi whispered to Shrewsbury.

Number One laughed. "And us for you. Tonight at dancing, maybe."

CHAPTER

Seventeen

The senior members of the expedition were invited to Geisler's house for dinner. The house was cozy and tidier than the former trapper's appearance had led his guests to expect. More surprising was the profusion of books crammed into the dwelling, weighing down shelves improvised from packing crates, stacked around the immense if somewhat decrepit polar bear rug spread-eagled on the parlor floor. "Man has to have something to do in the long winter," Geisler explained when he saw his guests' expressions. "Go mad otherwise."

Places were set on a frequently patched tablecloth of embroidered linen that served to conceal the irregular surface of the table, which had also been cobbled together from salvaged imported lumber. The service was a collection of odds and ends of cutlery and assorted earthenware plates, each of which Podluq painstakingly licked before placing it in front of the thunderstruck guest.

"Take it easy," Rafe said under his breath, nodding and smiling as she came to him. She beamed at him and put a plate down before Kampfer, who looked at it as if it had come with a toad in the middle of it. "She's showing us great honor."

"Great God," Shrewsbury said in a strangled voice.

Podluq went happily off to the kitchen, pleased with her

observance of punctilio. Billi gagged. Axel popped up, collected the plates, vanished into the kitchen to rinse them off.

"Poor girl," he said, returning to redistribute them. "I try to make her understand, but she never seems to catch on."

"Savages," muttered Kampfer in an audible undertone as Podluq returned with bowls of dinner. In further honor of the guests it was that rarest luxury, tinned food imported from Europe and Canada. She began to serve them with a spoon surreptitiously eyed by all, even Rafe.

The Dane paused to deposit a spoonful of canned peas on his plate, took a bite, masticated as deliberately as a devotee of Horace Fletcher. "Interesting you should say that. Because, of course, they think we're savages too."

"Then the brutes should be taught otherwise."

Geisler's eyes narrowed. "In what way are we savages?" Rafe bustled into the conversation before Geisler could decide to take umbrage at the pronouncements of outraged German digestion.

"They have a lot of food taboos," Geisler said, always ready to hold forth on the folk among whom he'd spent most of his life. "A young man or young woman isn't permitted to eat reindeer meat, hare, ptarmigan, eggs, or lungs. A young husband can't eat partridge, and so forth—crazy stuff."

"How do they explain our ignoring these taboos without showing any ill effects?" Billi asked.

"There's a funny dichotomy in Eskimo attitudes toward white men. On the one hand, they think we're awesome beings who don't have to obey the laws. On the other, they view us as less than people." He gave her a sideways grin. "According to Eskimo legend, little one, the whiteman was sired along with seals, wolves, and the wicked spirit-folk called Tornit by a man made of dogshit."

Billi fell back in her chair laughing. Shrewsbury resembled a glum frog. Kampfer and Waldmann were exchanging dark glances from opposite ends of the table, united for one brief moment in their distaste for the barbarians they'd fallen among.

Dinner finished, the tableware cleaned away, Geisler served brandy of uncertain pedigree but undoubted ferocity. While his guests politely attempted to cover their choking,

Podluq bounced in and sat on Geisler's lap. He gave her a hard slap on the rump and grinned at Billi.

"Your wife seems very devoted to you."

"She should be. Her first husband threw her out when she produced a deformed baby. She had no place to go, and she was viewed as cursed. If I hadn't taken her in, she would probably have starved."

"What happened to her baby? Did it die?"

"In a manner of speaking. She killed it."

Billi caught her breath, clutched for Shrewsbury's arm. He gave her hand a soothing pat, staring hard at the trader. "That's quite monstrous. Doesn't the Danish government take steps to halt such atrocities?"

"You've got a European's sensibilities."

"And you don't?"

He shook his head. "Not anymore. None of us do after a few years up here. Can't afford them. It's a different world, Professor. Harsher than anything you can imagine. These people live on the knife's edge between subsistence and starvation. They can't afford to carry an unproductive member of the community. And isn't it really kinder to kill a child at birth before it can know the agony of starving to death slowly?"

"No," said Billi in a low tone.

Geisler shrugged.

Fortuitously Lindhof materialized at the door, affecting not to overhear Geisler's none-too-sotto-voce remark about the specter fortuitously appearing too late for the feast. "Number One and his wife, Ice House, would be honored if you'd come to the dance house for a little while after dinner," the colonial official said.

"It's traditional in Eskimo villages to hold a dance in honor of visitors," Geisler explained. "Maybe you'll find it interesting. The music and dancing isn't exciting like the Charleston, but sometimes the *angakkoq*—that's the shaman—uses a dance as an opportunity to demonstrate his powers."

"All nonsense, of course." Lindhof sniffed. "But it does offer a fascinating insight into the primitive religion they cling to so obdurately."

"I'll go," spoke up Billi.

"And I too. It isn't often one is given the opportunity to observe an almost Stone Age people," said the professor.

Rafe just nodded his assent and looked to Kampfer. "Thank you, no. I will rejoin my men. I have no interest in capering savages." He and Waldmann rose as one.

Billi shot Kampfer a smoldering glance, but Rafe had the feeling that even her cherished liberal attitudes were being strained by her first encounter with a truly alien people. He'd seen her face when Podluq licked her plate.

Faintly they heard the dull beat of a drum. Rafe pushed back his chair as Lindhof indicated the door and said, "Shall we go?"

Geisler dumped Podluq onto the floor. She skittered off, trailing giggles. "Why not?" said the professor.

He tucked Billi's arm beneath his. Sometimes such possessiveness had the effect of driving up her back like an overly handled cat, but this time Rafe noticed that she drew in closer to his side.

The ex-trapper paced Rafe as Lindhof led them off to the dance house like a schoolmaster taking his class on a field trip. "I'm concerned about your friend," he said, low and serious. "The German lieutenant. If he goes too far out of his way to offend the natives, he'll end up with a skinning knife in his guts."

"What do you mean?" Rafe turned back to see Billi straining on Shrewsbury's arm behind them with her ears drawn up to little points. "I thought the Eskimo were peaceful people who loved everybody."

"So much for your happy, noble, and friendly natives, Rafe, my boy," Shrewsbury said.

"I never said they were."

"Were what?" Billi asked.

"Friendly. At least not Greenland Eskimos. Not that they're actively hostile. But they're a rougher, bleaker lot than their Canadian cousins—the ones you always read about in *National Geographic*."

"Igloos made of mud, hostile Eskimos," Billi said, shaking her head despairingly. "The Arctic is bunk."

Geisler nodded to the trading post—European music

blared from it, tinny and off-pitched, and Rafe thought to recognize "The Varsity Drag." "In any event, your lieutenant won't escape the savages by joining his men. Some of the unmarried villagers have brought their ancient hand-cranked gramophone and their record and are having their own party."

"'Varsity Drag'?" Billi asked.

"*Ja.* The top tune in Eastern Greenland. Also the only one." He guffawed gustily at his own wit.

"But none of the Eskimos speak German," Billi pointed out, "and the Master Race most assuredly does not speak Eskimo. Why are they entertaining them?"

"You must understand, lovely lady, that nothing much ever happens up here, except the slow cycle of seasons and the occasional catastrophe. Besides, the Eskimos think there's a chance they can cadge booze off the Germans—or, better, chocolate.

"Chocolate?"

"Sugar's a ruling passion with the Eskimos since their contact with white men," Rafe explained. Billi turned up her nose. "Before, the closest thing they had to candy was cubes of seal blubber. Somehow I can't blame them for preferring chocolate."

"Since you put it that way, neither can I."

The dance house was a somewhat larger igloo set in the center of the village. A large sleeping platform occupied one end of the low-ceilinged chamber, and here in the place of honor Billi, Rafe, Shrewsbury, and the Danes were seated on a pile of caribou robes. Two large blubber lamps maintained an even level of heat, but once sixty odd Eskimos crammed into the confined space, the temperature began to climb.

It wasn't the only thing. Billi's mouth puckered into a tight bud, and she groped inside her loosened parka for a handkerchief bearing traces of perfume. She caught Rafe's amused glance and blushed. "Well, it *is* a little overpowering."

"Considering the lack of water for seven months out of the year, it's a wonder they don't smell worse."

"There is the *oddest odor,* however," Shrewsbury whispered, taking an exploratory sniff.

"Urine," Rafe said bluntly. "They wash their hair in it."

Billi let out a sound like a stepped-on mouse. "You enjoy upsetting me, don't you, you son of a bitch," she hissed.

"Just broadening your horizons."

For an hour they reclined on the fur robes, listening to monotone chanting accompanied only by a drum while various dancers pranced and shuffled in the center of a ring of singers in the cleared center of the room. As one dancer would tire, his place would be taken by another, women alternating with men.

Thinking perhaps of his friend Tolkien, Shrewsbury leaned across Billi to inquire of Lindhof, "Haven't these people been Christianized?"

Lindhof made a mouth. The subject was clearly a sore one. "Many of us have tried, Professor, but so far our attempts have been blessed by small success. The best way to describe Eskimo conversion is 'skin-deep.' When they're near death, they almost always revert to the old ways."

"I consider myself a Christian man, Professor," Geisler said, "but me, I wonder if the introduction of Christianity into Eskimo culture isn't destructive."

Shrewsbury lifted a questioning brow. Lindhof looked pained, but there was little heat to it. This ground was clearly as well trodden as the paths between the peat houses.

"It's alien to them," the trader went on. "Also, I think it violates the Eskimo conscience. Eskimo society is a fighting society. Man against nature, if not much man against man. The Christian ideals of charity and renunciation of the world —they have contempt for them, if they even grasp them. The Bible says, 'Blessed are the poor in spirit.' Eskimo society says do away with them, for they are parasites. 'Blessed are the merciful—'" He shook his shaggy head. "Not bloody likely. The Eskimo code is retaliation."

"But wouldn't it be better to gentle them, civilize them with the Christian spirit?" Shrewsbury asked.

"No. I think it might destroy them. They don't have these ways because they are wrongheaded or ignorant, Professor. It's because they are *right* and *knowledgeable* about the kind of life they live. That life is one of the harshest necessity.

Their folklore and religion, primitive as you may regard it, arose in response to the reality of snow and cold and endless night. If Greenland ever becomes a new Eden, then perhaps they can afford your values, Professor. But for now, no."

He settled back. "But you'll understand better once you're out on the ice."

The singing died, and Number One stepped into the center of the ring. He made a short speech, but broke abruptly off with a cry of pain and covered his eyes with his hands. Lindhof's mouth compressed to a tight line, but Geisler sat forward, indigo eyes bright with interest.

"It's happening. Number One is going to spirit-speak on behalf of Putu's eldest daughter. She's been ill for several weeks. Lindhof's Western medicine hadn't helped, so now they fall back on tradition."

Shrewsbury frowned at him. "You speak as if you believe in this—well, rubbish."

Geisler smiled and shrugged.

Number One moaned syllables. "What did he say?" Billi whispered urgently.

His Indian eyes locked on the writhing figure of the shaman, Rafe replied, "He said he's summoned his protecting spirit. It's come, and now he's going to send it forth to bring back the stolen soul of the sick girl."

A series of low groans shook the Eskimo's body. Suddenly he raised his head, his eyes frenzied, and his mouth worked convulsively for several moments though no sound emerged. Then with a long, whistling sigh he collapsed onto the igloo's packed-earth floor.

Nervous murmurs rippled through the crowd. The sound of breathing was stertorous and loud in the overheated, stinking air. Billi shivered. "This is so deliciously exciting." Shrewsbury gave her a pained look.

For ten minutes Number One lay sprawled on the floor, not moving, not even appearing to breathe. When the foreigners were beginning to shift uncomfortably on their caribou skins, he climbed to his feet and began to stagger drunkenly around the igloo, muttering to himself in a high falsetto voice. Billi clutched the professor's arm. The spectators flung questions at the shaman, and he lurched from one to the other, shrilling prophecies, eagerly nodding his head whenever the answer was yes.

Questions flew like startled bats, but the headman stopped and stood staring thoughtfully at his fur boots. A long shudder rocked him. When he lifted his head, his eyes were strangely dulled; the possession had passed, the spirit had departed.

Billi screamed.

Rafe came bolt upright. The woman's eyes were fixed and staring, the muscles of her face twisted with furious tension. Shrewsbury reached for her, but she eluded him, crawled off the sleeping platform.

For an instant she knelt on the dirt floor, her breath coming in quick, whining pants, loud in the sudden heavy silence of the igloo. She sprang to her feet, walked stiffly across the floor, arms held rigid at her sides. Eskimos parted a path to the door. Rafe and the professor scrambled out of the furs after her.

She had almost reached the door when Number One stepped before her, blocking the exit. She screeched something incomprehensible at him. He responded with a single explosive word. She lashed her head left to right on her neck, uttered a shriek like a knife blade drawn over glass, collapsed. The shaman caught her as she fell.

"Her pulse is normal," Lindhof said, holding Billi's wrist as she lay pale and motionless on the big brass bed. The others were gathered around, the professor jittering nervously from foot to foot, Rafe perched on a heap of books. "She appears to be sleeping normally. Ah, here, she's coming around, even as we speak. Miss Forsyth, how do you feel?"

Tentatively she touched her forehead, as if uncertain what she would find, raised her head half an inch off the pillow, stared around the room with half-focused eyes. "Where . . . ?"

"You're back at Geisler's house, child. You fainted."

A tiny frown puckered the skin between her brows. "No,

I didn't faint. And I'm not a child. Melbourne." She reached out, gripped the professor's hand until the knuckles of her own stood whitely forth.

"There, there, you're fine," he said, not quite evenly. "You'll be right as rain in a few more minutes."

She stared up at a low ceiling patterned with smoke smudges from whale-oil lamps. "There . . . there was someone inside me. He was trying so hard to tell me something—"

"Nonsense. You're having an hysterical reaction."

Color exploded in her cheeks, and she snapped to a sitting position. "I am *never* hysterical. I'm telling you, something . . . someone tried to take control of me."

"What took control of you was the proximity of far too many unwashed bodies in far too close a space," Shrewsbury said irritably.

"Polar hysteria brought on by isolation and climatic extremes is a very real phenomenon here, gentlemen," Lindhof said sagely. "Woman are especially susceptible to the *perler-orneq,* as the Eskimos call it—"

Billi struggled off the bed. "I have been in Greenland all of seven hours. I sincerely doubt I am suffering from this *perly*—whatever you called it. There was someone *there,* dammit!"

Shrewsbury looked disgruntled, while Lindhof regarded the American woman with an interest usually reserved for entomologists studying a new species of beetle. Rafe pulled thoughtfully at his lower lip and said nothing. He was less inclined to take the older men's dismissive attitude. He'd encountered things, back in the Sangre de Cristos—

He was by no means ready to attribute Billi's collapse to hysteria or claustophobia. Just what he was ready to attribute it to, he couldn't quite say.

"I think what Miss Forsyth needs most is a good night's rest," Lindhof said, exhaling. "You are leaving early in the morning."

"Do you want me to stay with you?" asked Shrewsbury, all concern.

"No. If you don't believe me, you can just bloody well sleep by yourself tonight."

They had almost reached the bedroom door when she said in an absolutely flat and level tone, "It was trying to tell me something. Something important. *You'll* see."

Softly closing the door, Rafe tried to ignore the curious tingle running down his spine on centipede legs.

CHAPTER
Eighteen

Six in the morning and dead black. It would remain that way for hours yet. The cliffs that surrounded the village were looming indigo shadows against the gray-black sky. Number One, sucking thoughtfully on a cigarette, gazed impassively down at the steel runners on the six dogsleds while the other five Eskimos exclaimed in wonder and drew gloved hands across the gleaming blades.

"It was not to be anticipated that you folk, who are as backward children on the ice, would outdo us in this thing," the headman remarked. "These will run farther without needed resharpening than our bone runners, and be harder to break."

"We have our uses sometimes," Rafe said modestly in English.

Billi emerged from the house and stared uneasily at the fifty-four red, gray, black, and white dogs thronged out front. Their shrill yelps came echoing back off the cliffs, creating the illusion of several hundred animals baying out their varied hungers, to run, to mate, to kill. Number One regarded her for a long moment, then threw down his cigarette and raised a hand in grave salute. She looked away, embarrassed, pulled her parka closer about her body.

Doors slammed, boots crunched on snow and rock, and the dogs carried on as the expedition assembled. Here came

Waldmann, bluff and hearty as though headed for a hike in the Black Forest, belching steam like a locomotive. "Ah, it's a fine morning to set out," he exclaimed, rubbing mittened hands together.

"How can you tell," Billi asked, "when you can't see the sky?"

Strolling among the high-piled sleds, Shrewsbury gaped as Olipaluk's twenty-five-foot-long whip snaked out and caught one of his dogs neatly on the testicles. The animal yipped, sheepishly dismounted from the one female in the team, and cast a beseeching, fawning glance toward his master. The Eskimo threw back his head and laughed.

"Extraordinary," murmured the professor, and walked over to Rafe.

Kampfer barked orders, and the four troopers lined up with their rifles slung and their packs on their backs to have skis and poles inspected by Uurtamo. The young officer gestured to Rafe and Shrewsbury.

"To save weight on the sleds I have ordered my men to carry their skis until we're on the ice. I suggest you do the same."

"Sensible," Rafe agreed. "Especially seeing as how the things are so packed with ammunition the runners are bowed."

The young officer shrugged, grinned. "We are ordered to proceed so. And *Befehl sind Befehl,* as Herr Waldmann likes to remind us." The expedition's nominal head gave him a black look.

"The Eskimos aren't skiing," the professor said in a tone half hopeful and half pugnacious.

"They're trained to walk and run on ice and snow fields," Freiherr Chatenois pointed out. "We are not. It will be easier on us if we ski."

"It doesn't hurt so bad after the third time you fall," said Kurt Hoff, grinning through the gap in his teeth.

"Thanks awfully, old man." With a heartfelt sigh Shrewsbury hefted his skis.

Billi bounced off the provisions lashed to Mitsoq's sled and held out her hands. "Well," she prodded after a moment or two, "give me my skis."

"It is not necessary that you carry—" Kampfer began.

"I *want* to carry my skis. I said I would pull my own weight on this trip, and I will."

"Miss Forsyth—"

"Give her her skis," grunted Waldmann as he stopped and collected his own gear. Billi blinked at him, startled by support from so unlikely a quarter.

Lindhof emerged from the residency and clasped Rafe's hand. "The best of luck, Herre Springer, and you, too, Professor. I hope you find your archaeological treasure trove, but I doubt it. There's nothing beyond the coastal ranges but ice." He glanced quickly around, then inquired, "Is Miss Forsyth better today?" in a low tone.

"She seems none the worse for her experience," Shrewsbury said. He glanced at Billi, who was attempting by mime and sign language to get Iggianguaq to explain the intricacies of the bone and leather traces attaching dogs to sleds.

Eskimos emerged from the low igloo entryways like furry brown-and-white gumballs rolling from a machine. After the previous night's loud excitement they seemed strangely subdued as they said farewell to the six guides.

Ice House, Number One's round, jolly wife, fussed over her husband, checking his bearskin boots and pants and his *qulitsaq*, his deerskin jacket. She pressed a package of bone needles on him, and even the non-Eskimo speakers took the gist of her conversation: stay warm, dry your wet clothes, be careful, hurry home.

Stocky Iggianguaq swung his four-year-old son high into the air over his head. Cuddling the boy against his shoulder, he fished in his pocket, brought out a chunk of chocolate, a gift of Kampfer's soldiers. The boy's expression as he held the candy on his tongue was sheer blissful enjoyment, and Billi leaned quickly in and pressed a kiss on his plump cheek near his chocolate-smeared lips.

The child's immediate howl of fear sent her into quick retreat. She looked wildly over at Rafe.

"Eskimos kiss only on the nose," he explained. "Just be glad you didn't get his mouth; they consider that especially disgusting."

"Oh. I'm sorry." She patted the boy on the cheek. He

subsided. She tipped her skis jauntily over her shoulder. "Well, shall we? Last one to Gungnir's a rotten egg."

Number One raised his whip and cried, "*Aak! Aak!*" With a snap of teeth filed to bluntness the *naalagaq*—lead dog—urged his fellows to their feet. They lunged into the collars of their side-by-side harness. The other teams followed, yipping and grunting with exertion. The crunch and *skree* of steel runners over rock blended with the Eskimos' cries of farewell.

Number One set a brisk pace toward Waltershausen Glacier, spilling down through the coastal cliffs to the sea. Waldmann shouted an order, and the ten Europeans plunged after their guides.

"I hope the flat-faced devils don't simply disappear onto the ice with all our supplies and return after they think we've gone away," the Gestapo man said, chugging after the sleds.

"They've been hired and paid," Rafe said. "They won't desert us. They do have a sense of honor—even if it's not the same as ours."

Waldmann replied with a doubtful noise at the back of his thick throat.

The expedition went up the cut the glacier had rammed through the coastal mountains, the sleds up the slow slope of the ice, the Europeans scrambling on the stony fringes. It was a reasonably arduous climb, and even the soldiers were trying to hide their panting when they reached the top in the light of the rising sun and the party stopped to strap on their skis.

"We're out of shape from the boat trip," Rafe said. "This was just the warm-up; here's where it gets serious." The others eyed him with hatred.

An hour away from the mountains the Eskimos had established a routine that seemed so smooth and effortless that Billi was soon cursing Rafe and Kampfer for their insistence on skiing. Her calves ached already, the muscles stretching with each thrust forward, then snapping back into a tangled knot like a rubber band as her weight came down. The cold was intense, but between the sun, which clung to the horizon like a shy kitten hugging the walls of a new house, and brute physical exertion, her man's shirt was soaked with sweat within her parka.

Better to be an Eskimo, she reckoned, perched half seated on the front of a sled, feet tucked under you, jumping down now and again to run easily beside or in front of the dogs, calling encouragements. Blearily she watched Number One riding like a northern Buddha on his sled and imagined herself mushing her dog team on to an effortless glide while behind them the low mountains sank slowly into the ice. Before them lay an unending plain of white, rising gradually into the sky.

Abruptly Number One came out of his bodhisattva placidity, jumped into the loose snow as Mitsoq and Qavianguaq, who had also been riding, raced around to the backs of the sleds. All six drivers seized the *napariaq,* the rear stanchions. Each began to heave at the sleds, whipping up the dogs as they pushed for all they were worth.

The ice field looked level, but when Billi drew closer to the sleds, a line of hummocks suddenly resolved out of the snowfield glare, a barrier of knife-sharp ice ridges that cut at the feet of man and dog alike. Grunting Eskimos manhandled the sleds across the hummocks behind whining, slipping dogs.

Climbing crabwise up the low ridges, Billi was all at once very glad she was not handling a sled. Maybe it wasn't all riding serenely or running with the apparent grace of an ice skater. With each step he took, a man would mash his foot against the ice to keep from slipping, push with his knee at the rear of the sled's frame to avoid series of snow-filled furrows in the ice where the runners would stick and freeze.

Going down the hummocks' long backslope, the Eskimos braked by clinging to the *napariaq* and skidding along on the heels of their boots. Their whips snapped constantly before the dogs' eyes, splitting the teams to either side of the sledges so that the sleds were actually leading, with the slower-moving beasts anchoring them from behind.

Past the ice ridges, the chill increased. Billi had begun to worry about the lack of feeling in her cheeks. Now, after the exertion of climbing, the cold bit into her eyebrows and nose. Curiously it made her feel as if her face were cooking.

Letting one pole dangle from its wrist strap, she cupped a mitten and tried to blow some warm air from her mouth over her nose. Rafe pulled up beside her.

"Flex your fingers in your mittens to stimulate circulation, then slap your face. It'll help—" she smacked herself and let out a yelp "—after the first time or two, when it just hurts." She glared.

They broke briefly for a meal at midday. Billi was shocked to see that the dogs were given nothing.

"No, Aningaaq Pania," Number One told her through Rafe, whose comprehension of the Greenland dialect was much better than his ability to fit his tongue and palate around the Eskimo syllables. The headman's knowledge of English worked the same way, so he preferred to speak in his own tongue. "It cannot be done. To feed the dogs too often makes them weak and lazy. They pull harder when they're hungry, in the hope that once we arrive, they'll be fed."

"Well, when *will* they be fed? Surely you're not going to wait until we get to Eyjolfson's mountains."

"Tomorrow."

"Tomorrow!"

"Every two days in winter. Every three days in summer."

"That's awful."

"It's no wonder they lose a child or two every year to the dogs," Rafe added in an undertone as Number One went off to check the wrappings on his sled. Shrewsbury looked sick and set aside the remainder of his dried meat. "And now you see why I'm always warning you to give the beasts plenty of room."

They resumed their journey. Three hours later the sun eased below the horizon, leaving the twilight of the last hour or so almost undisturbed. Number One shouted a command. The dogs tumbled to a halt, tails waving like exotic fans over their backs. One hapless member of the shaman's team had been trying desperately for the past hour to defecate; now he groaned and hunkered down to work. When the reluctant turd finally fell into the snow, the other dogs fell on him, nipping unmercifully, seeming to ridicule him for his difficulty.

Number One pushed back his hood and sniffed like a caribou buck testing the air. "We will camp."

Kampfer slid forward with a whisper of skis. "We should press on. If we break this early every day, spring will have passed into summer before we reach our destination."

"The *quallunaaq* has tents, but the Eskimo must build his shelter. Unless the *quallunaaq* thinks the Eskimo should sleep outside with the dogs?"

The remark was delivered in Number One's ˙customary flat tone, but the sarcasm still cut like sandpaper through old varnish. Kampfer stiffened, but Rafe settled the argument by walking away from his interpretorial duties to unlash a tent and throw it into the snow. Even the soldiers didn't bother to hide their relief as they began to set up camp. There was something about the immensity of the ice dome that sapped the spirit, so that physical exertion, so far no worse than what they'd faced on the Great Aletsch, made them feel as weak as newborn puppies.

To Billi's delight the Eskimos began to build a "real" igloo, hacking large blocks of the snow out of the field and laying them with an artist's precision. The troopers worked fast, and soon had three tents up for the Europeans. Under Rafe's supervision they piled up a wall of snow blocks to a height of three feet all around the tent as added insulation.

Inside the tent, Rafe lit a camp stove to drive away the worst of the cold. "It seems strange," Billi said, pulling off a boot and giving her toes an experimental wiggle. "To use snow and ice to stay warm."

"It's absurd," sniffed Shrewsbury in a strained, high voice. "Why don't these savages move south and live like civilized—"

"You're just crabby because it's damn clever, and these *savages* thought it up all by themselves."

Shrewsbury shook his head with a certain desperation. "Billi, please. I'm far too tired for a wrangle tonight."

"I suppose that means you're far too tired for a tumble, too, hmm?"

The professor's chapped cheeks turned an even brighter shade of red. "Oh, please, don't mind me," said Rafe, calmly rolling out his sleeping bag. "I'm sure you won't be

too noisy, and as tired as I am tonight, I probably won't
hear—"

"Rafael!"

There was a discreet scratching at the tent flap. Billi un-
tied it and thrust her face out, right into a pair of furry white
bearskin trousers as flamboyant as seventeenth-century pan-
taloons.

"You wish to join us, share food?" Number One asked,
stooping to peer into the tent.

She shoved her foot back into her boot. "Thank you, I'd
be delighted. And they—" a quick jerk of the head at the
two men "—can come if they want to."

She tagged along as Number One stopped to extend the
same invitation to the other tents. Looking none too pleased
about sharing his shelter with the Gestapo man, Kampfer
brightened considerably when Waldmann accepted. Uurtamo
set aside the rifle he was cleaning and also nodded. That left
the young Wehrmacht officer to enjoy the privacy of the
tent, free from the presence of savages—both the Arctic and
domestic German varieties.

The dogs had beaten nests into the snow and now lay in a
great pile, tails over noses for warmth just outside the igloo's
tunnel entrance. "Poor things," Billi murmured, but Rafe
noticed that she didn't try to pet the "poor things." She had
seen enough of their behavior during the day's journey to
discourage any attempts at intimacy.

The snow hut was about nine feet in diameter, with the
usual sleeping platform directly opposite the door. Just to the
left of the entrance burned a stone lamp, the wick, floating
in seal blubber, giving off a steady, smokeless light. Over
the lamp hung a stone cooking pot, and above that was a
breakdown rack hung with boots and mittens spread to dry.
Rafe had been careful to bring some tins of whiteman food
to add to the feast, for aside from hunting weapons, there
was no private ownership in Eskimo culture. Everything was
shared evenly. Including women—Rafe hoped Billi's alien
status would exempt her in the Eskimos' eyes; otherwise, he
could foresee trouble.

Black Peter and the Freiherr crawled into the igloo, and
things definitely began to heat up. There were now twelve

people cramped into the room, and Rafe, who had lugged along the Primus stove, noticed that the roof was beginning to drip. He prepared boiled rice flavored with sugar, and hot tea also well laced with the sweetener. The troopers added a bag of dried fruit. Impressed by the foreigners' openhandedness, the Eskimos produced their greatest delicacy.

A strong, fetid odor filled the ice chamber, reminiscent of a particularly well-aged gorgonzola cheese. Billi frowned down at the tiny and unusually dead-looking bird Number One had deposited on her palm with the greatest solemnity. "Rafe, what do I do? It smells awful. I think it's spoiled."

Rafe swallowed hard, banishing his stomach back where it belonged. "It is."

Shrewsbury held his bird out with obvious relief. "Quite right. Explain to the chap that it's too well hung and we can't eat it, there's a good boy."

"It's *supposed* to be that way, Professor," Rafe said with a certain diabolical relish. "It's *kiviaq*. A choice dish reserved for guests. It would be improper to refuse it."

"What on Earth have they done to it?"

"You don't want to know."

Glumly Shrewsbury stared at his bird. It was a little Arctic bird called a guillemot, which the Eskimo hunters caught in nets, killed with a quick blow to the head, and stuffed, unplucked and uncleaned, into bags made of sealskin from which half the fat had been scraped. The bags were then stored under stones where the sun could not reach them. The fat melted slowly in the heat, and as the birds' flesh rotted, it marinated in the rancid grease. Rafe was right: Shrewsbury *didn't* want to know.

Everybody's eyes were on Rafe. His five companions stared at him with the expression of a dog confronted with some new and outrageous species of animal—a platypus, perhaps. The Eskimos watched him closely to see if the man who spoke their language also understood their manners.

He cobbled together a smile for Number One and pulled on one of the former bird's legs. The carcass slipped free of skin and feathers. A reeking mass of flesh, guts, coagulated blood, and fat ran into his hand. "Mmm. Looks well done." He lapped up a mouthful, allowed the decaying meat to melt slowly in his mouth. He thought it might be less of a shock to his stomach that way. He popped the rest inside.

When it was finally down, he faced his companions. "And *that's* the bravest thing you'll ever see me do," he said with a ghastly smile. The fastidious Freiherr gagged and bolted from the igloo, leaving his bird lying on the snow floor. From outside came the sound of vomiting while the dogs howled derision.

Billi shoved her *kiviaq* at Rafe. "I thought you were game for anything," he said.

She recoiled from his breath. "There are limits, Rafe!"

"You're going to insult these people."

"I for one, don't care," Shrewsbury enunciated with great care. Placing his bird onto the floor, he crawled out of the igloo.

Waldmann looked over at Billi with an oddly mischievous gleam in his small, close-set eyes. He tugged his *kiviaq* free of its skin and quickly ate the rotted mess. Billi gritted her teeth, breathed heavily through her nose several times, and followed suit.

Her throat worked convulsively for several seconds. The spasm passed, and she glared triumphantly at Rafe and Waldmann. There was laughter and applause from the Eskimos, and Number One said to Rafe, "The Aningaaq Pania becomes one of us."

"He—" She had to stop to swallow the bird, which was trying to repeat on her. "He's calling me that again. What does it mean?"

"Daughter of the Moon. Apparently he was impressed by your performance last night and decided you deserved a real person's name." He passed along the headman's compliment.

"Why, thank you," she said to Number One. "I only wish I could thank you in your own language . . . for both."

"Maybe you learn," Number One said in English.

Dietrich looked from one European to another, set his big blue-shadowed jaw, and devoured his own bird. For a moment he sat, eyes wide, looking as if the bird had come to life in his stomach. He offered up a sickly smile, then lurched from the hut to puke.

With visible relief the foreigners began to spoon their own stew into tin cups. The Eskimos ate the sugary stuff with a good deal more enthusiasm than their guests had shown for the *kiviaq*. "Yesterday you said something about the 'evil to the north,' Number One," Rafe said, gulping tea to clear his taste buds. "What did you mean?"

"There's evil where you go, beneath the mountain that smokes like dirty seal oil. I've walked there in my dreams. Nerrivik says you have come to expunge it. And none too soon, for shortly it will reach out to the coast and beyond. That's why we agreed to lead you, though most of us will not return."

When Rafe had translated this, Billi shivered. Waldmann jutted his jaw and chewed ruminatively on the inside of his lower lip. "You see, Herr Springer, this is no fool's errand, after all. The natives know of this 'smoking mountain'—this volcano you said couldn't exist."

Rafe grinned at him. "Oberführer, at this point I'm not going to be surprised at anything that happens." He sipped tea. "I wonder, when the time comes, if you'll be able to say the same."

The impromptu dinner party broke up soon after that. The wind hit them like a moving wall as they emerged from the igloo, and Billi staggered, grabbing Rafe's arm for support. "This storm certainly came up out of nowhere," she shouted. Swirls of snow danced around them like maddened moths.

"That's why Number One wanted to make camp."

At their tent she halted and dragged him into the dubious shelter of its leeward side. "Rafe, you can be so irritating when you're reasonable and open-minded about *everybody*. Don't you know how small and mean that makes the rest of us feel?"

"Don't sell yourself short. It took a lot of nerve to down that *kiviaq* tonight."

"No, that was an example of stupidity masquerading as bravado."

"If you think of a better definition of courage, let me know. Now let's get out of this damned weather."

Shrewsbury reared up out of his sleeping bag as they entered the tent. "Did you eat something?" Rafe asked as he tied shut the flap.

"Yes. Something civilized."

"I think it's a function of the cold. People who live in this part of the world tend feel a great need for the strong flavor of tainted meat—"

"Rafe, my boy, kindly do not try to justify this quaint Eskimo custom to me. I find it most irritating."

"Funny, that's what Billi just told me. I'll go to sleep and stop irritating people." He turned down the lantern and wormed into his sleeping bag.

He heard a handful of furtive, dragging noises, and assumed that Billi was pulling her bag closer to the professor. "Kiss?" he heard her whisper.

"Billi, my dear, I would sooner kiss a public jakes. Your breath really is enough to knock one down."

"Well!" And more dragging sounds as Billi and her bag humped to the other side of the tent.

Three days passed in a white grind of monotony. Weariness became their constant companion, a ferocious exhaustion that made their limbs tremble and their minds drift, that seemed only to mount and mount despite the lengthy nights when the drop in temperature turned progress from difficult to impossible.

Even in the feeble light of day strong winds down off the ice dome to the west often raised clouds of blown snow dense as a London pea-souper and plunged the temperature to −60°F. Frostbite affected everyone, and Billi took to checking her nose in her hand mirror every time they called a halt. Like all of them, her cheeks and chin had been blackened by frost, and the tip of her nose and the wings of her nostrils were peeling, the flesh raw and red.

"Will it get well?" she asked Rafe in a little-girl voice as they slogged along, a hint of tears lurking in the background.

"Yes. Think of it as a sunburn. After you peel and get out of the cold, you get back to normal."

"I wish I *had* a sunburn. I wish I were down in the Caribbean lolling on a white beach with—" Rafe shut her out. He knew it was exhaustion talking. But he was tired, too, his patience wearing thin as an old pair of pants.

"My foot is really beginning to bother me," the professor said, straggling along at Billi's side. "The cold seems to just creep inside that bullet wound. It's devilishly painful."

"What about my nose?" mourned Billi.

"You don't ski on your nose!"

"Oh, Mel, I'm sorry, don't be mad. It's just that I'm so tired."

"Perhaps we'll call an early halt today."

But they didn't. Waldmann drove them on, brushing aside Number One's fear that a storm was coming. When the order finally came to halt beneath black, turbulent skies, Billi was trembling with exhaustion, and her longing for the comfort of a stove-warmed tent was physical pain.

Fingers numb, she yanked at frozen sled knots until they came free. Throwing back the covering, she grasped the tent and heaved.

It didn't move. Encased in a hundred pounds of ice, it just lay there, adamant as a dead elephant. She pulled again: same result. And again. And again, each tug accompanied by an angry, hopeless sob. Sweat ran down her torso, freezing in seconds. At last she covered her face with her hands, collapsed in the snow, and wept, the tears freezing into transparent armor across her face.

"Here," Rafe said, bending to help her up. "We'll take care of that."

"I want to pull my own weight," she wailed.

"Well, that tent's probably twice your weight. That lets you out of having to pull it, wouldn't you say?"

Suspecting him of laughing at her up his sleeve, she glowered at him, but it took the combined efforts of three men to throw the tent off the sled. Number One shook his head gravely. "This is no good. It's too hard on the dogs. We'll have to leave the tents behind."

"Leave them? And then what do we sleep in?" Waldmann demanded, jowls aquiver.

"We'll build more *illuliaq*."

"But those tents cost money!"

"No amount of money will buy more dogs out here in the middle of the ice cap if these give out," Rafe said, joining the debate. "For my money we ought to dump the extra guns and ammunition too."

But Waldmann wouldn't hear of it. He pointed out that the Eskimos were packing *their* rifles, the brand-new Mausers that had been provided as part of their fee. Rafe had no come-back for that. So it was decided the ice-encrusted tents would be abandoned; the machine gun and the two rifles intended for Rafe and the professor would come along.

It was nearly nine before the four snow huts were completed and dinner cooked. Billi and Shrewsbury had both stubbornly insisted on helping and were now in terrible shape. The professor could endure no weight on his wounded foot, and Billi sat like a tiny zombie, too tired to eat.

Rafe ranted and cajoled, got a few mouthfuls of boiled white beans and some fruit down them, and put them both to bed. He crawled out of the igloo for a quiet smoke. The storm, which blessedly had held off till now, came howling up about him like a banshee army.

Number One was a dark silhouette against the whirling snow. Rafe joined him in the shelter of his own snow house, stuck two cigarettes in his mouth, finally got them lit. With a grunt of gratitude Number One accepted one, took a long drag.

"Tomorrow the older *qallunaaq* must ride on a sled," he said.

Rafe nodded. "I only hope his pride doesn't get up on its hind legs and make him refuse. He'll slow us down and probably kill himself."

The cigarette burned down until the wind was sucking the strength from Rafe's body at a lot brisker clip than he was sucking precious smoke from the fractional butt that remained. He pitched it away, nodded good night to Number One, walked to his own igloo. The inrushing storm had bricked it solidly from view behind a wall of snow, though it lay only feet away. He sensed Number One hovering at the mouth of his hut, watching him; men had wandered to their deaths under just such conditions.

The swirling white closed around him, shut him off from the rest of the universe. He seemed to be floating in a separate plenum, knew a moment's peace and a moment's panic. *How easy it would be just to . . . slip away.* He felt as if the bonds that held him to this Earth were dissolving in the cold.

Then the igloo's mouth was yawning right before him, welcome and welcoming, and he dropped to his knees and crawled inside.

Not even halfway there, he thought. *Can we really make it?*

"Billi," the professor said fretfully, "do please go and ski alongside one of the other sleds. It makes me feel like a useless old hulk to lie here while you're striding along beside me."

"Shut up. I didn't get shot in the foot. And you were right." She flashed him a smile. "I *don't* ski on my nose."

"This trip hasn't been very conducive to romance, has it?"

She caught both poles in her left hand, rubbed frost out of her eyebrows with her right. "No, but maybe that's good. Warts and all, and all that," she added vaguely.

"I've missed you, Billi."

She leaned in close to keep Waldmann, skiing just behind, from hearing. "And I've missed you. And just as soon as we get back to civilization, I'm going to keep you in bed for the next year or so. I just hope it doesn't fall off."

"Billi!"

Squatting on the front of the sled, Mitsoq grinned over his shoulder at them. Though the words were gibberish to him, the snaggletoothed veteran of many seasons' hunting knew the *qallunaaq* were making man and woman talk.

Cheeks burning with embarrassment more than the stinging of the wind, Billi veered to her right, letting the sled gain on her. It took all her strength to keep from screaming curses at the Eskimo. She knew at the core of her that he meant no harm, but to have him leering at her when she felt so vulnerable and small and very, very tired—

With a high-pitched hollow crack like the pillars of heaven giving way the world broke open in front of her. Madly she torqued her body right. She sprawled on her belly as with a soft sigh a thousand tons of snow, the sled, and Melbourne Shrewsbury went dropping away into the earth before her eyes.

CHAPTER

Nineteen

"Melbourne!" Billi shrieked.

The cloud of snow thrown up by the opening of the ice subsided. A pair of mittens clung to the crevasse's edge. Billi clawed her way frantically forward, dragging her skis behind her like the legs of a crippled mantis.

From behind came harsh cries of alarm and warning. Dogs raised a keening, dismal wail. Across the fifteen-foot abyss, Kampfer and Eblinger stood pointing back, faces scarcely a different color than the snow, as Number One fought the lead sled to a stop. They had missed by inches going in along with Mitsoq and his team.

The right hand slipped, leaving behind a long gouge in the snow. With a sob Billi kicked free of her skis and wriggled forward like a snake, clutching for the hand that remained.

Rafe was tearing at the straps of the third sled in line, going for an ice ax and a rope. With agility that belied his bulk, Waldmann shot forward, spun broadside to brake at Billi's heels, pulled his feet free of the bindings, and dropped to the snow. Planting his ski pole as deeply as he could, he wrapped one arm around the slender steel rod, stretched, and caught Billi by the ankle just as her hand closed around Shrewsbury's wrist.

Billi's head hung over the edge, inches from Shrewsbury's upturned face. His deathly pale skin, smudged with the bruiselike frostbite spots, lent him the look of a dying harlequin. His weight pulled her inexorably toward the brink.

"Let me go, girl," he gasped. "You'll fall!"

"Don't—talk like—an idiot," she gasped.

The fingers of his left hand failed. Billi screamed as his full weight almost jerked him from her grip. As his legs windmilled wildly above blue-black depths, she commended her fate entirely to the Gestapo officer and grabbed Shrewsbury's arm with her other hand.

"*Scheisse,*" Waldmann grunted. He had both legs braced, heels dug into the ice, but he was skidding forward now, the curved tip of his stick insufficient to hold back the combined weight of all three.

Then Rafe was at his side with a rope coil. The others anchored the line as he whipped a bend around Waldmann's thick waist. Billi squeaked as her strength began to fail. Rafe flung himself to the brink of the precipice, practically on top of Billi. With one hand he drove the spike on the back of the axhead deep into ice, while the other pitched the rope far out over the abyss so that it wouldn't strike the professor in the face.

Shrewsbury jammed one toe hard into a vertical split in the sheer ice face, grimaced; it was his left foot. As if blind, he reached for the rope, found it, wound it once about his wrist. Slowly, agonizingly, the three began to draw him up.

The sun shining through the ice filled the crevasse with an opalescent light reminiscent of early-morning sun through cathedral windows. As the crevasse deepened, the light faded to indigo and then to blackness. An agonized whining echoed up from the shadowed depths.

By inches Shrewsbury emerged from the pit. Billi's palms were cramping with the effort of holding him, the sweat streamed down her forehead, stinging her eyes and freezing in her eyebrows. Tiny ice ridges, unnoticeable on skis, cut into her belly and breasts like tiny razors. Rafe lay full length at her side, chest working like a bellows, upper body hanging over nothingness, eyes rolling like those of a frightened horse as he hauled on Shrewsbury. He was rancid with sweat, both stale and brand-new.

The professor wasn't idle on his own behalf. As soon as his elbows reached the surface, he dug them in and humped forward like a bull seal climbing onto an ice floe. Then the wiry Uurtamo was standing astride Billi, grabbing a handful of parka between the professor's shoulder blades and dragging him bodily onto the ice with surprising strength.

They scrambled back out of danger. Once clear of the crack, Billi flung herself onto Shrewsbury's chest, plucking frenziedly at his disordered hair, covering his face with kisses. He lay for a moment with arms outspread, gasping like a landed carp. Then he gathered her hungrily into his arms.

—In a moment both became aware of Rafe shouting across the crevasse in strangled Eskimo syllables. Number One answered, and then Rafe exchanged more shouts with Kampfer. He turned to the others, and his face was white and drawn.

"Get back farther from the edge. And make it snappy!"

Billi and Shrewsbury joined Waldmann and the Finn in an undignified scramble back to Pualuna's sled where the German soldiers and Eskimos thronged around, clapping them on the backs. Billi glanced across the crevasse to see Kampfer sidle up to the edge, toss something in that looked like a vegetable tin stuck on the end of a dowel. A moment later a sharp *crack!* came ringing up from the innards of the earth, muffled all at once by the soughing rumble of a cave-in.

"Grenade," Rafe spat. "I don't know why they want them in the God-damned Arctic, but I guess they've come in handy."

Billi looked at him. The color that had begun to return to her face abruptly fled. "Mitsoq—?"

"Dead. Or injured too badly for us ever to get him out; that hole's a hundred feet deep if it's an inch." He grabbed her hands, squeezed them until they hurt. "I know it's shocking. But it's the Arctic. Number One didn't want his old friend to suffer needlessly. And the dogs—"

She cut him off. "Hard as this might be for you to be-

live," she said, "I understand. This world isn't always the
way it looked back at Vassar."

She slipped from Shrewsbury's hold and walked to where
Waldmann sat in the snow, head between knees, breathing
sonorously. She reached a hand, hesitated, pulled back,
reached out again to touch the Gestapo officer's shoulder.

"Are . . . are you all right?"

"Ja, ja, Fräulein."

She thrust her hands deep into the pockets of her parka
and turned away with shoulders hunched. She got two steps
before whirling back to face him. "You saved him . . . saved
both of us. Thank you." She struggled with herself before
adding, "Ernst."

He gazed at her outstretched hand with a thoughtful, ru-
minative expression, as if he didn't understand the gesture,
or perhaps the implications inherent in it. Finally he picked
himself up with an embarrassed grunt, took her hand, and
gave it a quick shake. She hung on to him for a moment,
said "Thanks" again, wheeled away, her face a study in con-
flicting emotions.

Kampfer and Eblinger had followed Number One and his
sled around the end of the split three hundred feet away and
back to their comrades. "We've lost seven hundred pounds
of supplies," the lieutenant was saying, his young face
grave.

"It was just a sixth of our provisions," Waldmann pointed
out.

"Doesn't leave us much margin for error," Rafe said.

"Couldn't we have tried to recover at least part of it?"
asked Shrewsbury, still shocked by Kampfer's tossing down
the grenade.

"Too dangerous," said Number One in English. "Might
close, open deeper, ice fall. Better leave it."

Waldmann nodded. "We'd best see to the professor's condition, then continue. We can't afford to stay out any longer
than necessary."

Billi turned then, and looked wildly back at Rafe.
Number One had begun to weep, big tears rolling down his
seamed face. The remaining four Eskimos were crying too.
Billi ran to the shaman, hugged him.

He snuffled, drew the back of his mitten across his nose, and gathered his dignity back around him like a cape. "Once home, we'll make a proper grave for the lost one, appease his spirit. Please tell the Moon's Daughter this, so she'll know we know right behavior."

Rafe translated. "Was Mitsoq married?" Billi pressed.

"Please, Aningaaq Pania. It's forbidden to speak the name of the dead until he is born again. We'll make a little chant, then go on. Grief on the ice is unwise."

"Born again?" she repeated.

"An infant born this year will bear his name. Then it will be safe to mention him again."

"Well, I hope he gets to come back soon. Poor—the poor man."

Dinner that night was a cheerless affair. On the advice of both Rafe and Number One, Waldmann had reduced rations to stretch the remaining supplies. Given that they had carried a small quantity of extra provisions as insurance, a loss of fifteen percent was not catastrophic—if nothing untoward happened. Unfortunately the untoward was the norm on Greenland's broad, white back.

Depressed by the sudden loss of their companion, the Eskimos kept to themselves. Feeling none too giddy themselves, the foreigners all ate together in one igloo. Even Kampfer seemed subdued by the death of what was to him a mere *untermensch*—whether from true feeling for Mitsoq or in reaction to the unsubtle reminder of his own mortality, Billi charitably chose not to speculate.

After the meal she, Shrewsbury, and Waldmann compared war wounds. Billi's left ankle bore the imprints of Waldmann's viselike grip, and her wrists were shadowed with bruises. Waldmann's inner arm, from the biceps down into the forearm, was an ugly mottled black and purple. Shrewsbury, of course, walked off with the honors. "You look as if the frost-giants have been using you for a football, Professor," Rafe said admiringly.

They took out the cardboard tube containing photostats of Bjørn Eyjolfson's account of his trip, unrolled them on the packed-snow floor. "According to this, Eyjolfson's party

tramped across the ice for two whole weeks to reach the
cache—that is, the hiding place of Gungnir. With our sleds
and skis Rafe informs me that we should make the journey
in eight to ten days."

He tapped his fingers on the map Himmler's RuSHA
gnomes had prepared. It didn't consist of much—the coast
around the site of modern-day Narwhal, near which the researchers and Shrewsbury agreed the Vikings must have
made landfall, Walterhausen Glacier rising like a ramp
through the rocky mountains, and then a dotted line stretching across a white void to a stylized drawing of a mountain.
Rafe had thoughtfully doodled in a curl of smoke rising from
its peak.

"You know," said Billi, draped over the professor's
shoulder, "I am for the first time beginning to come to some
kind of understanding as to just what hardy sons of bitches
those Vikings *were*." So exhausted was Waldmann by the
day's events, he didn't even have the energy to be scandalized by her language.

Bone-weary as they were, the travelers were in no hurry
to try to sleep. They sat up late, listening to the professor
talk about the wars of Aesir and giant (and troll), of the
deeds of the gods, of frost-giants and stone-giants and the
fire-giants of fearful Surt, whose final irruption from Niflheim and Muspellheim would bring about Ragnarøk, the last
battle in the world.

"Niflheim and Muspellheim—the 'home of fog' and the
'home of the destroyers of the world,'" mused Billi after
Rafe translated the names. "Boy, what cheerful imaginations
the Norsemen had."

Chatenois laughed. "I feel this Niflheim must be very
nearby, Fräulein."

"Don't say that!" Rafe snapped at him. The handsome
Alsatian jerked back, startled by his unwonted vehemence.

"I'm sorry, Rafe, I meant no offense—"

But Rafe was holding up his hand and shaking his head
slowly, as if it weighed a great deal. "My fault. Fatigue, the
day's events—no excuse for rudeness, of course. . . ." His
voice trailed to a mumble, and tears glittered in the corners
of his eyes. A stubble of whiskers stood out from his wind-

burned cheeks, and Billi was shocked to see that they were touched with gray. Somehow the knowledge that hardship was wearing down even Rafe Springer unsettled her.

Shortly thereafter the Germans and Uurtamo made their way through the standard nocturnal gale to their own snow houses. They needed all the sleep they could get—uneasy as it might have been.

Next morning, they saw the smoke.

Uurtamo saw it first. He was skiing ahead of the little column and came to a halt on the lip of what the others thought from below was a plateau in the ice cap's steady rise toward the center of the landmass. He rocked back on his skis, humming a little tune that the wind carried in rags to his comrades, then turned and schussed down the slope.

"Smoke," he said in his curiously accented German. "Come." Then he turned and herringboned up again.

Rafe was the first to join him. He rested his weight on his poles and let out a low whistle as Kampfer, Waldmann, and Billi arrived. A tiny dirty-white appendix hung into the sky off the northwestern horizon. To his surprise Rafe felt no particular emotion. It was as if the ice had leached it from him like body heat.

Panting dogs pulled the sleds at a bias up the incline, Professor Shrewsbury querulously demanding more speed from Olipaluk, his driver for the day. "My word," the professor said to no one in particular as the sled coasted to a halt where the ice field leveled out. "The volcano's actually there."

Arms folded across his chest, Number One nodded. "The evil place," he said with satisfaction.

That night a storm came in and didn't leave for three days. The snow houses were well insulated and became more so as the storm raved on, piling ever more snow around them. A paraffin lamp and the breathing, sweating bodies huddled within kept the temperature bearable. Unfortunately the igloos quickly came to feel crowded to the point of insanity. The foreigners took little time to become heartily sick of each other's faces and the stink of their own and one

another's bodies. What felt like hundreds of little manner-
isms nobody had even noticed before became intolerable ir-
ritations.

Under the storm's unstinting assault it was virtually impossible to leave the igloos, even to go from one to another.
During the lulls, when the wind dropped to a mild eighty
miles an hour, there would be a mad scramble to adjoining
snow houses. So ferocious was the storm that the dogs were
sheltering in the tunnel entrances of the igloos, but even they
lacked the energy to snap at the house-hopping humans.

The third day Rafe made a pilgrimage to the Eskimo
igloo. Uurtamo was there, sitting in a corner watching Olipaluk, who had a dead eye that looked off nowhere in particular, make endless cat's cradles from a loop of sinew. Dour
Pualuna, the harpoon artist and allegedly the greatest
walrus-slayer on the eastern coast of Greenland, sat by himself carving a piece of tusk from one of the big marine
mammals. Iggianguaq, as short and broad as a keg, listened
with an expression of tolerant amusement to the exuberant
brags of Qavianguaq, the baby of the group, who had a faint
shadow of mustache on his upper lip and a face round as a
pie.

Number One greeted Rafe with a hint of a smile. "I knew
you'd come," he said.

Rafe raised a brow as he pulled himself up to sit beside
the tunnel's mouth. "Spirits tell you?"

"Imaka." Perhaps—the Eskimo's all-purpose response.

"What else do they tell you?"

"The storm will lift tomorrow. After that you should carry
your rifle with you. The Tornit lie ahead, though they aren't
yet aware of our coming."

Rafe huddled down, the fur of his collar rasping his beard
stubble, and regarded the shaman. His first pronouncement
wasn't particularly startling; you didn't get to be as old and
well respected as Number One without having some feel for
the ebb and flow of Greenland weather. But the other...

"Number One, nobody lives this far into the interior. An
old hunter like you should know that better than anyone,
especially an upstart pup like me. *Nothing* lives on the ice

cap: no ptarmigan, no seals, no bears, no plants, nothing to eat for man and beast."

"The Tornit do. And the strayed men who serve them."

Rafe gestured in exasperation, and Iggianguaq grinned at him with a rugged, clean-shaven face that would have been ugly but for its appearance of great strength and two of the most splendid eyebrows Rafe had ever seen. Family man Iggianguaq was a master of the difficult art of stalking basking seals with a rifle, a discipline requiring not only vast patience and stealth but also a particular sort of marksmanship: shots were taken at no great range, seldom more than fifty yards, but bullets were precious, and if the first shot didn't penetrate the seal's brain and kill it instantly, it would be gone, injured or otherwise but irretrievable, back under the ice.

"You speak with great authority, Almost-a-Person." The nickname the Eskimos had bestowed on Rafe was intended as a high compliment, and he accepted it as such. "Have you been there?"

"No, I can't say as I have."

The Eskimos laughed. "Then you can't contradict Number One, for he's walked there with Nerrivik."

Number One didn't join in the merriment. He merely rocked back and forth and said, "You shall see, my friend."

"*Imaka,*" Rafe said, and slithered out into the storm.

CHAPTER

Twenty

"It's impossible," Rafe Springer said.

"Rocks and dirt," Billi said with a shrug. "What so special about it? Other than the fact that after days of nothing but ice and snow and snow and ice I feel like falling down and kissing the first pebble I come across."

"Because the nearest solid ground should be at least a mile away," Rafe said, leaning heavily on his poles. "Straight *down*." He jammed the point of one pole into the snow for emphasis.

True to Number One's prediction, the storm had played out in yesterday's early hours. Before daylight the travelers were under way again, eager to be free of their ice-walled prisons, and had done the same today. The sight of the smoke plume on the horizon had spurred everyone's eagerness to reach their destination—and the storm delay had forced another precautionary cut in rations.

Now the expedition had halted at the crest of a particularly treacherous incline. Before them the land seemed to fall away to the level, rather than maintaining its often imperceptible, but invariable, rise toward the ice dome's apex. Far away a line of dark serrations broke the smoothness of the horizon; from a larger tooth than the rest trailed a wisp of smoke into the blue clear sky, indication that here was more than mirage or a line of ice cliffs.

They hardly paid any attention. Closer to hand—thirty yards away—a boulder jutted gray and unmistakable from the ice, and beyond it were visible other rocks sticking up like beast heads from burrows; far ahead gray patches were visible, suspiciously like bare soil.

"Clearly that Royal Dutch Shell expedition you accompanied a few years ago expected to find something of this nature, Rafe," Shrewsbury said.

"Yeah. But what they *did* find was ice, ten thousand feet thick. Greenland's a giant bowl, heaping-full of ice. In the middle of the island the earth's actually-compressed to one or two thousand feet below sea level."

"Could this be a spur of the coastal range, Herr Springer?" Waldmann asked. Given the blistering heat of the day—it must have been over freezing—his hood was thrown back, and he was wearing a colorful red knit cap that made him look like Santa Claus shaved and wearing mufti.

Letting one pole hang from its wrist strap, Rafe rubbed his jaw. "You could be right. You probably are."

"You don't sound convinced," Billi said. He shrugged.

"We'd better move along," Number One, practical as always, pointed out. "The going will be slower crossing rocks and bare ground."

Rafe cocked his head at him. "This doesn't surprise you one damn' bit, does it?"

The headman just looked ineffably superior and whipped his dogs to their feet.

As they moved out, the Eskimos pulled their rifles, encased in sealskin scabbards, from beneath the sled wraps and lashed them to the rear stanchions—*napariaq*—with their buttstocks close to hand. Pualuna had his harpoon slid under a strap atop the cargo mounded on his sled. Less attuned to the niceties of dogsled packing than Rafe, the others showed no sign of noticing. The kid Qavianguaq saw him studying the weaponry, gave him a grin.

Rafe single-sticked forward on his short, broad touring skis, rummaged among the cargo on Number One's sled. The outlanders watched with surprise or amusement as he pulled out a web belt and his big Colt in its ancient flapped Army-issue field holster and buckled it around his waist.

"I thought you said we wouldn't need guns, Herr Springer," Kampfer said with a coprophage grin.

"Just thought I should get used to wearing it again," Rafe said. "We'll be going back to face the hazards of civilization one of these days, you know."

They trudged on toward the distant sawtooth of mountains. More and more bare ground began to break out around them, despite the looks half of wonder and half of outrage Rafe kept scattering about him. "It's turning into tundra," he muttered to himself. "It *can't* be turning into tundra."

"How can you be so crabbed as to complain on a lovely day like this?" Shrewsbury demanded from Iggianguaq's sled. "Eyjolfson's account is true, by Jove, it must be—the volcano proves it."

"So, you admit Gungnir exists?" Waldmann asked, not without irony, perhaps.

Shrewsbury frowned briefly. "Well . . . let us say that I feel we're on the verge of a momentous discovery." He brightened. "And who can say? Maybe Gungnir awaits us at the cache, after all." He laughed like a delighted schoolboy.

"What about the trolls?" Billi asked. "If Gungnir's there, doesn't that mean the trolls are too?"

Too buoyant to be sucked into an argument, Shrewsbury just laughed again. Number One looked back, his face creased with interest. "Trolls?" he asked.

"*Trold*," said Rafe, giving the Danish word. "A race of malevolent manlike beings."

"Ah." He nodded. "Tornit."

Shrewsbury clucked and shook his head. He was warming to the Eskimos. His natural curiosity had begun to overcome his distaste for their strange ways. He didn't feel, as Kampfer still seemed to, that they were subhuman, just that they displayed a to-him inexplicable fondness for revolting habits and silly superstitions. The journey's rigors had worn him down to a state of tolerant amusement.

"Imagine. They believe such creatures actually exist," he said.

Rafe looked at the patches of gray around them and shook his head.

Twilight caught them crossing a field of jumbled gray

rocks interspersed with patches of snow and ice. Several hundred yards ahead of them a low hillock crowned with gray boulders humped up out of a snowfield. Rafe guessed they would make camp there; crossing the stony ground with the sleds was an arduous process, and it would be nice if they didn't have to forage for snow to make igloos. *Maybe we shouldn't have been so hasty about abandoning the tents,* he thought. But he knew the dogs could never have held out, pulling the hundreds of pounds of water that had soaked the tents and frozen.

The foreigners had shed their skis and packed them on the sleds; here it was easier to walk across the snowy spots than ski through the rocks. Shrewsbury was up and walking, puffing his pipe and using a ski pole as a walking stick, for all the world like a country squire on a morning stroll about the grounds.

Everyone kept especially alert around the dogs; they were in a savage mood from the extra effort of hauling the sleds over bare earth. The Eskimos had to be alert with their whips to keep fights from breaking out among the teams.

"I had begun to doubt it was possible," Billi said, picking her way over a hump of ice. "This is sort of exciting, with this mysterious tundra that's so upset poor Rafe and all."

"What was it you doubted was possible, my dear?" asked Shrewsbury around the stem of his brier. He'd lost the thread of her conversation while picking his way across a particularly stony patch of ground.

She waved a hand at the landscape around. "This. To have a *benign* sort of adventure. We had so much trouble back in Germany, I was about to give up on the idea of adventure."

Grunting his sled gratefully up onto an expanse of ice ahead of the three, Pualuna stopped, seemed to stumble. Billi pointed. "What's happening?"

"I don't know," Rafe said, frowning. He started forward.

Pualuna leaned forward, whipped the bone-headed harpoon from beneath the lashing, pulled his arm back, and threw. The harpoon arced ten yards and struck behind an ice-capped rock as high as a man's waist.

With a horrendous scream a man erupted from behind the

rock, clutching at the harpoon buried at the base of his neck. A bone bow dropped from his hands.

Pualuna's right leg gave way. He turned as he dropped to the knee. Billi screamed.

A black arrow jutted from the socket of his right eye.

The rocky plain erupted men. "Run! Run for the hill," Rafe shouted, while the thunderstruck outlanders watched Pualuna pitch forward to lie unmoving in the snow. The Eskimo drivers had their teams on the run, whipping them on as they jerked rifles from scabbards.

Rafe hauled out his pistol and fired at a man running toward him, harpoonlike spear upraised. The man stopped, made swimming motions with his arms, fell backward. Black-dyed arrows of bone moaned past Rafe to both sides.

One struck Billi just below the left breast. "Oh, my," she said weakly but distinctly.

"*Billi!*" Shrewsbury grabbed her. His face was paler than when he'd dangled over the abyss.

She shook him off. "It didn't penetrate," she said in a wondering tone. She tugged at the shaft. The barbs held the carved-bone head fast in her parka, but it hadn't even pierced the shirt she wore beneath.

The flat barks of Mausers surrounded them as the Germans opened fire. Rafe stood as if transfixed, staring at the stubby, fur-clad forms rushing toward him. For a moment he was back on that hill outside Nijni Gora, while the White Russian gunners fled their emplacements with a Canadian sergeant bellowing after them to stand and fight, and the Bolshevik militia rolled forward like a storm front shouting their war-cry. . . .

"*Rafe!*" Billi screamed. At once he was back in the present, staring into the round, hate-twisted face of a man raising a bone club to brain him. He threw himself at the man, grabbed his wrist. For a moment they struggled, the Eskimo's fetid breath seeming to fill Rafe's head, and then he kneed the man hard in the crotch and broke away as he doubled over. He snapped a shot at a knot of men charging him and raced to join his companions.

That there was no obvious route saved them. The ambushers had hidden themselves in clumps all over the snowy, rock-strewn plain. Now that their trap was sprung, they streamed toward the intruders in ragged waves. Rafe caught up with Number One's sled, clawed at the wrappings, uncovered his rifle.

As he jerked it free he heard the heavy rap of a grenade, saw half a dozen Eskimos roll screaming into the snow and dirt. Then the MG34 snarled like all the huskies in the world rolled into one. Pistol holstered, Rafe went to his knee and began squeezing off shots.

Whoever the attackers were, they were clearly unprepared for the fury of their intended victims' firepower. The assault began to falter as survivors nearest the caravan dropped into hiding places among the rocks and flopped into the snow where their white parkas rendered them almost invisible.

The sleds had reached unbroken snow and shot ahead. The animals of Pualuna's team, hopeful of reaching camp and food, followed their fellows. Kampfer had sent a couple of men plowing through the snow, pacing the sleds as best they could, and Waldmann and another soldier escorted the unarmed professor and Billi. Uurtamo sat in the snow, pulling on his skis as calmly as if on a pleasant weekend tour.

The rear guard of Kampfer, Rafe, and the trooper lying prone behind the MG watched the attackers melt into the landscape. "That's settled them," said lanky Eblinger, giving the machine gun's receiver an affectionate pat. He climbed to his feet, picked up the weapon. "These devils weren't prepared for—"

An arrow transfixed his throat. He broke off, stared almost comically down his long nose at the shaft sticking out from under his chin, uttered a strangling sound, and fell over kicking as the attackers barraged them from cover. Rafe grabbed him, tried to pull him to his feet as Kampfer reeled in the machine gun. Supporting him between them, the two men slogged for the hillock.

The ambushers hadn't overlooked it. A shower of darts and arrows arced down as the sleds raced up to it. An arrow in the belly tumbled Freiherr Chatenois off his skis but failed to penetrate. Kurt Hoff halted on the slope of the rise, prepared a stick grenade as black missiles hissed past his ears, tossed it up into the rocks. The blast evoked screams and flushed half a dozen enemies from the boulders like quail. Number One whipped his dogs straight up the slope. A foe-man heartier than the others stood up to hurl a harpoon, went down with a scream as Number One's lead dog hit him in the chest. The rest of the team swarmed over him like soldier ants, tearing at him with happy savagery.

Uurtamo glided up to Rafe and Kampfer. Kampfer waved him away; no way he could help move the injured trooper. He turned and sped to the base of the hillock, from which Hoff, Chatenois, and the Eskimos—with some help from the dogs—had routed the ambushers. He sat down with his feet still in the bindings and methodically began to pick off any enemies bold enough to stick any major body parts out of concealment.

Professor Shrewsbury was limping badly now, unable to keep from grimacing at the pain of every step on his injured foot. Billi had his arm slung around her neck, and several of the Germans huddled watchfully around, weapons ready, now eyeing an expanse of snow deceptively innocent of hostile figures.

Burdened though they were with the machine gun and the still feebly struggling Eblinger, Rafe and Leutnant Kampfer passed them up just before they reached the hill. Kampfer dropped off halfway up the incline to set up his machine gun while Rafe put on a burst of speed, hauling the wounded man to the relative safety of the rocks on top.

The attackers came boiling out of the snow again in a fresh storm of arrows. "Let me go," Shrewsbury yipped as a barb raked his cheek. "I can make it from here!"

"You aren't being heroic?" Billi breathed.

"For the love of God, *go*."

They all ran flat out for the hill. The ambushers pursued them in the lethal silence they'd maintained throughout the attack. With fresh impetus the professor ran like a gazelle, hurt foot or no, and the others had difficulty keeping up with his lengthy strides.

Kampfer was having trouble with the machine gun. Somewhere its drum magazine had been jarred loose, and several metal links of the ammunition belt inside had gotten twisted. The lieutenant carried no spares. He'd torn off the faulty links and had the cover open, fumbling a fresh end of the belt into the feedway.

At the foot of the hill a rock turned beneath Shrewsbury's foot. He fell heavily. "*Melbourne!*" Billi shouted. Already halfway up she turned and raced back to haul frantically on his arm. An arrow hit her in the forehead, an inch above the plucked arch of her right eyebrow.

She sat down hard. *I'm killed*, she thought. And then: *No, I'm not, or I wouldn't be thinking this. Would I?*

Another arrow moaning past her ear snapped her back from the verge of hysteria. Driven by a short bow, the bone-tipped arrow hadn't had the force to penetrate her skull. She tore the missile out of her forehead and threw it away.

Shrewsbury was struggling to his feet beside her. He froze at the sight of her blood-washed face. "Billi—?"

She jumped up and grabbed his arm again. "Don't just stand there gaping, you son of a bitch," she shouted. "We've got to *move!*" And they scrambled up into the boulders as Kampfer finally got the MG34 working again and sent a wave of attackers tumbling away from the very foot of the prominence.

CHAPTER

Twenty-one

A sound rose up around them like the twilight gray, a pulsating cicada drone. "Bullroarers," Melbourne Shrewsbury said. "Quite remarkable, really. It's generally theorized that just such noisemakers of carven bone caused the Vikings to name the inhabitants of the island *skraelinga*, meaning screamers."

Billi lifted her bandaged head and looked at him. "Professor," she said sweetly, "will you kindly shut up?"

He sniffed.

The hilltop was crowded. Seven Europeans, two Americans, four Eskimos, five sleds, and forty-three dogs—two had been killed, one from Number One's team and one from Qavianguaq's—were cramped into a rough circle ten yards in diameter, stacked any which way among sharp-edged basaltic rocks.

"Would you like me to kill the man with the noisemaker?" Uurtamo inquired with great seriousness, in his curious singsong German.

Shrewsbury raised his head from the receiver of his own rifle to stare at him, wondering if he could be serious. He was. Respectful of the interlopers' firepower, the attackers had withdrawn to a distance of four hundred yards. To Uurtamo, a marksman of terrifying precision, that was scarcely a stone's throw.

"Better save your ammunition," Rafe grunted from the other side of the perimeter. "They might try again."

The Finn nodded. Since the party had gotten ensconced on the hilltop, their attackers had tried one assault, which the machine gun and the big 7.92-millimeter magazine rifles had easily repulsed. But the unknown enemies still had them surrounded and showed no sign of losing interest in the proceedings.

"You seem awfully bloody matter-of-fact about the business of killing a man," Shrewsbury said.

Uurtamo shrugged.

"They are determined," Kampfer said, shaking his head. "Why don't they give up?"

A good thirty forms lay in the snow, along the travelers' line of march and around the base of the low hill. Most of them weren't moving, though some had been as recently as a few minutes ago. Whoever these squat Eskimolike men were, they showed little interest in caring for their own casualties.

"They want to see the color of our guts," Passauer said. "Begging your pardon, Fräulein."

"It doesn't bother me if you call a spade a spade," Billi said, sitting up from the roll of bedding she'd been using as a pillow. "And don't give me the fish eye, Rafe Springer. I'm not making a target of myself; even *I* know we're not in range of those silly bows and arrows."

"Not that silly, Fräulein," Black Peter said. "They finished for the stamp collector." He jerked his head at the edge of the hilltop from which they had rolled the *Braunschweiger* Max Eblinger. He'd been dead by the time Rafe got him to their position.

"God, this is awful of me," Billi said, smoothing back her sweat-matted hair and picking at the bandaged wound around her forehead, "but I'm glad it's so cold. It means the bodies will keep. I don't think I could stand it if all those dead men began to smell."

"Not awful, Fräulein," Waldmann said in a voice far removed from his usual tones of bumptiousness or menace. "Had you been in the trenches during the Great War, you would feel no guilt at being glad to escape the stink of death."

"I don't understand why we don't break out of here," Billi said. "We've got the guns."

"There are still at least two hundred of them out there," Rafe said. "And we don't have an infinite amount of ammunition. That machine gun has an enormous appetite. And even these bolt guns eat ammo fast in a fight."

"But they're afraid of the guns. They've shown that. And the guns have so much greater range than their bows and arrows. They'd never stand up to us. I never thought you were a coward, Rafe." Bitterly: "Before."

"It's not that we fear a mere several hundred savages, Fräulein," Chatenois said blandly, "for you are surely correct: we'd go through them like a hot knife through butter. And then they would hide in the snow and behind rocks and snipe us down as we passed."

"And don't forget," Dietrich said, "sometime we have to sleep."

She put her head in her hands. "I just can't stand this waiting."

Rafe drew a deep breath, exhaled explosively. "It's only going to get worse."

For a fact, they were stuck. Their firepower and the enemies' manpower had produced a classic Mexican standoff. The attackers weren't willing to spend the lives necessary to storm the height; the defenders didn't have enough ammunition for a counterattack, and even if they broke the circle of besiegers would face the dangers the Freiherr and Black Peter had pointed out: constant harassing attacks, the danger of a rush under cover of night or blowing snow.

"It's getting dark," Number One said. "We must build a snow house."

"He's right," Rafe said. "It's not going to be any warmer just because we're surrounded."

"What about *them*?" Billi demanded.

"They build them, too, Aningaaq Pania," Qavianguaq said, and pointed. It was true. All around them circular shelters were sprouting in the gloom.

There was room for only one igloo on the hilltop, and

given the danger of attack at night, nobody even suggested moving off it. Under cover of the outlanders' rifles, the Eskimos moved down and cut blocks from the snow at the hill's base, lugged them up to assemble the shelter. By the time full dark arrived in the middle of the afternoon, the snow house was complete.

The tough part was setting lookouts. Rafe and Kampfer decided they could get by with three spotted at equal intervals around the hill. They would have turns of half an hour each, with a newcomer coming out every ten minutes to check on them and spell the one who had been out longest. Even at that everyone shared the unspoken dread of facing the awful cold that night brought, eighty miles into the ice.

Billi and Shrewsbury both insisted on taking their turns, so Rafe went out with them to form the first rotation. After ten minutes Billi gave no argument when Kampfer came out to spell her, nor did Shrewsbury balk when Waldmann— who, to everyone's surprise, had declined to pull rank and exempt himself from the arduous duty—came for him after twenty minutes. After many hours had passed in ten more minutes, Rafe Springer wasn't exactly grudging when Number One came and tapped him on the shoulder.

He had barely settled in with a cup of steaming tea when Kampfer wriggled through the ice tunnel. "Rafe, you'd better come. Something's happening."

The soldiers started up, trying to disentangle their weapons from the limbs and bodies crammed into the shelter. Kampfer shook his head. "No attack—at least, I think not."

The professor and Billi followed Rafe out. "My God," the professor said, hunkered behind a rock at Kampfer's side. "Bonfires? Whatever do they find to burn?"

They stared out at the mostly invisible ring of besiegers. At the four points of the compass open fires burned—not big, but shocking in a treeless land where sea-mammal fat was used for illumination.

"I don't even know what they bloody well find to *eat*," Rafe complained, putting a pair of binoculars to his eyes.

"The Tornit give them food and dried plant matter to

burn," Number One called from the far side of the circle. "In return they guard the spirit folks' realm against intruders."

"Bah," Shrewsbury said. But it lacked conviction.

Billi leaned her lips close to Rafe's ear, whispered, "Does he—" She faltered, tried again. "Does he *know* that, or is he just guessing?"

"You'd have to ask him," Rafe said, fiddling with the focus.

She bit her lip. "I can't. I'm . . . afraid."

A camp fire swam in a yellow-orange haze, resolved into image: figures sat around it, their natural stockiness exaggerated by their thick *kapataks*. One man danced by the fire waving what even at this range looked suspiciously like a human thighbone with feathers tied to the knob at the end. On the fire's far side stood a pole of bones joined end to end, capped with what might have been the skull of a polar bear —in the jittering light Rafe could not be sure.

"I don't believe it," he said. He shook his head. "I'm starting to sound like a stuck record. I'm no anthropologist, but I'm damned sure it violates the strongest taboos for them to make use of dead human bodies in those shaman sticks. And that skull standard—I've never heard of Eskimos anywhere doing anything like it." He slapped his cheeks. Already the cold seemed to be flaying the skin from them.

"These men are tainted by the evil of the Tornit. The Tornit have given them many gifts, and it has made them mad things. There—" Number One pointed. "There's great magic being worked out there, something to hurt us. I feel it."

Rafe felt the short hairs at the back of his neck stirring like crawling insects. Even the professor had nothing to say. They turned and retreated into the comparative warmth of the snow house.

"I know we find ourselves faced by an extraordinary concatenation of events," Professor Shrewsbury said, "but that does not mean we should fall back upon superstition. We're civilized men."

"But if we really are faced with otherworldy influences," Maurice Chatenois said, "then it's surely no superstition to believe in them?" He smiled slyly; he had a well-earned reputation as a barracks lawyer.

"Nonsense. A non sequitur. We've faced nothing in the least otherworldly. Just savages with Stone Age weapons."

"Who live where there's no food and burn fires where there's no fuel," Passauer said. "Nothing out of the way at all, Herr Doktor Professor."

"Bourgeois fantasies," Black Peter said, stirring a tin of beans bubbling atop a Primus stove with his bayonet. The stove's halfhearted shine accented his black brows and the dense fur on his cheeks, lending him a Neanderthal cast. Passauer tossed a sardine tin at him. He caught it easily and laughed.

To one side of the igloo the Eskimos were all asleep in a single mound; they slept jumbled together like puppies. While fatigue, fear, and their own unwashed state had done much to mitigate the foreigners' distaste for the natives' smell, they weren't yet prepared for such immediate proximity. They had spaced themselves out as best they could in the nine-foot-wide shelter's other half.

Rafe sat huddled inside his parka, staring moodily at Black Peter's stove. "Maybe we shouldn't be so quick to dismiss what Number One says as superstition."

"Good heavens, Rafe!" the professor exclaimed. "And you have scientific training."

"When I was a small boy," Rafe said, not seeming to hear him, "my mother's uncle was a member of the Catholic cult called *penitente*. I remember him; a tremendous old man, tall and broad, with a splendid white beard growing down his chest. It was the wonder of the Sangre de Cristos; people with so much *indio* blood didn't usually get hair so white— nor beards that bushy, for that matter.

"Every once in a while the popular press gets hold of the *pentitentes*—Archbishop Lamy specifically tried to suppress them as part of his general campaign to wipe out the Spanish culture in New Mexico during the last century. The sect gets its name from the penances the faithful take upon themselves, which can be pretty gruesome; not only do they flagellate themselves to bloody ribbons on various holy days, but every Easter the most devout among them had the honor of being crucified."

Lying with a cloth over her face, Billi gasped. "Delightful people," the professor murmured. The Germans—including Kampfer, who'd been spelled by Kurt Hoff—stared at Rafe with round eyes, avid to hear stories of the legendary American West where Rafe had grown up. This was great stuff—the Karl May Westerns of their own boyhoods were stuffed chock full of Red Indian mysticism.

"It's usually not a fatal process, I'm told. Anyway, the lurid rituals that occasionally make the papers aren't the heart of the *penitente* faith. The inner mysteries, as it were, have a good dose of gnosticism to them." He sipped melted snow from a cup, carefully moistening lips burned raw by wind and frigid cold. "I remember, back when I was a kid, staying with my great-aunt and uncle sometimes in summer, in the hills up above Las Vegas. Sometimes my great-uncle would go out into the mountains at night and not come back till morning. And we knew what he was doing: going up onto the mountaintop to summon down demons of the air, so that he could test his strength against theirs."

He stared off past his drawn-up knees, as if looking through the half-translucent walls of the igloo, away through time and space. For a while the silence was thicker than the smell inside the snow house. Then with a moan Billi rolled to face the wall. "This is a hell of a time to tell camp fire ghost stories, Rafe Springer."

The night passed like a glacier marching to the sea. Billi dozed fitfully, and the rest took advantage of the fact to deal her tacitly out of the rotation. Rafe kept an uneasy eye on her. The skin around her arrow wound was pink, inflamed, and he thought the tip of the head may have broken off in her skull. Unlike frostbite, which carried the constant threat of gangrene, open wounds posed little danger in the almost germ-free Arctic, but the wound persisted in weeping. Infection or no, having a chunk of stone embedded in her head couldn't be too comfortable, and Rafe wished he could do something for her.

Number One came in from his second watch while Rafe

was still warming his hands against his body. The two small-
est toes on his right foot had turned white, a dangerous sign;
from his reading of Santesson he knew not to do anything
stupid like massage or rub snow on them. Using his own
metabolic warmth was best. When his hands were warm, he
would hold his toes until they warmed as well.

"There's a lot of power here," Number One said, as
though he were saying it was about to snow again. "I feel it
all around."

Billi made a mewling sound in her sleep. The professor
was shrunken in on himself, apparently likewise asleep.
"Can you do anything?"

The shaman shook his head. "We are far from Nerrivik's
sea. And the magic of the mad things is very potent. Sometimes I have the power to prophesy, or see things far away,
and as you know, Nerrivik has told me of certain things in
dreams. But I have never had the power to send or dispel
magics."

Kampfer sat up, rubbing his eyes. "What's he say?"

Rafe translated. To his surprise the officer did not ridicule
what the old man had said.

"Well, what does he see for us?" Kampfer asked.

Number One frowned when Rafe relayed the question.
"A great whiteness fills my vision when I try to look ahead.
More I cannot see."

An hour later Hoff crawled in to wake his commander
and Rafe. "Better come look. A storm's coming in."

They emerged out of the tunnel to see a white wall, like a
glacier agleam in starlight, spanning the northern horizon.
Kampfer made a sound between his teeth. "Looks bad."

Qavianguaq, taking his turn on watch, pointed at the
low-lying cloud front and spoke too rapidly to understand.
The fear on his round face was unmistakable.

"I'd better get Number One," Rafe said.

As he emerged from the tunnel into the chamber Billi
came upright with a shriek that curled his spine. "It's coming!" she screamed. Her eyes were wide open, but she gave
no sign of seeing Rafe or the others, slammed from sleep by
her cry, who huddled around her. "I feel them out there—

their hatred burns like the fires. But cold, cold will cover them—cold will cover the world—"

She doubled into a fit of violent sobbing. "She's feverish," the professor said, forcing his hand between hers and her face to feel her skin. He looked at Rafe, the darkness of the sockets lending his pale eyes a wild intensity. Rafe bared his teeth with an emotion he could not begin to name, and went back out with Number One right behind.

Outside, the dogs were howling. "Is Fräulein Forsyth all right?" Kampfer asked. "We heard her scream. It woke the beasts."

"Scream not wake them," Number One said in his halting English. "Magic wake them."

Kampfer eyed him narrowly. "Magic?"

Number One pointed north, to the whiteness that rolled upon them like a tidal wave. "Magic. There."

"A hell of a storm," said Passauer, who'd been sharing the watch with Hoff and the young Eskimo.

Kampfer sniffed. The cold made his nose run, and he didn't dare rub it; he'd told Rafe that in cold-weather training he'd seen a man do that and have his nose come off in his hand. "At least we can all go inside. No one's going to attack us in *that*."

Rafe nodded. He'd feared a mild storm—Eskimos could forge ahead in weather no white man would dare, or survive if he did, and the besiegers might use the cover of blown or falling snow to overrun the little hilltop redoubt. But the sliding wall of white, already perceptibly nearer than moments before, showed every sign of being a classic Greenland hell-bender in which nothing exposed could survive.

A thought hit with such force that it staggered him, a mad thought, he knew, but still—he snatched the binoculars from Hoff, adjusted the focus with fingers that felt like lead within his thick mittens, found the glow of a fire.

The besiegers were all on their feet, dancing as if in ecstasy. Faint cries drifted across the snow. From within the igloo came Billi's cry: "*It's coming! Out of the dark lands*—"

Eyes wide and burning in the cold, Rafe faced Number One. He felt as if his sanity were about to be torn apart, like a sail caught by a violent gust of wind. *"Did they bring this storm?"*

Black eyes met his. *"Imaka,"* the shaman said.

The storm came with fantastic speed. Quickly they called the dogs into the long entrance tunnel and blocked the door just as the wind exploded around them like a bomb. The wailing seemed to beat from the walls like agony from an open wound.

Sobbing, Billi clung to the professor. He stroked his eyes and stared at the king-block of the shelter. *"Mein Gott,"* Waldmann breathed. "It's like all the lost souls in hell."

Kampfer crossed himself.

The wind raged, now a high, tearing shriek, now booming like giant muffled handclaps. "When you were in Greenland before, did you ever hear a storm such as this, Herr Springer?" Chatenois asked. His attempted tone of agnostic brashness flaked away like dead skin even as he spoke, leaving the last words naked and fearful.

"I've never heard anything like this, anywhere on Earth."

"Never been a storm like this on Earth," Uurtamo said, staring as if hypnotized at the lone blubber lamp.

"In a storm this bad even the snow house might not help us," Iggianguaq said.

"Against bad magic, nothing can help us," Qavianguaq said disconsolately.

"We've been in some bad spots before," said Passauer, trying to lighten the mood. But Black Peter shook his head.

"Not this bad. Not even training in Russia," he said.

The storm sound crescendoed, making talk impossible. Rafe stared at the tiny, undulating flame. The import of the former miner's words had already slipped from his grasp. The storm made it hard to think, hard to concentrate on anything but that mind-killing din. Yet there was something about the pounding waves of sound, something strange, a thing he could not quite place—

Uurtamo seemed to catch his thought, and stripping off a mitten, laid his bare hand against the wall of the snow house. "I can't feel the wind," he said.

Blank faces looked at him. They could not hear, or perhaps they could not comprehend what he was saying, but

Rafe grasped it at once. "A wind this hard, you can feel through the blocks—the impact when it changes direction—"

"And it should be colder in here," added the Finn.

"You're raving, both of you," Shrewsbury said.

Rafe turned and disappeared into the tunnel like a ferret. "He's mad!" Shrewsbury cried, and lunged after him.

The professor saw the soles of Rafe's boots receding down the tunnel past the huddled dogs, saw his legs from shins down as the American stood erect. And then Shrewsbury realized that the expected blast of cold wind had not hit him in the face.

He joined Rafe standing outside the hut. One by one the others emerged to take their places gazing around in disbelief too deep for words.

They stood on an oasis in a white infinity. A roiling, howling, turbulent whiteness as solid as paint completely walled in the hill. It was as if a great bell jar had been placed above the hillock, keeping the terrible wind at bay.

Then Kampfer was pointing upward, his face the same color as the turmoil that surrounded them. Their eyes traveled up and up, and they realized that the hill formed the base of a shaft of clear air that stretched up to the open sky.

And wheeling in that tiny circle of night, just visible against the star field, were two winged shadows.

Like ravens.

CHAPTER

Twenty-two

At dawn the storm dissipated with the same abruptness with which it had descended. Feeling weightless after a sleepless, eerie night, the travelers resumed their watch on the enemy encampments circling them. Billi insisted on helping, though she kept slipping away into a peculiar trancelike state. She turned aside questions as to what had happened to her the night before with a queer smile that was somehow more unnerving than her raving.

By noon they had seen no movement from the snow houses, dotted around them like half scoops of ice cream under a foot of new snow. Rafe and Kampfer took Number One and a couple of soldiers and went out to investigate, leaving Chatenois with the machine gun and master sniper Uurtamo with his rifle to cover them. Waldmann stayed back. Shrewsbury was still in no shape to go trooping off on a risky reconnaissance, and Billi, though she ached to go along, elected to stay behind and keep an eye on him.

Half an hour later the patrol was back, faces gray and grim. "They're there," Rafe said. "Every mother's son of them. Frozen stiff as crowbars."

"Inside their igloos?" Shrewsbury said.

"Except for that bear-skull shaman," Rafe said. "He's still out by the pole and the dead camp fire. His face looks like the devil had him by the tail."

Chatenois stretched a grin across his teeth. "Maybe their magic came back on them, like, what's the word? Boomerang."

"*Imaka*," Rafe said.

They pulled out within minutes, eager to be clear of the frigid village of the dead. Max Eblinger they covered with stones and left to lie; the earth was frozen too hard to bury him. They had four sleds now. Their supplies were depleted sufficiently that the load from Pualuna's sled could be distributed among the others, and likewise the dogs from his team. The sled itself was abandoned.

Perhaps through some trick of the icy air the mountains before them seemed to grow with unnatural speed, as though they were rushing toward them much faster than sleds or skis could possibly move. They did not appear enormously tall, but their peaks were quite sharp, giving the horizon the appearance of a shark's jaw, jagged and forbidding. Dominating the range was the dogtooth-shaped volcano, from which white smoke seeped into a sky decked with a high, gauzy overcast.

That night they could hear the mountain grumbling like a dyspeptic giant. From time to time lightning flickered across the peaks, orange, violet, red. Hints of orange glow sprang up sporadically among the valleys, faded.

"Great," Billi remarked, standing outside a snow house in a night that felt almost mild. "We're marching right into a live volcano."

"You have any premonitions on that subject?" Rafe asked, more than half seriously.

She shrugged. "Nothing definite," she said slowly. "They come and go."

Next day the land began to pitch up into foothills. The temperature rose, and the snow almost vanished. Surprise reflexes thoroughly dulled, the travelers scarcely commented on the phenomenon, simply loosened the thongs on their parkas and trudged on, leaving their skis strapped on the sleds.

Two hours after they'd set out, Number One called a halt. "The ground is too rocky, and there are too many ridges and gulleys to cross," he said. "We must leave the sleds."

The foreigners exchanged looks. The sleds were their lifeline, and they were reluctant to be parted from them. On the other hand, there was no question of the dogs pulling the sledges over the broken landscape, and the runners, metal though they were, would quickly be battered into uselessness by the rocks.

"You're willing to abandon your dogs?" Shrewsbury asked with keen interest. "I thought you valued them as you do life itself."

"We must go on," Number One said in English.

"Number One feels you can drive the evil from these mountains," Iggianguaq amplified. "We're willing to take the risk of leaving them behind for the days it will take us to go in and come back. Who's to molest the dogs, after all?"

"The people who attacked us, for one," Kampfer said, when Rafe had translated.

Iggianguaq shrugged. "I don't think we have to worry about them anymore."

Billi sat slumped on Olipaluk's sled, massaging her temples. Shrewsbury hovered nearby. "I'm afraid Billi's still suffering ill effects from her injury," he said. The wound in her forehead continued to weep, to Rafe's dismay, and she seemed to be running a fever.

She shrugged Shrewsbury's solicitous hands off in irritation. "I'm fine. I'm just . . . fine. Only, I feel . . ." She paused and stared at the mountain. It seemed to hang over them like a threat, bleeding smoke gray as lead across high, thin clouds. "I have this feeling we have to press on no matter what."

Shrewsbury rolled his eyes toward a distant heaven. "Lord, she's gone visionary on us."

"Look, dammit, hasn't it occurred to you that there are things going on here that just don't follow the normal course of nature? Or not the nature that we're accustomed to, anyway. Professor, I'm not entirely sure we're still *in* our world."

"Hey. An alternate dimension," Rafe said, beaming at the tantalizing, if chimerical, prospect of actually living a favorite conceit from the fantastic fiction he loved.

Shrewsbury shook his head. If he'd fallen among madmen—and women—he could at least gracefully acquiesce in fate.

They divided what they could into backpacks. Rafe's silence when the Germans loaded themselves down with ammunition and grenades was eloquently loud; without comment he picked up a fifty-round drum for the MG34 and stuffed it into his own pack, thrust a couple of stick grenades through his belt. He and the professor carried their rifles slung, and Billi wore Eblinger's Kar-98k strapped across her back. Leutnant Kampfer had appropriated the machine gun.

Rafe regretted that they had left the tents behind, but already the temperature seemed more that of the coast than the icebox interior. Unless there was a repeat of the witch-storm of night before last, their nights would be livable, if not exactly comfortable.

They took several days' worth of food, medical supplies, bedding, and all the water they could carry, though there were postage-stamp patches of snow dotted well into the mountains. The rest they cached under some large boulders jumbled together to form a sort of cave. They tethered the dogs in the lee of another heap of boulders under which they could shelter, next to an expanse of snow they could lick for water. They left frozen chunks of walrus meat on the ground for the dogs to eat and pressed on.

Professor Shrewsbury made heavy going of it. But he had a ski pole to use as a walking stick, and more than that, he had the lure of the mountain and Bjørn Eyjolfson's fabulous Viking trove to draw him onward. "Really, I'm fine, my boy," he said when Rafe asked him how he was doing, after half an hour's hike. "I feel as if I'm walking on air."

Two hours later the sun was diving for the tag end of the mountains when they saw the bird turning lazy circles in the sky. "What are those things?" Passauer demanded. "Why do they keep following us?"

"Are you sure you want to know the answer to that question?" Rafe asked.

They kept on their track toward the volcano, following the draws between ridges to save energy, working gradually toward their destination. Presently a second black bird joined the first, and then the two flapped to an ungainly landing ten yards in front of the party.

"We've come a long way since the Ku'damm," Rafe said, raising a hand in greeting.

The nearer of the birds cocked its head at him. The party started to walk by the birds. They flew up in their faces, uttering ragged raven cries and making a great commotion with their wings.

"Forward brutes," Shrewsbury said, fending one off with his rifle.

"Take it easy, Professor," Rafe advised. "These are old friends."

The birds once more planted themselves directly in the expedition's path. When Shrewsbury walked by, they fluttered up into his face again.

"They want us to go this way, Mel," Billi said softly, kneeling to stroke the larger bird's rounded head. It hopped aside, glaring at her in outrage.

"Wilhelmina, can't you see how preposterous it is to speak of what the beasts want?"

"No. And if you call me Wilhelmina ever again, I'll break that upper-crust nose of yours."

One of the ravens took off, flew to a landing just below the crest of the ridge that rose to their left. He fixed the travelers with a beady, expectant stare.

"I can take a hint," Rafe said, starting up the slope, unslinging his rifle—the events of the last few days had left him in no mood to take chances. The bird watched him with what he could have sworn was grudging satisfaction: *say, Mac, you're not as dumb as I thought you were.*

"If you run into any trolls, give 'em my regards," Billi said, resting her Mauser on her shoulder.

Trudging to the top, Rafe frowned slightly. *There shouldn't be an echo here,* he thought, listening to the crunch of his footsteps, which seemed to be repeating themselves a beat late. He reached the crestline—

—and found himself face-to-face with a creature on furlough from some child's nightmares.

It was taller than he was, heavier, manlike but by no stretch of the imagination a *man*: a being with coarse blue-

green skin, a snouted face, two boar's tusks curving upward
from a mouth that was black-lipped like a dog's. The appari-
tion had a conical steel helmet and a hauberk of coarse mail,
a sword and shield strapped to his back and—an incongruity
that almost rooted Rafe to the spot—an ancient Danish Krag
military rifle in its black-taloned hands.

Its eyes started from deep sockets. It produced a grating
sound, swinging the rifle toward Rafe. Frantically he
thumbed the Mauser's flange safety to the off position,
snapped a shot from the hip even as he stared down the
eight-millimeter tunnel of the Krag's muzzle.

Steel rings popped over the creature's sternum, and a
cloud of black mist exploded behind it. The thing bellowed,
dropped its rifle, and went rolling down the backslope while
Rafe lunged up to look down that side of the ridge.

What killed the cat almost bagged a New Mexico
Springer. There were a bunch more down there just like the
one he'd shot, and at least four of them had rifles. At least
that was the number he counted in the split second before he
turned and dropped out of sight with his back to the cold,
stony slope.

A tatterdemalion volley spattered him with pebbles and
dirt from the ridge line. He pulled a grenade from his belt.
"Trolls," he said to no one in particular. He twisted the cap
and lobbed the grenade backward over the top.

The *Jägers* were pausing to fix bayonets while everyone
else came booming up the slope. "Rafe, what on *Earth* was
that frightful creature?" Billi yelled, throwing herself down
beside him.

The grenade went off with a noise like a big door slamming. "A troll," he said earnestly. "I shot a troll."

"You're shocky."

"You're right."

There were wounded-beast bellows from the far side of
the ridge, and the trolls came swarming over. Billi gasped
and swung up her rifle both-handed as a squat creature with
a face like a vampire bat's swung a broadsword at her. Blade
rang on barrel, and the rifle dropped from Billi's numbed
fingers. Showing delighted fangs, the troll raised the sword

again, and the right half of its head was sheared away by a shot from Uurtamo's rifle.

With his Mauser Black Peter slugged aside a short spear thrust at his chest, swung the butt up with all the force of his miner's back and shoulders, and knocked the creature in a back flip over the ridge top. Kurt Hoff plunged his bayonet through a troll's hauberk and deep into its belly. The being smiled, black blood welling around filed teeth, and split the German's skull with a hand ax. Hoff's dying reflex spasmed his hand shut on the trigger and blew the thing's chest apart. The two rolled downhill together in a lifeless sprawling dance.

Leaving his rifle on the ground beside him, Rafe drew his pistol and rolled up onto his knees in time to fire at a troll coming for him with buckler and sword. The slug hit the shield on its metal boss, punched through to break the arm beneath. Undaunted, the troll swung a vicious, whistling cut at Rafe, who had to throw himself full length on the slope to avoid it. As it closed in, young Qavianguaq moved in behind it, thrust his Mauser into the thing's kidneys, and fired. It went down squalling like a branded calf.

Uurtamo and Iggianguaq, the seal hunter, stood down the incline, picking off trolls trying to rush upon the travelers' right flank. Holding his MG34 by its pistol grip and the perforated shroud of its barrel, Kampfer blasted a troll with a bone-jarring burst from the hip at ten feet, flung himself down to try to enfilade the creatures from the left. Waldmann stood at the crest, toe to toe with a being a head taller than he, parrying blows from a crude halberd with his bayoneted rifle. Number One was rolling down the hill clinched with a troll in leather armor with metal plates sewn into it, fending its claws with his injured hand while gamely trying to plant his knife in flesh with his right.

Qavianguaq was still grinning in triumph when a troll raised a trapdoor Springfield that had to date from the Apache wars and shot him through the lungs. He uttered an enormous choking sob and fell.

Kampfer caught three trolls climbing the backslope to get into the fight, butchered them with short bursts from the MG34. A troll suddenly reared up beside him. He tried to swing the weapon to bear, but it was too long. A mace tipped with a baseball-sized lead head whistled down. Desperately the lieutenant rolled, whipping up an arm. The mace splintered his forearm. The troll uttered a gobbling, triumphant cry, cocked its arm again, and Rafe shot it under the ribs. It staggered, turned to face its new antagonist with madly rolling eyes. Rafe shot it again through the chest.

Waldmann, his parka laid open by a stroke that was nearly good enough, stepped back out of the way of a two-handed cut, then, with surprising speed, lunged forward and ran his bayonet through his antagonist's throat. The being seized the Mauser's forestock with both hands and sank down strangling on its own blood. Shrewsbury shot a troll who had been incautious enough to poke his head up over the ridge through the mouth. The professor was congratulating himself when a clawed hand grabbed the barrel of his rifle just above the hooded front sight and hauled him bodily over the top of the ridge.

Rafe was caught in the middle of a magazine change. Shrewsbury groaned as an ax bit into his right thigh. Billi raised her .45 both-handed and emptied it into the gigantic troll before he could strike again, the slugs driving him step by step back down the incline until he collapsed. She dropped the pistol, crawled to the professor, and began to tourniquet his leg with her belt.

Quite suddenly they were out of trolls. At the base of the ridge Number One stood up, covered in black gore and wearing an altogether uncharacteristic grin. "Bears are tougher," he observed. "See? I still have my thumb."

Billi cradled the professor's head in her lap. His lips were set, and his face was drained of color.

"You will—forgive me," he gritted, "for doubting your ability to h-handle that gigantic pistol, dear girl."

She looked down at him, her face wet with tears. "I know this is a hell of a time to ask, Professor," she said, "but will you please marry me?"

"Yes," Shrewsbury said, and fainted.

CHAPTER

Twenty-three

Rafe turned the rifle in his hand with an expression of disbelief. As he had thought at first, it was an 1889 Krag, in terrible condition, rusty, with a split forestock that had been wrapped tightly with some sort of thin, light-colored hide whose origin he had a feeling he didn't want to know, and bound with crisscrossed leather thongs. "Amazing."

"I don't know much about Norse mythology," Billi said, "but I do damn well know the old sagas don't say anything about trolls having *guns*."

"They must have gotten them from the Eskimos we tangled with," Rafe said. "God knows how they convinced them to stick with bows and arrows and let them have the guns."

"Who knows what cunning lies the Tornit tell?" Number One said.

"Trolls," Shrewsbury said. His leg had been bound, he had regained consciousness, and he now sat with his back to a rock and his leg stretched before him. "Who would have imagined? Actual trolls. *Trolls*."

"You're starting to sound like Rafe," Billi said.

The Germans had scavenged foodstuffs, weapons, and ammunition from Kurt Hoff, collected a few personal items to take back to his family; he had a wife and a son and a daughter living with his in-laws in Munich. Rafe wondered just how his comrades would explain what happened to his family. Come to that, he wondered how any of them were going to explain any of this to anybody.

Well, maybe we won't have to, he thought. *We're not out of this yet.*

The Eskimos had finished weeping over poor Qavianguaq, so happy, willing, and inexperienced—and some over Pualuna, whose initial mourning had been delayed by the press of sheer survival. They and Rafe rigged up a rude travois out of rope and troll pole arms to carry the professor on. Shrewsbury could no longer walk.

Now they were examining the booty of the fight. The Eskimos left that part to Rafe and the Germans; they were none too keen on handling human corpses, and aside from the fact that these were evil-tainted Tornit bodies, they smelled horrible. The outlanders weren't exactly eager for the task, but they wanted to learn what they could of these impossible beings.

It wasn't much. The trolls were decked out in a bewilderingly random array of armor, skins, bits and pieces of modern machine-loomed fabrics. They, themselves, were none too uniform, seeming to come in an assortment of sizes, shapes, and complexions. Some were smooth-skinned, some scaled, some had hair on their heads or sprouting in tufts from various parts of their bodies, and most seemed to have a marked greenish or bluish cast. Beyond that they showed no particular point of similarity except that they were all pretty ugly.

"Imagine what we must look like to them," Rafe mused, gazing thoughtfully down at a century-worn gold coin in his hand.

"Why?" Kampfer asked. He wore his damaged arm in a sling and made a brave show of pretending it didn't hurt.

Rafe made a face and flipped the coin. It landed with the reverse uppermost, displaying the heraldic image of a stallion rampant and the legend, *Mundus vult decipi.* He nodded and tucked it into a pocket.

He turned to face the others. "Folks, I have to admit I'm unsure where we go from here."

They stared at him. "Why, we press on, of course," Shrewsbury said. "Whatever else might we do?"

"Go back."

"Even your sense of humor isn't strange enough for me to think you're joking," Billi said, sitting next to Shrewsbury. "So you'd better explain yourself."

"Too much dying, too much killing. I'm beginning to wonder if the game is worth the candle."

Everyone stared at him as though he'd started speaking in tongues. "G-go back?" sputtered the professor. "Preposterous."

"Rafe, what's gotten into you?" Billi asked, shaking her head.

"We've lost five men since we came to Greenland. Brummbär Bauer never made it out of Germany—"

"You'd throw away their deaths, then?" demanded Waldmann.

"You think maybe getting more people killed off will bring them back somehow, Oberführer?"

He sat down on a rock. "There's something else. These beings are pretty manlike, tool users, possessed of intelligence on a roughly human level. I'm not happy about charging in and killing lots of them just because they've got something and we want it."

"I didn't notice you being very backward about that during the fight," Passauer said sullenly.

Rafe nodded. "When somebody shoots at me, I shoot back. That doesn't mean I go looking for people to shoot at me so I can plug them."

"Rafe," Billi said, "we're not the conquistadors riding in on a village of simple, happy, pastoral trolls. These people —these creatures—aren't innocents. Wasn't that human skin on the stock of that rifle you were looking at? And, anyway . . . they started it."

"Billi, you start killing people because they aren't nice, it gets mighty hard to know where to stop. And after a while maybe you don't look so nice yourself." He shook his head, which was displaying a tendency to hang on the weary muscles of his neck. "And, speaking of people who aren't so nice, do you really want to go on with this just so Reichsheini Himmler will have his very own, genuine, certified one-hundred-percent-authentic mythical artifact?"

That got everyone shouting at everybody else. Waldmann's face looked like an eggplant. Professor Shrewsbury's cheeks showed more color than they had in a week at the hint that they might not press on the last few miles. He'd devoted his life to Norse mythology, and here it was turning real before his eyes, and only death was going to keep him from seeing what lay at the base of that smoldering mountain. Kampfer just looked sad and perplexed that this man he so ardently desired to hero-worship had found yet another way to disappoint him.

Black Peter Dietrich, the intellectual ex-miner, backed Rafe. Billi sat there while the professor bubbled and spouted like an alchemist's retort, the corners of her green eyes turned more than usually down, gloomily smoking a cigarette.

"You've made your point, Rafe," Billi said, "and I want to agree with you. I can't even make myself say anything that begins, 'We've come all this way...'"

"*I* can," Kampfer put in.

She ignored him. "But there's something—*someone*—inside me saying we have to keep going. I don't know who or what it is, but I can't ignore it, so with you or without you *I'm* going ahead."

One of the ravens had gone flapping off toward the deep pass through the mountains that led to the tallest peak. The other had been perched on the chest of a dead troll, appearing to listen to the proceedings with interest. Now it spread its wings and hopped onto Rafe's right shoulder, looking at him as if contemplating taking a chunk from his ear.

Rafe eyed the bird sidelong. "Are you Hugin or Munin?" he asked. At the second name the bird nodded twice, in the encouraging but not overemphatic fashion of someone trying to urge a sixteen-year-old second-grader to leap the awful gulf between *L* and *M*. "Seeing as you're named Memory, is it possible you're trying to jog mine?"

"I say, Rafael, are you actually attempting to converse with a bird?" Shrewsbury said.

The raven looked at him, shook a peremptory wing, and went *skrawk*!

"I think you've just been told to butt out, Melbourne," Billi said.

Rafe regarded the creature. Actually, sitting there talking to a bird struck him as pretty weird too. Even if this was not your common raven off the Kurfürstendamm.

"And you're trying to remind me, in your inimitable way, that what we're trying to take from the trolls doesn't belong to them."

The bird clacked its beak, nodded. "Bingo," Billi said, blowing smoke through her nostrils.

"Whether or not you go on, Almost-a-Person," Number One said urgently, "we have to proceed. That which you seek is what holds the evil ones here. We must wrest it from them if the evil is to go."

"Well . . ." Rafe rubbed his chin. Stubble rasped his palm. "You feel this is pretty important for your people, Number One. And we'll be recovering a stolen item, after all. That lends us a certain moral justification, though I'm not sure it would've satisfied Aquinas."

Ernst Waldmann slung his Mauser. "With you or without you, Herr Springer, I'm going on."

"Oh, I'm with you." An uneasy sidling glance. "Besides, I'm afraid that if I hold out any longer he's going to take out my eye."

The other raven—Hugin, by default—came winging back through dusk dense as fog, skimming low across a hilltop with a low cry. At the same time Uurtamo, who'd been keeping aloof watch on the pass from the ridge top, whistled softly and pointed.

"Company coming," the Freiherr said. "Somebody heard our little party and intends to invite himself."

Black Peter stooped, picked up the end of Shrewsbury's travois, and set the poles on his wide shoulders. "Once again the intellectuals are borne on the backs of the proletariat," he said with a sardonic smile. For once Shrewsbury had no rejoinder.

The others gathered up their packs and weapons and set off.

* * *

The patrol passed at a trot, weapons and accoutrements from a dozen centuries clattering. Loose stones of a dry streambed squeaked under horny feet. Lying on their bellies, peering over the lip of a low bluff, Rafe and Leutnant Kampfer traded looks in the dark. The trolls were nothing if not confident in their domain.

Of course, they had every right to be—not knowing of the aerial reconnaissance provided by the low-flying ravens, who helped the travelers steer clear of their search parties.

The trolls rattled off around a bend in the draw. When they had gone, Rafe and the lieutenant slithered quietly back off the bluff and moved out to rejoin their companions.

As quietly as possible, with Black Peter dragging the professor, they picked their way along the flank of the narrow pass. For about fifty yards to either side of the streambed that ran along its floor the walls of the valley sloped at angles varying from thirty to forty-five degrees. Past that they hurtled up into sheer, mullioned cliffs that rose hundreds of feet.

For a time the German soldier, with Rafe's help, had tried to carry the travois like a stretcher. Shrewsbury himself put a stop to that. "I say, if you keep this up, you'll break an ankle, scrambling across these wretched rocks. And even if you don't, I can't say I fancy being dumped on my head. I'm afraid—" He'd started to say, "afraid you'll have to leave me," but his throat wouldn't pass the words.

"Can't leave here," Number one said flatly. "Them find."

The ravens began to flap and fly at the party from behind, growing more impatient by the second with delay. Rafe shrugged and let down his end of the travois. "Can you manage it yourself?"

Dietrich nodded. "But not quietly," he added.

"The birds can warn us if anyone comes this way," Rafe said.

The mountains grumbled like a vast living organism beneath their feet, and here and there the lava rock gave warmth to the touch. The perpetual stirrings and basso groans, and a distant muffled throbbing like some great steam engine hidden away in the earth, helped cover the noise of their passage. But Rafe was afraid of encountering canny troll sentries familiar enough with the background noise to pick out the sounds the interlopers made like ants on a tablecloth.

Uurtamo, agile as a leopard, led the way. Rafe followed, with Kampfer behind him. Next came Number One, then Waldmann, burly Passauer, Black Peter hauling his working-man's burden with Billi keeping pace, then the other two Eskimos and a watchful Freiherr Chatenois bringing up the rear with the MG34. The little column had an inchworm tendency to stretch out over easy going and bunch on the rough, but that couldn't be helped.

A tortuous quarter mile from the foot of the pass they stopped to catch their breath. "There's a perfectly good path down there at the bottom of the valley," Billi said, gesturing through the boulder behind which they sheltered. "Why don't we follow that? This lava's cutting my feet to shreds."

"How badly do you want to meet the people the path is meant for?" Rafe asked quietly.

"Oh."

The birds uttered low, evil croaks, stirred their wings with rustling sounds. "All right, all right," the Freiherr said, getting to his feet. "You birds are worse than a Prussian drill-master."

Fifteen minutes later they were rounding a gradual bend in the valley, keeping to the rocks well above the tempting path, when Uurtamo stopped and held up a hand. "What is it?" hissed Shrewsbury from the travois. His frustration and shame at being reduced to the state of baggage and his fever-ish desire to confront whatever legendary sights awaited them had him in a virtual frenzy.

"Hush," Billi whispered. "I hear something. It sounds like—" she looked up "—thunder."

Everyone looked up. *"Himmel Herr Gott,"* Waldmann shouted. Crashing chaos rushed down on them like a de-railed train, mocking their attempts at stealth. Rebounding with prodigious splintering bangs from rock to rock, a boulder the size of a Mercedes sedan bounced a final time and arced ten feet over the heads of the scattering travelers, to land with a prodigious thump in the middle of the path.

Staring up, Rafe caught a flash of image that made his head spin: the figure of a man standing on the brink of a cliff right above them, raising a rock two-handed over his head. But the cliff was at least a thousand feet high, and the figure many times larger than any human.

Another boulder finished pounding its way down the mountainside and squashed Hannes Passauer so quickly and completely that he never made a sound. A barrel-sized rock dislodged by its passage struck Waldmann glancingly on the back and sent him tumbling downslope in a miniature avalanche of gravel.

"A stone giant," Shrewsbury breathed as the huge being readied its rock. "Marvelous. Simply marvelous."

"I'm so glad you think so, Mel," Billi said in her driest tones. "You can die happy."

Uurtamo's rifle flowed like quicksilver to his shoulder. He fired. The giant arched back, winding up for a good toss, and then he dropped the rock from his great hands, doubled about himself, and spun back from the verge as the boulder went leaping off like a spastic rabbit down the steep slope, bound for nowhere near the travelers.

"He hit him," Rafe marveled.

"Uurtamo's the best," Black Peter said.

"How could he miss him?" Billi demanded. "It's a giant, for Christ's sake."

"Billi, he was a thousand feet up," Rafe pointed out.

"More to the point, *where* did he hit him?" Shrewsbury asked. "He seemed rather big to be bothered by a puny rifle bullet."

Distance-delayed, a bellow of agony like an oak tree splitting open struck their ears. "Shot him in nuts," Uurtamo explained.

"The Tornit surely heard that," Iggianguaq said.

Chatenois, Olipaluk, and Billi skidded down to where Waldmann lay moaning almost in the trail. He gasped when the Freiherr touched his arm; his right shoulder was broken. But with their help he was able to get to his feet and climb painfully up the slope with his left arm locked around Olipa-luk's thick neck. Painfully the party moved on.

They had just gone far enough to catch sight of a reddish glow spilling around the bend in the valley when the ravens, who had flown ahead, came flapping back in a state of agitation. Kampfer signaled the party to take cover with his good arm, then he, Rafe, and Uurtamo moved rapidly forward to see what had upset the birds.

Around the curve the pass opened up to a flat floor perhaps a hundred yards broad. Across the valley from them the smoking mountain challenged heaven, huge and black, like a monstrous being with many red eyes and a gaping red mouth. The black exudate from its crest covered half the sky.

The three gazed at the mountain in silent wonder. The eyes were vents, a score or more, and the mouth was a great opening at its foot. Yellow torchlight leapt on the rock of the vents and portal, but it danced against a backdrop of pervading red glare that came from a source the onlookers couldn't see. From within the mountain came a multitude of noises, cyclopean gurgles, creaking and clattering, raucous troll voices, and overriding everything a titanic pounding, metallic, that seemed to resonate in their bones.

Sentries stood silhouetted in some of the vents, shadows armed with spears or rifles. A number of trolls moved in and out of the great entryway, engrossed in various errands, but they weren't what tore the watcher's attention from the wonderful, terrible mountain. Forty trolls, heavily armored and bristling with weapons, moved toward them along the path, alert and watchful as though expecting trouble. In front of them crawled a pair of outlandish beings. These were similar to the trolls, but their bodies were diminutive to the point of absurdity, while their heads seemed to consist almost entirely of long, snoutlike muzzles with grotesquely flared nostrils. The creatures snuffled noisily at the rock as they crept over it like beetles.

"They're trying to sniff us out," Rafe said quietly. "Go back and tell the others to get ready for Custer's Last Stand."

Kampfer nodded, melted into the rocks behind. With a single shared glance Uurtamo and Rafe settled themselves into sheltered firing positions overlooking the trail. Nothing left to do but fight until the ammunition ran dry. Rafe suspected he'd be well advised to save the hackneyed last round for himself. He didn't think the trolls would follow the Geneva Accords.

He focused himself along the black barrel of his rifle. Barely thirty yards away, one of the tracking trolls raised its outsized head and seemed to look directly at him. He captured a section of the head in the semicircle of the foresight hood, so that the squinting, wrinkle-wrapped eye seemed to rest on the front blade, and took in the slack of the trigger.

From far behind came the rolling boom of an explosion.

CHAPTER

Twenty-four

The blast was still echoing when a machine gun's roar cut it across like a circular saw. Rifle shots rapped like the hammers of a hundred carpenters. A troll wearing a splendid crested helmet and holding a bolt-action Lee Enfield pointed down the valley, and the patrol set off at a clanking run.

Leaving Uurtamo to hold his position, Rafe practically ran back to the others. "What the hell? Did reinforcements arrive?"

Everyone was staring off in the direction of the valley's mouth, invisible around the curve. "Sounds like it," Dietrich said.

"It sounds like a whole platoon," said Chatenois, cocking his head to the sounds of an enthusiastic firefight, complete with grenade blasts.

"From the rate of fire, that machine gun's an MG34," Rafe said. "You boys have any little secrets you'd like to share? Like sending a rifle regiment to back us up?"

Kampfer was staring up the valley as though trying to force his eyesight through solid rock. Clutching his crushed shoulder, Waldmann barked a laugh. "If we planned to mount a whole invasion, do you think we would have taken such trouble with foreigners like you?"

Shrewsbury cleared his throat. "I say, while everyone is

sitting about discussing our great good fortune, no one seems to be taking advantage of it."

"Good point, Professor," Rafe said.

None of the trolls in sight at the foot of the volcano or standing sentry in the vents appeared to be paying attention to the commotion from the head of the pass. It was likely they couldn't hear it for the noise that beat up out of the mountain like waves of heat. Chatenois set the machine gun up among rocks overlooking the trail just out of sight of the smoking mountain, to cover while the others crossed. They all crossed safely, even Black Peter and the professor, then the Freiherr joined them.

They worked their way up the far wall, along it until they were moving across the face of the black mountain itself. Below them, around the skirt of the mountain, the trolls went about their business, oblivious to their presence. None of them had any particular reason to look this way, and even if they had, the light within the mountain had ruined their night vision so that they were unlikely to make out the shapes edging among the clumps and outcrops of volcanic rock.

The vent nearest them opened out eighty feet above the valley floor. They picked their way to within fifty feet of it, then several of the uninjured members of the group crept forward to investigate.

A troll sentry in mail and helmet stood just inside the vent. He was armed with a spear and shield, no firearm in evidence. "If we want to get a look inside, we've got to take care of him," Rafe observed when they drew back.

Chatenois and Dietrich looked at him. Iggianguaq stood silently to one side. With a sensation inside him like an elevator car with a broken cable, Rafe realized that *he* was the veteran, and these two soldiers, a decade or more younger than he, had never known battle before this trip. And the Eskimo, stealthy, seasoned hunter though he was, wasn't exactly skilled at this sort of furtive murder, either. And *that* left—

"Lend me a knife?" he asked. Chatenois handed him his bayonet. Rafe stood next to the vent and reflected that he didn't really have much experience at this sort of thing, himself. But some.

He tossed a chunk of lava rock onto the ground eight feet below the vent. The sentry stepped forward, coming out onto the slope, spear lowered to the ready. Rafe stepped out behind him, grabbed him by the head, and stuck the bayonet into the side of his neck.

He felt blood cascade over his arm. The troll started thrashing furiously, trying to break free. Rafe sawed the knife from side to side, trying to cut the being's throat and feeling like a real son of a bitch for doing it. The troll dropped his spear and clawed for him.

They toppled, went rolling down the slope. Rank black blood spurted all over Rafe. Trying to cut the being's throat was like trying to cut a cluster of wet, slippery surgical tubing. It horrified him, and the choking, mewling sounds the troll made as it fought for life were worse.

Finally they fetched up against a rock, halfway to the valley floor. Either because it had struck its head or because it had lost enough blood, the troll subsided to lie breathing stertorously and docilely bleeding to death. Rafe crawled a few feet away and was violently ill.

Everybody came up to peer into the vent. Professor Shrewsbury moved his lips like a communicant at prayer. Billi clung to his arm. The Eskimos muttered excitedly at each other. A thick stink of sulfur made everyone's eyes water.

Waldmann summed it up. "It's real. The whole crackpot story is true."

They looked out over an immense cavern. The far wall was striated with catwalks hewn out of stone and honeycombed with tunnel mouths. Trolls scurried across an irregular floor lower than the valley bottom, black stone polished by myriad feet and gleaming in the light of torches in twisted iron sconces like Art Nouveau gone wrong. That hellacious red glare welled up from molten stone bubbling in a fumarole in the floor's center.

Above the lava pit squatted a humanoid figure that must have stood twenty feet or more when erect. It was naked and hairless, and the ever so slightly translucent skin was a red that seemed illuminated from within. A pair of horns swept upward from its temples. As they watched, dumbfounded, it drew a glowing ingot of metal as long as a man from the lava with a pair of tongs, laid it on a large, flat rock and began to forge it with a huge hammer. The sound of that forging threatened to burst their eardrums.

They pulled back. Shrewsbury stared at Rafe with lemur's eyes. "This is fantastic, utterly fantastic. A fire-giant, possibly even Surt himself." He shook himself. "I'd say this was a dream come true, except I've never dared dream anything so farfetched. Actually to encounter creatures from the legends I've studied for so long—"

"Could be the death of us all, Melbourne," Billi reminded him.

"Not much doubt Gungnir's in there," Rafe said, pulling back. The heat washing off the lava raised a sweat even up here. "The problem is where to find it."

"We could always ask someone," Chatenois suggested facetiously.

Rafe nodded. "We could, at that."

Twenty minutes later an unarmed middle-sized troll came sauntering along the catwalk. It noticed that the sentry was missing from his usual position. Thinking the sentry had slipped into the darkness to get drunk, the creature stepped forward to the edge of the light.

Black Peter Dietrich's huge fist wrapped itself in the front of his leather jerkin and yanked him on out into the night, where Billi laid him out with the butt of a Mauser. They bundled their malodorous captive up and carted him off into the rocks.

He proved to be able to speak a crude dialect of Greenland Eskimo. It didn't take much effort to persuade him to do so. Perhaps the shock of being plucked right out of the stronghold of his kind unnerved him. Or maybe he didn't have a lot of intestinal fortitude.

"Yes, we have spear," he said in a voice reminiscent of a dog's snarling. "Steal from One-Eyed Enemy many year ago. Hide here, out of own world."

"Surely you must have known you'd be, ah, traced by the spear's rightful owner," Shrewsbury said.

"Aesir no come here. Valley protected by strong magic. Outside own world, One-Eye not have much power, not smart like troll."

"Where is it?" Waldmann asked. Rafe translated.

The troll looked stubborn. He had a wide, flat face, more humanoid than some, but no nose to speak of beyond two vertical slits in his face. Judging from his breath, he would have found the taste of *kiviaq* insipid. "Why I should tell you?"

Black Peter held up a broad-bladed knife. "Because we'll kill you if you don't."

"It's in the armory," the creature said promptly. "Go down tunnel . . ." He sketched a route he claimed would take them to the chamber where Gungnir was kept.

"Well, that was certainly simple," Billi said. "So much for modern police interrogation techniques."

"I'd think you'd be pleased we didn't find it necessary to resort to those," Waldmann said.

Billi frowned. "You know, I'm finding out a lot about myself on this jaunt . . . and I don't know if I like everything I learn. You could have treated this critter a lot worse, and I would have gone along with it. That makes me ashamed." She brightened. "On the other hand, *most* of what I'm finding out is convincing me I'm pretty damned swell."

"Good for you," Rafe said without irony. He looked at the troll. "Just for the record, if you've steered us wrong, one of us will survive long enough to kill you."

The troll squirmed in his bonds and swore on the genitals of various prominent troll personages that he was telling the truth. Not all the names were familiar to Rafe, and the professor scribbled madly in a pocket notebook.

"Dear God, the monograph I'll write," he said, eyes fever-bright. "I don't dare submit it for publication, but it will make my biographers' hair stand on end when they root through my effects."

They bound the troll still more securely, gagged him with Billi's handkerchief so his sharpened teeth would have trouble working on the sealskin straps, and stashed him behind a chunk of lava. "Now our only problem is, how do we get in?" Rafe said. "We can't reach the entrance to the tunnel leading to the armory without crossing a hundred feet of open floor."

"Acolyte's robes," Billi said.

Everybody looked at her. "I beg your pardon," Waldmann said.

"Acolyte's robes. In the serials the heroes always hit the devil cultists over the head, then infiltrate their temple wearing their robes with the hoods pulled up."

"When did you ever see serials?" Rafe demanded.

"Wilhel—Billi," Shrewsbury said gently, "may I remind you we haven't *seen* any trolls wearing hooded robes? They wear armor or crude clothing, or go naked."

"Betrayed again by popular culture." She shook her head. "When we get back, I'm entering a convent."

"Billi!"

"Just kidding, just kidding."

"Armor." Freiherr Chatenois tugged at his narrow chin. "Pity we didn't scavenge some from the patrol we shot up."

"I didn't see you volunteering to carry the smelly stuff," Billi said. The young Alsatian laughed.

"There's the sentry Herr Springer killed," Dietrich pointed out. "Perhaps we could take care of a few more, outfit several of us—"

Rafe gagged. "It would take too much time, and it would increase the risk of our being found out here," Waldmann said. His voice was strained; as his adrenaline levels fell off, pain flooded into his injured shoulder.

"Herr Springer could put on the armor, at least."

"I hope you're not suggesting I could pass for a troll, there, Dietrich."

"It's pretty dark in there," Billi said. "The lava and the torches don't give off that much light, and there are plenty of protrusions to cast nice big shadows. Besides"—she touched his jawline with her fingertips, turned his head a few degrees—"in a certain light you *do* sort of look—"

"I haven't slugged a woman in several years, Billi. I'd like to keep my streak going."

"Right, Captain Springer, sir."

Number One, who was managing to follow the gist of the

conversation largely through intuition, said in English, "Man think he see seal, he see seal; don't look closer 'less he hunt him."

"Which means nobody'll give you a second glance," Billi supplied.

Feeling put upon, Rafe, with Dietrich's help, stripped the mail byrnie from the dead sentry. Reeking black gore had begun to clot on the woven links in front. "Good thing hygiene isn't these trolls' strong suit," Billi observed as Rafe shrugged the metal garment on.

He made a couple of carp-gulps, swallowing air to try to keep from throwing up again. The stink of the byrnie was enough to kill the hair in his nostrils. "Who's coming with me?" he asked, tucking the helmet under his arm.

Number One stepped forward. "I'm coming," Kampfer said. The two *Jägers* jostled each other getting to their feet.

"You can't both come. Somebody has to help watch the wounded and give us covering fire."

The two drew straws. Black Peter won. "Damned Bolshevik," Chatenois grumbled.

"You're going down armed with just a pistol, Leutnant?" Rafe asked. "You sure can't work a bolt-action rifle with that busted wing."

Kampfer grinned. "I've got something even better." He muttered something to Chatenois, and the two retreated to one side.

"So how are we going to disguise ourselves—the rest of us, that is?" Billi asked.

"*We?*" Rafe asked.

"You don't think I'd miss this one, buster? What do you think I've been kidnapped, shot at, and possessed by spirits, not to mention tramping across a thousand miles of ice for?"

Rafe sighed. "Fine with me." He forbore to point out she'd exaggerated the distance by a factor of ten. It *felt* like a thousand miles. "But we don't have any disguise other than this goddam armor you made me wear. We trust to the bad lighting, and when that or our luck plays out, we run like hell and shoot anything that moves."

"Spoken like a true hero, Rafe. I knew you had it in you."

He showed her his teeth.

Shrewsbury struggled further upright. "Billi, I absolutely forbid—"

She looked past him, out across the floor of the valley, where trolls by dozens scurried about their affairs unaware of what was going on in the rocks overhead. "I didn't hear you, Melbourne. It's just as well, because I have a strong suspicion that if I had, the engagement would be off, and we'd have to settle for a mere beautiful friendship."

The professor dropped his eyes. "You—you're right. I have to accept you for what you are. After all, what you are is why I . . . love you."

She leaned forward, kissed him quickly on the cheek. "I wondered if you'd ever get around to saying that. I love you, too, Professor—Melbourne."

"I hate to interrupt you lovebirds," Leutnant Kampfer said, stepping up, "but we'd best be moving. I'm ready."

Rafe looked at him. "You're out of your mind."

The Lieutenant wore the MG34 around his neck on a sling long enough that the heavy weapon rested horizontal at the level of his right hip. The curious double drums of a seventy-five-round saddle magazine hung to either side of the receiver. "Oh, no, Rafe," he said cheerfully. "This isn't like one of the old-fashioned water-cooled guns you needed a mule to lug around. It was designed to serve as an assault weapon."

"A damned heavy one," Rafe said, "and for someone with all his hands. You're never going to control that son of a bitch."

Kampfer shrugged. "Who needs much control? I'll be shooting at close range. And I daresay the trolls might not be too happy about facing an automatic weapon. They don't seem to have any themselves."

"Shouldn't we emplace the gun on the catwalk, to cover you crossing the floor?" old soldier Waldmann asked.

Chatenois scratched his cowlick. "We have grenades and magazine rifles for that. And if they run into trolls in the corridor—" He shrugged. "That *Maschinengewehr* could prove a quite efficient broom to sweep the path clean."

"What the hell." Rafe tried the helmet on, winced as it cut into his skull, put it against a rock and stomped on it until it conformed a bit better to the shape of his head. He pulled it on. "We can't stand here all night arguing. Let's go."

CHAPTER
Twenty-five

The black lava catwalk zigzagged crazily down into the cavern. Steps hewn into the porous stone joined it at intervals, leading from the vents. Here and there rooms opened onto the walkway, naturally occurring bubbles or chambers rudely hollowed out by troll artisans.

"Haven't they ever heard of safety rails?" Billi grumbled as they picked their way down the uneven path. The weird, ever-shifting light made the footing especially treacherous.

Kampfer walked in the lead, since if they were discovered, he was best equipped to clear the way for them—and no one wanted to be in *front* of him when he cut loose one-handed with that thing. Dietrich walked behind, holding his rifle across his belly, then Number One, Billi, and Olipaluk —though not the shot Uurtamo was, blocky Iggianguaq was marksman enough to be of most use covering from above. Finally, Rafe stumped along in the rear, with the shield slung over his back and his own Mauser in his hands. He hoped vaguely that if anybody noticed the distinctly nontrollish appearance of the others, they would take them for prisoners.

Since they were blatantly armed, that wasn't much of a possibility, he had to admit. *What the hell, a man's entitled to dream*. They had to play the hand they'd been dealt.

To his astonishment at least, it seemed to be a good one. Whether hammering away on anvils next to the fumarole, or scurrying this way and that in response to commands delivered by the giant in a voice like boulders grating together, or just bustling across the floor on whatever errands trolls did, none of them glanced up. Either they were an incurious lot, or nothing new had happened in Trollville time out of mind. *If that's the case,* Rafe thought, *we'll be doing them a service. Things are about to liven up no end in these parts.*

He was just thinking how glad he was that they wouldn't be passing closer than a hundred feet from the two-story fire-giant when a squatty little blue troll popped out of a cubbyhole and stuck a short spear into Peter Dietrich's belly. The soldier gasped, grabbed the shaft, his big blue jaw locked against agony, the muscles standing out in relief from his columnlike neck with the effort it took him not to cry out. He took two steps backward and fell off the walkway.

He plummeted thirty feet without making a sound. Unfortunately he landed on a troll in a leather apron. The troll trotting at its side dropped the scrolls it held under its arm and screamed like a soprano klaxon. Many, many heads turned to look.

Rafe shot the troll who'd speared Black Peter before it could duck back. Kampfer was already bounding down the ramp at breakneck speed, the others running behind. The lieutenant hit the final switchback, turned, saw half a dozen trolls crowded at the foot of the walkway, trying to elbow their way up to attack the intruders. He aimed at their feet and pulled the trigger.

Trolls screamed in terror and pain as the first burst skipped off the stone and scythed through their legs. As the muzzle rode up, Kampfer fired another burst, and two trolls came apart as though hit by a buzzsaw. Three fled, leaving two more writhing in pools of blood, legs broken.

Kampfer hit the floor at the run with the others behind him as a grenade exploded in the lava pit, spattering gobbets of white-hot stone for twenty feet. Workers scattered. The fire-giant dropped a huge stone ladle and fell over, batting at itself and squalling in a hurricane voice. Apparently live lava was too much even for a fire-giant.

Taken utterly by surprise, trolls ran in all directions, most of them not knowing what the hell was going on. Rafe saw one who did aim a rifle at them from the far side of the room, tried to bring up his own weapon in time, knowing with sick certainty he was too late. The creature's head snapped back as a bullet from Uurtamo's rifle drilled through its skull, and the rifle barrel dropped and blasted a shot into the rock at the being's feet. The ricochet screamed over the heads of the five humans as they ran flat out for the floor-level tunnel that led to the armory.

A troll hurtled down from the catwalks on the far side of the cavern, his rifle turning lazy cartwheels by his side; the riflemen up in the vent were on the job. Rafe and the others scattered shots to both sides as they ran, aiming at nothing but increasing the trolls' confusion. Another grenade lobbed from above went off somewhere to the right as Kampfer popped into the tunnel mouth.

The others followed. Illuminated by dispirited lamps that gave off the distinctive fishy stink of seal oil, the tunnel was clear for thirty feet until it curved out of sight. Panting, Rafe cranked open his Mauser's bolt and began stuffing in fresh cartridges.

"It can't be this easy," Billi said, reloading her own weapon. "Nobody's even following us."

Rafe grinned at her, teeth shocking white in his smudged face. "Would you?"

"Come on," Kampfer urged with a jerk of his head.

They pelted down the passageway, their footsteps echoing around them. As described by the helpful captive, the tunnel described a hundred-yard S-curve; the five peered at the low, round-topped doorways to both sides as they passed, trying to decide behind which one the armory might lie.

A party of trolls came around the bend toward them, not forty feet ahead. Kampfer opened up. Billi let her rifle drop to hang from her arm by the sling and slapped her hands over her ears to shut out the hideous racket.

Supported by its sling and one hand, the machine gun wasn't terribly accurate. But then, it didn't have to be. Chips and black lava dust peppered the trolls, and they turned and ran, leaving two lying on the rough floor. The flame and blast and richochets shrieking past their pointed ears must have seemed as fantastic to them as the fire-giant outside seemed to the humans.

Number One paused to cut the throat of a still moving troll as they passed. Billi swallowed hard but didn't complain. By now she knew she didn't want live enemies between them and the door, even hurt ones.

"By God, the monster told the truth." The passage had opened up into a vaulted chamber at least twenty feet high and twenty wide. Letting the MG hang, Kampfer stood before a huge double door of oak, feeling the crudely dressed wood with his hand.

He tried a big latch of black iron, set in a thick iron plate. "Locked. Stand back, everybody."

"You're not thinking of—" Billi began.

He raised the machine gun so its muzzle was two inches from the wood next to the latch plate, fired a burst. The gun reared back like a randy stallion. "I always wanted to do this," the lieutenant grinned.

He lowered the unwieldy weapon, fired again while the others cowered unashamedly at the mouth of the chamber. The machine gun didn't make a very good saw, but it ripped hell out of the wood. After several bursts the door was pretty well splintered next to the plate. It sagged when Kampfer kicked it, sprang open on the second try.

He led the way inside. The chamber inside was big, oil lamps dribbling light grudgingly across rack upon rack of weapons of all descriptions, from halberds to magazine rifles of Great War vintage. "So how do we recognize Gungnir?" Kampfer asked.

Billi was shaking her head as if that would clear her ears of the ringing the machine gun blasts had left. "You don't think they'd just hang it on a rack with the everyday stuff, do you? Try that door to the left."

To Rafe's relief—Kampfer could use his field-expedient power saw trick only so many times before a round bounced back and killed somebody—it was unlocked. The next chamber was just like the first but smaller. "Next door," Rafe said.

Kampfer threw it open. He, Rafe, and Billi crowded through—and froze.

It was a chamber identical to the last, except for one
detail. In a man-high niche chiseled high in the far wall
stood a spear, held upright by iron staples. Its six-foot shaft
was gleaming ash wood, its broad, leaf-shaped head white
metal that glowed with a blue-white light of its own.

"*Gungnir,*" Billi breathed. "Jesus Christ, it's *real.*"

"Ought to be ostentatious enough even for old Heinrich,"
Rafe commented. They stepped into the room—then noticed
the other detail in which this chamber differed from the last.
A small, stooped, and evidently quite deaf troll in a dirty
white smock sat hunched over a writing desk, scribbling
away at a ledger with a pen carved of bone.

It looked up, saw them, leapt from its stool, and spun to
grab at a rack of rifles on the wall behind the desk. Number
One shot him in the back. He uttered a hoarse cry and fell to
the basalt flagging.

Curious, Billi bent over him. His pointed skull was
fringed with stringy white hair. "Poor thing. He was just an
old guy."

"Old man with gun, Aningaaq Pania," Number One said.

Rafe stood below the spear, gazing up. The blade's shine
bathed his face in harsh light. An acrid smell of burned
powder and gun oil tickled the back of his throat.

"Don't think I can reach it," he said. "Olipaluk, Leutnant, watch the door. Billi, put your gun down and climb up
on my shoulders. See if you can get it."

"How am I supposed to get it out of those brackets?"

"Maybe you can wiggle it out. Or pry it loose with a
knife. Come *on.* We don't have all night."

Looking doubtful, she laid her Mauser down. Rafe hunkered. She clambered up on his back. Steadying herself on a
weapon rack, she got to her feet with her boot soles resting
on his shoulders.

"I'm sure glad you don't have hobnails," he said. Leaving his own rifle on the floor, he caught hold of her ankles
and slowly straightened.

Billie reached. "I can't get it. It's just beyond my fingertips."

"Stand on tiptoe."

"Doesn't work. You try standing on—"

A sound from the door made her turn with her fingers still quivering two inches from the butt of the ashen haft. A scaled blue hand with talons like black sickle blades was clamped over Olipaluk's face, and a blue arm reached over his shoulder, claws sunk into his thick jacket. His struggles made no impression on the eight-foot monstrosity stooping in the doorway. Its shoulder muscles writhed under heavy blue scutes, and it tore Olipaluk's head from his shoulders as though picking a ripe fruit from a vine.

It tossed the head contemptuously aside, let the blood-geysering body fall. It looked like a great, tailless iguana that walked on its hind legs, head a nightmare of spined crests, rubbery lips peeled back to reveal a mouthful of pointed teeth two inches long. It produced a strange, shrill tittering sound and took a step into the weapons room.

Kampfer stuck the muzzle of the MG34 in under the greyhound-great rib cage and pulled the trigger. Bullets screamed off the wall behind it and splintered spear hafts in their rack.

The creature's tyrannosaur grin widened. It tittered again. A hand lashed out and swatted the machine gun from Kampfer's hands, bending the barrel as if it were a New Year's noisemaker made of cardboard. A backhanded blow knocked the lieutenant flying into a rack of pole arms. He slumped.

It took a step toward Rafe and Billi. Number One interposed himself, breaking his Mauser butt across its face to no effect. It batted him aside, eyes locked on Billi's. They were enormous eyes, night stalker's eyes, fire yellow with barred pupils like a goat's. Eyes that lusted with no hunger she could bring herself to name.

She screamed with a throat already raw from screams she'd never heard, launched herself from Rafe's shoulders in a desperate leap. Her fingers closed around Gungnir's shaft.

The spear leapt out of the niche, ripping the heavy staples right out of the lava wall. Billi dropped it as she fell. When her feet hit, she let her legs fold beneath her and rolled, tucking herself into a ball to take the fall.

The monster lunged at her. Rafe threw himself in a body block at its legs. It kicked him aside. He grabbed a short sword off the rack and lunged for it, swinging. It blocked the blow with its bare arm. The steel refused to bite.

The creature plucked the weapon by the blade from Rafe's hand, stuck it in its mouth, and bit it in two. Sweating heavily, Rafe backed away. It swung at him with raking claws. He danced back in time to avoid disembowelment, but the long black claws had slashed the mail like wet tissue paper.

"Run, Billi," he shouted past the thing. "I'll try to hold it." But even as he spoke, it swung away from him, heavy head pivoting to seek out Billi with those terrible eyes.

She cowered against the wall with Gungnir lying several feet away. The monster advanced on her, step by step. The eyes held hers like hooks. She felt a strange psychic pulling, as though the monster were trying to tear her soul out of her body.

A Mauser roared. The bullet passed through the thing's chest and shattered on stone above Billi's head. Cursing, Rafe worked the bolt. Bending forward, the creature reached for Billi.

She lunged for the shining spear, grabbed it. She thought it would be too heavy to lift, but it whirled up as if of its own accord, point toward the massive scaled chest. The monster recoiled, "You *bastard,*" Billi screamed, and thrust.

The point sank in as though the monster's chest were cheese. "Oh, God," she moaned, thinking that the horror's flesh would pass the spear blade as easily as it did bullets.

Instead the horror staggered back. Gungnir seemed to draw Billi along with it. The creature grasped the haft just behind the glowing head. The blue flesh smoked. The blade's gleam began to grow, mounted to intolerable actinic brilliance. The creature threw back its vast, misshapen head and shrieked.

And crumbled away to blue-gray ashy dust.

The terrible glow died. Gungnir's point clashed on the floor.

Rafe took the spear from Billi's trembling hand. "That was heroic, Billi."

She shooked her head. "The spear—the spear did it—"

Her nails bit into her cheeks. Her spirit still seemed tenuously moored within her.

"The spear of Odin, which never fails in the attack and never stops attacking until the foe is vanquished. Or words to that effect. But you had the courage to use it, Billi. Without a hand to wield it, even Gungnir's useless."

Groaning, Kampfer picked himself up off the floor. Billi helped Number One to his feet. He grinned at her like a monkey. "*Eee*, Aningaaq Pania, I was right! You are truly one of us."

"That only leaves several thousand trolls between us and the outside," Kampfer observed. He drew his Luger, thumbed down the safety. "At least bullets work on *them*." He cast a last look at the MG34 lying twisted and ruined on the floor, shook his head, and walked toward the corridor.

Number One stood a moment over Olipaluk's headless body, tears rolling down his weather-cured cheeks. Retrieving her rifle, Billi came to him, touched his arm. Then they fled the chamber.

To their relief they encountered no more trolls in the S-shaped passageway. A din of battle echoed to them from the great cavern. "Sounds like our friends are still holding on," Rafe commented as they rounded the final bend at a run.

And stopped. Two huge clawed feet stood just outside the tunnel's mouth, two muscle-knotted thighs rising out of sight like red banyan trunks.

The fire-giant had them trapped like mice.

CHAPTER

Twenty-six

"Give me the spear," Billi said.

Rafe held it away from her outreached hand. "Whoa, just a minute, here. Let's not do anything hasty."

"Give me the goddam spear. It made short work of that other hoodoo. Let's see what it does to that horned joker."

"That other hoodoo wasn't twenty-odd feet tall."

"Listen, this is Odin's Spear. It doesn't stop till it wins, remember?"

"We don't know all the fine print, Billi. What happens if its wielder dies in the middle of the fight? If it could act totally of its own accord, do you think it would have spent the last eight or ten centuries hanging on a wall being a troll trophy?"

She jutted her lip. Number One laid a hand on her shoulder. "Listen to him, Aningaaq Pania. Stout though your heart may be, you have not the strength to overcome such a foe as this, even with a magical weapon."

She pulled away. "Oh, you're just being a *man*."

"No. My magic tells me this."

Kampfer cocked his head. "Listen." His face was grave.

From behind came a raucous babble of voices, the metal crackle of firearm actions being worked. "Well, the cavalry's arrived," Rafe said. "Unfortunately it's on the wrong side."

"You must get the spear away from here at all costs,"

Number One said. "Tell my wife I sorrow that I could not return to her."

Before the others could react, he bolted out of the tunnel and straight between the fire-giant's legs. Once past the creature, he turned, raised his rifle, and shot it in the ass. Its bellow made dust fly out of the tunnel walls, and the Eskimo darted aside with an agility that belied his years, as a hand like a steam-shovel scoop raked the spot where he'd stood, the nails raising sparks off stone.

Number One's Mauser cracked again, and once more a bellow answered it. "He'll be killed," Billi shouted.

Rafe was slinging his rifle so he could hold the spear in one hand and his pistol in the other. "*Don't you think he knows that?*"

Behind them, the tunnel flooded with armed and shouting trolls. They ran.

Number One was leading the giant a merry chase off in the general direction of the fumarole. His magazine was empty now, and at every shot he pulled a fresh cartridge from his sealskin pouch and crammed it up the Mauser's breech. The eight-millimeter bullets could have been no more than hornet stings to the fire-giant, but hornet stings *hurt*. He had the being's undivided attention.

Billi grabbed Rafe's arm, pointed off toward the vent through which they'd entered the cavern. Several dozen trolls were trying to fight their way up the catwalk to get at their companions. The foremost attackers were shooting from behind a heap of bodies not twenty yards from the vent, while others huddled behind them. As Rafe watched, Chatenois leaned around and tossed a stick grenade over the barricade of corpses. The blast projected three trolls screaming from the walkway, and the soldier ducked back from a hail of bullets.

Iggianguaq and Uurtamo were popping around the edge of the vent to shoot and dodge back to safety. Less agile, Shrewsbury and Waldmann scattered rifle shots among the trolls running hysterically for cover on the floor or trying to shoot from the tunnel mouths on the far wall. The professor saw the three—Billi, Rafe, and Kampfer—pointed and waved.

A troll blundered into Rafe from his blind side, squeaked, ran as fast as he could in a different direction. A shot from the tunnel mouth behind cracked past Rafe's ear, making him duck belatedly.

"Where do we go?" Kampfer shouted.

"The portal—we'll never get up that walkway!"

"We'll never make it," the young German said.

Billi jerked her thumb at the trolls streaming out of the tunnel they'd vacated. "I don't think they're in a mood to negotiate." She started running for the yawning cavern mouth.

The others followed. They saw the fire-giant stalking the impertinent Eskimo around the rim of the fumarole. Number One kept the bubbling pit between the furious giant and himself and kept stinging its thick hide with rifle shots.

From a large tunnel on the far side of the lava pit appeared a large party of trolls. They trotted forward to cut off the travelers, their manner distressingly businesslike. "We're not going to make it," Rafe panted.

Far above, Uurtamo stepped out onto the catwalk, cocked his arm, threw. It was a beautiful lob, the height from which the grenade was thrown permitting it to sail a good eighty yards. It bounced in front of the fresh squad of trolls, bounced, began vomiting dense white smoke.

"Smoke grenade!" Kampfer yelled. They redoubled their pace. Chatenois lay on his stomach in full view of the trolls behind the barricade, driving shot after shot into their faces as Uurtamo primed another smoke grenade and threw it.

The charging trolls faltered, seeming fearful of the smoke. Several fired at the fleeing humans, but the smoke was already drifting across their field of fire, hampering their aim. The second bomb landed, added its own white billows to the smoke screen.

The Finn reared back to hurl a third grenade. A troll rose up behind the barricade and shot him through the throat. He pitched off the catwalk and fell a hundred feet to the cavern floor. The grenade went off beside him, shrouding him in smoke like a flameless pyre. Chatenois rolled back into the cover of the rocky wall as bullets cratered the catwalk about him.

The Finn's sacrifice had served its purpose. They reached the ramp leading up to the cavern mouth behind thick curtains of smoke. Their firearms scattered the few trolls there in all directions, and they plunged up to the verge of night.

Though the outside air was vastly warmer than the frigid air of the ice cap, it seemed bitterly cold after the hot brimstone-laden air of the cave. "Number One!" Billi yelled. She turned back in time to see through a rift in the smoke as the fire-giant reached down, caught up the hogshead-sized ladle, and plunged it into the lava. Before Number One could move, it dashed a great blob of molten stone onto the shaman.

Billi shut her eyes till the muscles at the back of her neck quivered with the strain, squeezed both hands hard on the stock of the rifle.

"Here come the trolls," Rafe said, hoarse with exertion and emotion. They fled the glare of the cave entrance, went flying down the valley as fast as they could run.

Something flashed up out of the rocks, straight at Rafe's face. He whipped up the .45 and fired. An outraged squawk echoed the gunshot, and a raven settled down at his feet, aggrievedly shaking a wing pierced by the bullet.

"Sorry," Rafe said. "But you shouldn't jump out at a man like that." It made a rude-sounding noise.

An answering cry came from upslope, and the three looked that way to see Chatenois and Iggianguaq helping the two injured men clamber down to the trail. "Is it safe to follow the path now?" Billi wanted to know.

"The birds herded us down here once you reached the cave mouth, Fräulein," the Freiherr said. "They haven't steered us wrong yet."

"Where's Dietrich?" Shrewsbury demanded. "And Olipaluk and Number One?"

"Dead," Rafe said.

"Dear God."

A bullet cracked off a rock nearby and bansheed off into the night. "No time for mourning just yet," Rafe said as armed trolls poured out of the cavern. He and Billi each got one of the professor's arms around their shoulders, and they set off briskly, the professor sort of poling along with his good leg. The punctured bird perched on Shrewsbury's fore-arm next to Rafe's left ear, while its comrade winged over-head.

Periodically Freiherr Chatenois and Iggianguaq paused to fire back at the pursuers, to keep them from getting too en-thusiastic. Slowly they gained on the trolls.

"Say," puffed Billi, as the valley opened up before them, revealing the dark foothills beyond, "that damned Viking map talks about fabulous treasures."

"That's—true, my dear," the professor said, wincing as his dragging foot banged a rock.

"Well, *I* never saw any fabulous goddam treasure. All I saw were rooms full of rusty old weapons and one magic spear."

"And a monster," added Rafe.

"Well, yes, a monster," she agreed. Shrewsbury looked from one to the other, then realized they probably weren't daft, after all. "But I definitely wouldn't call *him* a treas-ure."

"No doubt you missed the treasure rooms," Shrewsbury said.

Billi moaned. "And I had my heart set on finding some nice jewelry—nothing fancy, a modest solid-gold torc, say, or an emerald-studded broach made of electrum."

Rafe tipped his head forward to look at her. "You can always go back."

She glared at him. "Spoilsport."

They left the valley at last. "Now we can find places to hide from our pursuit if we have to," Waldmann said. Even in the starlight his face was an unhealthy gray.

With a sharp cry the raven jumped from Rafe's shoulder and went hopping toward a humped boulder thirty feet ahead. The other bird swept down and lighted on the rock.

The "rock" rose. Instead of a boulder it was a man in a wide-brimmed hat, not tall but enormously broad. He wore an ermine-trimmed cloak wrapped around mighty shoulders, on one of which a raven perched. The second bird fluttered up to the other. The stranger stepped forward, smiling through his gray-shot black beard. Starlight danced in his single eye.

"Thank you for recovering my property," he said in a voice as deep as the roots of the mountains.

They stopped. "Odin, of course," Shrewsbury said. He came forward, using Billi's rifle as a cane. "I suppose I guessed quite a long time ago—those ravens, don't you know—but I wouldn't admit the obvious to myself. I'm afraid I didn't think you really existed."

"Oh, I don't." He laughed at their expressions. "Rather I do, but not customarily on your world. Or in your universe, as I gather it's now fashionable to refer to such things."

"Uh, I beg your pardon, Mr. Odin, sir," Billi said, "but I think we'd better be moseying along. There's a little matter of about a thousand trolls baying after our blood, and one very angry fire-giant."

"Fear not," the god said.

"That's easy for you to say," Billi started to say, but Rafe ground his heel on her instep.

"Had that been Surt himself you faced, they might be so bold. But they sense me here. They'll pursue you no farther.

"In fact"—he gestured to the spear Rafe held rather limply in his right hand—"since they've lost Gungnir, they no doubt will quit expending the mystic energy needed to maintain this little slice of *Jötunnheim* in your realm. A clever hiding place, but in the end not clever enough." He shrugged. "Within hours—minutes, perhaps—this whole region of rocks and tundra which so perturbed Mr. Springer will no longer exist. Or, at least, not here."

"You knew the spear was here?" Waldmann said. Odin nodded. "Then why didn't you fetch it yourself?"

The god frowned, and a wind seemed to rise chill about them. Then his great brow smoothed. "You've had a trying experience, so I shall forgive your rudeness and ignorance. Neither I nor the giant kindred possess full powers in your world, which fact you may thank for your lives. The trolls did have power enough to erect wards around their stronghold. I am able to penetrate the outskirts of the land they have translated into your world, but even I could not enter the valley itself. Fortunately mortals could—as well as my friends and valued servants, Hugin and Munin." The ravens preened.

"This is the most incredible moment of my life," Professor Shrewsbury said reverently.

"Yes, it is. Now, if you'd hand over my spear..." He held forth his hand.

"Now just hold on a minute, here," Billi said, stepping forward. A shaggy eyebrow rose. "*We* stole your precious spear back from the trolls. Finders keepers, Mac."

"Billi," Rafe said out of the side of his mouth, "you had enough sense to keep a civil tongue with Heinrich Himmler. This is a *god,* Billi. On't-day ake-may im-hay ad-may."

"To hell with you, Rafe Springer. And to hell with you, too, Odious or Odium or whatever your name is. We sweat blood to get this spear. Melbourne got his leg half amputated, the lieutenant got his arm busted, Herr Waldmann had a rock dropped on him. Eight good men *died*—not even counting poor Count Kinski. What makes you think we should just hand it over?"

The deity seemed to be experiencing difficulty breathing. His eyebrows formed a continuous band of bushy hair above his eyes. "Forgive this young woman, Odin," Professor Shrewsbury said hastily. "She doesn't realize whom she's dealing with."

"Oh, yes I do, Melbourne. This is Odin, chief of the Norse gods, and he doesn't like people to talk back to him. And I don't give a damn. We've been kicking supernatural critters in the fanny pretty damned well today, if I do say so myself. I don't see any reason to stop now."

"*Madre de Dios,*" Rafe said.

Odin's eyes were slits. The divine lips writhed inside the beard; the massive frame shook inside the cloak. The world itself seemed to shake beneath their feet, the ravens spread their wings and voiced dismal, doomful cries, the wind howled round as Odin raised himself to his full height—

—and laughed. "You've got courage, girl," he boomed. "I've always been a god who admires courage."

"I'm not a girl."

He frowned, and she wilted ever so slightly.

"Perhaps I should remind you that you didn't precisely accomplish your task without help—*my* help, to be exact.

I've had my ravens watching over you for quite some time, you know."

"You weren't much bloody help on the train," Billi said, subdued but still game. "Nor in Bremerhaven, for that matter."

"I, myself, entered your world not far from here, and my influence on this plane dwindles with distance from that entry point. At any rate, there was scarcely any way I could have aided you in either of those instances without tipping my hand—as well as causing you a good deal of embarrassment. And you came through both splendidly without my assistance, I might add."

He looked at Rafe. "I was able to render your Mr. Springer here far more tangible help on the ship—you really must get him to tell you truth about that knot on his head, someday." Rafe gazed off across the landscape, as if hoping to spot Halley's Comet coming back early to surprise everyone.

"I tried to give you a few hints when you were still in the village on the coast—a bit of improvising, I grant, but Miss Forsyth's susceptibility to the trance state was too prime an opportunity to pass on." She blushed. "And who do you think was behind that storm that saved your bacon on the hill? The *skraelinga* shaman summoned it, actually, using magic gotten from the trolls, but I turned it around on them. Rather a clever bit of business, you will admit."

"Oh, yes," Rafe said.

"I dispatched Hugin and Munin to guide you past the trolls and make sure you reached your destination safely— and I'm willing to overlook the fact you punctured poor Munin, Mr. Springer, since I know it was inadvertent. And when your run-in with the stone-giants alerted the trolls, *who* was it who produced a splendid imitation of a pitched battle out here at the entrance to the valley, to draw the pursuers off your track? Me, that's who." He shook his head. "Really, you owe me an immense debt of gratitude for the help I've given you."

"That's true enough, ah, Odin," Rafe said. "But I hope you will forgive me for asking what *we* get out of this."

Odin held up a thick finger. "You get the personal favor

of a god, which isn't all that easy to come by in this world of
yours, let me tell you. Also you get to collect all the various
rewards that wretched little Himmler creature promised you
in Berlin. And because you have returned to me that which
was lost to me for ages, I shall throw in a little extra. Behold!"

He struck the ice that had formed in the lee of a boulder.
It shattered, fell away to reveal an open chest of age-stained
wood bound with brass. It overflowed with jewelry, massive
Norse goldwork inset with gems, huge and roughly cut.
Even in the tundra murk the treasure had a warm and
wealthy glitter.

"Now—the spear."

Waldmann pushed forward. "Herr Wotan, may I point out
that if we give *you* the spear, we will not be able to give it to
Reichsführer Himmler?"

"So you still feel you owe that thick-necked little maggot
loyalty? I thought better of you, Herr Waldmann. Surely
you're not so obtuse that you don't realize that he fails, shall
we say, to fully appreciate you."

Waldmann stared at his boots. "The Reichsführer isn't
particularly known for his sense of humor where major dis-
appointments are concerned, Herr Odin," Freiherr Chatenois
pointed out.

"The spear," Odin said pointedly.

Rafe looked at Billi. She shrugged. He stepped forward
and laid Gungnir across its master's palm. A ripple of energy
seemed to run through the weapon.

"Thank you," Odin said. "That wasn't so hard, now, was
it?"

Rafe tore the shredded and befouled armor off over his
head, threw it onto the ground, and kicked it twice for good
measure. "The hard part's going to come in when we get
back to Berlin," Billi muttered under her breath. "I wonder
when the next tramp steamer bound for Perth puts in at Narwhal."

Odin smiled. "You don't really think I'd reward you so
poorly, you who have served me so well. Besides—" He
reached behind him. "You provide a perfect opportunity for

me to square accounts with a slimy creature who's bringing nothing but discredit to my good name."

He brought forth a spear that looked exactly like Gungnir. "This one was not made by dwarves, but your Herr Himmler won't know that. On the other hand, *this* one is cursed. Himmler won't know that either—" He showed eyeteeth. "Until it's too late."

"Will it turn him into ashes?" asked Billi hopefully, remembering the creature in the armory.

Odin shook his head. "My power is not that great on this plane. It will work slowly. But very, very surely. Behold."

He held the false Gungnir forth. Blazing runes appeared along the spine of the blade. "Disgrace—and—death," Shrewsbury translated, frowning with concentration, "shall —befall him—who wields this spear—to dishonor— Odin's—name."

"So it shall be done." Odin pronounced in a voice that echoed around the corners of the universe. The runes blazed forth, blindingly bright, and then were gone without a trace.

As were the mountains, the ravens, and Odin himself. The travelers stared about them. Iggianguaq's homely face creased in a smile. "The sea—I smell the sea!"

They stood on rocky ground. Dawn was building up in gray increments around them. Shrewsbury stood holding the spear with a foolish expression on his long, donnish face.

They heard excited barking, ran toward the sound. Behind an outcrop of rock they found the sleds and the tethered dogs, sniffing uncertainly at the ground beneath their feet. Beyond the rock the land fell away, and they saw the tarnished-silver glint of water under starlight.

Billi ran to the edge of the headland. "Look! Look there. It's Narwhal. There's the ship!"

They crowded up around her, Shrewsbury now using the spear to help him walk. There was the familiar grubby clump of peat igloos, a few wisps of smoke wavering in the face of the dawn that whitened the eastern horizon. Riding at anchor out in the bay lay *Holger Danske*, softly breathing steam as its crew came to life.

"There's a way down here," Chatenois said, pointing out a path that ran down from the headland.

"The injured can ride the sleds," Iggianguaq said. "The dogs don't need drivers now that they can smell home."

"We did it." Billi turned away as if she could no longer bear the sight. "We actually did it."

Shrewsbury gimped over and put his arm around her. "At quite a cost." He looked down at her, gave her a funny little smile. "Though I suppose the trip has had its compensations . . ."

She stood on tiptoe and kissed him on the nose.

Iggianguaq turned and gazed wistfully back at the ice dome, rising huge and silent behind them. "Now we may grieve for our lost ones and give them proper songs." A tear glittered on his cheek.

Without even thinking about it Rafe translated. Kampfer looked thoughtful. "Ask him if outsiders will be welcome at the ceremony."

Billi tipped her head. "You mean you'd rub elbows with subhumans?"

Kampfer closed his eyes. His fine skin looked very pale. "Forgive me, Fräulein. These people helped us, fought with us, gave their lives for us. They are men, not animals. I will grieve for them almost as much—" his voice faltered the tiniest fraction. "—almost as much as I will grieve for my men—my friends."

He cocked his head and looked at her. "Perhaps it takes me time to learn some things. But I learn eventually, yes?"

She came to him and kissed him on the cheek.

Rafe stood on a rock, gazing out along Fosters Bucht with his hands in the pockets of his pants. The wind ruffled his hair, blowing the last of the troll treek away. "So, Herr Waldmann," he asked without turning, "are you really willing to hand that spear over to the Reichsführer, knowing what it signifies?"

Waldmann looked at the spear in Shrewsbury's hand for a long moment. Or toward it; his eyes seemed far away. "Yes," he said at last. "Yes, I do believe I shall."

And they whipped up the dogs and went down to greet the rising day.